Failing is not an option . . .

"I've been watching you, wondering, waiting to see where you'd end up. After all, there are other demon law schools," Seknecus said, making a moue of distaste that showed me exactly what he thought of them. "But I was happy to see that you chose St. Lucifer's."

Technically my mother chose St. Lucifer's . . . But there seemed no reason to interrupt to clarify that bit of misinformation. Seknecus wandered around the room, picking through papers, flipping open and quickly shutting the front covers of various leather-bound books, never meeting my eye. I had no doubt, however, that his attention was fully focused on me.

"So, you see, seeing your name on my list wasn't exactly a surprise, although it appeared much later than I would have liked."

He glanced at me then, with a frown of disapproval. I did my best to look expressionless because none seemed appropriate. It wouldn't do to look amused, bored, or, Luck forbid, rebellious. Seknecus stared at me with narrowed eyes and then went back to wandering.

"You've got some catching up to do," he said, addressing a copy of *Sin and Sanction: Codification & Case Law.* "It doesn't matter why or what excuses you've got for yourself. You will be held to the same standards as everyone else, regardless of whose daughter you are. And you've missed a lot of class already."

I opened my mouth to protest, but he cut me off with a wave.

"Manipulation class," he clarified. "You're going to have to work ten times as hard as everyone else just to pass. Quintus Rochester doesn't go easy on students and he's likely to see your absence during the early part of the semester as a challenge. You know, failing is not an option. Not if you want to live . . ."

DARK LIGHT OF DAY

JILL ARCHER

ACE BOOKS, NEW YORK

THE BERKLEY PUBLISHING GROUP
Published by the Penguin Group
Penguin Group (USA) Inc.
375 Hudson Street, New York, New York 10014, USA
Penguin Group (Canada), 90 Eglinton Avenue East, Suite 700, Toronto, Ontario M4P 2Y3, Canada
(a division of Pearson Penguin Canada Inc.) • Penguin Books Ltd., 80 Strand, London WC2R 0RL,
England • Penguin Group Ireland, 25 St. Stephen's Green, Dublin 2, Ireland (a division of Penguin
Books Ltd.) • Penguin Group (Australia), 250 Camberwell Road, Camberwell, Victoria 3124, Australia
(a division of Pearson Australia Group Pty. Ltd.) • Penguin Books India Pvt. Ltd., 11 Community
Centre, Panchsheel Park, New Delhi—110 017, India • Penguin Group (NZ), 67 Apollo Drive,
Rosedale, Auckland 0632, New Zealand (a division of Pearson New Zealand Ltd.) • Penguin Books
(South Africa) (Pty.) Ltd., 24 Sturdee Avenue, Rosebank, Johannesburg 2196, South Africa

Penguin Books Ltd., Registered Offices: 80 Strand, London WC2R 0RL, England

This is a work of fiction. Names, characters, places, and incidents either are the product of the author's imagination or are used fictitiously, and any resemblance to actual persons, living or dead, business establishments, events, or locales is entirely coincidental. The publisher does not have any control over and does not assume any responsibility for author or third-party websites or their content.

DARK LIGHT OF DAY

An Ace Book / published by arrangement with Black Willow, LLC

PUBLISHING HISTORY
Ace mass-market edition / October 2012

Copyright © 2012 by Black Willow, LLC.
Cover art by David Palumbo.
Cover design by Lesley Worrell.
Interior text design by Laura K. Corless.

ISBN: 978-0-425-25715-9

ACE
Ace Books are published by The Berkley Publishing Group,
a division of Penguin Group (USA) Inc.,
375 Hudson Street, New York, New York 10014.
ACE and the "A" design are trademarks of Penguin Group (USA) Inc.

PRINTED IN THE UNITED STATES OF AMERICA

10 9 8 7 6 5 4 3 2 1

ALWAYS LEARNING   PEARSON

Almost twenty years ago
my mother gave me a hurricane lamp.
Its pewter base was engraved with the words
"May Your Light Shine Bright."

This one's for you, Mom.
I love you, and always will.

Acknowledgments

A huge heartfelt thanks to Lois Winston, fellow author, mentor, and awesome agent. Lois was the first person to see promise in Noon's story, and I will always be grateful for that. Throughout this whole process, she has been extremely accessible and extraordinarily tenacious. Her frank words of caution or encouragement are always well received. Thanks to Ashley and Carolyn Grayson as well for all of their advice and early enthusiasm.

Mega thanks to Jessica Wade for being such a dedicated editor. Revisions are kind of like boot camp for novels. At the end, the manuscript should be leaner and meaner (or, in *DLOD*'s case, stronger and kinder). Jessica's an excellent trainer! Thanks also to Lesley Worrell, the art director, and David Palumbo, the cover artist, for bringing Noon visually to life. I love Noon's slightly defiant expression as well as the other details! Nice work.

I'm also incredibly grateful to Michelle Kasper, my production editor; Mary Pell, my copy editor; and the rest of the folks over at Penguin who made this book happen. A big thanks to Joan Havens too for assisting with the Latin phrases.

Finally, thank you to my family and friends who have supported me with love, affection, education, passion, curiosity, and commitment. To my free-spirited mother, who passed on her fierce independence and artistic aesthetics. To my pragmatic father, who was always there for me even when we lived apart. My dad loves books as much as I do, and we've spent large chunks of time discussing novels, characters, and authors, and visiting bookstores together. To my stepmom, who was the one who suggested I take the LSAT and encouraged me to apply to law school.

To my mother-in-law for always helping out around the house and with the kids. She's my fairy godmother! To my father-in-law, who's also a lawyer, for not thinking I was absolutely insane to quit practicing law to write about it (especially when he heard I was adding demons and magic to the mix!). To my brother, best friends, and daughters for being a part of my life. A writer's life is much richer with people to love, laugh with, and take care of.

And to my husband, whose unwavering support over the years is awe-inspiring. Sometimes he has more faith in me than I do! I couldn't have asked for a better, more steadfast, and more dauntless partner in life's endeavors, including this latest of mine.

I

*Deep into that darkness peering,
long I stood there wondering, fearing,
Doubting, dreaming dreams no mortal
ever dared to dream before . . .*

—EDGAR ALLAN POE

Chapter 1

ʅ

The wind whipping across my face made it feel as if I'd just scrubbed with camphor and bits of glass. My eyes watered and my nose ran. I sniffled and kept walking, my boots crunching over the ice and snow. Stars winked high above me like baby's breath thrown into an inky sea, but the main light came from small umber streetlights tucked into the stone wall beside me. The Asters' front gate was just thirty yards ahead. I tried not to think about how cold the walk home would be if they refused to let me in. Inside my pocket, I squeezed my letter, forever wrinkling it. I knew some people framed theirs. I didn't care. I planned to burn mine.

The wall I'd been walking along ended and a massive iron gate rose up in its place. To its side was a call box. Giving the letter one final vicious squeeze, I withdrew my hand, opened the box, and turned the crank. It stuck at first and I had to wrench it free from a brittle crust of snow and ice. Finally I heard a pop and some clicking. But no one answered. I stood for another half minute or so, blowing breath into my cupped hands to warm my now-frigid mouth and nose. I turned the crank again. It was too late for dinner and too early for bed. Someone would answer. After a while, Mrs. Aster did.

"Hello?" squawked the box.

"Evening, Mrs. Aster," I said, trying to keep my voice pleasant. "It's Nouiomo Onyx."

A moment of silence passed as I tucked a strand of hair back into my hood. The frost on my mitten brushed my cheek. The spot burned as if someone had just nicked me with a metal rake.

"Good evening, Noon."

"Is Peter home?"

"I haven't seen him since dinner." This may or may not have been true. The Asters' house was as big as a castle and I knew Peter spent most of his time studying either in his room or in the family library.

"I need to talk to him about something," I said, still managing to keep the impatience out of my voice. "Would you let him know I'm here?"

"Can't it wait until tomorrow?"

"No. I'm leaving tomorrow. That's what I want to talk to him about."

There was a long pause before she answered again.

"Noon, I have two hundred poinsettias, five holly trees, and a dozen *live* mistletoe sprigs in the house. You can't come in. I'm sorry."

I fought for calm and swallowed the lump in my throat. What had I expected? It was Yuletide and the Asters were Angels, for Luck's sake.

"Can you tell him to come out?"

Another long pause and then, "He's studying."

I sighed. The lump was gone, replaced with resignation. I had lived next to Peter for twenty-one years, my whole life. And I could count on one hand the number of times this gate had opened for me. I cleared my throat, wanting my voice to sound stronger than I felt.

"Tell him I stopped by then, would you?"

"Of course. Good night, Noon." The squawking stopped and then the static and the box went completely silent.

I turned and started crunching my way back, stepping carefully, and clutching my hood beneath my chin to keep the wind from my ears. I was so focused on how cold and miserable I was that it took me a while to notice the warmth spreading from the pocket of my cape. Just as I started to smell burning wool—disgusting!—warm turned to seriously hot and I glanced down to see that I had set my cape on fire. *Brilliant.* I hadn't inadvertently set anything on fire since puberty. I waved a flat hand over the flames and quickly smothered the fire. I looked around to see if anyone was watching. Someone was.

Luckily, it was Peter.

He was leaning against the stone wall I had just walked along. The same stone wall that ran for miles along the Lemiscus, a lane as old as the Apocalypse which separated our families' estates. The Asters had a wall running along their side. On ours? Nothing. My father, Karanos Onyx, was one of the most powerful Maegesters in the country. We didn't need walls to keep our privacy.

Peter's hood was down, his cloak unbuttoned, and his hands bare—obviously he'd rushed to meet me. In the deep twilight, his white blond hair was the color of snow and ash, nearly the opposite of my midnight colored tresses. He pushed off the wall with his shoulder, his lanky frame ambling over to my shivering one, and put his arm around me. His smile was friendly but his frost blue eyes were disapproving. He'd seen the fire.

"Shall we?" he said, motioning toward a small wooden door that was half-hidden in the wall.

"Is it safe?"

"As safe as it always is. I cast the spell just before opening the door."

Huddled together we stepped through the doorway. Peter closed the door behind us and I stared ahead, remembering the first time I had stepped through that door. I'd been five and it was the first time I'd ever stepped foot in a garden. I'd been so in awe, *so overwhelmed*, by the life growing within these walls. The dark, destructive waning magic I tried so desperately to keep hidden deep inside of me had pulsed in response to the rich magentas, bright clarets, and cheerful fuchsias of the blooms and buds. Within seconds of my entry, I had killed three hydrangeas, two hostas, and a mulberry tree. Instantly, they'd become black silhouettes against the garden's remaining ruddy colors.

It was the single most horrifying day of my life. And the most hopeful. Because a moment later Peter had cast a protective spell over the surviving plants so that I could walk among them—green, growing, *living* plants. I dared not touch anything now, but at least I could look.

The place would have been magical even without a spell. Yew topiaries shaped as Mephistopheles, Beelzebub, and Alecto warred alongside Gabriel, Michael, and Mary. They were all dormant now, the yews buried under an inch of fresh snow, but I could feel their presence. Alive and well, they waited for spring to resume their fight. Behind the wall, shielded by hedgerows and distant cypress trees, the snowflakes felt less like bits of glass and more like cold confetti. Peter and I sat down on a small cement bench, which was nestled back nicely in a cut-out niche of the hedgerow. He spread one side of his cloak around me and cast a spell of warmth over us. My shivering subsided.

"What's wrong?" he asked.

He'd seen the fire so I couldn't very well say, "Nothing." But I'd burned the letter so I couldn't just shove it at him in way of explanation either.

"I've been accepted to St. Lucifer's Law School."

Peter's face went still. It could have been surprise. It could have been anger. With Peter, you could never tell.

"Luck, Noon, did *you* apply there?"

I rolled my eyes. "My mom sent in the application for me. She swears she didn't tell them about my magic. She thinks I should tell them. Her exact words were, 'It's your power, you have to decide to use it.'" I snorted, remembering.

My power. As if it was something positive. People like me, who possessed waning magic, were a menace. Not only could I kill something just by touching it, my presence alone had the potential to harm growing things. Plants, pregnant women, gardens, greenery—all could suffer disastrous consequences if I came too near. Worse than that though, was what we were expected to become: Maegesters, or demon peacekeepers. Because waning magic was the only type of magic that could be used to control demons. Becoming a Maegester meant learning all of the Byzantine laws that Halja's ruling demons idolized and then training to become their consiglieres, their judges, and even their executioners.

Worse than *that* though, was that I was the only female with waning magic that I knew of.

Unfortunately, I had to live with it, which was why I'd spent my whole life wishing I possessed the waxing magic of a Mederi healer, rather than the waning magic of a future Maegester.

"So are you going to go?"

I shrugged and made a helpless gesture. Ever since I was five, after that first disastrous entry into the Aster garden, Peter and I had been plotting a way to reverse my magic. Peter thought the answer was to find a rumored long-lost Reversal Spell. But, so far, we hadn't found it and my time was running out. Law and scripture required us to use our talents for the greater good. The demons who ruled Halja had no patience for rule breakers, and so under Haljan law, anyone with magic had to declare it by Bryde's Day of their twenty-first year. That day, the day I'd been dreading my entire life, was now just weeks away.

"I don't know, Peter. It's a big gamble, not declaring by the deadline. I'll be *killed* if they find out I have magic and didn't declare it."

Peter scoffed and I bristled.

"Peter!" I said, suddenly angry. The snow on the branches above us instantly melted and dribbled down on us, a chilling reminder of the combustible magic I was trying to hide. "You act as if the demons, the Council, and the law are of no concern."

Slowly, he rubbed the back of his bare neck, swiping at the cold drops that had fallen there. He stared out into the snow covered garden, his lustrous blue eyes never meeting the soft smokey bronze of mine.

"Noon, I'm so close," he said finally, turning to me. "You've got to trust me. I know I'll be able to find the Reversal Spell before Bryde's Day. Can't you convince your mother to let you stay home for a few more weeks?"

I shook my head. "She kicked me out, Peter. My own mother."

Peter grimaced. "Is there anyone else you can stay with? Just until I find the spell?"

I stared at him and then smirked. "I'd move in with you, but your mother hates me."

"She doesn't hate you . . . Wait, you'd move in with me?"

"I . . ."

I didn't know. Peter was my best (and only) friend, but I'd given up my adolescent dreams of anything happening romantically between us years ago. I'm not even sure Peter had known I'd felt that way about him.

"Peter, I need my own place. And I need a job. I need to figure out what to do with my life."

"Well, I guess you could go to St. Lucifer's temporarily, just until I find the spell. If your mother didn't declare for you, your secret's still safe. Some people might suspect, but I think they're too afraid of your father to speak openly of it or to declare for you. Just enroll in the Barrister classes, *not* the Maegester ones. Instead of learning how to police demons like a future Maegester, learn how to help Hyrkes follow the Demon Council rules like a future Barrister."

"There will be others with waning magic who are there to train as Maegesters. They'll be in the Barrister classes too. There won't be any way to avoid them." Members of the Host who had waning magic could often sense one another. It was a magical remnant of the days when our ancestors had been Lucifer's warlords.

"I can cast a cloaking spell over you that should last for a few weeks," Peter said. "I'll reinforce it when I get there."

Peter was twenty-four. For the last three years he'd been attending the Joshua School, a prestigious Angel academy that shared a campus with St. Lucifer's. Angels, whose power came from their beliefs rather than their birth, were different than waning and waxing magic users. They cast spells, instead of using innate power.

I raised my eyebrows at him. "You can cast a powerful enough cloaking spell to hide me from *any* Maegester at St. Lucifer's?"

For the first time that night, Peter grinned. "Have a little faith, Noon. Have you ever sensed your dad's magic before?"

I frowned. Not that I could remember. Peter nodded and smiled.

"That's because he's always cloaked. I can do the same for you."

"Do you really think you can find the Reversal Spell in less than a month?" I said, still worried. "Most people think it's a myth."

"It's not a myth!" Peter grabbed my arm as if I hadn't heard his next words quoted from him a thousand times already.

"'He will wipe away every tear from their eyes, and death shall be no more, neither shall there be mourning, nor crying, nor pain, for the former things have passed away. And He who was seated on the throne said, "I make all things new. *Write this down, for these words are trustworthy and true.*"'"

"Noon, somewhere out there is an ultimate spell of reversal, a spell that makes things the way they were meant to be. The old book of Revelation doesn't give us the spell, but we know from it that the spell once existed. Someone wrote it down at His command and I'm going to find it."

I stayed silent, not knowing what to say. *Did the Reversal Spell really exist?*

"What does Night think?" Peter said, cutting into my thoughts.

Night was short for Nocturo, the Maegester's name my parents had given to my twin brother. Within a day of our birth, it became clear that our names were completely inconsistent with our magic. Because magic and gender were so closely related in Halja, our birth mix-up was something we Onyxes almost never discussed. The fact that I had been born with the waning magic of a Maegester and Night had been born with the waxing magic of a Mederi embarrassed my father, shamed my mother, and caused Night and me no end of grief.

"Night left two weeks ago to join one of the Mederi tribes," I said.

Peter stared at the Alecto topiary, frowning. I brushed snow from my knees.

"That's going to make it hard."

"Tell me about it. My mom and dad weren't speaking before. Now they can't even stand to be in the same room with each other."

"I meant your brother's choice to openly train as a Mederi healer might make it harder to cast the Reversal Spell once we find it."

Peter stood up, taking his cloak with him and breaking the spell of warmth he'd cast over us. The wind whistled in my ears again and I shrugged. Night hadn't consulted me. He'd just left. Now, our mother obviously thought it was my turn.

"I think Night just looked at the calendar and decided a few more weeks weren't going to matter. He got tired of waiting."

"Don't declare, Noon. Once you declare, it'll be that much harder for us. Even if I found the Reversal Spell, the Council might not let me use it."

"Don't worry," I said, laughing bitterly. "Declaring my magic and training to become a Maegester is the *last* thing I want to do."

I pulled my hand from my pocket. The ashes from my burned acceptance letter spilled out into the wind and then settled on the garden's snowy white coating. By the time Peter finished casting my cloaking spell, the little black bits were gone.

Chapter 2

❧

If Halja, my country, was the lone man left standing in a battlefield after a long and brutal war, then its future would be the spilled blood under his feet—expected, yet somehow still startling, slippery and shifting, a sacrifice for peace in a world full of demons. Real ones. Because it was here in Halja that Lucifer's army, the Host, beat the Savior's army in the last great battle of the Apocalypse.

And yet . . .

Life goes on pretty much the way it did before. People still get married, have babies, and pay their taxes. Many things were destroyed, but many things have been rebuilt. We have mechanized cabriolets, electro-harmonic machines, winder lifts, pots of lip gloss, and nail lacquer. We have time to do our hair. Because the Apocalypse happened over two thousand years ago. Armageddon is old news and in the days, years, centuries, and millennia since, we've mourned our dead, buried them, and even forgotten where their graves were.

Lucifer's Host, which consisted of his warlords, their
wives and sisters, and the demons they controlled, evolved.
Not physically, but culturally. The warlords became Maegesters, or peacekeepers. The wives and sisters became
Mederies, or healers. And the demons broke into two groups:
those that value Halja's future and those that don't.

Well, like it or not, expected or startling, my future began
at five the next morning when the tinny ring of my alarm bell
woke me. In the cold blackness of predawn I dressed hur-
riedly in slim wool pants, a linen undershirt, and a heavy
gray sweater with a large cowl collar that could double as an
extra hood if needed. I grabbed my leather backpack and
crept downstairs to see if I could find something to eat before
I had to leave to catch the ferry that would take me to St.
Lucifer's.

Our house was as big as Peter's (maybe even bigger) so it
took me a few minutes to reach the kitchen. My fingertips
brushed the walls as I went, each turn illuminating memories
of events that occurred in these darkened rooms long ago.
There was where, at eight, I'd tripped on one of the carpets
and smashed my head into the side of *that* table, nearly slicing my ear off. Night had tried to heal me, but my father had
stumbled upon us before he could and had bellowed for my
mother. She'd patched me up, with catgut stitches instead
of magic, and Night had never tried again. At least not in
this house. *There* was where I'd thrown my first fireball. At
my mother. I hadn't meant to. I hadn't even known I could.
Thank Luck, I'd missed and hit the wall instead. She'd
grabbed me by the ear (the one she'd sewn with catgut four
years earlier) and marched me upstairs to look out the window at her blackened garden.

"Do you want the whole house to look like that?" she'd
asked, shaking me by the ear.

She'd made me paint the wall white again, but I swore I
could still see the black spot, even in the dark.

There was a light on in the kitchen. I hoped it was Estelle,
our housekeeper. But when I rounded the corner and entered,

I saw my mother at the end of the long wooden table, scraping the tops of several white iced petits fours into a trash can.

"I've told Estelle," she said, almost to herself, although she had to know I was there, "*no flowers*. I've told her bells, stars, arrows, hearts . . . whatever she fancies, but *no flowers*." With each word, my mother's scraping became more violent. The last petit four crumbled into the trash can, icing, cake, and all. She stood for a moment looking down at it, unable to meet my silent gaze.

Why was she upset? She was getting what she wanted. Me out of her house. I sighed. It was probably a good thing. For both of us.

I grabbed one of the last unviolated petits fours. In the red light of the kitchen's brick oven fire and the overhead iron chandelier candles, the white icing looked orange. The little flower flickered on top, almost like a tiny flame.

"She doesn't make them for you," I said, popping the little cake into my mouth. "She makes them for me."

My mother looked up at me frowning. *Had she been crying?* In this light, it was hard to tell. And why didn't she have the electric lights on anyway? My mother had always been far too fond of fire.

Two score and five years or so ago, my mother, Aurelia Onyx nee Ferrum of the Hawthorn Tribe, had been the most beautiful and powerful Mederi the south bank had seen in at least three generations. She'd cured countless diseases, scoured scores of unnamed pestilence, helped crippled children walk again, and the blind to see. She'd birthed hundreds of babies, healed new mothers, and brought blue babies back to life. No one miscarried with the young Aurelia Onyx attending. She'd been a superb midwife. Not only beyond reproach, but a shining example of what all young, dutiful Mederies aspire to be.

Her garden had been legendary. Bluebells, bog lilies, and cattails had bloomed next to sand verbena and prickly pear. Wisteria blossomed next to bougainvillea, passion flowers sprouted amongst sea holly, four o'clocks opened at dawn, and the night-blooming cereus flowered not just on midsummer's night, but every night of the year. People never spoke directly to me about it, but I'd gathered that, in its heyday, my mother's garden had been something of a fertility shrine. Hyrkes—humans with no magic—came from as far as the New Babylon suburbs just to spend the day in it. Losing a day's work and traveling for hours was nothing in trade for the chance to soak up all that life and to possibly see her. Or even to have her touch you. Because Aurelia Onyx had had the gift of life.

But as her marital years wore on and she created no new life of her own, folks began to wonder. Fewer and fewer people traveled from New Babylon to the garden. Fewer Hyrkes hired her as a midwife. It was impossible for a Mederi of her strength to be barren. Wasn't it?

I have no idea what happened then or how it did. I only know that my brother and I were born twenty-one years ago and the day after our birth my mother burned her garden to the ground. With a can of gasoline and a match, because Mederies didn't have destructive power. But every day of my life that I'd woken to my view of the charred garden that never grew back, I knew different. You didn't need magic to destroy.

My mother had certainly proven that again with Estelle's poor petits fours.

"I think your brother has joined the Demeter Tribe," she said, setting her knife on the tabletop.

"Demeter sounds like a good choice," I said, scrambling to remember what I knew about that tribe. My mother pressed her lips together, showing me what Hawthorn likely thought of Demeter. Still, beggars couldn't be choosers. As a male Mederi, Night wouldn't exactly have his pick of tribes to choose from.

I walked over to the table and surveyed the decapitated petits fours. I selected two more and walked over to the icebox to find some juice. I didn't think I had the patience to boil water for tea this morning.

"How do you know he joined Demeter?" I asked, peering

into the dark, ice-cold box. Several glass bottles in varying shades of red, pink, orange, and yellow were neatly lined up on the top shelf. I grabbed the pink one—pomegranate juice—and went to fetch a glass. Even though there was only enough left for one person, I knew better than to drink straight from the bottle in front of Aurelia.

"They had an opening. One of their Mederies disappeared recently."

"Disappeared?" Disappearances in Halja usually didn't have happy endings.

"Linnaea Saphir, Demeter's Monarch, sent her best midwife up to New Babylon last week. She'd received an unsigned note from a messenger requesting immediate assistance with a difficult birth in a neighborhood to the east of the city. Amaryllis Apatite, the Mederi midwife she sent, climbed on board the North-South Express at 2:00 p.m. last Tuesday and hasn't been seen since."

No need to ask how she knew all this. My mother might not practice medicine anymore, but she still kept in touch with Hawthorn's Monarch. And news of a missing Mederi would be something for *every* tribe to be concerned about.

"They're not afraid it's another Ionys situation are they?"

Ionys was the Patron Demon of Wine, Winemaking, and Vineyards. Last year, the demon's favored drink had turned one of the local vintners mad. Over the course of five weeks last spring, he'd abducted and murdered six Mederies. He'd sprinkled their blood across his vineyard in the hopes that Ionys (despite the demon's prohibition against such practices) would reward him with an excellent vintage. Needless to say, the follower was caught, tried, condemned to death, and his vineyards confiscated and burned.

I shoved the uneaten petits fours back onto the table, feeling suddenly ill. My mother's silence was answer enough.

"Are you worried?" I said. "About Night? Because we haven't heard from him?"

Aurelia stared at me with her dark, red-rimmed eyes.

"Yes," she said simply, picking up the knife again. "Of course I'm worried about him. *Him*. The Apatite girl. *You*."

And with that last word she took her knife and swept every bit of Estelle's ruined petits fours into the trash.

I wanted to tell her we'd be all right. Night. Me. The missing Mederi. But this was Halja. The land of demons. A place where our footing, and our future, was always slippery, shifting, treacherous, and unsure.

Chapter 3

ૐ

We lived in a small village called Etincelle on the south bank of the Lethe. The river flowed between Etincelle and New Babylon, Halja's biggest and only city. The Lethe's south bank had been settled sometime after the Apocalypse by the Host, some Angels, and their Hyrke servants. How the Host and the Angels managed to occupy the same ground without continuing Armageddon is no small mystery. Perhaps the Angels were too bereaved by the death of their Savior to continue their holy war. Certainly the Host was disorganized. Killing the Savior had weakened Lucifer to the point of near annihilation. It was said he collapsed on the field in his armor, no longer able to bear its weight. Lilith rushed to him, but it was too late. He transformed before her eyes, first into a serpent, then a dragon, and then finally a star in the firmament of Halja.

His star, the Morning Star, winked down at me now as I trudged to the edge of the Lethe in the slowly lightening dark.

The wind and snow from the night before were gone, re-

placed with a still crispness. The air smelled almost sterilely
clean, at least until I came within a few yards of the dock
when the stench of dead fish, wood rot, and engine fuel became too concentrated to ignore. I told myself it was the foul
smell that slowed my steps but I knew it was fear. Last night's
determination to attend St. Lucifer's masquerading as a
human Hyrke with no magical powers disappeared with the
clean smelling air. The brief burst of raw grit that had seen
me through the tearless farewell with my mother was gone.
I clung to the thought of Peter's cloaking spell and mentally
pulled it around myself for warmth and courage. No one
knew that I'd been born with waning magic. There was no
reason, yet, to declare my status and start training as a Maegester. Maybe I really would be able to hide until Peter found
a way to reverse my magic.

I looked across the wide gray expanse of the Lethe. Today,
I knew it for what it was: the choppy, white capped boundary
between my childhood home and my uncertain future. It
was dotted with all the tiny, muted-colored ferries that ran
between Etincelle and New Babylon. The only people who
worked in Etincelle were the Hyrke servants of the Host and
Angels. Everyone else worked in New Babylon, which was a
bustling hub of cosmopolitan urbanity, similar in many ways
to the old world cities that existed before the Apocalypse.
New Babylon offered myriad opportunities that Etincelle did
not—shopping, entertainment, the diversity that comes from
a large population, as well as employment. So travel between
the two areas was brisk.

My mother had booked me on the 6:06 a.m. ferry. She
hadn't told me its name. We'd said little to each other after
our discussion about Night's possible whereabouts and the
missing Mederi. The bulk of our remaining conversation had
been taken up with logistics. She'd arranged to have most of
my things sent ahead to St. Lucifer's, there was an orientation for new students tomorrow morning at nine, and she'd
purchased a one-way ferry ticket for me. I wasn't to be late.

It was 5:42 a.m. I wasn't late.

The ferry wasn't even there, so I dropped my leather

backpack beside a wooden bench and slumped down into it. I huddled under my bulky layers of clothing, the gray collared sweater, my dark winter cloak, and my heavy snow boots. I pulled the sweater's cowl collar up over my mouth and nose for warmth and looked out across the water, searching for my ferry.

The other ferries hustled about. They all had names like *Absence*, *Veracity*, or *Courage*. Like a little augury, I thought. Would my ferry bear a name of inspiration, enlightenment— or dread? The water lapped at the pier beneath me and boats' horns and bells sounded in the distance. Hyrke captains yelled things to mates, dock boys shouted at each other, and then, as more and more ferries approached from the north, the dock got busier. Ropes thumped as they were thrown to the dock, rubber bumpers squeaked as boats lined up and were tied off. Feet thudded down the pier as commuters and shoppers prepared to board.

I recognized most of them. Marius Steele, a Maegester whose clients were almost exclusively winged imps who barely had the power to light a match, boarded the *Absence*. He glanced in my direction, recognized me, and gave a startled little wave before scurrying onto the boat. Mark Grayson, a Hyrke mechanic who lived on the Petrificai estate, boarded the ferry *Honor*. The Petrificai, despite their ominous surname, were more relaxed than most Host families. They allowed Grayson to accept work from other sources—both in Etincelle and New Babylon. Though a Hyrke, Grayson was well respected on the south bank. He had no magic, but magic wasn't necessary to work with machines. Grayson gave me a polite nod, which I returned, before he nimbly jumped on board *Honor*. Soon it would be my turn. It should be easy. Just step on board. After all, I'd crossed the Lethe countless times already.

But this time was different. For one thing, I'd always had a return ticket. And for another, I'd never been trying to pull off the near impossible. Hiding my magic at St. Lucifer's would be infinitely more difficult than it had been at the Ajaccio Academy, my Hyrke high school, or Gaillard University, my Hyrke undergraduate college. But declaring I was a woman with waning magic would not only brand me as the freak I didn't want to be, it would also set me on a career path I most emphatically did *not* want.

Just before six, a tiny beat-up boat chugged across the water toward the dock. Its paint was faded and its engine sputtered, but it was as fast as it needed to be and soon a scrawny boy of about twelve was jumping to the pier and tying it off. I sat on my bench and stared. The boat was about fifty feet in length. A cabin occupied almost half of the deck. The rest of the deck was covered with benches. The boy gave a wave to the captain and the engine shut down. The captain, a short, stocky, gray-haired old man, came out and they exchanged a few words I couldn't make out. Likely about something insignificant like fuel or fees. I heard more thumping on the dock. I guessed I wouldn't be the only one taking the 6:06 this morning. Someone with a determined step approached. But when I looked up to see who it was, I wasn't prepared for my reaction.

Instead of cold, I felt suddenly hot. Like my body was the letter I'd inadvertently burned last night. I could feel Peter's spell kick in. It acted as a counterforce and I realized my magic had flared up unbidden. It would have been only horrifyingly frightening had it stopped there. But the magic tug-of-war continued in my body unabated. My waning magic wrestled with Peter's spell. The battle raced across my skin, over my scalp, into my fingertips, skittering into the pit of my stomach where it roiled there, threatening to boil over. I clenched the arm of the bench and gritted my teeth. The man with the determined steps slowed, then stopped and turned, looking straight at me. I didn't recognize him but he stared anyway, making no movement except, perhaps, a slight widening of his eyes.

Whether it was Peter's spell or my own sense of self-preservation that prevailed, I don't know, but the electric revolt of my stomach stopped, moving out as a feeling of pins and needles in my legs and arms. The feeling finally settled into a numbing coldness that I might have mistaken for simply sitting too long if I weren't still looking at the man who had been the mysterious catalyst of the whole incident.

He was young, around my age, and good-looking in a dark, imposing way. This was a man who would feel at ease threatening, or possibly even torturing. But I got the impression he'd turn the screws with a smile, which made him seem even more sinister. His hair was short, very short, as if he'd just come from the barber. Was he a Hyrke? I didn't think he was an Angel or a member of the Host. I'd memorized every face in the *Etincelle Register* (it was easier to avoid other waning magic users if I knew what they looked like). His face hadn't been in there. I would have remembered. But his eyes were more piercing than any Hyrke's I'd ever seen. They were so brown they were almost black and they bored into me with an intensity that made me feel as if I were a butterfly pinned to a box frame. Then the moment was broken and he walked over to me.

"Are you crossing on the six oh six?" he asked. His voice was deeper than I'd expected.

I cleared my throat and pulled my hand free of the armrest. I opened my mouth but no words came out. I'm sure I looked like an idiot. Like I was fourteen again and someone had just asked me to the school dance. Part of me actually wanted to get on the boat if he was going to be on it.

"No," I said, surprising myself. What else was I going to do? Of course I was getting on the boat, which would make me look doubly stupid after this response.

He nodded but kept staring down at me, frowning.

"What?" I snapped. He was undeniably attractive but right now I just wanted him to go away. I had to figure out what I was going to do.

He shrugged, turned around, and walked toward the ferry. I watched him the whole way. He was tall and solidly built. He moved gracefully for his size and, too soon, he bounded over the rail of the ferry, into the cabin, and out of my sight. A few other passengers boarded. None were strangers but there was no one I knew really well either. At 6:05 a whistle sounded and I knew it was the last call for boarding. I stood up and grabbed my leather backpack, lacing one of the straps over my right shoulder. But I did nothing else. I just stood there.

The stranger emerged from the cabin just as the scrawny boy was untying the ferry's ropes from the dock. The boy threw each rope to the stranger, who caught them easily and stowed them under the benches. The boy jumped aboard and entered the cabin. I knew the boat was seconds from leaving.

If I was going to go, it had to be now. What other choice did I have? My mother had made it clear I wasn't welcome back home. Night couldn't take me in. My waning magic would stunt or kill everything his tribe would try to grow. At least Peter's cloaking spell gave me a chance to hide at St. Lucifer's, passing as a Hyrke, while Peter continued to look for the Reversal Spell that might turn my destructive waning magic into the nurturing waxing magic I was supposed to have been born with.

I started walking across the pier just as the ferry was leaving. I hurried my pace. The boat's bumpers squealed as it began to maneuver out of its spot. The engine rumbled and the ferry slowly started to pull away.

I wasn't going to make it. I started running and covered the last few yards in seconds, but in those seconds the ferry had moved almost as far. It was now at least five feet from the pier. I stood paralyzed with all manner of emotions— anger (at myself), disbelief (at the situation), and fear (my constant companion).

Someone yelled.

"Throw your pack!" It was the stranger. He was motioning impatiently with his hands to underscore his advice.

Without thinking I unshouldered my pack and tossed it into the air. It sailed over the water in a great big arc and landed in the stranger's arms. I should be so lucky, I thought. Now I was committed. I stepped to the edge of the pier and jumped out over the water as far as I could.

It wasn't far enough.

I slammed into the side of the ferry and almost fell into the water. I would have too if the stranger hadn't caught both of my hands with his own. The jump hurt a lot more than I thought it would. I'd naively thought that I'd either land on the boat with both my feet under me, or I'd fall in the water unharmed. Landing only halfway, smashing my head into the side of the railing, and then being dragged by the ferry, now gaining speed at an alarming rate, with my legs half-submerged in the water, just hadn't occurred to me.

"Are you okay?" the stranger yelled to me. "Try to drag yourself up."

My head was still pounding and I think I was partially in shock at what I'd just done. I vaguely registered that my hands hurt too. The stranger was squeezing them so hard I thought he'd crack the bones. Fear replaced dazed confusion as I realized I might actually drown if he let go of me. We were now hundreds of yards from the dock. With my water soaked snow boots, a heavy cloak, and a banged up head, my chances of surviving the ice-cold water were maybe fifty-fifty. *What in Luck's name had I done?*

I took the stranger's advice and tried to drag myself aboard. But my arms were weakened by pain and shock and the drag of the water on my boots was greater than my resolve. After a few seconds' effort, I fell back and let myself go limp again. I felt my hands slipping from his.

"Come on! You can do it," the stranger shouted. "Don't give up now!"

I looked up and met his gaze. He was so determined. His ruggedly handsome face was grimly set with the effort of holding my weight against the side of the boat. He wasn't going to let me fall into the water. I was no one to him, but I could tell that he would do anything and everything to make sure I made it into the boat. And from what I'd seen, *anything and everything* included more than most Hyrkes had to give.

He let go of my left hand. I screamed. But then he leaned over the rail, putting himself at substantial risk of falling in too, and shoved his hand under my armpit. It was awkward because of my cloak, but somehow he managed to get his arm almost all the way around me. He started pulling and I finally started helping. It suddenly mattered what this man thought of me. I'd lied to him on the dock and now here he was trying to save me from a drastically stupid, ill-timed jump to the boat I'd sworn I wasn't boarding.

After a full minute of further struggling—obviously everyone inside the cabin was oblivious to my plight—we managed to get me over the railing and onto the boat. We collapsed together on deck, entangled in each other's arms, my cloak billowing out and settling over us like a blanket. For a few seconds neither of us said anything. We just lay there, panting from our efforts. I had no idea what he was thinking, but my thoughts were positively racing. *What, in all of Luck's scorched Hell, was I going to say to this man?*

I disentangled first, and hauled myself up from the deck. I thought I saw a flash of disappointment in his face but I couldn't be sure. Then he rose too and stood in front of me. His frank assessment of me was unnerving. His gaze swept over me as if he already knew every one of my secrets. That would be dangerous, I thought, and doubled my resolve to play the part of a credible Hyrke.

"Thank you," I gushed. At least my gratefulness wasn't fake. I stuck out my hand. "I'm Noon."

"Ari Carmine," he said, shaking my hand. His grip was gentle and he turned my hand palm side down and rubbed his thumb across my bruised knuckles. "I'm sorry I hurt your hands," he said, and for a moment I thought he might raise my hand to his lips in some antiquated chivalrous gesture. But he switched his gaze from my hand to my face and something he saw there must have made him change his mind. He released my hand and let it drop.

"Do you have a last name, Noon?"

I hated that question. My last name produced reactions in people that I'd rather avoid. I paused and thought about making something up, but I'd lied to him once already. Now that he'd saved me from possibly drowning, I didn't want to lie to him any more than I had to.

"Onyx."

He nodded. Like he'd expected it. Which wasn't what *I'd*

expected. Hyrkes who didn't know me usually looked wary when they first heard my last name.

"I know your father," he said.

Doesn't everyone? I thought, but just nodded. The Demon Council, that body politic that ran Halja and everyone in it, had an executive head. The executive position was always held by a Maegester. For the past twenty-one years, that Maegester had been Karanos Onyx, my father.

"So you're the executive's daughter. One of the Hyrke twins born to Host parents."

I couldn't be sure, but it sounded like he might have put a little too much emphasis on the word *Hyrke*. On the other hand, it seemed more likely that deciding to attend St. Lucifer's was increasing my normal paranoia.

"That's right. My brother's Nocturo," I said, careful to use the Maegester's name Night had been given at birth instead of the nickname he'd adopted later.

"So, what brings you to cross the Lethe, Noon?"

I could have just told him. Hyrkes attended St. Lucifer's too (otherwise my plan to masquerade as one wouldn't work). But this guy seemed a little too well informed of my background and I didn't want to get into any discussion about demon law or anything to do with Maegesters, executives, demons, or otherwise.

Still, I was trying not to lie.

"You," I blurted out. He looked surprised for a moment and then grinned. What a sight. I couldn't help thinking of that pre-Apocalyptic nursery tale, something about a wolf and the line, "the better to eat you with." He looked positively carnivorous.

"I wondered why you changed your mind," he said, chuckling. The rumbling sound of it made me swallow. I shook my head. This whole introduction had gone horribly wrong.

"No. I just meant if it weren't for you, I wouldn't be crossing at all," I said, with as much dignity and sincerity as I had left. "Thank you, again." I turned to go.

There was something about him that made me nervous. I

couldn't say whether it was a bad nervous or a good nervous. But I had too many other things to worry about to stick around figuring out which one. I walked over to the cabin door and reached for the door handle. His hand closed around mine in a way that was becoming too familiar, too fast.

"Mind if I sit with you?"

I stared down at his hand over mine wondering what to do. I would look seriously horrible if I couldn't just sit with someone who had recently rescued me from falling into the Lethe.

"On one condition," I said.

"Anything," he said. I raised my eyebrows. He grinned again. I fought a tickly feeling in my stomach—fear or excitement?

"No more questions."

He looked disappointed but then brightened. "Fine," he said. "We can talk about me instead," and he locked his arm in mine and led me over to a seat near a heater.

True to his word, he told me about himself. He'd been raised in Bradbury, a working-class Hyrke neighborhood in the southwest section of New Babylon. He had a younger brother, Matt, who was seventeen and trying to decide where to go to college. The top contenders were my alma mater, Gaillard, and the Engineering Institute. Apparently Matt was some kind of mechanical genius. I told Ari that I'd gone to Gaillard.

"You're kidding?" he said, sounding genuinely surprised. Was he surprised at finding a connection between us, no matter how tenuous? New Babylonians tended to do that when they found they shared something in common with a stranger. That's what happened when you lived in a city populated with a million people. Or was he surprised that someone who'd willingly jumped off a pier to a moving boat would be accepted at Gaillard? Gaillard wasn't for academic slackers. You had to have excellent grades just to get in, let alone stand out against your peers. My parents had sent Night and I there before the ink was dry on our Ajaccio

Academy diplomas. It was the perfect solution for them. The urban campus had no plants for me to kill and the Hyrke curriculum offered no occult training to confuse (or educate) us.

Ari told me he'd gone to Etincelle last night to stay with his aunt. She was his mother's sister and I gathered they were close. He'd brought her a birthday present—a garnet pendant on a silver chain—because the sisters' favorite color was red.

"What's your favorite color?" he said suddenly.

I opened my mouth to answer but then realized I'd be opening the door again to further questions about myself so I said instead, "What's yours?"

"Black," he said slowly, looking at my hair and then bringing his gaze back to my eyes. My heart skipped a beat. I hoped he'd think my rosy cheeks were due to the cold.

"Who's your aunt?" I asked, thinking I would probably know her.

"Judy Pinkerton."

"Oh, right," I said. "She lives on the Decemai estate." He nodded. The Decemaus family lived off the Lemiscus too but miles from us.

I felt myself opening up a little as we talked. Ari wasn't the type to burst into spontaneous laughter. But I had fun. It had been a long time since I'd chatted it up with a Hyrke. Their conversations always seemed so *normal*. Maybe pretending to be a Hyrke at St. Lucifer's wouldn't be so bad after all.

Too soon the crossing ended and our little ferry started docking on the north bank. I grabbed my pack from underneath my seat and prepared to go. Ari grabbed my hand—a not unpleasant habit he had adopted over the last hour or so.

"Let's get together again," he said.

"I don't think that would be a good idea."

"Why? This crossing was one of the best I've ever had."

Wow. Really? Surprisingly, I felt the same, but I knew he wouldn't have said that if he'd known he'd been sitting next to someone who could instantly turn him to ashes.

"Come on, I want to hear more about you, Noon. You made me talk about myself almost the whole time. Next time, it's your turn."

I just stared at him, speechless and nearly numb with the power of my wanting things to be different.

"Come on, you can't hide forever." *Was that my plan?* I hope I didn't look as pained as I felt.

I shook my head. "I'll see you around."

I resisted the impulse to hug him. Sure, he'd maybe saved my life and we'd spent a pleasant hour crossing the Lethe, but I didn't even really know this guy.

"I'm sure you will," he said and smiled. Then he turned around and walked in the opposite direction of where I was headed.

I watched him for a while, wondering if I'd made a mistake. I'd had Hyrke flings before. He might be a welcome distraction from all the stress St. Lucifer's was sure to heap on me. On the other hand, it was more likely the guy would become an unwanted complication. I turned away. I walked for a while and then couldn't help myself. I glanced over my shoulder. Ari was gone. I could see our ferry though, tied up and loading passengers bound for Etincelle. Its name was as faded as the rest of it, but I could just make out the lettering: *First Light.*

So much for the augury idea. A boat named after its arrival time told me nothing about my future. I turned my back on it and kept walking.

Chapter 4

꒤

My boots squished with every step so I took a cabriolet
from the waterfront instead of walking. My cabbie, a
polite nontalker who expressed zero reaction to my destination, dropped me at a courtyard in front of what appeared to
be the main building. I tipped him extra for his reserve on the
way over. He looked at the money, grunted, and sped off. I
turned to face my new home.

My first reaction was that it looked like a bigger version
of some of the Etincelle estates. Lots of heavy, clunky, gothic
architecture with an emphasis on pointed arches, flying but-
tresses, and gargoyles. But there were a lot more people
milling around here than there would be on a private estate.
And there were more buildings. The campus took up at least
five city blocks. That seemed about right, I thought, mentally
checking off the buildings I'd read about in the orientation
materials—Megiddo, Abaddon, and Infernus (dormitories),
Marduk's (eating hall), Corpus Justica (library), Lekai Auditorium, and Rickard Building, where the main classrooms
were. There were probably a few I'd forgotten. On the other

side of the courtyard from where I stood was the Joshua School, where Peter went. But he wouldn't be arriving for a few weeks so, for now, I was on my own. I trudged into the Warenne Tiberius Rhaetia Administrative Building in search of the student affairs desk. Someone there would be able to tell me where my dorm room was and who I'd be sharing it with.

On the way, I checked out my new surroundings. For the most part, everything was exactly how I'd imagined it. The lounge at student affairs looked pristinely comfortable, with deep couches, overstuffed chairs, and large tables. The walls were a freshly painted beige and the furniture had been recently reupholstered in tastefully coordinated patterns of honey, russet gold, and burgundy. Thankfully, there were no plants. I hadn't expected to see any in a school where they trained future Maegesters but I was relieved nonetheless. Students were milling about in small groups. More than half of them seemed to be paying more attention to the people around them than the group they were with. I hurried through the room, wanting a hot shower and a dry pair of shoes more than anything.

The Hyrke working the student affairs desk had a cold. A box of tissues, a bag of throat lozenges, and a bottle of aspirin lined her desk like charms. If the charms were supposed to ward off students, it wasn't working. The line was at least six students deep when I took my place. The woman in front of me mumbled something under her breath to the man in front of her. He turned around to reply and caught me staring. I didn't want to be rude and was just about to look away when he winked at me and then said to the woman in front of me, "Ivy, she's *ill*, for Luck's sake. Give the woman a break."

"Like Hell," Ivy muttered. "That bottle of aspirin has been sitting there since summer and those lozenges look so old they're probably from the pre-Apocalyptic days."

A few of the other students snickered. I gathered from their collective impatience they'd been there awhile. The man in front of Ivy interpreted my staring as an invitation to chat. He pushed past her and extended his hand to me.

"I'm Fitz," he said.

"Noon," I replied, shaking his hand. His grip was firm and quick. The woman named Ivy turned around. With flaming red hair, a mottled complexion, and light green eyes, she looked every inch a Mederi. And with that name I had to wonder . . . but what would a Mederi be doing in law school? They were all about healing and growing.

"This is Ivy, my cousin," Fitz said. The family resemblance was strong, although Fitz's hair was a few shades deeper and his complexion ruddier.

"So, what section are you in?" Ivy asked. All first years were in one of three sections. You did everything with your section—took classes, studied, ate, and even slept in the same dorms together. The orientation materials had made it sound as if your section was a fishbowl. You'd be able to see the world around you but you wouldn't be living in it. The only people who were going to share your life during the next year were the people in your section. I had the feeling my answer to Ivy's question would determine exactly how much longer this conversation would last.

"Section three," I said.

"Us too," Fitz said, grinning.

Ivy's expression changed from impatient annoyance to one that was half-interested, half-wary. I was now someone who mattered, an academic competitor who would have a direct effect on her future. I wanted to reassure her that my only goal was to live in the fishbowl without being eaten by the cat but since saying something so revealing was out of the question, I settled on asking if they'd heard anything about our professors.

"Ben Copeland teaches Sin and Sanction," said Fitz. "He's young. Overcompensates for it by being overly strict. Any perceived slight and you are on the outs for the whole semester. Darius Dorio teaches Council Procedure—"

"A real performer," Ivy cut in. "Turns every class into a

show." That could be interesting, I thought, provided I stayed part of the audience.

"Promises and Oathbreaking is Telford," Fitz said, rolling his eyes.

"Ah, yes," said Ivy. "The professorial equivalent of *Dionaea muscipula*. He lures students into a false sense of security by repeating test questions every year. He even puts the questions *and the answers* on file in the library. But every now and then—and you never know when—he asks entirely new questions. So you have to study everything anyway or risk complete failure."

"For Evil Deeds, we've got Sarah Meginnis," continued Fitz. Listening to the two of them was like listening to two simultaneously played dueling piano performances. My head bobbled between them, trying to keep pace.

"Very dusty," Ivy said, flipping her hair and taking a peek at the front of the line. There was only one more student in front of them.

"She's ancient and has been at St. Luck's forever," Fitz said. "Rumor has it she just went straight to teaching without any time in the field. She's out of touch with real practice, but since evil deeds haven't changed much since Azazel first defined them in the hundred days following Armageddon, she's still teaching what we need to know."

I nodded, acting like some of this was old news and the rest was of no concern, but inside I was sweating. Forget about my concerns over training to become a Maegester. Studying to become an ordinary Hyrke Barrister was starting to sound near impossible too.

"Who'd I leave out?" Fitz asked, stepping up to within sneezing distance of Lady Lozenge. He was next in line.

"Erdman for Analysis and Application," Ivy said. "We don't know much about her, except she's new. I did hear that A and A is a lot of case briefs, though, endless reading and a lot of writing. The only other first year professor is Quintus Rochester. But he's a Maegester and only teaches Maegester classes."

I hoped my cheeks weren't burning. It was so much easier playing Hyrke at Gaillard where no one talked about stuff like this. Was I imagining the hush in the room? Mercifully, Fitz was called up and Ivy, naturally, went with him. I knew they were cousins but they acted like siblings. I watched as they poked and prodded each other, trading little barbs back and forth while Lady Lozenge pulled up their info. A few seconds later, all three of them turned toward me.

Oh no.

"Are you Noon *Onyx*?" Lozenge asked.

"Yes," I said. Now I knew I was not imagining the hush. The room had gone deadly silent.

"You're not signed up for Manipulation," Lozenge said.

"Manipulation—?" My voice squeaked and I refused to look around at anyone else. What was she talking about? How stupid was I for not even reading the Maegester part of the course catalog. I'll bet even the Hyrkes who were training to become Barristers did that.

"I need to know where to put you." Lozenge said, exasperated. "Are you here to train as a Barrister or a Maegester?"

Up until this moment, I'd managed to avoid situations that put me in awkward positions such as this. Positions where I'd have to lie outright about who and what I was. Oh, I'd omitted the truth a countless number of times. But I had never stood in front of an administrator at a demon law school and denied being something the demons valued. The demons might view it as stealing. That's why Maegesters had to declare themselves by Bryde's Day of their twenty-first year. A Maegester's adult life was either spent serving the Council or it was spent . . . not at all. I cleared my throat.

Would Peter be able to find the Reversal Spell? If so, when?

"I'm . . ."

"Apparently, you're my new roommate," Ivy said, staring at me. She gestured behind her with her thumb. "She said you're in Megiddo. Room one twelve, same as me. You did know that the Hyrkes here have roommates, right?"

Oh. Right. Of course. Only a handful of students would have the necessary magic to become Maegesters, but hundreds of Hyrkes were here to become Barristers. The school would have to assign roommates or they'd never be able to house them all.

I nodded and Ivy smiled.

She turned away and walked over to the exit with Fitz. I stepped up to the student affairs desk wondering what other info Lozenge and I had to exchange. I still wanted a warm shower and dry boots but I would gladly have traded those for some new friends. Lozenge and I wrapped pretty quickly—my bill was paid, my room assigned, and my status no longer in question. I was free to go. I squished over to the door.

Fitz and Ivy were still standing there.

"We're headed to Marduk's for lunch. Want to come?"

Marduk's was as warm and cozy as you'd expect an underground pub in Halja to be. The windows were at street level so the light wasn't natural. Little spots of yellow glow hung suspended over each heavily scarred wooden table. Bench backs were high, tablecloths were nonexistent, and the walls were exposed brick. But for all its age and roughness, Marduk's felt like an old pair of canvas trousers, comfortable and well-worn. We chose a table near the back, by a huge fieldstone fireplace that was blazing with heat and orange light.

I ordered a large bowl of potato soup and a small meat pie with mushroom sauce and both Fitz and Ivy ordered some sort of salad and a blueberry crisp. I had to be careful around salads and fresh fruit. It wasn't that someone with waning magic couldn't eat fresh produce, but you wouldn't want to hold it in your hand for too long before eating it either. Cautious as I was, well cooked, heavily smothered in sauce food was a habit I'd had since I'd cut my first tooth. When the food came we hungrily tucked in until there was nothing left but the crust of my meat pie and a few radishes on Ivy's salad plate. I pulled out the unoccupied fourth chair and put my feet up—it seemed like the kind of place where that was more than okay—and undid my laces, hoping my boots would dry better closer to the fire. Neither Ivy nor Fitz seemed inclined to leave, and the place wasn't crowded so we ordered some coffee.

Ivy was short for Ivana Jaynes and she was here to study riparian rights and the law of navigable waters. Her family owned and operated a whole fleet of ferries, the flagship of which was the *Alliance*, a sturdy double-decked vessel that took mechanized cabs, as well as passengers, to the outposts up and down the length of the Lethe. She was well educated and well traveled. Fitz's education and experience, on the other hand, seemed a bit more piecemeal. He had grown up on the Seknecai estate, one of the very few Host estates here in New Babylon. His mother—Ivy's aunt—was the house-keeper for Waldron Seknecus, the dean of demon affairs here at St. Lucifer's. I gathered from the looks exchanged between them that Seknecus might have pulled some strings to get Fitz accepted here.

Both Fitz and Ivy were unbelievable gossips. They had the goods on everyone. But nothing they said was malicious, and they seemed genuinely interested in me, as I was them. I made sure to keep my answers vague though, although I soon found myself wishing I could confide in them. They were as warm and comfortable feeling as the place they'd invited me to for lunch.

I had just finished lacing up my boots when I started to feel the prickly, skittering feeling along my arms and back like this morning. This time Peter's spell doused my magic faster but left my half-digested meat pie feeling like a mound of red-hot lava rocks searing through my stomach. *I have to get out of here,* I thought. I stood up to go and that's when I saw him—Ari, the Hyrke who'd saved me from drowning in the Lethe not two short hours ago.

What was he doing here?

He looked better than I remembered. Here in the underground warmth of Marduk's, his strong features looked even more ruggedly handsome. In this small space, the bulk of his body appeared twice as big. On his arm was a tall, statuesque woman with hair the color of Ivy's. But that's where the similarities ended. This woman was a showstopper, a real knockout, with pouty red lips, porcelain skin, and sky blue eyes. But just above her sternum were two nasty red burns—two wounds the size of thumbprints pressed into the slender hollow of her throat. Immediately behind her was another woman, a pretty brunette with ash-colored eyes and a dimple in her chin.

"Ah," said Ivy quietly, following my gaze, "That's Ari Carmine."

"I know," I said, slumping back down in my seat. Her eyebrows shot up.

"You do?"

"Uh-huh. We shared a ferry ride across the Lethe this morning."

"He always dates the beauties—powerful Mederies from the Gaia Tribe," Fitz said, looking over with a frank look of half-admiration, half-envy.

Ari and his companions slid into a booth along the wall near the front. Ari reached for the redheaded beauty's hand in a gesture that was all too familiar. The sick bubbling feeling in my stomach wouldn't go away.

How had she gotten those burn marks? And what was Ari doing at Marduk's? Was he a student at St. Lucifer's too?

If so, it was surprising that it hadn't come up during our discussion this morning, but then I'd steered purposefully clear of any talk about where we were headed after the crossing. More surprising—and infinitely more disappointing— was my reaction to seeing him with the beautiful Mederi. It irritated me. It irritated me even more that it irritated me at all. I sat in the half darkness at the back of Marduk's stewing. I grudgingly realized that Ari was even more confident than I'd given him credit for. Handsome, charismatic Hyrkes dated Mederies, sure, but not many from the Gaia Tribe.

"The redhead was attacked by a *rogare* demon two days ago," Ivy said.

Surprise turned to outright shock. "Here? *In New Babylon?*"

Ivy nodded. Fitz grimaced.

In Halja, demons came in all manner of sizes, shapes, ages, classes, and types, but there were really only two kinds. The *regulare* demons, who loved rules and the adoration of their followers more than they loved anarchy and chaos, and *rogare* demons, who didn't.

"Did they catch the demon who did it?" I whispered, my throat suddenly dry at the thought of what it would be like to have a demon grab me by the neck.

"No," Ivy said. "Not yet. But the Council's been alerted. I heard that some of the upper year Maegesters-in-Training here might help track it down."

I said nothing. All of my focus was on trying to keep my breathing steady and my hands from shaking. Knowing Halja was full of demons was one thing. Seeing one's brutal handiwork was quite another.

"What was he like, during the crossing?" Ivy asked.

"Who, Ari?"

"No, the captain," Ivy said, rolling her eyes and grinning. "Of course, Ari."

"He was nice," I said, finally tearing my gaze from Beauty's burn marks.

"Nice," Ivy repeated flatly.

Fitz barked out a laugh. "You just called one of your dad's demon executioners *nice*." He laughed again.

My blood turned to ice. "Demon executioner?"

"Yeah, you didn't know?" Ivy said, frowning. "That's how he pays for his education. He executes *rogare* demons. Last fall he declared and chose to train at St. Lucifer's to become a Maegester. Lucky us." She spoke the last two words completely without sarcasm. And from the way she was looking at him, she meant it.

"So he's Host, not Hyrke," I said, confused. "But I've never heard of him. Where did he come from? Was he spawned from Lucifer himself? Members of the Host don't just pop up out of nowhere. They grow up in Etincelle."

There was an uncomfortable silence as my new friends processed my mildly profane outburst. Then Ivy said, "Well, he didn't."

"I know," I said, shaking my head in disbelief. "He said he grew up in Bradbury." There had to be a mistake. They had to be talking about someone else, although the remaining sinking feeling in my stomach told me otherwise. I risked another peek toward the front and wished I hadn't. My gaze suddenly locked with Ari's and he stilled. My cheeks flushed and I looked away, embarrassed to be caught staring.

"He said he had a younger brother," I mumbled, turning back toward Ivy and Fitz. "Who's considering going to Gaillard."

"Right," said Fitz. "I heard that too. Or at least about the younger brother. He was raised by an adoptive Hyrke family somewhere in the southwest. So Bradbury fits."

Ivy kicked my chair. "He's coming over," she hissed.

Every emotion I'd had—petty jealousy over the beautiful Mederi, incredulity over Ari's surprising background, irritation over my own attraction—suddenly turned to liquid fear. If Ari was training to become a Maegester, I could have nothing to do with him. Those with waning magic could sense it in others. Peter's temperamental cloaking spell now made perfect sense. But bolting now, while Ari was on his way to the table, would only call more attention to me. So I sat, forcing a bland smile, hoping he didn't already suspect.

"Hi, Noon," Ari said, smiling down at me. "I had a feeling we'd see each other again."

I shrugged. "You didn't mention you were a student here."

"Neither did you," he said pointedly, his smile disappearing. "Did you get your room assignment yet?"

"Megiddo," I said, inwardly breathing a sigh of relief. He'd be over at Infernus on the floor reserved for the rest of the Maegesters-in-Training. At least I wouldn't be seeing him walking to the bathroom, toothbrush in hand. "This is my roommate, Ivy, and her cousin, Fitz," I said, motioning to them, wanting his attention directed anywhere but toward me. He turned toward Ivy first and extended his hand.

"You're Ivy Jaynes, right?" Ari said as they shook hands.

"Yes," Ivy said, clearly surprised that he might know who she was.

"Your family's *Alliance* has given me safe passage along the Lethe many times," he said warmly, grasping her hand with two of his. His touch and the tone of his voice had its effect and Ivy smiled back openly at him.

"And Fitz?" Ari said, offering his hand to the right. "Is that short for something?"

"Fitzgerald," Fitz said slowly, pumping Ari's hand. Fitz had the look of an alpha dog under attack. He wasn't growling but his ruff was up and his tail was wagging a whole lot less furiously than before. "We were just leaving," he said, standing up.

Ivy looked like she wanted to stay but I leapt up as if on springs. Ari was quicker than me though and grabbed my cloak off the back of my chair before I could. He opened it for me to step into. I paused, not wanting to meet his eye, and then turned so that he could drape the heavy cloak over me. He did, softly laying it across my shoulders and running his hands down my arms as he did so. I shivered and repressed a longing to fall back into his arms. *Was I crazy?* He was a demon executioner who'd come here to train as a Maegester. He had waning magic. Apparently, a lot of it. But even worse, so did I.

Even if I could get used to the fact that he'd killed demons to pay for his tuition, he'd never get used to the fact that my magic was as deadly as his.

I broke free, mumbled good-byes to all, and launched myself toward the door. On the way I had to pass Ari's table where Beauty and her pretty friend waited for his return. I stared. Beauty stared. Mederies were not usually vengeful creatures but she didn't look happy. Somehow I didn't think it was the burn marks. More's the pity for both of us. She only reminded me of everything I wasn't. Everything I could have been. If I'd been born as I should have. I stomped out in the direction of Megiddo. Time to dig my trenches deeper and settle in.

Chapter 5

ͽ

Every waning magic user had a demon mark. I was no exception. The marks were usually dark spots of pigmentation just above the left breast—right above the heart. Mine was light but it was there. When I was nine, I'd tried to cut it off. It had been a disastrous, bloody mess. But the mark had grown back, a shade darker, with no scarring. It was the waning magic in me, I knew, and I hadn't tried to remove it since. What I did do, however, was cover it up. Even in the summer. My entire wardrobe was primarily designed for one purpose—to cover my demon mark. In the winter it was easy. I wore a lot of high-necked sweaters. In the summer, I wore a lot of high-necked, sleeveless shirts. On the rare occasions when I had to dress up, my frocks were startlingly conservative. Or they bared skin somewhere other than my décolletage. Even that morning, heading to student orientation, I was wearing one of the twenty turtleneck sweaters my mother had shipped ahead for me.

My clothes were always serviceable, as Mrs. Aster would put it, and today it was more of the same. My sweater was a

sharp, almost shiny gray and my canvas pants were very
dark and very new, not at all faded or fraying. It was freezing
so I had on a black hooded snow vest lined with ermine and
a different pair of snow boots. The ones from yesterday
hadn't dried out completely yet. And they reminded me painfully of Ari, who I had sworn to put out of my mind. Funny
how people you'd waved off as irrelevant before suddenly
became irresistible.

The sidewalks were covered with a thin coat of brittle ice.
Ivy and I crunched along, our breath coming out of our
mouths in puffs of white as we discussed the start of the semester. Fitz had been assigned to a room in Abaddon and
he was saving seats for us in Lekai Auditorium where the
new student orientation would take place. I raised my hood
against the wind and shoved my hands deeper into my pockets. A light snow fell. Every now and then a flake would
touch my face and melt, a tiny pinprick of ice exploding on
the warm surface of my skin.

Off the sidewalks, the snowfall was deeper, at least a foot,
which gave the benches a rounded, blanketed look. Timothy's Square, the courtyard in between St. Lucifer's and the
Joshua School where the cabdriver had dropped me yesterday, looked stunningly bright with all that white. I was glad
to see the gray cement of Victory Street, one of the main
thoroughfares dividing the campus. Mechanized cabriolets
in every shape and size rushed by, some with beeps or honks,
all with the slushy sound of rubber tires carving through wet
snow.

Ivy and I stood clear of the splash while we waited for an
opening to cross. During our wait five more students joined
us. Students from every direction were converging on Lekai
Auditorium, which was now directly in front of us. A steady
stream of dark jackets, heavy cloaks, bright scarves, hats, and
hoods moved into Lekai. When the traffic cleared enough for
us to cross Victory Street, we joined them and pushed our
way inside Lekai Auditorium.

The lobby was unbelievably crowded. It was like the
Warenne Building's lounge yesterday, but with infinitely

more people. Some people looked like they'd arrived at dawn, while others still had their cloaks and hats on. The outer doors kept opening and closing as students endlessly circulated, searching for their friends, their seat, the bathroom, nonexistent coffee, or just an end to their anxiety.

It was going to be a long morning.

The crowd had an odd scent. One I wasn't used to. Many of the students were wearing perfume or cologne, which was unpleasant but familiar. Some even smelled of nicotine. But I froze when I realized the unfamiliar smell was *pine*.

"What's the matter?" said Ivy, tugging me along by my sleeve. She sensed my hesitation and looked back at me, perplexed. "Let's go!" she said. "Orientation starts in a few minutes. If we don't find Fitz, we'll have to sit apart, or worse—stand for an hour."

I nodded and scanned the room, desperately searching for the offending green. If I spotted it first, maybe I could avoid killing it and giving myself away. The din was tapering off as more and more people found their seats. Through a gap in the crowd, I spotted a Yule tree. *What in Luck's name would a Yule tree be doing at a school for Maegesters?* It could *not* be real. I started to move toward the auditorium entrance farthest away from it, but Ivy grabbed my hand and started dragging me toward it, shouting, "There's Fitz!"

I was just about to yank my arm free when I got close enough to see it was a fake. The annoying pine smell must be artificial too. I was so angry that I almost set the damn thing on fire, but I caught myself just in time. Peter's spell hummed at the edge of my fingertips. *Would it have stopped me? Could it have?* I doubted it. Peter had been clear that the more time spent around things that tested it—Maegesters, plants, demons—the more its magic would fray. His final advice: "Just stay away from them. All of them." As if avoiding Maegesters at a school for Maegesters would even be possible.

Still, I was determined to try.

We followed Fitz down the left aisle of the auditorium. The space was large enough to seat about three hundred people. Now that everyone was filing in, I estimated that the place would be packed. That meant about one hundred students in each section and a two-thirds chance that Ari would be in one of the other two. *Luck, be with me.* I ignored the impulse to start scanning the room for him. It was disconcerting to know that there were others with waning magic here as well. Fitz led us toward the front, weaving in and out of the students who were still standing.

"Ari's saving our seats," Fitz called back to us. "You know, Noon, you were right. I mean I wouldn't necessarily call him *nice*, but he's more personable than any member of the Host I've ever met . . . well, I mean except for you, although you're not really Host . . . It must be the Bradbury thing for Ari. That's a good Hyrke neighborhood. Lots of *nice* people there . . ." I had to tune out Fitz's monologue and concentrate on wiping the shell-shocked look off my face. The skittering feeling starting up my arms told me we were almost there. The feeling wasn't so bad this time, more of an itch than an electric jolt. I wasn't sure if repeated exposure to Ari was wearing down Peter's cloaking spell or if I was learning to control my magic. I desperately hoped the latter.

Ari had positioned himself on the aisle. Fitz and Ivy filed into the seats he'd saved leaving one empty seat between Ivy and Ari. I squeezed by Ari, only too aware of how close he was, and slipped into my seat. He chuckled.

"What? No 'Hello' this morning, Noon?"

I mumbled salutations. He leaned in close and whispered in my ear. The itching feeling ratcheted up a notch and became very, very hard to ignore.

"No full disclosure. I think that was *your* policy for the trip over here. You can't be upset that I didn't tell you about St. Lucifer's. You weren't exactly forthcoming yourself."

I opened my mouth to respond and then immediately shut it. What could I say that was appropriate? I couldn't figure him out. His interest in me if he were a Hyrke would be understandable. I knew from other guys that I was considered attractive. But other members of the Host had never wanted anything to do with me. *What was he doing here? Not here at St. Luck's, but here, sitting beside me?* Then a sneaky, insidious thought formed and I couldn't shake it. I looked up and our gazes locked.

He knew.

Before I could say anything more, the dean of student affairs, Donald Shivel, took the stage and asked everyone to quiet down. The hush was almost total. Shivel launched into orientation immediately with nary a clearing of the throat, a warm-up anecdote, or even a personal introduction. We all knew him anyway, by reputation at least. Shivel was a Hyrke but he was well respected by both the Host and Hyrke communities for his work at St. Lucifer's. It was said he was fair but tough, zealously guarding the school's reputation or aggressively recruiting potential star students as circumstances required. Always the last warning on everyone's lips about Shivel was that he took academic violations very seriously.

"The law school has two tracks," Shivel began. "One for future Barristers and one for future Maegesters. Everyone takes the same core classes together—Evil Deeds, Promises and Oathbreaking, Sin and Sanction, and Council Procedure, but the fifth class will differ depending on which track you're on. Barristers-in-Training will take Legal Analysis and Application and the Maegesters-in-Training will take Manipulation." Shivel paused and peered out at the crowd. I wondered if he was looking for the future Maegesters. I kept staring straight ahead, refusing to look at Ari.

"The classes are similar in a way," Shivel continued. "Each is a hands-on clinic class that will allow you to directly interact with a real client while you are learning the methods of representation, as opposed to the substantive law that you will be taught in the other classes. Hyrke students taking A and A will work in either the Council Procedure clinic or the Sin and Sanction clinic. You will be assigned to one or the other; it will not be an elective choice."

There were several groans. No one wanted to be stuck in a clinic they weren't interested in.

"Maegesters-in-Training may be assigned a demon client." This time there were murmurs, a lot of them. Demons were by no means rare. Halja was full of demons. But Hyrkes almost never directly interacted with them. The fact that some might actually see a demon—perhaps for the first time ever—was one of the reasons St. Lucifer's was such a prestigious Hyrke law school. In the Hyrke community, the perception was that St. Luck graduates were ready for anything.

My parents had been careful throughout our childhood not to expose Night or me to any of the usual Host education lest our uncanny switched-at-birth magic be discovered. So demon interaction had been strictly taboo. None of my father's clients had ever come to our house (as if Aurelia would have wanted demons visiting) and we'd never accompanied my father to the Office of the Executive in New Babylon. Demons remained as much a mystery to me as to Hyrkes. Conveniently, I didn't have to fake my fear of them either. Sure, I had waning magic, but I had no idea how to use it, which meant I had no idea how to control a demon. And demons were nasty creatures, individually given to spiteful pettiness at best and horrifying, stomach turning atrocities at worst.

I realized I hadn't been paying attention when I noticed Ari staring at me out of the corner of my eye. I risked a glance at him. He frowned and narrowed his eyes. Shivel continued to lecture us on the dangers facing us at St. Lucifer's.

"Host students with magic should understand that the euphemism 'sink or swim' does not mean 'pass or fail' at St. Lucifer's. It means 'live or die.' "

All the twittering died down and the audience became deathly still.

"The *regulare* demons that seek Maegester representation respect Halja's laws, but they are still demons. They are likely to be . . . upset . . . about whatever matter has driven them to seek representation in the first place. The demons who seek Maegester representation may not be *rogares*, but they are likely to be unstable. Maegesters-in-Training will be expected to control them . . . for *everyone's* sake."

Shivel smiled. "That having been said, our Admissions

Committee is very good at what it does. St. Lucifer's hasn't had an on campus incident in years." There were a few chuckles over Shivel's self-congratulations but mostly, it seemed, the students were relieved. "This year, we have five Maegesters entering St. Lucifer's and each and every one of them has been thoroughly vetted. Their raw power is substantial, their prior demon experience impressive, and their discipline and control evident. Hyrke students, be assured, you are safe at St. Luck's."

I bit my lip and felt the accusation in Ari's stare. I suppose he thought I should declare so I could learn how to control the unstable-teetering-on-the-brink-of-madness demons that sought representation here. *Um, no thanks.*

The rest of orientation passed in a blur. After the talk, students filed out, most talking in hushed tones. I took my leave of Ari, Ivy, and Fitz, complaining of a headache, which was actually true. Fitz and Ivy were headed to the bookstore and I told them I was going back to Megiddo to lie down. Less than five minutes after I returned to my room, there was a knock on the door. Before I could even open it, Ari strode into the room.

"You could have waited until I opened the door, you know."

"Would you have?"

I stood in the middle of my room, staring defiantly at him. He stared back.

"You know I've done a lot of jobs for your father," he said.

I glared. I really didn't want to know how many demons he'd killed.

"He never mentions you," he continued.

Wow. Ari really knew what to say to a girl. But then it wasn't exactly like he was trying to woo me. He had his wounded Beauty to look after. What could he possibly want with someone whose magic was as deadly as his?

"Now I think I know why."

With each sentence, he'd taken a step closer to me. And I'd taken a step back, maintaining the distance between us.

But with this last statement, Ari moved more quickly than I did and he caught me before I could step back again. His hands gripped my shoulders as he looked down at me. I turned my head.

Despite the fact that he was a demon executioner, he'd saved my life. He'd also been fun to talk to yesterday (albeit, we'd both been pretending to be people we weren't). And, there was no denying, especially not now, when what we were doing was so dangerously close to embracing, that I found him physically attractive. Unfortunately, inordinately so.

I didn't want to lie to him. In fact, I would rather have told him the truth. Ari was the first person I'd ever met who made me want to share my secret.

But I couldn't. It would jeopardize the plan Peter and I had come up with. And even though I'd only known him for a day or two, I didn't want to see the look on his face when I finally admitted what he already knew. That I was far from being a harmless human Hyrke. That I was further still from having the fruitful, abundant, overflowing waxing magic of one of his preferred Mederies.

I tried to shake him off.

"What are you doing here, Noon?"

I sputtered for a moment, incredulous. First, what right did he have to barge into my room and ask intrusive questions? Second, wasn't it obvious?

"I'm a student here, just like you."

Ari shook his head. "Not here at St. Luck's, here at Megiddo. Why aren't you over at Infernus with the rest of us?"

"The rest of . . . ? Ari, I don't know what you're talking about." But instead of sounding angry, I sounded scared.

I sounded like a liar.

"Tell the truth, Noon," he said. His voice had a strange intensity to it. He put his finger under my chin and lifted my face. He looked . . . angry? Anxious? I tried to pull away, but his grip was tight. He wasn't hurting me, but he wasn't letting go either. I remembered how strong he'd been when he was pulling me into the ferry after my disastrous jump. I knew if he didn't want to let go, he wouldn't. I stopped struggling. I didn't want to fight.

"Ari, please go," I said, but he only shifted his position. Taking both of my hands in his, he pulled me close.

"You're playing a dangerous game, Nouiomo Onyx."

I was trapped, in more ways than one. What did he want from me? Why did he care what I did? Ari stared at the spot just above my left breast, right above my heart where my demon mark was. He hesitated, as if weighing a decision to a question only he knew, and then slowly he placed his palm over my mark. Even through my sweater I felt the effect of his touch there. It felt like a brand. I cried out. Ari's eyes widened in disbelief. He took one look at my face. (I have no idea what he saw. Fear? Anger? Uncertainty?) His jaw hardened with resolve. He lowered his face to mine.

What was he doing? He couldn't possibly be thinking of kissing me. And kissing him was the last thing I should be doing.

My demon mark burned beneath his hand and my magic flared, rushing over me as a searing wave and then crashing against the confines of Peter's spell. The jilted force of it would have knocked me flat if Ari hadn't been holding me. He pulled back and grunted, tightening his grip. This time it did hurt.

"Let go," I said through gritted teeth.

"You need to declare," he said roughly, releasing me with a shove. "Soon, it's going to be too late."

"I'm leaving," I said suddenly and recklessly. I'd never wanted to come here. St. Lucifer's was just a place to hide while Peter continued to search for the Reversal Spell. But if I left, I wasn't sure where I'd go next. With waning magic, any work at a restaurant, hospital, or farm was out. Maybe I could become a dockworker or a cabdriver.

"Leaving won't solve the problem!"

"But it isn't *your* problem so you don't need to worry about it," I said, rubbing my shoulders and turning toward the door.

He snorted. "You've been my problem since yesterday. You think I couldn't sense your magic on the boat?"

So why hadn't he said anything then? Why was he cornering me now?

"I don't understand you," he said, circling around to stand between me and the door. He didn't understand *me*?

"You should *want* to declare. If you declare, you'll be taught an honorable career. You'll be taught to control your magic, instead of having it be a potential danger to yourself and others. You've got raw power. I can feel it. We could use you."

Ah, I thought. Finally. I got it. And him. Ari's motivation in coming here was that of a good shepherd. He was trying to bring one of the wayward back into the flock. Well, Ari might be a good shepherd, but I'd never been a very good sheep.

"I don't *want* to," I snapped. "I don't want any part of declaring. I don't want *any* part of demons, demon law, or Maegesters. I can't *stand* waning magic."

Ari winced. "That's blasphemy. You can't mean that."

"I can and I do," I said, forcing my voice to sound angry instead of pathetic. "You don't know what it's like. You were born the way you were supposed to have been."

He blinked and stared at me in surprise. For a moment, neither of us spoke.

"Noon, why do you waste one second on what might have been? What is, is. That's the only thing that matters."

"Well, what *is*," I said with false bravado, "is that I don't *want* to declare."

Ari said nothing, just stared at me with a hard look on his face. "Just don't leave."

I groaned.

"Please," he said. I got the impression he didn't use that word a lot.

"Are you going to declare for me?" I asked.

After a while, he shook his head.

"*You* need to declare," he said ominously and walked out.

* * *

Classes started the next morning. I didn't leave and I didn't declare, and over the next few weeks Ari and I seemed to work out some kind of unspoken truce. He was in section three, of course—because I could feel Luck starting to turn against me—but he always sat down in front while I back benched it. Ivy and Fitz always sat somewhere in the middle rows.

"I feel like a referee," Ivy said one day. "What gives? I thought you two were friends."

"Friends?" I said, laughing nervously. "No, we just shared a ferry ride, that's all."

"Uh-huh."

In those first few weeks I didn't really think (much) about Ari and declaring because, honestly, it was all I could do just to survive the basic Barrister classes.

Demon law school was hard enough all on its own without the added headache of Manipulation, which is what the Maegesters-in-Training were required to take. Five classes were held two to three times per week and most of them were a minimum of ninety minutes each. The prep time for each ninety minutes, however, seemed to take ninety days. I worked at becoming more efficient, but every time I found myself with three seconds to spare, the professors seemed to smell it and filled the time with more work. We read cases, briefed cases, discussed cases, and argued cases. I lived, breathed, ate, and slept endless cases. No two were alike and each had multiple parties, confusing procedural history, irrelevant facts, inconsistent holdings, nonsensical rules, hidden issues, poor judgments . . . The work seemed to go on forever.

Because it did.

Ivy and I were both late-nighters, but Fitz was an early riser so we had all worked out a schedule. We met at Corpus Justica an hour before our first class to go over the day's assignments. We ate lunch at Marduk's, discussing cases, classes, professors, and other students' answers the entire time. After lunch we had our last two classes—together, a three hour grueling ordeal that was only possible because of the coffee breaks—and then went back to Megiddo. Ivy and I always crashed then and slept for at least a couple of hours. When we woke up, it was already dark and we met Fitz for dinner, sometimes at Marduk's, sometimes somewhere off campus just for a change. Fitz would leave after that to sleep and Ivy and I would hit the books until early morning, sleep for a few hours, and then get up the next day to do it all over again. Our entire world was quickly reduced to four buildings and one hundred people.

It was impossible, since he was one of the one hundred people, to stop thinking about Ari entirely. Occasionally I wondered if he would keep his word and not declare for me. I had no further incidents with plants, other Maegesters, or losses of control, and I never saw my name put up on the Maegester's List outside Waldron Seknecus' door, so I had to assume my cover was still holding. Around the second week of classes, my magic stopped flaring up around Ari. Maybe it was constant proximity; maybe it was a lack of reciprocity. I knew I shouldn't miss the flare-ups, but I did. It seemed like the connection between us had been broken. But it was stupid to mourn for something I'd never had and, besides, hadn't I told him I wanted nothing to do with him?

During the third week of school, Peter called me. The electro-harmonic machine that had been installed on the wall of our dorm room had to have been one of the first five ever made. Connections were often horrible, even on the newest machines, but this one made Peter sound like he was calling from under the Lethe, not across it.

"—on, ss— Peter. How—" Static burst from the receiver so loudly I had to hold it away from my ear, which precluded me from hearing the next ten words Peter said.

"Peter!" I yelled into the box on the wall. "It's a bad connection!" *When weren't they?* "I can't hear you—"

But his connection must have been even worse because he just kept talking. I knew if I didn't calm down and listen, I'd burn the box right off the wall.

"—ou? 'z . . . 'ell Holding up? . . . I—"

After seven dropped connections and as many call backs I finally understood that Peter wasn't coming as planned. It was impossible to hear his entire explanation. But the gist of it seemed to be he'd found a new lead and he was staying in Etincelle to pursue it. He'd contact me (hopefully by letter, messenger, or in person!) once he was here in New Babylon.

In an effort to distract myself from the constant anxiety created by Peter's absence and what it might mean, I threw myself into my classes with renewed vigor. I stopped back benching and joined Ivy and Fitz in the middle rows. I participated more and my answers were articulate. I stopped verbally stumbling when I didn't know the answer and got better at modifying my arguments midsentence. Verdicts that had seemed unfair or illogical on the first day of class became clear when reread within the context of the entire body of law known as demon law.

Under demon law, rules were gods not to be crossed. Lucifer was king and in his absence no other demon could take his place. Halja—our very existence—depended on following, to the letter, the rules laid down in the aftermath of Armageddon, the last battle of the Apocalypse. Halja's *regulare* demons were capable of wreaking havoc, but they knew what they were about. They did not want chaos or anarchy. They'd had enough of that prior to Armageddon. Now, all they wanted was adoration. So the *regulare* demons and their Maegesters set up a very strict form of government. No clemency, no leniency, no second chances—that is if you're a demon.

If you're a Hyrke though, pick a demon to appeal to. They *loved* that. They *lived* for that. A demon wanted you to state your case, they wanted to hear your pleas, they wanted to aid in your defense. So most Hyrke families appealed to a single hearth demon. It was kind of like an inherited deity-client relationship. Hyrkes almost never saw their hearth demon. But so long as a Hyrke's pleas were respectfully spoken and accompanied by the required sacrifice, pleas were usually granted. Problems happened when demons started fighting over their Hyrke clients—or anything else. That's when the Maegesters stepped in. But Barristers didn't have to worry about that. Their job was mostly preventing the Hyrkes from abusing their client privileges and reporting any activity that could lead to demon fighting.

Training to become a Barrister was rigorous work. I wouldn't say I was happy, but I'd settled into a rhythm.

Arrhythmia struck a week before Bryde's Day.

We were between afternoon classes and I was in Rickard Building on my way to my locker to change out my books. We'd just endured a particularly painful session with Meginnis in Evil Deeds. My mind was positively reeling from all the archaic rules on defamation, false light, and alienation of affection. Personally, I thought it all boiled down to "don't mess with another man's demon" but I knew sweeping summaries would never do. Scrupulous rule following was *praeceptum primum, praeceptum solum. The first rule, the only rule.*

Ivy and Fitz wandered down to the coffee kiosk in search of caffeine and sugar. I dropped my stack of books in front of my locker. Around me, students were also dropping books, slamming the metal doors of their lockers, and trying to talk over each other. I was bumped from behind by elbows, shoulders, and, occasionally, a backpack. The hallways of Rickard were filled with the blood of students coursing from one class to another. I grabbed the silver catch on the front of my locker and pulled it up and out. My locker door swung open. There, sitting in the middle at the very edge of the top shelf, was a small unadorned evergreen tree.

A real one.

It was only about four inches tall and no more than three inches at its base, but this tiny tree meant the end for me. I stared at it, numb from too many emotions, felt all at once. Who had left it in my locker? And why? In and of itself, the thing was fairly innocuous. Hyrkes sometimes gave them as gifts this time of year. But that tradition was frowned upon here at St. Luck's in deference to the Maegesters. Still, it hadn't been strictly forbidden either. Hyrkes brought plants to St. Luck's at their peril—and apparently, mine. Did I have a secret Hyrke admirer? One who was oblivious to what this "gift" might mean to me? But figuring out who put it there and why was irrelevant. My immediate problem was how to get rid of it without giving myself away. I knew full well Peter's cloaking spell wouldn't help. There wasn't a spell in Halja that would allow someone with waning magic to actually touch a live plant without killing it. I'd have to come back later and get rid of it when there were fewer people.

I was just about to close my locker when a thick, pasty white arm stretched across my face and reached up for it. Short, stumpy fingers closed gently around the tree, killing it instantly. I turned.

Standing beside me was a barrel-chested man with a longish blond beard that was just a shade lighter than dirty dishwater. He gave me a twisted smile and chucked the dead plant into a nearby trash can. He waved a slightly plump hand in the air in a fluttering, dismissive gesture.

"Plants have no place at St. Lucifer's." His voice was so deep, I thought I might be in danger of falling into it.

"Who are you?" I asked, involuntarily taking a step back. Recoiling from him just seemed like the natural thing to do. His expression was simply *not friendly*.

"Sasha de Rocca," he said, keeping his hands clasped behind his back. "I'm a Maegester-in-Training in section two." He stared at me, as if daring me to say something. But I was speechless.

"I'm also a distant cousin of yours," he said blandly, "Our grandfathers were brothers."

Oh, right. I remembered who he was. His mother was Livia, my mother's first cousin, but they'd never been close—even before Night and I were born. Sasha was one of seven. Most of his siblings had magic. He had two older brothers who were already Maegesters and one sister who was a Mederi. His two younger sisters had been born without magic and were living as Hyrkes. I think I'd actually met one of them during my last year at Gaillard.

But I'd never met Sasha. I would have remembered. And

now seemed an odd time for a family reunion between two distant relatives who'd never met and didn't want to. Sasha's face said it all. He'd been forced to come talk to me. But by who? Aurelia? Livia?

"Ari thinks we should talk," he said.

"About what?" I said, narrowing my eyes.

Sasha arched an eyebrow. "Oh, you know—evergreens, gardens, babies—the usual." He snorted. "What do you think he wants us to talk about?"

I stared blankly back at him, proud that he couldn't see how hurt I was that Ari had betrayed my trust.

"And if I refuse?" I whispered fiercely. "Another tree for me tomorrow?"

Sasha shrugged. "Where do you want to meet?"

I gritted my teeth, staring down at my books.

"Timothy's Square, after our last class."

Chapter 6

ও

Class after that was excruciating. Feeding off my hurt and anger, my magic flared up for the first time in weeks when I walked past Ari. He looked up at me with a stone-cold expression on his face, which I gave right back to him. Marching up the aisle, I sunk down in a seat next to Ivy and spent the rest of the time alternately sweating and clenching my fists. I did not take one note. Thank Luck I wasn't called on. It was all I could do not to burn the place down. I knew I had control issues but it felt like Peter's spell was barely working. When class ended, I bolted to the ladies' room.

In the mirror, my face looked flushed but otherwise all appeared normal. I splashed cool water over my cheeks and waited for my natural pallor to return. When it did, I walked out to the square. Sasha was already there, waiting.

The sun was sinking, but I couldn't see it. It was hidden somewhere behind all the buildings. Moments like these, I missed Etincelle.

Sasha sat on a bench facing the Joshua School. A few inches of his chin-length thick blond hair stuck out of the dark red knit cap he was wearing. He turned to face me when I sat down, his full lips nearly as red as his hat from the cold. He raked his gaze over me, top to bottom, and then pursed his lips together disapprovingly. I tucked a stray piece of hair back into my hood and stuffed my hands deeper into my pockets. A few other students crossed the square, scurrying through the cold on their way to dinner.

"Ari's obsessed with you, you know. And I don't understand why. I mean, look at you. All I feel from you are weak bursts of magic. It's like you're sputtering."

Peter's spell must finally be in tatters from all the abuse I'd heaped on it.

"He wants you to declare," Sasha said peremptorily. When I didn't respond, he continued. "He thinks we could use someone with your . . . *talent*." He cleared his throat and flicked a piece of imaginary lint from his trousers to show me what he thought of my "talent."

Beside him, I stewed.

"Ari took last month's demon attack on one of his old girlfriends personally. As if it was directed at him." Sasha scoffed. "I think that's why he wants *you* to declare. He's convinced that every scrap of waning magic in Halja can be useful. Even waning magic found in the most unlikely and unwilling places."

I bristled, but elected not to rise to Sasha's bait. Instead, I asked a question I'd been wondering about since I saw Beauty's burn marks that first night I'd met Ari weeks ago.

"Where was she attacked?"

Sasha looked at me like I was a Gorgon with snakes coming out of my head. "Where was she . . . You don't actually think you're going to track that demon down, do you?" Sasha laughed, a great big belly burst of laughter that sounded like a hole opening up in the ground. "Ari just wants you to declare. He didn't mean you should start hunting demons *now*." He laughed again and shook his head. "He said you were conflicted about who and what you are. No kidding."

Where did Ari get off confiding all these thoughts about me *to Sasha?* I'd been surprised and, I couldn't help it, a little bit pleased, that Ari was obsessed with me, but I was beginning to understand he was obsessed about me the way you'd be obsessed about a cowlick you can't quite smooth down. And the plant in my locker was a low blow. I started to feel itchy again and knew beyond the puff of a demon's breath at midnight that Peter's spell would not be able to contain my magic if I allowed it to heat up.

"Just answer the question, Sasha," I said blandly, flicking an imaginary piece of lint off *my* trousers.

"At the train station."

Interesting. And somewhat worrying. Amaryllis Apatite, the Demeter Mederi that had gone missing the week before classes started, had last been seen boarding the North-South Express. The place where Amaryllis had been headed, and the place where Ari's burned Beauty had been attacked, were one and the same: the New Babylon train station, which was just one block from here. I was suddenly glad my brother, Night, had decided to go south, with no plans to return north. Still, if the *rogare* demon responsible for the attacks was still out there, then anyone using the New Babylon train station might be at risk. I told Sasha as much. He rolled his eyes, which told me exactly what he thought of my concerns and then got back to the matter at hand.

"So what should I tell Ari about you? Are you going to declare?"

"Whether or not I declare is my business, not yours. And not Ari's."

"Wow. You just don't get it, do you? If you don't declare by Bryde's Day, the demons will eventually find out. The fact that your magic is so weak you couldn't control an imp won't matter. You will have broken the rules. And the demons hate that. They won't stand for that. They will find you and they will kill you.

"I told Ari this conversation would be a waste of time." Sasha sighed dramatically. "I told him if you didn't have waning magic, we didn't need to talk. And if you did—we *still* didn't need to talk. Because anyone with waning magic who seriously considers not declaring, *especially* a weird mutant gender bending *freak* who has waning magic, isn't worth working with."

The itchy feeling I was experiencing turned fiery. Everything Sasha said may have been true, except for the part about me being weak. I had to leave *now*, before I set him on fire. But he beat me to it.

"I feel like I'm talking to a corpse," he said. And then he got up and walked away.

I sat there on the bench for a while. The sun set and the night grew dark. Fewer and fewer students walked through the square. My cheeks got cold and my toes grew numb. The fact was, like it or not, declaring was starting to sound like a viable option. Oh sure, I hated thinking about making any choice that someone like Sasha might have suggested. But my life was different now than it had been even one month ago. My days of growing up in secluded Etincelle or hanging out in relative anonymity at Gaillard were over. Bryde's Day was next week and Peter still hadn't contacted me. The likelihood that he'd find the Reversal Spell in the next seven days was about as likely as Lucifer guest lecturing for Meginnis.

My magic control had been tested more in the past four weeks than it had been in the past four years combined. If this was my new normal, I was in big trouble. Eventually, I would give myself away, or worse, hurt someone. Maybe it was time I started learning how to control my magic instead of hiding it. I hated possessing waning magic because it was destructive and deadly. But *I* didn't have to be, right? Some people—the Mrs. Asters and Sashas in the world—would view me with disgust. But others might not. Ari hadn't.

The temperature dropped. My breath puffed in and out in small white clouds. The square's lamp lights came on. Finally, I got tired of just sitting there. I got up and walked back to Megiddo. Back in my dorm room, I took a good look around. Our room was more cramped than cozy, little more than a ten by ten space crammed with two twin beds, two desks, and two wardrobes. Ivy had plastered her side of the room with pictures she'd taken during her frequent travels: panoramic vistas of Halja's western mountains, sepia-toned shots of her posing with various crew members who worked on her family's ferries, whimsical pictures of her fishing from docks, rowing in dragon boats, and sunbathing on da-habeahs. There were even a few of her and Fitz at the Sekne-cai estate.

On my side of the room? Peeling paint and crumbling plaster. Maybe it was time to put some pictures up there, even if they weren't the pictures I'd always dreamed of.

Maybe it was time to declare. The jangly sound of our room's electro-harmonic machine wrenched me out of my meditation. I walked over to the wall and picked up the receiver. It was Peter. And this time the connection was clear as lark song. He was at the Joshua School and he wanted to see me.

"Noon, can you come over now?"

I didn't even spare Ivy's pictures or my blank walls a second glance as I hung up and rushed over to meet him.

Unlike at the Aster estate, Maegesters and those with waning magic were always welcome at the Joshua School. In modern times, Maegesters and Angels worked together all the time. Mostly, Angels were hired as consultants. Angels were experts on Apocalyptic knowledge, the history of Armageddon, and its aftermath. They were also fluent in all three of the primary demon languages. Angels were the ultimate linguists. Any case involving a matter of interpretation, whether it was historical or linguistic, was likely to have an Angel involved. Their spell casting abilities were an added boon.

The inside of the Joshua School was more modern than I expected from people who made their living off of ancient knowledge. In fact, the lobby was very contemporary, all slick lines with whitewashed walls and curvy bleached wood trim, funky colored, oddly shaped furniture, and lots of tables made of bubbled glass and oiled iron. I walked up to a long counter that ran along part of the side wall. The setup reminded me of a hotel. Behind the counter, along the wall, were little niches for the Angel students, full of mail and packages.

A man stood behind the desk. He had one of those boyish faces that never seem to age. He watched me approach, expressionless and silent.

"I'm here to see Peter Aster," I said.

"Is he expecting you?"

"Yes." The lobby was so quiet and deathly still, it felt like a tomb. The ageless man walked over to the lobby's small harmonic and cranked the handle.

"Mr. Aster? There's a woman down here to see you . . ." A moment later, the man nodded, replaced the receiver, and looked at me. "Go on up," he said. "Thirteenth floor, room seven."

I nodded my thanks and walked over to the lift. It was self-operating and opened immediately, which was a relief. At the top, Peter was waiting for me.

His smile disappeared as soon as I stepped out.

"What happened to the cloaking spell?" he said, putting his arm around my shoulders and leading me down the hallway. "It's practically gone. Did you have a brush with a demon over at St. Luck's?"

I didn't bother answering him. There'd be plenty of time to catch up later.

"Did you find the spell?" I asked breathlessly.

"Not yet," Peter said cavalierly, not realizing the effect his words would have on me. The giddiness I'd experienced when he first called evaporated.

Peter pushed open the door to his room and led me in. Small, gleaming silver ensconced white glow lights hung around the room, reflecting off white walls and waxed wooden floors. Its brightness was jolting. Peter turned toward me, his face a mixture of concern and expectation.

"So how are things at St. Luck's?"

Horrible. Frightening. Awful. And yet, if I were being 100 percent truthful, I'd also have to add interesting, intriguing, and challenging.

I walked over to him and put my head on his shoulder. I'd missed him. He was my oldest friend and I needed one right now. I wanted something comforting, something familiar. But there was nothing comfortable or familiar about resting my head against Peter's chest. He stood stiffly beneath me for a moment and then slowly put his arms around me. After a moment of awkwardly embracing, I pulled away.

Peter's room was nothing like I expected. It was in fact a suite of rooms, but clearly built for just one occupant. Apparently, Joshua School students didn't have to bunk up like the Hyrkes at St. Luck's. It was also flawlessly clean. The living area was defined by a spotless white love seat and a black leather chair. On the floor between them was a thick cream-colored area rug and, on top of that, another glass and iron coffee table. The only thing on the table was a piece of mail. "Masquerading as a Hyrke has been a lot harder than I thought it would be," I said. "I thought I could do it. Now, I'm not so sure. Honestly, Peter, if you haven't found the Reversal Spell yet, I think I'm going to declare."

"What? How can you say that? You don't want to be a Maegester."

"Yeah, I know. I've always hated the thought of having to use waning magic." Peter nodded. When he wasn't frowning, which was a lot of the time, Peter was handsome, almost beautiful.

"But it might be good to learn how to control it," I said slowly, gauging his reaction.

"Learning how to control waning magic means becoming a Maegester," he said, motioning me over to sit on the couch. I sat, teetering on its edge. He took the chair and faced me.

"You won't be allowed to learn how to use your magic and then say, 'no, thanks' to the job. You'll be required to serve the Council."

I grimaced and Peter's face softened.

"Do you really want to be someone whose job is to advise, judge, and possibly execute demons?"

We stared at each other for a long time. Peter could be very convincing. I sighed.

"No," I said finally. "But it's not just about me, is it?"

"What do you mean?"

"I mean if I don't learn to control my magic, someone could get hurt. I do know that I don't want to spend the rest of my life as someone who's afraid to lose her temper for fear of burning something . . . or someone."

I thought of Sasha and how much I'd wanted to hurt him. He might have said horrible things, but no one deserved to be burned. I'd never burned another person before, but then I'd never felt as cornered as I had lately. And if I didn't declare my magic by Bryde's Day, the cornered, panicky feeling I'd been holding at bay would turn into a full-fledged fight for my life.

"No one will get hurt," Peter said impatiently. "I'll cast another cloaking spell—"

"Peter!" His eyes widened and he leaned back from me. I lowered my voice. "I don't want another cloaking spell."

He moved to the edge of the chair. Our knees touched. He took my hands in his.

"What are you saying?" he asked. "That you're going to declare?"

I pulled my hands free and sank back into the couch. "You can't cloak me forever."

"I would, if I had to. But I think I can find the Reversal Spell before Bryde's Day."

"It's next week, Peter," I said, groaning, covering my face with my hands. "When we first came up with the plan to search for the Reversal Spell, we had nine *years*. Now we have seven *days*. Don't you think it's time we called the search off?"

"Absolutely not. I found something. Another reference." I took my hands off of my face. He came to sit beside me. This time he was flush with excitement.

"Remember I was telling you that the ancient book of Revelation referenced the Reversal Spell? That the spell had been written down in the immediate aftermath of the Apocalypse at His command?" I nodded. "Well, I did some digging. Most people believe that Armageddon was the last battle of the Apocalypse. But I don't think so."

It was my turn to frown. How could that be? Peter was arrogant, and he spent more time studying the archives than anyone I knew, but even he couldn't rewrite history.

"I was in the Divinity Archives and I found a working draft of a manuscript titled *Last Stand*. It was never published. The draft was pretty rough, but from what I can tell it was an account of the end of days. The true end. According to *Last Stand*, a small portion of the Savior's army survived Armageddon and holed up on the far shore of some river. They huddled there, dejected and weary, waiting for the Savior to rally them for the final battle. But he never came. Instead the Host did. But instead of killing them, they offered a truce. The terms of the truce were recorded by scribes on both sides. The Savior's scribe was the same person who wrote the draft of *Last Stand* . . . Jonathan Aster."

Our eyes met.

"Do you know where the Savior's army made their last stand?" Peter asked. I shook my head.

"In Etincelle. Think about it, Noon. It makes sense. The far shore of some river has to be a reference to the Lethe. Everyone knows Armageddon was fought here, on the ground that became New Babylon. And it would explain why Etincelle was settled by both Angels and Host."

What he said made sense, but still . . .

"You're losing me, Peter. What does this have to do with us—here and now?"

"If the Reversal Spell was recorded after the end of the Apocalypse, then it may have been recorded as part of the truce terms between the Host and the Angels. And if Jonathan Aster was the scribe who recorded the truce . . . where would you search for it?"

The Aster estate. It was almost too much to hope that the

spell that could make everything okay was right next door to where I grew up. Could Luck be that cruel? That kind?

"Your house," I said.

Peter nodded. "Or, more precisely, the Aster Archives in the crypts beneath it. I'm headed back to Etincelle tomorrow morning." He pointed to a duffel bag beside the door that I hadn't noticed before. "Want to come?"

I hesitated. "I don't know . . ."

"If you help, we'll find the spell twice as fast."

"Maybe . . ."

Finding the Reversal Spell was what I wanted, right? I didn't want to be a Maegester. Heck, I didn't even want to be a Barrister, although I'd miss Ivy and Fitz. The three of us worked well together. Each of us had our strengths and weaknesses. Fitz loved all the idiosyncratic rules of Council Procedure, but was hopeless at Evil Deeds. Ivy seemed to intuitively understand all the confusing promise doctrines like oath estoppel and unjust empowerment. Whereas I'd become surprisingly adept at Sin and Sanction. Fitz and Ivy depended on my near perfect recall to quiz them on the hundreds of sins the residents of Halja could be found guilty of. I suppressed my guilt over the upcoming Sin and Sanction midterm. It wasn't as if Ivy and Fitz were helpless without me.

Peter smiled. It was the first real smile I had seen from him in a long time. It transformed him from a dour, hand wringing intellectual into a beautiful, bright, and highly capable young Angel. I smiled back.

"Have you eaten yet?" he said. "I'm hungry."

I shook my head.

"Want to go somewhere on your side of campus? How about Marduk's? It's been ages since I've been there."

I ate there every night. But it wasn't every night that Peter was in such a good mood.

"Okay," I said, slipping my arm through his as we walked to the door.

"Oh, I almost forgot," he said, turning back to the coffee table and grabbing the piece of mail I'd noticed earlier. He handed it to me. "This is for you. It's a letter from Night. I brought it for you from Etincelle."

"He's okay, right?"

He nodded. "That's what your mother said when she gave me that to give to you."

Well, at least that eased one of my concerns. I grabbed Peter's arm again before his good mood could change and marched him to the door.

"So," I asked, "what time is the ferry leaving tomorrow?"

Marduk's was crowded. Peter and I waited for a table. One finally opened up, a deuce near the front door, and, regardless of the constant draft creeping in, I finally began to relax. How could I not? We weren't leaving tonight—the last ferry had left hours ago—so I shrugged off my remaining unease about our planned early morning departure. I reminded myself I hadn't wanted to come to St. Luck's in the first place. When I began to think about how much work I'd put into school already, I concentrated on the menu. As I skipped over a baby spinach salad in favor of grilled vegetables, I remembered the evergreen in my locker. Which led me to think of Sasha again and the things he'd said to me. And that reignited my earlier anger.

I feel like I'm talking to a corpse.

If the Reversal Spell worked and I retained only half the amount of magic I currently had, no one would ever associate me with death again. My healing powers would rival my mother's, before her mysterious decline. My touch would be a balm to the sick and soothing comfort to expectant mothers. At the very least, I'd be able to eat a bite of fresh salad without it rotting on the way to my mouth. *I vowed to look up Cousin Sasha after I had blessed my one hundredth crop of wheat so that I could dare him to look me in the eyes and call me a—*

Three things happened almost instantly. I set my napkin on fire. Peter knocked over his water glass, putting out the flames, and Ari walked through the door. If I had doubted before whether there was any vestige of Peter's cloaking spell left, I knew then that every shred of it was gone. The feeling I experienced when Ari walked into Marduk's was as different from the prickly, skittering feeling I was used to experiencing around him as demons were different from Angels. It was as if a small sun had entered the room. Heat, or something like it, radiated from Ari. The intensity of it left me feeling blistered and burned. I instinctively reacted, putting up the magical equivalent of a hand to repel the force assaulting me. But I had no idea what I was doing or how much counterforce I used. I only know that Ari turned toward me then, first with a look of shock and then one of absolute focus, as he made his way through the crowd toward our table.

Peter shoved the half-burned sopping wet mess that had been my napkin into his pocket. He scowled at me, his earlier winsome expression completely gone.

Ari arrived. He wore a long dark wool cloak over a charcoal gray, thick weave sweater. Small snowflakes glistened in his hair, melting in the heat of Marduk's. In the warm underground glow surrounding us, Ari's dark eyes appeared almost entirely black, devoid of pupils and eerily intense. I concentrated on controlling my emotions. I felt like two people. The first was a wannabe Mederi who was desperately infatuated with a seriously hot, super powerful Maegester in the making. Having Ari stand this close to me when for weeks we had done nothing but ignore each other was difficult. I couldn't help remembering how it had felt the day of Shivel's orientation lecture when he had put his hand over my demon mark. What would it feel like now, without the barrier of Peter's cloaking spell?

What would it feel like without the barrier of clothes beneath his palm?

I turned away, blushing. When I turned back Ari stared at me, a set expression on his face.

The second person I felt like was a real-life she-devil. I wanted to crisp Ari on the spot for his little tree trick, but doing so in such a public place was hardly a good idea.

"Did Sasha find you?" he asked.

"Yeah."

"And?" Ari said, completely ignoring Peter.

"And," I said, my voice betraying my anger, "I told him to go to Luck with my blessing."

Ari inhaled sharply and leaned over the table toward me.

"I was hoping he'd talk some sense into you. I'd have thought you'd have come around by now."

"Excuse me," Peter said, placing his hand on Ari's chest and physically pushing him back from the table and away from me. "Who the hell *are* you?"

Ari looked at Peter, almost as if he were seeing him for the first time.

"Ari Carmine," he said, offering his hand. Peter waved it off, declining to take it.

I knew Peter's feathers were likely smoothed by Ari's Hyrke surname but I didn't want Peter getting any ideas that Ari was a friend.

"Ari's a Maegester-in-Training here, Peter." I lowered my voice so that only the three of us could hear what I was saying. "Ari left a special present for me in my locker today—didn't you, Ari?" I said, smiling up at him with syrupy sweetness and, I hoped, a murderous look in my eye. "And then he sent one of his minions to come talk to me."

"Sasha's not one of my minions," Ari snapped. "He told me he was your cousin. Wait—what present? I didn't leave anything in your locker for you."

"Sasha as in Sasha de Rocca?" Peter asked, his tone both incredulous and angry, but Ari and I ignored him.

"The evergreen," I hissed. "That was low, Ari, even for you."

To his credit, Ari blanched. "I didn't leave an evergreen in your locker. Is that . . . do you actually think . . ." He shook his head as if to clear it.

"Let me get this straight, you left a *plant* in Noon's locker? Why? How did you even . . . ?" Peter was slow to the party but he played catch-up fast. He realized in seconds what had taken me a day to figure out.

Peter's cloaking spell had never hidden me from Ari.

"Who are you?" Ari asked Peter. "I haven't seen you around. Are you a friend of Noon's from home?"

"Peter Aster," Peter said. He stared at Ari with narrow, calculating eyes.

Ari's nonplussed look continued. "Aster . . . You're an Angel?"

"That's right."

The two men sized each other up. Ari likely saw a thin, anemic looking academic while Peter likely saw a hulking, shabbily dressed demon beseecher.

"I didn't—wouldn't—leave a plant in your locker, Noon," Ari said finally, turning to me. "Come on, how would I even get it in there without killing it myself?"

"Just stay away from me," I said. Ari looked away. "Come on," I said to Peter. "I just lost my appetite."

Peter stood up, looking grumpy. He tossed his napkin to the table. "Fine. I've got some more research to do and you still have to pack."

"Pack?" Ari said, his voice low and deep. I'd never been afraid of Ari, but just for a moment I could imagine what it must be like. "Where are you going, Noon? Did you forget our deal?"

"What deal? We never had a deal."

"We had an understanding. You said you wouldn't leave."

"Any understanding you think we had was broken when Sasha showed up at my locker today."

"Let's talk outside," Ari said, looking straight at me, ignoring Peter again. I shrugged and got up slowly. I didn't want him to think I jumped at his command. Ari turned and made his way to the door. I followed, purposefully staying a few feet behind him. Peter trailed me, looking peevish.

The entrance of Marduk's fronted an alley. All of the other doors along the street were back doors to buildings already closed. Outside, it was cold and dark. One streetlamp glowed but it was some ways away. We climbed Marduk's outer steps to street level, crossed the alley, and stood in front of another door, likely locked for the night. There was a small awning over the door that kept most of the falling snow off of us.

"Where are you going?" Ari said, wasting no time in launching back into our interrupted conversation. "You can't just skip class like that."

"There are more important things to worry about than class," I said, refusing to look at him.

"Like running away."

"I'm not running away."

"The hell you aren't, Noon. Bryde's Day is next week. You're twenty-one. The *only* place for you right now is *here*," Ari said, pointing at the ground beside him. "You know what you have to do."

Peter stood absolutely still. He was no longer peeved; he was livid. Out here, his face appeared translucent. His lips moved slightly, as if he was talking to himself, but I recognized what he was doing—getting ready to cast a spell.

"If you leave, I'll declare for you," Ari said, forcing all of my attention back to him.

"What?" I said, stunned. "But you can't . . . I . . . We're so close. I just need more time."

"You don't have it."

"Give her until Bryde's Day," Peter said.

"Why?" Ari said, his patience clearly wearing thin.

"Why can't you just leave her alone?" Peter said. Two angry spots of color appeared on his cheeks.

"I can't," Ari said, looking surprised at his own admission.

"All we're asking for is a couple of days," Peter said. *"Pacta sunt serv—"*

Instantly, Ari waved his hand in a slicing motion across Peter's throat. Peter made a strangled noise and grabbed his neck with both hands. He tried to talk but no words came out. He just stood there, his mouth opening and closing, his lips smacking and his tongue clicking, while his eyes grew wider and his face redder. Ari had leeched the oxygen from around Peter, making him breathless and, more importantly, speechless.

"Stop!" I cried, shoving Ari. How had the situation deteriorated so quickly? Luckily, Ari did stop. He looked down at me and a little sliver of fear ran up my spine.

"Set your spellcaster on me again, Noon, and I'll rip the larynx right out of his throat."

I nodded, shaken by the exchange, not wanting to make things worse by continuing to argue.

"Why do you need a couple of days?" Ari said. "What are you up to?"

"Looking for something," I said.

"What? Come on, Noon. I don't feel like dragging this story out of you. Give me a good reason not to go up to Seknecus' door right now and write your name on The List."

"We're looking for a spell."

"A spell?" Ari snorted and made an impatient motion with his hand. "*What* spell?"

I was reluctant to reveal what we were doing because Peter might get into as much trouble as I would. I'd never really thought about it before, but what if we found the Reversal Spell and the demons killed Peter for casting it over me? The demons might view casting the spell in the same way they viewed not declaring—that we'd stolen a valuable asset from them. But it was clear that Ari wasn't going anywhere until he got the full story. And after his stunt with Peter just a minute ago I knew he probably *would* declare for me if I didn't tell him everything.

"Peter thinks he might know where the Reversal Spell is."

Ari's eyebrows shot up and he looked over at Peter with renewed interest. Peter, on the other hand, shot Ari a lethal look.

"The Reversal Spell is a myth," Ari said.

"No, it's not," Peter said with exaggerated patience. He probably hadn't forgiven Ari for the choking incident but he likely knew he'd brought it on himself by attempting to cast an unwanted spell over someone as powerful as Ari. Peter's expression told me he hated Ari but that he wouldn't do anything stupid like trying to cast another spell.

"Then it's a dangerous truth," Ari said. "If the Reversal Spell exists—and that's a big if—no one has cast it for thousands of years. Legend says it's the biggest spell of all time. Regardless of whether you might be able to find it, do you really think you could cast it?" Ari spoke directly to Peter, all former antagonism gone. He spoke with a theoretical tone, as if discussing whether or not Professor Telford would repeat last year's test questions.

"Watch me, firestarter," Peter said contemptuously. Ari glanced over at me to see my reaction to Peter's insult. I didn't give Ari the satisfaction of seeing me break ranks with Peter but I couldn't help wondering if "firestarter" was how Peter viewed me as well.

"Easy, spellcaster," said Ari. "All I'm saying is that casting something that big shouldn't be rushed into. Noon's working with a pretty tight deadline. Do you really want to risk botching the spell?"

"I haven't botched a spell since I was a kid," Peter said viciously, clenching his fists.

Ari shrugged. "Search for the spell. But leave Noon out of it."

"I'm doing it for her."

"Are you? Any Angel who locates and successfully casts the Reversal Spell could likely do anything he wanted, become dean of the Joshua School, maybe even head of the Divinity—"

"Enough," I said, cutting into the conversation and physically placing myself between the two men. I was tired of being talked about as if I weren't standing right there. I had told Peter earlier tonight that if he hadn't yet found the spell, I was going to declare. The only reason I'd started wavering again was his continued insistence that he could find it by Bryde's Day. But I hadn't thought about what casting the spell might mean for Peter. So what if Peter was hoping to cast the spell out of ambition? That didn't make it any less dangerous for him.

Peter must have sensed my commitment wavering because he grabbed my shoulders and shook me.

"Noon, you're a woman," he said. "Don't you want to have the power to create something instead of destroying it?" I shook my head. I did *not* want to have this conversation right now. But Peter misinterpreted my look as argument. "Don't you want to hold life in your hands? To grow things, instead of killing them?

"You're a *woman with waning magic* for Luck's sake!" he cried.

I cringed. Peter had never spoken to me like this before. But his next words were even worse. "Without a spell to help you, you'll *never* have a child. *Never* have a family. Is that what you want?"

I stepped back as if struck. Suddenly what I wanted most was another cloaking spell to hide me. I wanted to run and run and never look back. Peter's recitation of my deepest, most private fears, in front of Ari, someone I'd been more than mildly infatuated with, someone who likely viewed me as a repulsive mutant who was too cowardly to do what was necessary, undid me. Tears welled and I turned away, embarrassed, hating myself for being weak. But I didn't have to be. If I declared and started learning how to control my magic, people would no doubt say all kinds of things about me. But *weak* wouldn't be one of them.

Chapter 7

I left Ari and Peter. I have no idea what they said to each other after I left. I didn't care. It didn't matter. The only thing that mattered was taking charge of my destiny and stopping all these feelings. I refused to be weak or scared—for myself or anyone else—again. And the only way I could do that was to declare and accept what Luck had given me.

I walked from the back alley where Marduk's was to the front of Warenne. The administrative building was dark and the doors were locked. Frustrated, I jiggled the handle. In seconds, the doorknob became too hot for me to hold. I stared, half-horrified, half-satisfied, as it melted before my eyes. Hot dribbles of molten metal dripped down the front of the door. A few drops fell to the ground and sizzled, cooling into a small piece of charred metal. I stepped over it and pushed open the door.

Waldron Seknecus' office was on the third floor. Since he was the dean of demon affairs at St. Luck's, he was the individual charged with rounding up that year's current crop of potential Maegesters. To facilitate matters, Seknecus always kept a piece of paper pinned outside his office door. It was referred to simply as, "The List." Any student with waning magic who entered the doors of St. Luck's was obligated under demon law to put their name on The List.

I walked quickly, took the steps three at a time, and arrived outside of Waldron Seknecus' door breathless and shaking. There it was. The List. The thing I'd spent the last four weeks—well, really my entire life—avoiding. I stared at it long and hard. It was incredibly mundane for something with such a monumental purpose. For something that would turn my whole world upside down. A few black pen strokes spelling out five names on a piece of plain white paper. I couldn't even use lack of a pen as an excuse. Some helpful person had conveniently tied one to a string and tacked it next to The List. Not wanting to stall any longer, I reached up to add my name, but my hand was shaking so badly I couldn't write.

I lowered my hand and it grazed something sharp sticking out of my pocket. The corner of Night's letter. I'd forgotten all about it. I pulled it out to read. Night's familiar script raced across the page.

Noon—

I made it to Maize, the Demeter Tribe's southern outpost, with little incident. As you may have guessed, my appearance here—without any introduction—kicked up some dust. It's mostly settled now. I'm sorry I didn't tell you my plans before I left. I wasn't sure I'd really go through with it until I got here.

Don't wait to start your life, Noon. Peter may never find the Reversal Spell, and even if he did, who knows how it would work. Leave the believing to the Angels. Those in the Host have to do what we were born to do, as Luck would have it.

I hope this reaches you before Bryde's Day. You know what you need to do.

Night

I folded the letter back up and put it in my pocket. A feeling of acceptance, if not peace, came over me. *I could do this.* Before I could change my mind again, I scrawled my name across the bottom of The List.

It was done.

When I got back to my room, Fitz was pacing in front of the window and Ivy was sitting on her bed biting her nails.

"Where have you been?" Ivy asked. She rushed over to me and gave me a great big hug, and then, just as quickly, she let go and shook me by the shoulders. "Seriously, where were you? There's been another demon attack. And this one happened *on St. Luck's campus.* We heard there's going to be an announcement posted about it sometime tomorrow. Fitz and I were worried! We thought something might have happened to you when you didn't show for dinner."

Her gaze swept over me as if she were searching for signs of an attack. Probably because of everything going on at that moment—my recent declaration, this new news that there'd been another attack, the fact that Ari had trampled my trust into the dust—Ivy and Fitz's concern for my well-being almost made me feel like crying.

"Noon, you're not hurt, are you?" Fitz asked, leaping up from Ivy's bed where he'd been sitting.

I shook my head and motioned for him to sit back down.

"Then what's wrong? What happened to you?" Ivy asked, stepping back.

"Tell me about the attack," I said, ignoring Ivy's questions. We'd get to my unwelcome news soon enough.

I sat down on the edge of the bed facing Fitz. "What happened? Who was attacked? And when?"

"We're not sure yet who it was," Ivy said. "But, about an hour ago, some second year Hyrkes heard screaming outside of Corpus Justica. They ran out to see what was going on and saw a woman dressed in a Mederi's green traveling cloak engulfed—that was the word they used—by a dark mist. She was struggling against it, but, before they could reach her, the mist burst into a fireball and she was gone, mist and all."

Corpus Justica was across the street from the New Babylon train station. If the Mederi was wearing a traveling cloak, it wasn't too much of a stretch to think she may have been coming from there. I told Ivy and Fitz about Amaryllis Apatite's disappearance and shared my worry that the events were somehow related. Unlike Sasha, they didn't belittle my concerns.

"You should tell Waldron," Fitz said. I'd nearly forgotten that Fitz had grown up on the Seknecai estate. Of course he would be on a first name basis with our dean of demon affairs. I nodded and swallowed, getting suddenly quiet. Fitz and Ivy were too. I think they sensed my no-show at dinner was related to something important. And they were waiting for me to tell them what it was and where I'd been.

I cleared my throat. "Speaking of Seknecus . . . I have to tell you something."

Luck, why was it so hard?

I'd just declared to all of Halja. It shouldn't matter what Ivy and Fitz thought of me. My whole life I'd been a loner. I'd had some Hyrke friends at Gaillard, but those friendships had been surface only. No one had ever known who I really was. There was Peter. But our friendship was always strained by the fact that his mother hated me. It was only fear of my father that dissuaded Mrs. Aster from revealing my secret or publicly showing her antagonism toward me. So, here I was. Ready to tell the two people I'd spent almost every hour of every day with for the past four weeks, that I wasn't really who I said I was. That I was really the product of some odd Host birth defect.

"Actually, I just got back from Seknecus' office. I . . . ah . . . put my name on the list outside his office door."

"You mean 'The List'—the one for Maegesters?" Fitz asked, totally confused. "Why would you do that?"

I bit my lip and felt my cheeks flush. My magic never heated up though. It stayed coiled inside me in a tight, little, easy to control ball. I wasn't mad at Ivy and Fitz after all. I was afraid of them. Afraid of their judgment, or worse, their pity.

"Because my name belongs on The List," I said.

"I don't understand," said Fitz. "You have to have magic to become a Maegester. And don't you have to be a man?"

I sighed. "Yeah. That's how it usually works."

"Noon, what are you saying?" Ivy said. "That you've got magic and it's waning, not waxing? How's that possible?"

I made a hopeless gesture. All I wanted to do was crawl under my covers and go to sleep. Pretend this day never happened. Wake up tomorrow and realize this whole day had been a nightmare.

"I don't know," I finally said. "I don't get it any more than you do. But I was born with waning magic and my brother, Night, was born with waxing magic. I don't know why. I only know that's how it is."

I remembered Ari's words on the first day of the semester when he'd told me he knew. *Why do you waste one second on what might have been? What is, is.*

Well, what was *now*, was that I was just about to lose the only two friends I had here. I realized that I should have told them the truth from the beginning. They still might have thought I was a freak, but at least they wouldn't think I was a freak *and* a liar.

"You're going to be a . . . *Maegester*?" Ivy asked, clearly horrified.

The three of us stared at each other for another minute or so without speaking and then I blurted out, "I'm sorry."

Fitz still looked confused. "For what?" he said.

"For not telling you the truth in the first place."

Ivy nodded, looking miserable.

"Look, I just . . . well . . . I just wouldn't want you to think I'd burn the place down or something." I was trying to make a joke, but the problem was, with my lack of control, there was an outside chance I might.

"Wow. You really could, huh?" Fitz asked, looking at me, really seeing me—*me*—for the first time. It was weird, but not as bad as I thought. I could tell he viewed me with a mixture of awe and morbid curiosity. "What else can you do? How powerful are you? Who else knows? I guess everyone will by tomorrow." Fitz didn't even wait for me to answer his questions. He just kept asking them and answering every third one himself. Ivy just sat there, still looking hurt and upset.

"Fitz!" I finally said, stopping his verbal hemorrhage.

"Oh," he said, ceasing. He seemed to realize that Ivy had been oddly quiet.

"So I guess this means you'll be moving out," she said.

"Do you want me to?"

"Why didn't you tell us?" Ivy asked.

"I've never told anyone," I said. "My family doesn't even talk about it. I was raised as a Hyrke. I've learned to live life as a Hyrke. But I realized tonight I couldn't keep living that way."

"Because of the demons," Ivy whispered. "Were you really going to lie to them?"

I shrugged. "What does it matter now what I was or wasn't going to do? I declared by the deadline. I've broken no rules. I doubt I'll ever be some kind of Maegester wunderkind, but at least I'm here, walking, talking—breathing." I knew I was trying to convince myself more than them but they seemed to appreciate what I was saying. In some small way, it made me feel better. Fitz was even nodding. But then his eyes narrowed.

"Are you still going to be in the study group?" he asked.

I couldn't keep the surprise off my face.

"Oh, I guess not," he said. His face fell.

"No, I am!" I said. "I mean, I'd like to, if you still want me to be."

"Well, sure," said Fitz, in a tone that suggested everything about this discussion was obvious. "How else am I going to pass Sin and Sanction? But you're on your own for Manipulation." Fitz and Ivy shared a look of horror.

"Ivy, I can move to the Maegester floor at Infernus if you want me to," I said. "But . . . I'd rather stay here."

"You would?"

"Yes," I said, nodding emphatically.

Fitz left soon after and Ivy and I fell gratefully into bed. This had been the longest day of my life. Just before I dozed off, Ivy's voice came from the darkness.

"It must have been hard for you, growing up. Not being able to talk about your magic or let anyone know you had it."

"Yeah," I said. I wasn't sure what else to say. I'm sure others had it worse.

"Still, maybe your parents had their reasons. Maybe they just wanted to shield you from what was to come for as long as they could. Keep your childhood as normal as possible."

A cold, tight feeling burned like ice inside me. I'd never thought of it that way. But then, who knew what my parents thought or why they did what they did? My childhood had been anything but normal.

But Ivy continued, oblivious to my conflicted thoughts.

"You have a good heart, Noon. Fitz thinks so too. No matter what happens, don't let the demons and what you'll be expected to do for them or to them ever take that away from you."

The Host *never* said prayers. But if we did, I'd have said *Amen* to that.

I woke up before sunrise the next morning. There was something I had to do before my declaration was made public—tell Peter. After all the years of plotting a way to reverse my waning magic, he deserved to hear from me that I'd finally gone and declared that I possessed it and would now start learning how to use it. But when I showed up at the Joshua School, he was already gone.

"Where did he go?" I asked the boyish-faced man from last night. Was the man ensorcelled? If he didn't age, maybe he didn't sleep either.

"Etincelle."

So I was too late. News of my declaration would spread to Etincelle by lunchtime. Peter would hear it from someone else after all.

"Wait," said the man, turning back to the wall of cubbies behind him. "He left something for you." He pulled out a crisp white envelope, similar to the one I'd received from Night, and handed it to me. I stepped outside and read it while walking to class.

Noon—

I know what you did. I wish you would have waited. If you were an Angel, I would tell you to have faith. Instead, I shall keep it for both of us. I've taken a leave of absence from my studies at Joshua School to continue my search for the spell in Etincelle. You'll be the first to know of any progress. Don't get too carried away with following the road you've been forced to travel. The farther you go, the harder it will be for me to help you find your way back.

Peter

I crumpled up the letter and threw it in the nearest trash can. Readjusting my hood and backpack, I clutched my cloak at the collar, crossed Angel Street and Timothy's Square and entered Rickard for my first class of the day, Sin and Sanction with Copeland.

Walking into the classroom was about what I expected it would be like. I lowered my hood and all of the preclass hum—much of it about last night's demon attack—stopped. All eyes turned toward me. People's faces showed all sorts of different emotions. Some students were openly gawking, like they were looking at something from a street fair or sideshow. Some people wore an expression of frank assessment, obviously recalculating their academic chances against me now that the new information about my declaration was in. A few looked as if they'd been sucker punched. Those wore a green-around-the-gills expression that suggested my doubling the odds for a chance demon encounter didn't sit well with them. Ari smiled at me, but smartly withheld any sign of smugness.

Ivy and Fitz had thankfully saved me a seat between them. I sat down and some of the buzz returned to the room. I couldn't help thinking most of it was probably about me. When I sat down, Ivy slid a cup of coffee my way. The gesture reminded me uncomfortably of something a Hyrke servant might do for a Host employer until I remembered it was her turn to buy today and that I'd be buying tomorrow. She was proceeding with business as usual. Maybe everyone else would too. I grabbed my books out of my backpack just as Copeland entered the room.

As law professors went, Ben Copeland was young. He was probably in his late thirties. Physically, he was nothing remarkable. Intellectually, however, he was a powerhouse. He taught class primarily by asking questions, not answering them. He used one case as a jumping-off point from which to start a freewheeling discussion on whatever set of sins we were discussing that day. Usually, he would pick one student and torture them for the entire class. If they couldn't formulate answers to his increasingly hypothetical questions he would pounce on their nearest neighbors. But he would always return to his original victim, gnawing at them, worrying them, until they were little more than a pile of shaking bones and scrambled brains by the end of class.

Last night's cases had all involved theft and varying forms of theft like conversion. I'd read most of them but, due to my own late night sin of breaking and entering Warenne Building to declare, I hadn't had time to prepare as fully as I would have liked. I took a fortifying sip of coffee, flipped open my notebook, and uncapped my pen. I nearly choked when Copeland barked out my name.

"Ms. Onyx, please state the case of *Creswell v. Henn.*"

Stating the case meant tell the class who the parties were, what the sin was, and whether the accused was eventually found guilty or innocent. Sometimes it was helpful to state other useful information such as whether either of the parties was a demon, Host, or Hyrke (Hyrke mercy pleas were granted more often than others) and what the consequence of a guilty verdict was. In modern day Halja, consequences were given for some sins as a means of deterrence, not punishment. But for certain egregious sins, the demons still demanded retribution in the form of suffering. I imagine these consequences were a bloodletting of sorts, a release valve for all the pent up evil in Halja. In any case, knowing the consequence of a particular sin gave you an indication of how serious the demons believed the sin to be.

The case I'd been asked to state was fairly straightforward, although I'd only had time to read through it once. Around the turn of the century, somewhere on the outskirts of New Babylon, a farmer named Henn had leased some land from a man named Creswell. Included in the lease were a house, grounds, meadow, woods, and a cleared area for planting crops. The lease was vague as to how much authority Henn had to implement changes around the farm.

"Creswell was a landlord who leased land to Henn for farming," I said. "Henn farmed the land successfully for eighteen years but then sinned and was evicted, just prior to winter, and denied his share of the crop."

"Henn's sin?" Copeland prodded from the front.

I had to think for a moment, but then I remembered.

"Waste." It was some obscure sin related to theft.

Copeland looked expectant and then made an impatient gesture with his hand. "And . . . what is waste?" he asked, enunciating each word to underscore how slow he thought my responses were.

"Waste occurs when one destroys, neglects, spoils, or otherwise wastes the asset one has been entrusted with. Waste can be either voluntary or permissive. Voluntary waste is similar to theft in that it requires an act. Permissive waste can occur simply by not acting—by not taking care of the asset to which one was entrusted. In the Creswell case, Henn's act of waste was voluntary. The farmer cleared an additional six acres of woods to experiment with a new crop."

Copeland nodded. "And was he found guilty?"

"Yes."

"Was the experimental crop a failure?"

"The casebook doesn't say."

"What if the crop had been successful? Do you think the landlord would still have evicted him?"

"It's impossible to say," I said, wondering where Copeland was going with this line of questioning. "Was the landlord an entrepreneur or an arborist? Did Creswell prefer money to trees?"

"Does any of that matter?"

Well, sure it did, to rational people. But we lived in Halja and were ruled by demons obsessed with rules, not reasons.

"No," I said. "Henn committed waste when he cleared the additional acres absent Creswell's permission. The failure—or success—of Henn's crop experiment is irrelevant. Henn didn't have the authority to decide how to best use the land he was entrusted with."

Copeland made a noise, something between noncommittal and murmuring assent. He stared at the ceiling for a moment and I knew the next question would not be about *Creswell v. Henn*. Most students made it to this point without getting too thoroughly trounced. But when Copeland started hypothesizing, only the most erudite students kept up.

"What if, instead of a farmer, the accused had been a musician?" Copeland said, "A virtuoso. What if, at an early age, this musician is given to the family's hearth demon to be trained as a master pianist?"

I was listening, and following with an academic ear, but part of my brain was sounding an alarm. I had a sinking feeling about where Copeland was going with his waste hypothesis and why he had called on me today.

"What if," Copeland continued, "the musician doesn't want to make music? What if he prefers to paint landscapes?"

I remained mute, despite the direct question. I didn't want to go where Copeland was leading me. Of course, by not answering I left my friends open to attack.

"Mr. Fitzgerald," Copeland said, abruptly turning to Fitz. "What if the musician refused to play music?"

Fitz was lost. He shuffled through his notes, seeking inspiration, but finding none. Finally, he asked weakly, "Does the hearth demon like art as much as music?"

Copeland brushed him off with a wave of his hand. "Ms. Jaynes?" he asked, addressing Ivy, who snapped to attention. She cleared her throat.

"What if the musician changes his mind?" she said. "And agrees to go back to playing the piano?"

Copeland frowned. Apparently having the tables turned on him, with students providing more questions than answers, didn't suit him. He pounced on me again.

"What if, Ms. Onyx, instead of bestowing the gift of a virtuoso, the boy's parents hid him from the demons? Would that be waste?"

It was classic Copeland. He had boxed me into a corner. *Damned if I answered, damned if I didn't* . . .

"What if by the time the boy was found and trained it was too late? What if the years of neglected training had reduced his talent to shreds and tatters? Would that be waste?"

I swallowed. I was going to have to say something. Copeland wouldn't stop asking questions until I did. But while I was dithering about whether my sense of self-preservation was more important than my sense of academic competition, Copeland got to the point.

"What if the boy was no virtuoso, but a future Maegester? What if the boy—*or girl*—was hidden from the demons for so long that her waning magic had atrophied by the time she declared? Would *that* be waste?"

I opened my mouth to speak, but before I could, Ari's hand shot up. Copeland looked amused. "Yes, Mr. Carmine?"

"It wouldn't be the student's sin, it would be her parents'," Ari said, turning to look at me briefly before directing his gaze to the rest of the section. I realized what Ari was about to say was as much for them as for Copeland. "And no sin will have been committed if the value of the lost asset can be restored within a reasonable time." He turned back toward Copeland.

"The farmer's problem was that he didn't have access to a Mederi to regrow the woods. And the musician's problem was that he refused to accept the talent that Luck had given him. But Maegesters are far more valuable assets to Halja than dirt diggers or entertainers. No Maegester will be accused of waste if she can prove herself, regardless of any act—or omission—that occurred prior to her declaration."

Copeland narrowed his eyes, apparently mulling over what Ari had said, and then he looked at me. "Ms. Onyx?"

"The doctrine of reasonable restoration can be invoked for the sin of waste," I said slowly, gathering my thoughts. "But reasonable is defined by the person against whom the waste was committed. For the farmer, the landlord would judge whether Mederi-born new wood was comparable to virgin forest. For the musician, the familial demon would determine when artistic license becomes sinful rebellion.

"For the future Maegester," I added, forcing my voice to stay clear and strong, "the Demon Council will judge her fate."

Copeland pursed his lips together and nodded.

"You have a clear grasp of Sin and Sanction, Ms. Onyx. Let us hope that you do as well in your Manipulation class."

He moved on to someone else and I felt the sweat trickle down between my breasts. I'd heard Copeland's message on levels both academic and personal because that's how he'd meant it. Just because I'd declared, didn't mean I was out of danger.

After class, I headed to Corpus Justica. It was Friday and the only other class we had was A&A in the afternoon. Since I was dropping it, there was no point in going. On Monday, I would start Manipulation with the other Maegesters-in-Training. I was dreading that almost as much as I had dreaded declaring. It was bound to be awful. The only other waning magic users I'd ever had any interaction with were my father (hardly ever saw him), Sasha (couldn't stand), and Ari (completely conflicted about). And then there was the class itself. Manipulation was supposed to teach Maegesters how to control demons. I could barely control my own magic.

The somber mood of Corpus Justica suited me just fine. The hush and stillness, the solemnity, the sheer gravity and immenseness of the place fell around me as thickly as my winter cloak. Walking through the stacks of the library made me feel insignificant. It calmed me. Insignificant people could not make significant mistakes.

I chose an empty study carrel as far away from the main entrance as I could get. No one was around so I wasn't very quiet taking my books out of my bag. Two thumps later there were five collective inches of leather-bound material for me to cozy up with. I draped my cloak over one side of the carrel, sat down, and flipped open my books. We had Oath-breaking on Monday, right after Sin and Sanction. I was determined to master remedies over the weekend. Twenty minutes later I was deep into monetary damages versus specific performance when I felt Ari approach. I say felt because it was impossible to mistake that burning, blistery feeling he gave off now that I was free of Peter's cloaking spell. I turned around.

Ari was standing a few feet from me, staring.

"I can feel you," he blurted out.

I frowned. *So? I could feel him too.* It was no secret that those with waning magic could sense one another's presence.

"It's different now," he said. "It's more acute."

He seemed to be having trouble talking. Like he wasn't sure what to say. If I didn't know his confidence was as high as the heavens that once were, I would have said that he was nervous. I suspected he felt awkward, just like I did.

"Peter cast a cloaking spell over you before you came here, right?"

I hesitated, than nodded. Any evidence of it was long gone. Mention of Peter's name made me think of the scene in the alley from last night. I felt my cheeks flush. Ari grabbed a chair and pulled it over next to mine.

Why was he sitting down?

Once, we might have been friends—maybe, if things had gone differently. He'd been so easy to talk to on the crossing. But that was *before*. Before, when we were pretending to be Hyrkes, before the lie of St. Luck's, the Sasha betrayal, and the threat of forced declaration. Before the scene in the alley last night, when Peter voiced all of my most private fears and darkest insecurities right there in front of Ari. It was like having your clothes ripped off in front of the hottest guy at school. And then having him see that you have this hideous birthmark you've been trying to hide. One he knew about but had never really *seen*. I knew I should learn to love the birthmark, but it was hard when it marked me as a destroyer of men—and women and children, gardens and greens.

"I'm glad you declared," he said.

Of course he was glad. He'd threatened to do it for me.

I hadn't been this close to him with no one else around since the day of orientation. It was unnerving. Law school had left little time for personal grooming, but with Ari it only added to his attraction. His hair had grown longer since our first meeting. It was as thick as mine, but not nearly as straight or dark. He hadn't shaved and his chin and cheeks were covered with dark stubble. In the glaring overhead light of Corpus Justica, his eyes appeared rimmed with black, intensely deep. I was afraid to stare into them for too long for fear he would know my thoughts. Despite last night and the unbelievable foolishness of it, I was still hopelessly attracted to him.

I shrugged and looked away. "I didn't do it because of you."

"I know," he said. "It's better that you did it for yourself."

Ari wasn't a large man, but he was tall and powerful looking. He dwarfed the small library chair he was sitting in. He looked down at the floor. It was an odd moment, almost as if he was bowing to me, but then he looked up and there was nothing submissive in his look. It was predatory and very determined. It was a look that sat comfortably on Ari Carmine's face. I licked my lips and forced myself to be still. Every emotion I had, I wanted to hide from him. *When would he go away?* He was making me feel things that would be difficult to forget.

"Noon, you're going to need someone to help you catch up."

"Catch up? I'm doing fine," I said huffily, leaning back and narrowing my eyes at him. He was the last person I felt like studying with.

"I don't mean with your regular classes. I mean with Manipulation. Copeland's right. The Council is going to be watching you very closely now. I want to help."

"What's with you, Ari?" I said, suddenly annoyed. "You think that the performance of every Maegester-in-Training somehow affects you? That somehow your future success as a Maegester becomes less likely if another fails?"

"No—"

I cut him off. "Whether I succeed or fail has nothing to do with you. Stop worrying about me. I'll either be fine or I won't," I snapped, "but it won't affect you."

I was prepared to grab my books and leave, but before I could, Ari reached out and put his hands on my knees. The effect of contact was immediate. A blast of desire shot through me and I suddenly wanted Ari's hands in more intimate places than just my kneecaps. I tried to brush his hands off, but he grabbed mine and leaned toward me.

"Your success or failure has everything to do with me," he said softly. I scoffed and looked away, but he brought his hand up to my chin and gently turned my face back toward him. "I knew you had waning magic the first time I met you. And I knew we'd meet again, I just didn't know how soon. I thought you were younger. That you would have more time to figure things out before you had to declare. But then when I realized you were a student here—at St. Luck's—in my class and still pretending, I knew there was no more time. You had to declare."

"I know, Ari," I said, reaching up to remove his hand from my face. "Why are you rehashing the obvious? That's all yesterday's news, literally."

He refused to move his hand and, in fact, reached up with his other so that my face was cupped between them. It was impossible to look away. It would have been a delightful precursor to some very pleasurable academic distractions if I didn't feel so awkward and embarrassed around him.

"Noon, I would have declared for you, if you hadn't," he said, his breath tickling my lips, teasing them. *It was so unfair. Why couldn't we be two Hyrkes? Why hadn't I been born a Mederi?*

"I couldn't let you be killed," he continued, "and not because I know your father or because we could use your magic, and definitely not because your failure to declare would reflect badly on me." He snorted. "You know full well the reason I don't want you killed, but you refuse to accept it. You're still trying to hide," he murmured and I shivered beneath him. "But I won't let you."

He kissed me then and it was unimaginably different than any other time I'd been kissed. I surrendered completely. Despite the awkwardness I felt, this was what I had wanted. I felt like a weak, knobby kneed girl who'd just swooned in her lover's arms, but Ari's kiss made me feel deliciously feminine. His mouth came down on mine insistently, his lips soft but firm, his grip quickly moving from my chin to the back of my nape as he tilted my head back to gain greater access. His tongue darted across my lips, an unmistakable question.

Would I yield to him?

I did. What else could I do? I wanted him in the worst way. He assailed me both physically and magically. The skin beneath my demon mark burned, my whole being coursed with heat. Waning magic swirled around us and Ari stood up, pulling me to him.

"I've wanted to do this since the first time I saw you," he said. His voice was gravelly and rough, rumbling deep within his chest. There was an unusual rawness to it. I would have rolled my eyes and made a joke about the bounds of his arrogance being so great that he was determined to have every conceivable sexual experience, even those that bordered on the exotic or bizarre. But there was something eerily serious about his gaze as he looked at me. A joke seemed inappropriate. I settled for an incredulous look.

"Noon, don't you know how beautiful you are?"

Men had called me beautiful before. But they'd all been Hyrkes, unknowing of my true nature, of what I was really capable of. If they'd only known what was lurking beneath my pretty porcelain shell . . . My magic flared up, vicious and strong, all soft edges made sharp again, the last few minutes almost forgotten.

"Let me help you," Ari said gruffly. "Let me teach you how to control your magic."

"What's in it for you?"

"You, I hope," Ari said, meeting my magic with his own. He didn't try to soften my edges; he just parried them with his own.

"I can't stop thinking about you, you know," he said, squeezing me to him. "You *fascinate* me."

He followed up his declaration with another kiss, this one more scalding than the last, and then dropped me back into my seat, breathless and wanting.

When I left Corpus Justica that night, I saw Waldron Seknecus' announcement up on the corkboard to the right of the main exit.

St. Lucifer's Law School

ALERT
FOR IMMEDIATE POSTING

- ☑ CORPUS JUSTICA
- ☑ WARENNE ADMIN BUILDING
- ☑ LEKAI AUDITORIUM
- ☑ RICKARD BUILDING
- ☑ DORMITORIES
- ☑ MARDUK'S

* POSSIBLE ROGARE DEMON SIGHTING . . .
* POSSIBLE ROGARE DEMON ATTACK . . .

WITNESSES RECENTLY SAW WHAT APPEARED TO BE A ROGARE DEMON ATTACK AND ABDUCT A TRAVELING MEDERI WHO WAS PASSING THROUGH ST. LUCIFER'S CAMPUS BETWEEN THE HOURS OF 6:00 AND 7:00 P.M. IN AN AREA TO THE NORTH-NORTHWEST OF CORPUS JUSTICA.

STUDENTS ARE ADVISED TO USE EXTREME CAUTION WHEN
WALKING ON CAMPUS AFTER DARK. IF POSSIBLE, TRAVEL IN
GROUPS AND DON'T GO OUT ALONE.

I pulled my hood up over my head, pushed the huge iron
doors of Corpus Justica open, and stepped out alone into the
cold dark of night.

Chapter 8

১

I had agreed to let Ari help me learn to control my magic. It seemed the sane thing to do. Luck knew, I needed the help. The fact that Ari had declared he couldn't stop thinking about me and I was madly over the moon about him was an added complication I could have done without. Despite how weak kneed our little romp in Corpus Justica had made me feel, the dalliance was unlikely to go anywhere good. The best I could hope for from Ari was what he had offered— help with my magic.

Infernus looked exactly like Megiddo. The rooms were the same; the only difference was that Maegesters didn't have roommates. Ari met me downstairs and escorted me up. We met no one on the way. Because it was Saturday, the floor was deserted. That suited me fine. I'd have pushed off the day of meeting my fellow Manipulation classmates as long as possible if I could have. As it was, Ari had insisted I spend the weekend with him in a crash course designed to get me up to speed for Monday. When I had mentioned my plans to conquer Oathbreaking remedies over the weekend, Ari had looked at me incredulously.

"Oathbreaking?" he said. "Forget about Oathbreaking for now, Noon. You need to put everything you have into Manipulation. You need to understand, starting now, that Manipulation is *everything*. You're going to be a Maegester, not a Barrister. You could ace every single other class here at St. Luck's, but if you can't pass Manipulation . . ." He let the silence speak for itself and then continued. "You still need to *pass* all your other classes, so you can't completely ignore them. But they're the background. Manipulation is the forefront. Maegesters have Manipulation class every day. In one week, you may be asked to represent a real demon." He paused, appearing to choose his next words carefully.

"Have you ever met a demon, Noon?"

I shook my head, not wanting Ari to see I was actually starting to get scared. I did want to do well. I prided myself on being strong. But I was so ill equipped for the task in front of me.

Ari sighed. "It'll be hard for you."

"You have though," I said. "Obviously, since you worked for my father as a demon executioner."

I'd meant for my words to sound casual, matter-of-fact, but the tone of my voice betrayed what I thought of demon executioners. A main reason (okay, the top reason) I didn't want to be a Maegester was that Maegesters were all about death and destruction. Maegesters *killed* things. And I hated killing. I wanted to heal, grow, and create, not destroy.

"It bothers you, doesn't it?" he said. "The fact that I worked for your father."

I shrugged.

"We weren't close," he said. "I told you we never discussed you, if that's what you're worried about. I was one of at least a dozen others."

"That makes it right? The fact that others did it too?" The words slipped out before I could think better of it. Ari stared at me for a long time, his face completely expressionless.

"Why did you do it, Ari? Why did you do it before you *had* to do it?"

Finally, he blew his breath out. "Because I could. Because I needed the money. And because I don't think it's wrong to execute *rogare* demons. *Rogare* demons are the worst Halja has to offer. They're lawbreakers, criminals, and unsanctioned sinners. They're torturers and murderers. They deserve what they get, Noon."

"Have you ever met a demon you didn't kill?"

He glanced over at me, his expression a combination of curious and wary. I think he was wondering if my question was serious or not. It was.

"Yes. Quite a few times. Last summer I actually stayed with the Cliodna, the Patron Demon of Waves and Waterbirds." His mouth quirked a bit and I remembered the three adjectives always used to describe Cliodna: lusty, busty, and bold. But those adjectives were said by Hyrkes, people who'd likely never seen a real demon before, people who likely would never meet a demon, and so could afford to be flippant with their descriptions—provided the descriptions were flattering.

"Why Cliodna?" *Beyond the obvious,* I thought, but didn't say.

"I was tracking a *rogare* demon near her main devotion site. I needed a place to stay. She's one of the demons my adoptive family adores so she offered me sanctuary for the night."

I remembered that he'd been adopted. Raised by a Hyrke family in Bradbury. But then Ari's ability to easily hang with Hyrkes was what had made our first meeting so comfortable. I sighed. There was a lot I didn't know about Ari, but did it matter? My greatest risk was that his predilection for peculiarities like me would grow cold before I'd learned what I could from him.

"Do you really want to talk about Cliodna?" he asked, smiling at me.

I shook my head.

"All right," he said, motioning for me to sit. I sat in his

desk chair, thinking it wise, after our encounter in the library, to avoid the bed. "Let's start with some basics."

I was more layered than usual today. I had on my usual turtleneck sweater over a buttoned tunic with a sleeveless cotton shell under that. My hair was tied back in a casual knot and my only makeup was petroleum jelly on my lips. The last thing I wanted was for Ari to think I would get gussied up for a study date with him. I tried to assume a look that was all business but it likely came across as a scowl. Ari started pacing the room, playing the part of an instructor.

"You know most people with waning magic can sense one another, right?"

I nodded. My parents had at least told me that.

"Well, that feeling is different for each magic user. It's called a signature."

"So does each signature have different characteristics that tell you something about the . . . uh . . . signer?"

"Actually, yes. You can tell a lot about another magic user by their signature. People with strong magic have strong signatures—they're better senders. They're also better receivers, so they can more easily pick up on a weak signature."

"What does my signature feel like?"

Ari smiled and looked at me. "It's intense."

"*Intense*. What does that mean?"

"Let's just say Peter's spell didn't have a chance of cloaking your signature from me."

"Does that mean I'm a strong sender?"

"Yes, but I'm also a strong receiver. Only the strongest magic users can sense a signature cloaked by a well-cast spell."

"So Peter's spell was well cast?" I said, trying not to get too hopeful.

"Noon, I know what you're thinking," he said, sighing. "But you don't need a spell to help you. Nothing is wrong with you."

I made some noncommittal noise and tried to figure out where to look. I didn't want to look at Ari. His stare was unnerving. But I didn't want it to look like I couldn't meet his eyes either. I settled for a quick glance and then looked out the window. A heavy mix of icy sleet and wet snow rained down. Every now and then, a splatter hit the window and fell, leaving a slurry, blurry trail. There was really nothing to see out there so I turned my attention back to Ari.

"Can Maegesters cloak themselves?" I asked.

"I wouldn't call it cloaking. It has nothing to do with a spell. But, yes, you can learn to control the wattage of your signature. Although you'd never be able to hide yours from me." He laughed, a short barking sound that made me think it had been involuntary. He resumed pacing. He reminded me of a caged beast, which did nothing to ease the anxiety I was starting to feel.

"Why not?" I said sharply. It suddenly dawned on me that my days of fading into the woodwork were over.

"Like I said, I'm a strong receiver," he said, but I sensed there was more to it than that.

"What? What aren't you telling me?"

He shrugged. "A signature is personal going out, but it's also personal coming in. How it feels depends on the subjective interpretation of the receiver."

I frowned. "I don't understand."

He struggled for a moment, apparently trying to find the words to explain. Finally, he pointed. My gaze followed. "Look at that book on my desk. What color is it?"

"Green. Dark green."

"And pretty much everybody would say that, right?"

I nodded.

"It's not red or blue. It isn't light green and I don't think you'd get many people arguing with you about that."

"Okay . . ."

"Well, Maegester signatures aren't like colors. You may say my signature looks—or feels—dark green to you, but not every Maegester will agree. In fact, most won't. Everyone will have their own interpretation of how my signature feels to them. And it's not because we're simply using different words to describe the same thing. Maegesters from the same family often experience tranquility in the presence of their kin's signatures. And their descriptions of each other's signatures are remarkably similar."

I considered this new information. *Tranquility* was never something I'd experienced in the presence of my father.

"So what does *my* signature feel like to *you*?" I finally said.

Ari stopped pacing and sat on the bed, across from me. It reminded me of how our library encounter had started. I fidgeted.

"Noon," Ari said simply, patting the spot on the bed beside him. His meaning was clear. Instead of blushing, this time I blanched. If I'd thought I'd just be able to use Ari for his knowledge and somehow keep my feelings separate, I'd been unbelievably stupid.

"Your signature, as you call it, feels like lots of things," he said. His voice had lost that dry professorial quality. It was now full of emotion. "But right now there's one feeling in particular that's dominant."

"What's that?" I said, swallowing hard.

"Arousal."

I had to stop this. I didn't want to be Ari's new fetish. I realized then that I felt too deeply about him to be anything but cruelly hurt when the inevitable rejection came. It was better not to let anything get started than to suffer that eventuality.

I cleared my throat. "Ari, I came here to learn. What happened yesterday was a mistake."

"Don't say that," he said, grabbing my hands and pulling me over to him. I yelped, from surprise rather than pain, and he flipped me onto my back and leaned over me. I lay beneath him on the bed, panting, trying not to get angry. He grinned at me.

"Do you want to get up? I'll let you up. Or, better still, you can unleash your magic and we can have our first real lesson." A fissure of alarm raced down my back. *He wanted me to lose control?*

"Noon, that day I laid my hand over your demon mark, I only wanted one thing. If you hadn't pushed me away . . ."

"But we're the same," I said, trying to instill a little sanity back into the conversation. That was really hard to do with Ari's hard body looming over mine. I squeezed my eyes shut to block out the sight of him. "We're like two negatives, instead of a negative and a positive. We're not made to fit."

"Like attracts like," he said dismissively.

"*Opposites* attract," I countered.

"Why is it so hard to believe that I'm attracted to you?" One of my hands was pinned at my side and the other was caught in Ari's grip. I made a fist and he squeezed back, somehow making the aggressive gesture affectionate.

"Noon, open your eyes." I did.

"Ari," I said, defiantly meeting his gaze and sitting up. "If you are attracted to me, I'm sure the novelty will wear off." We sat on the bed facing each other, no longer touching. "Before long, you'll go back to dating Mederies from the Gaia Tribe. They suit you. I don't."

To his credit, Ari looked confused.

"You forget," I said. "I saw you with her."

"Who?" Now he looked positively thrown. But I was losing patience.

"The redheaded beauty, the Mederi from Marduk's the night I found out you were a student here. The one who was attacked by a *rogare* demon just before classes started." Luck, I hated sounding jealous. I don't think I ever had been before. It was so unbecoming.

"Oh, her."

We stared at each other for a moment, all former feelings completely dashed. Ari looked upset, but I couldn't tell if it was because I'd mentioned the as yet unpunished *rogare* demon who was responsible for the attack, or because my words implied I had the right to comment on other women he'd obviously been attracted to.

"Her," I said, scooting to the edge of the bed, intending to get up.

Ari put his hand on my arm. He didn't grab me, only made it clear he didn't want me to go. "I stopped seeing her that night, right after I knew you were a student here."

I gave him what I hoped to be a sardonic expression.

"Noon, I swear I'm telling the truth. Mederies are all the same. None of them stand out. Not like you."

"Yep, that's me. I stick out like a sore thumb."

"That's not what I meant," he said, managing to sound frustrated. Neither of us spoke for a moment. Finally, Ari broke the silence with a complete non sequitur.

"Noon, did your mom ever bake coffer cookies?"

What . . . ? No . . . The thought of Aurelia baking cookies was laughable.

"You know what they are though, right?"

I raised my brow at him, but answered his question. "They're the ones with the jelly filling. The ones shaped like miniature baskets, or caskets, that people like to pair with coffee?"

He nodded. "Well, Hyrke mothers all across New Babylon bake them. To get the imprint in the center of the cookie where the jam goes, they push their thumb into it. That's why some kids call them thumbprint cookies."

Okay . . .

"Well, as I said, signatures are called signatures because each one is different. It's an easy term for something difficult to describe. Everyone with waning magic has a signature . . . so demons have them too." I nodded, and tried to ignore the fear I felt at the thought of feeling *any* part of a demon, even something as amorphous as its signature. "Which brings me to the other reason signatures are called signatures. The demons use them to mark one another."

"What do you mean 'mark one another'?"

He grinned. "Just what I said. Sometimes, when there's a strong enough attraction, waning magic can be used as a brand to mark someone. It's called a *signare*, which is the magical equivalent of pressing your thumb into someone else's heart. Not everyone can do it."

"Why would I *want* to do it?"

"Why do you want to do anything with someone you're attracted to?" This time his grin was positively ear splitting. "Because it feels good, for one thing."

He moved toward me and put both of his hands on my waist. He moved them under my sweater and up the sides of my shirt.

"What are you doing?" I cried, clamping my hands down on his through my sweater. That hot feeling that Ari called *arousal* relapsed as suddenly as a half-treated fever. The feeling washed over me, inflaming every part of me. My body wanted his hands exactly where they were. My mind knew I had to get out of his room immediately.

"Let me show you something," he said, inching his hands higher. I shook my head. "Please," he added. Again, that word. I'd only ever heard him use it one other time. When he'd asked me not to leave St. Luck's. I loosened my hold on his hands. He moved them slowly up my ribcage, brushing the soft curve of my breasts through the fabric of my tunic and undershirt. It made my breath hitch, which gave him a start, but he continued undeterred toward whatever purpose he had in mind. He raised my arms and removed my sweater, popping it off my head and tossing it to the floor.

"That's better," he murmured. He began to unbutton my tunic.

"Ari," I started to warn, but he shushed me and told me to trust him and to keep my hands at my side.

"Signatures can change," he said. "Depending on what the sender is experiencing."

I was having a hard time remembering our earlier discussion. Ari was throwing off massive amounts of heat, or at least that's what it felt like to me. I tried to shield myself as I had on other occasions by shoving a counterforce back at Ari.

"Don't," he said. "I'm not pushing magic at you. You're just experiencing my signature right now. *You're* actually doing this to *me*."

Very slowly, I ratcheted down the amount of force I was shoving toward him. As I did, the heat I felt became more intense. But the less I fought it, the less it felt like heat and the more it felt like energy. Yes, they were the same thing.

But the difference was in what it *felt* like. The one felt like blistering pain and the other felt like a warm, tingly glow.

"What you're feeling is your effect on me," he said.

His signature was tingly—*very tingly*. He unbuttoned the last button on my tunic and pushed the shirt from my shoulders. It fell softly behind me. "Do you feel that?" he said, placing his hand on my demon mark. The cloth of my undershirt was still between us and I was thankful for the barrier. Because Ari's touch there *hurt*. But the feeling it created elsewhere—lower down especially—was exquisite. I grabbed his hand and flung it off me.

"Stop!"

He chuckled, the sound low and deep in his throat. I swallowed, my mouth suddenly dry.

"Of course, it works both ways," he said clinically, as if what we'd just experienced hadn't happened. "I can feel my effect on you."

I blushed. This was embarrassing. I didn't want Ari to know how he made me feel. I turned away.

"Sorry, Noon," he whispered roughly. "There's no way I will ever not be able to tell what you're feeling. That's just the way our magic works."

I turned back to him and he tweaked my nose. "You could never hide from me, any more than I could hide from you."

"I'm not hiding anymore. Remember, I declared?"

"You're not? Good."

He reached for the hem of my undershirt and I grabbed his hand, my breath now ragged. Coming to Ari's room didn't seem like such a good idea anymore. Sure, I was no virgin, but I'd never truly given myself to anyone. Anything I'd done previously had been with Hyrkes, who had no magic. No Hyrke had ever *known* me, who I was, what I was. No Hyrke had ever felt me the way Ari was feeling me right now. I didn't like it. It made me feel vulnerable and exposed. I didn't want to be naked in front of him, physically or magically.

Ari brushed my mouth with a kiss and then bent to kiss

my neck. Hot breath and moist lips traced the blood in my veins. My pulse quickened and he bit me there, gently. I stifled a growl. *What was he doing to me?*

"I want to touch your demon mark," he said, "skin to skin."

I knew what he was really asking. *Was I willing to let him make his mark on my heart?*

"No." I was afraid. But even if I weren't, I wouldn't let him do that to me just in the name of fun. If I ever let someone mark me magically, it would be because I felt something for them beyond a magical or physical attraction.

"Fine. I wanted you to be first, but if you won't, I will." And with one fluid motion, he swept off his shirt so that he was sitting bare-chested in front of me, his eyes smoky and unreadable, his whole body as tense as a feral beast ready to spring. Ari had never looked overly bulky but, I realized now, the loose cut of his clothes had hidden hard, deeply sculpted muscles. It was hard to keep my hands off him. My instant reaction was that he looked much stronger than I'd suspected he was.

Ari made no move. He just watched me, watching him. He seemed to want to underscore the meaning of his gesture, that he was opening himself up to me, giving himself freely to me and whatever feelings came of this. My gaze finally settled on the spot of skin just above his left breastbone. His demon mark was large and dark. Mine looked like a tiny drop of spilled café au lait, whereas his looked like a huge inky stain. I knew I shouldn't, knew it was likely to set something free in this world that I wouldn't be able to catch and contain again, but I couldn't help myself. I raised my hand and reached out to touch the mark. I made contact with only two fingers but the shock of it was fierce. A swift current of energy traveled instantaneously from my fingers, up my arm, and into my chest where it exploded in a burst of electrifying heat. Ari hissed and I remembered how much it had hurt when he'd touched mine, even through my shirt.

"I'm sorry," I said, snatching my hand away.

"Don't be."

His voice was as rough as I'd ever heard it, like his throat was cut up from swallowing glass. His eyes smoldered as he looked at me. *Was it supposed to hurt?* I didn't want to hurt him. I hated that my magic had the power to hurt, instead of heal. Instinctively I pushed Ari down onto the bed and straddled him. He grabbed me at the waist and moved his hands up my back, pressing me toward him. I knew what he wanted. What he needed. Because I felt it too.

Our magic swirled around us, writhing and twisting, building and cresting, until the two parts of it finally crashed together, leaving a whirling vortex of swirling energies melded together in one great big roiling, boiling mass. Ari's hands were wrapped in my hair as he lowered my head to his chest. I brought my mouth down on his demon mark and kissed him there. He bucked under me, but held me tightly to him. All thoughts of gentle healing were gone as I raked my hands up his sides, my nails clawing smooth skin, my fingertips feeling hard muscle and sharp bones beneath. I finally raised my head and moved my lips from Ari's chest to his mouth, giving him a kiss at least as good as those he'd given me. After a while, I came up for breath.

"The lesson is over for today," Ari croaked and then laughed. "You're going to kill me, Noon."

He was smiling when he said it, but the joke still stung.

Chapter 9

❧

Safely wrapped once again in tunic, sweater, and cloak, I left Ari and walked back to my room at Megiddo. Ivy had left a note:

Noon—

Fitz and I are going to the Black Onion for lunch. If you can, meet us there. If not, see you later at Corpus Justica!

Ivy

p.s. Your mother rang and Waldron Seknecus wants to see you.

Terrific. I wasn't sure which part of the p.s. to respond to first. Neither option was appealing. I opted for visiting the dean of demon affairs, which said volumes about my relationship with my mother. Once again I trudged across campus in the cold and the muck, trying to ignore the feeling that, at any moment, I might feel the signature of the *rogare* demon who was terrorizing traveling Mederies. After I'd looked back over my shoulder for the fifteenth time, I decided to focus on something a little less frightening (albeit, only marginally less): Ari.

We'd made plans to meet later for dinner to go over more Manipulation. My stomach did a little flip thinking about what that had meant this morning, but Ari promised there would be fewer "distractions" this evening. I couldn't help but be a little disappointed.

I walked over to Warenne Building and stepped inside. The building's furnace obviously had only two settings: *hot* and *Hell's fury*. I quickly unwrapped myself, trying to ignore the fiery pain as my ears adjusted from sub-zero to sizzling.

There was a reason students had dubbed this building the "Rabbit Warren." Its passages were long, narrow, and twisty. There were lots of dead-ends and corridors that appeared to go nowhere. Windows were scarce and some of the hall lights blinked spasmodically, creating a surreal zoetrope effect as students wound their way through the aboveground maze. The Rabbit Warren was three-stories high but might as well have been three-stories deep for all the natural light it got. I remembered all too well where Waldron Seknecus' office was. My name was still the last name scrawled at the bottom of The List and likely to be the last for this year. I knocked on the door, my hand shaking only a little.

I heard rustling from behind the door and a shuffling sound as footsteps approached. The door opened and a white-haired, wrinkly old man stood in front of me. He had a hawkish nose and his eyes were glazed with age, but he was clean shaven and his hair was closely cropped. No flowing white locks or beard for this octogenarian. I suddenly understood what Ari meant when he'd said that everyone's signatures would feel different. Seknecus' signature felt like a piece of hard white oak—solid and strong. Something that could be used for many purposes: a sturdy bench upon which to prop a struggling student or the weapon by which they were dealt a death blow to the head.

It was hard to imagine that chatty, lackadaisical Fitz had grown up—and by all accounts happily—on the Seknecai estate. I wondered what Fitz's mother, Ivy's aunt, was like. The head housekeeper for a Maegester like Seknecus was unlikely to be meek.

The windows in Seknecus' office were large and expansive. After the dark and depth of the Rabbit Warren, stepping into the room felt like stepping out of a cave onto a high rocky plateau. New Babylon spread out beneath us, its blinking lights peeking out from under an icy layer of soot and snow. The dean of demon affairs' office was spacious but stacked floor to ceiling with books, both old and new, apparently in no particular order. Immediately, I spotted my Oathbreaking book, *First Year Oathbreaking: Cases, Questions, and Notes*, sitting next to what appeared to be an original copy of *A Maegester's Manifesto: How to Avoid Demon War* by Allighiero Lotharius. Lotharius was reputed to be a direct descendant of Lothario, one of Lucifer's fiercest battle lords. Reprints of the book were quite popular among Host and Hyrke alike and original copies were treated as devotional relics.

I stood front and center on a hand-woven wool rug with a motif of rosettes and stars. Its colors were somewhat faded but at one time it must have been an extravagant red. The room smelled dusty but not musty, like old leather, aged paper, and something else I couldn't quite place, smoke or some sort of acrid burning smell, though there was no fireplace that I could see.

"So, you're Nouiomo Onyx," Seknecus said.

I nodded. Then cleared my throat. And then finally spoke. "I am." I wondered what kind of vibe I was giving off in my signature. I was nervous but determined to show well.

"I've heard about you, like everyone else in the Host. I had my suspicions but, out of respect for your father, I've kept my distance. He and I were good friends once, but he made it clear after you and your brother were born that your mother was in no state to receive visitors. And that never really changed, did it?"

I had to work hard to keep the surprised look off of my face. I'd had no idea that Seknecus and my father were close. But then I hardly knew a thing about my father since I rarely saw him. It was true that Aurelia was somewhat of a shut-in, although she'd likely find the comment offensive.

"I've been watching you, wondering, waiting to see where you'd end up. After all, there are other demon law schools," Seknecus said, making a moue of distaste that showed me exactly what he thought of them. "But I was happy to see that you chose St. Lucifer's."

Technically my mother chose St. Lucifer's . . . But there seemed no reason to interrupt to clarify that bit of misinformation. Seknecus wandered around the room, picking through papers, flipping open and quickly shutting the front covers of various leather-bound books, never meeting my eye. I had no doubt, however, that his attention was fully focused on me.

"So, you see, seeing your name on my list wasn't exactly a surprise, although it appeared much later than I would have liked."

He glanced at me then, with a frown of disapproval. I did my best to look expressionless because none seemed appropriate. It wouldn't do to look amused, bored, or, Luck forbid, rebellious. Seknecus stared at me with narrowed eyes and then went back to wandering.

"You've got some catching up to do," he said, addressing a copy of *Sin and Sanction: Codification & Case Law.* "It doesn't matter why or what excuses you've got for yourself. You will be held to the same standards as everyone else, regardless of whose daughter you are. And you've missed a lot of class already."

I opened my mouth to protest, but he cut me off with a wave.

"Manipulation class," he clarified. "You're going to have to work ten times as hard as everyone else just to pass. Quintus Rochester doesn't go easy on students and he's likely to see your absence during the early part of the semester as a challenge. You know, failing is not an option. Not if you want to live."

"Death is certain, life is not," I blurted out without thinking.

Seknecus looked mildly shocked.

"I mean to do well," I said quickly. "I *will* do well," I added emphatically.

Seknecus grunted. "Do you have your Manipulation materials?"

"Not yet."

Seknecus rustled about on his shelves and located a couple of dusty volumes. "Maegesters hardly ever buy new Manipulation books. The margin notes from previous students can prove invaluable," he said, handing the books to me. I accepted with what I hoped was gracious thanks and he continued. "You should think about which Angel you might want to work with too. It won't be necessary right away, but next semester, you'll need to pair up with someone from the Joshua School."

"That won't be a problem," I said.

He stood there for a moment, pondering. Finally, he said simply:"You must take great care here, Ms. Onyx."

I blinked. *Take great care.* Of course. What student wanted to be accused of being careless? But then I realized he wasn't talking about any academic threat just now. He was talking about the recent demon attack.

I nodded and then remembered Fitz saying I should tell him about Amaryllis Apatite and my suspicions that the New Babylon train station was the link among the attacks.

"I saw your announcement about the Mederi who was attacked and abducted two nights ago. Do they know who it was yet?"

"Laurel Scoria from the Hawthorn Tribe. She rode up from Emmer last Thursday on the North-South Express."

"You know there was another Mederi, from the Demeter Tribe, who went missing the week before classes started. The last place she was seen was boarding the North-South Express at the southern terminal . . . around 2:00 p.m."

Seknecus grunted his acknowledgment. "Amaryllis Apatite."

"And there was another Mederi . . ." I realized I didn't even know the name of Ari's old girlfriend. "She was attacked three days before classes started. *At the New Babylon train station.*"

Seknecus looked at me with a gimlet eye. "You seem to be remarkably well informed for someone who just declared, Ms. Onyx." His eyebrow arched higher. "And for someone who seemed so reluctant, until recently, to participate in the policing of *rogare* demons."

Until recently. Was he kidding? I *still* wanted no part of policing demons. But I couldn't resist one last question.

"The Mederi who got away . . ."

"Bryony Ijolite."

"Right. Her. How did she do it? How did she get away?"

"Your father, actually. He's the one that saved her. Thank Luck he chose to walk back from here to the Council offices via the train station. Otherwise, Ms. Ijolite would likely be missing too."

"What was my father doing *here*?"

"He's the executive," Seknecus said, giving me a look that made me think he was doubting the academic scores my mother must have reported on my application. "Executives have always taken a keen interest in all of the MIT's trained here at St. Luck's."

Well, I was sure to be the exception to that practice. But Seknecus' next words belied my thoughts. "Actually, someone from the Office of the Executive stopped by this morning to inquire after you. He left something for you too," he said, his eyes glinting. "That's the other reason I wanted to see you."

"There must be some mistake."

Seknecus walked over to his desk and rummaged in one of the drawers.

"No, certainly not," he said, finally locating the object he was searching for. He held up a small silver ball, about the size of a Yule tree ornament. The ball was attached to a silver chain and it swung gently back and forth as Seknecus walked over and handed it to me. I took it and examined it more closely.

Mrs. Aster would have loved it. The silver had a lustrous patina that could only mean the artifact was as ancient as it looked. There were symbols and ciphers all over it, most of them I couldn't read. Someone had lovingly cared for this objet d'art. Though it was old, it shined as if recently polished, its filigreed scrolling metalwork a testament to some long dead artist. I was touched, but confused.

"He sent a letter with it," Seknecus said, tucking the note in with the books he'd just given me. "You're to open that first."

I tucked the little ball into my cloak pocket and left. On the way home, it warmed me better than a brazier. By the time I returned to Megiddo, I felt toasty and warm, almost happy. I dropped the Manipulation books on my desk and carefully pulled the ball out of my pocket. I took off my cloak, keeping one hand on the silver ball the entire time. I walked over to my bed and sat down, the ball in one hand and the letter in the other. I opened the letter.

Noon,

The familiar's name is Serafina. She is small, but powerful enough for practice. Read Chapter 9 of Alexios Skleros' Lesser Demons before you release her. Practice alone and for no more than two hours a day. The ball is for your protection . . . and everyone else's.

I never wanted this for you. A long time ago your mother made a foolish promise and we have all paid the price.

Your father, Karanos

p.s. push the button to open the ball

A familiar? My hand shook slightly as I held the ball up by its chain to peer at it more closely. *There was a demon in there.* No matter how small, the thought should have been mildly terrifying. But instead I felt wonderfully intoxicated and numb around the edges, like I'd drank too much wine at a party. I looked for the button but couldn't find it. I twisted and turned the ball, holding it up to the afternoon light streaming through my dormitory window, and finally found the catch. I pushed it gently with my thumb and the ball sprang open.

Immediately the intoxicated, numb feeling went supernova. Serafina's signature made me feel like my body had been liquefied and then turned inside out to congeal in the cold. I suddenly craved warmth and this demon was the only source that could satisfy.

I stared at her, hardly able to reconcile her with a lifetime of imagined fears. Haljan myths and legends spoke of brutish beasts hell-bent on fury and destruction. Haljan paintings, bas reliefs, and statuaries also often depicted demons as cruel fiends and vicious monsters. But Serafina didn't look dangerous. She looked ungainly.

She belched and stretched, glaring at me through two black eyes the size of beads. She was naked but it was no pretty sight. Her body, though diminutive, was bloated as though she'd died in the Lethe and been left too long. Her skin was a grayish, sickly looking green, and she rubbed her distended belly with one clawed hand as she grinned malevolently at me.

"Do you speak?" I said.

The creature cocked her head, a puzzled expression on her face. *Great. A demon who didn't speak my language.* I held out my hand, wondering if she would jump to my palm. I wanted to walk over to my desk to see if I had a reference book on one of the three primary demon languages, but suddenly five feet seemed too far to walk without her.

She jumped to my palm without hesitation. The sensation was like being bitten by a spider. My palm stung and a sharp pain started moving up my arm. At the same time though,

the all-over numb feeling I'd experienced before increased so
the pain didn't seem to matter. I cradled Serafina to me and
started riffling through my desk searching for a primer on
Vandalic, Venetic, or Vestinian. I found one and repeated my
earlier question in all three languages. Or at least what I
hoped was the three demon languages. I'd never learned
them and my tongue stumbled on the unfamiliar consonants
and odd guttural sounds. Eagerness turned to muted interest
and then finally to outright displeasure when it became clear
to Serafina that I wasn't going to say anything she could understand. She viciously clawed my palm and I transferred her
to my shoulder, absentmindedly sucking at the base of my
thumb where she'd cut me.

With Serafina safely ensconced on my shoulder and pumping out the magical equivalent of ten tons of serotonin in her
signature, it was time to call my mother back. I walked over
to the electro-harmonic machine that hung on the wall. I
picked up the receiver and cranked the lever. The line crackled as it came to life. The operator connected me with our
house line in Etincelle. Three jangling rings later I was on the
verge of hanging up when my mother answered. Her voice
was smooth and rich, like ice cream, and just as cold.

"I guess you heard the news," I said, skipping the pre-
liminaries that never went well between us anyway. I wondered who'd told her. *The school? Doubtful. Peter? Doubly
doubtful. Mrs. Aster? Luck forbid. Winifred Aster and Aurelia Onyx had never really hit it off.*

"Your father told me," she said.

That must have been an interesting discussion. I was glad
not to have been around for it. Watching my parents try to
talk to each other was like watching two towns try to destroy
each other through simultaneous siege. Their brand of psychological warfare was all about deprivation. Any real fight
would put them dangerously close to a confrontation where
talking and touching might occur. I had an instant vision—
my father passing my mother a note, "She declared," and my
mother crumpling up the note, tossing it in a trash can, and
lighting it on fire—with matches, of course—and my father

simply walking out. I'm sure the discussion hadn't actually taken place like that, but something similar had likely occurred.

"Have you heard from Night?" I said, grasping at something to say.

"Not since his last letter. I gave Peter the one he sent for you. Did you get it?"

"Yes. Thank you. But you haven't heard from him since?"

She must have heard the concern in my voice.

"No. I guess you've heard about the other Mederi who was taken."

"They put an alert up here at school."

"Laurel Scoria. I *knew* her, Noon. A long time ago. We trained at Hawthorn together. She was almost as good a midwife as . . . Well, it doesn't matter now."

"I'm sorry, Mother."

A few seconds passed and then she said, "I suppose you wouldn't believe me if I told you I wished you were here at home."

I had to hold the receiver away from my ear for a moment in disbelief. Nope. She was right. Wouldn't. Didn't.

"You were the one that enrolled me here in the first place."

"I know," she sighed. "It's where you need to be."

"Have you heard from Peter?"

"No."

I was running out of things to say.

"Someone put an evergreen in my locker," I blurted out. I don't know why I said it. Looking for sympathy in the most unlikely places, I guess. My mother was silent on the other end for so long I thought she might have hung up. But then she said: "I put the evergreen in your locker, Noon."

I exhaled sharply. Serafina snarled in my ear and started scratching my neck and pulling my hair. I tried to bat her off my shoulder but she avoided my swipes, getting nastier. Her magic had a poisonous feel to it and nausea replaced the numb feeling from before.

My *mother* had given me the evergreen?

"Why?" I croaked, finally managing to grab Serafina

around the belly. I squeezed hard and yanked her out of
my hair. She squirmed and tried to bite my hand. Did my
mother have any idea how that evergreen had made me feel?
Did she have any idea what it felt like to know you could kill
a thing just by touching it? I threw Serafina down on my bed
and blasted her with a jolt of waning magic to stop her squall-
ing. *Of course my mother didn't know—she was a Mederi.*
Leaving an evergreen, a symbol of eternal life, for me to kill
was unbelievably cruel, even for her.

"I told you," she said in that rich, creamy, cold as ice voice
of hers, "*you* were the one who had to decide to use your
magic. *You* were the one who had to declare."

"Well, if you wanted Night and me to use the magic we'd
been born with, why did you hide it from everyone? And why
did you raise us to be so ignorant about it?" I was practically
shouting, something I almost never did when speaking with
her.

"Noon, I—"

I stopped listening. Something was happening in my
dorm room. All of a sudden it was *hot*. Suddenly I remembered accidentally burning my admission letter and the napkin at Marduk's. Was I about to set the whole room on fire?
I raised my hands in front of me, palms up. A meaningless
physical gesture, the only purpose of which was to focus my
energy inward. I searched for the source of the surge. It
wasn't coming from me.

I hung up on my mother and walked over to my bed where
Serafina fumed. She flexed her small rapier-sharp claws and
snorted actual fire, singeing tiny little spots on my quilt and
pillows. *Must be a demon trick,* I thought crazily. *Even I
can't do that.* Serafina met my eye and her look was full of
dark emotion. Blistering waves of malevolence pulsed from
her, like sickening magical radiation. My stomach threatened
to revolt and I sat down heavily on the bed, my palms falling
out at my sides. Serafina took it as an invitation and jumped
back into my palm. This time, the sting of her touch was less.
And the numbness infinitely more welcoming. I sank back
into the pillows.

My dorm room's harmonic jangled again sometime later. I had no idea how long we'd been sitting there like that. I had the vague, unsettled feeling of being woken up from a dream too early. My mind was unfocused and my muscles were stiff. I got up, carrying Serafina like she was some live, grotesque version of a children's stuffed bear, and yanked the receiver off its hook.

"Noon, where are you? Aren't you coming?"

The voice was concerned. For a moment I couldn't place it. The feeling was frustrating, like when you're late and can't find your house keys. Finally, I realized.

"Ivy," I said, my voice slurring a little. I tried desperately to remember where it was I was supposed to be. Thankfully, her note to me was right in front of me. I read it, puzzled that I didn't remember reading it in the first place.

Was she calling from the Black Onion or Corpus Justica? What time was it?

It didn't matter.

"I can't come," I said. I sounded like I was underwater. "I'm meeting Ari to go over some Manipulation stuff for Monday."

I hung up and walked back over to the bed, disturbed. Something was wrong.

There were things I was supposed to be doing, but I couldn't remember what they were. And, if I did, I wasn't sure it would have mattered, which worried me more.

Curled in the crook of my arm, Serafina dozed contentedly, her signature drowsy and warm. I wanted nothing more than to curl back up with her. In fact, the more I focused on her, instead of trying to remember what I'd forgotten, the better I felt. But before I could lie back down, the harmonic's bell rang again. This time, the clanging jangle woke Serafina up and my sick, nauseous feeling returned. I wanted nothing more than to get rid of it. And whoever was on the other end of the line. Again, I dragged Serafina and myself across the room, and unhooked the receiver.

"Get some good studying in?" It was Ari. His voice cut through my haze like a metal shaft through water.

"No."

"You didn't?" His voice sounded sharp. "What have you been doing?"

I looked down at Serafina, who was rubbing her belly and glaring at me. I didn't want to tell him about her. There was something about the situation that made me feel guilty and defensive.

"I had other things to do," I said.

"Like what?" He sounded annoyed. *Now that our mutual interest was obvious, did that mean I had to account to him for every minute of my day?*

For a moment I debated telling him about the meeting with Seknecus, how it had been predictably terrifying, yet oddly heartening. I thought about telling him how hurt I'd been to find out my mother had been the one to leave the evergreen for me to kill. And I considered sharing Serafina with him . . . but then an inexplicable possessiveness took hold. I wanted her all to myself.

"I can't meet you tonight," I said.

"Why? Noon, what's going on? I thought you understood how precarious your situation is. Manipulation starts Monday. The Council is watching. You don't have a lot of time to catch up."

None of that seemed to frighten me anymore. Serafina was a demon and we were getting along fine.

"Seknecus gave me the books I'll need for Manipulation," I said, "and I told Ivy I'd study with her."

"*Seknecus* gave you your Manipulation books?"

"Yep," I said breezily. "So I'll see you Monday." I started to hang up.

"Noon, wait! What about tomorrow?"

Tomorrow? Today was all that mattered. And getting back to Serafina.

I hung up.

I was setting personal records. Today, I'd hung up on three people and hadn't cracked a single book.

What in Luck's Hell was the matter with me?

I went to bed early that night, with Serafina tucked in

safely by my side. I briefly considered trying to put her back in the ball for the night but the thought of not being able to feel her signature, vile though it was at times, made me uneasy. In fact, it would be fair to say that I had a minor panic attack at the thought. So I hid the ball deep in my desk drawer, absent the demon that went with it. I snuggled up to Serafina's cozy warmth—nasty, repugnant little creature that she was—and promptly went to sleep.

I woke prematurely. Two things alerted me that something was wrong. The relatively loud sound, in the hushed silence of my darkened dorm room, of Ivy dropping her keys and books on her desk and Serafina's suddenly rapid-boil signature. Still groggy from sleep, but acting on instinct, I threw the covers off me and swung my legs to the floor.

"You were sleeping?" Ivy asked, surprised. She looked down at the load of stuff she'd just dumped on her desk. "Sorry. I thought you'd still be with Ari. Speaking of which . . ."

Ivy's tone grew more concerned and I started to feel feverish in a horrible way. I knew Serafina didn't like Ivy. I could *feel* it. But that singular thought was the only coherent one I had. Everything about me was sluggish—my thoughts, my movements, even my magic. I tried to control Serafina by shielding her magic with my own but it was like trying to broadside someone with a sled underwater. My magic wobbled and swayed. It shimmied and swerved. It did everything but hit its target or work like it was supposed to.

"Noon," Ivy continued, as yet unaware of Serafina's tiny body beside mine and the danger she was in, "I know you're really worried about Manipulation—who wouldn't be?—and I don't blame you for wanting to spend Saturday night with Ari, but . . . Fitz and I were counting on you tonight to go over the differences between sedition, subversion, and incitement. Our Sin and Sanction midterm is next week. You said you wanted to stay in the study group. You have to pass . . ." Ivy enumerated her concerns on her fingers in typical Ivy fashion, but I was too panicked to pay attention.

Before, when I had pushed magic back at Ari, it had felt

like I was throwing out an array of kitchen knives. Ari had melted the knives or engaged in a bit of playful parrying. But Serafina multiplied and sharpened my magic and threw it back at me. The strike hit me with the force of a copper-pot blow to the head and the toxin of a thousand scorpion stings. I grabbed her and pulled her out from under the covers. I was desperate. Words wouldn't work; Serafina couldn't understand me. Magic wouldn't help; she just repelled it and sent it back with greater force.

A sick, awful feeling bloomed that had nothing to do with the toxic magic Serafina was throwing off. *What if she started directing her magic toward Ivy?* No Hyrke could survive a demon attack. It dawned on me how stupid I'd been and what I'd let happen. Serafina was a *demon*. I'd let her out of the ball, I'd kept her out of the ball, and now I couldn't control her. Ivy could die.

Ivy realized it at the exact moment I did.

"Noon," she said, her voice going soft, "is that"—she swallowed as her eyes met Serafina's—"is that . . . did you . . ." Ivy backed up until she hit the desk. I didn't need to speak Serafina's language to know that she saw Ivy as a threat. Serafina was a demon familiar, one of the most jealous demon species there was. And it was just occurring to her that I had a roommate, a friend, someone else who talked to me and spoke *my* language. Somebody else who I gave my attention to. Someone else who, in Serafina's eyes anyway, received a share of the adoration that was due to *her*. Cold, hard fear sliced through me, cutting the veiled haze I'd felt since opening Serafina's silver ball.

I felt Serafina's signature change just before she struck. Everything in the room seemed to stop—the sound of my breathing, Ivy's heart beating, the low rumbling in Serafina's chest. Even the light seemed suddenly static, as if the scene in front of me were a life-sized photograph instead of the real thing. The day's fugue fell away like a cloak cut from my body. The room seemed to contract and expand and then, a moment later, Ivy's hands were on fire.

She screamed and I reacted without thinking. Instead of

trying to ward off Serafina with the magical equivalent of a bunch of blunt butter knives, I thrust a razor-thin, needle-sharp shaft of magic at her. I could feel its strength. It was unlike anything I'd ever thrown before. All my life, I'd thrown defensively. This was instinctive and aggressive. What I'd thrown before was like aluminum or tin. This magic was as hard and clear as a diamond and directed to lethal effect. Serafina collapsed in a liquefied puddle of demon flesh. Anguish surged through me, but I had no time to dwell on it. Instantly, I leeched the oxygen from the air around the fire.

I was too late. Red, angry welts and blistery burns covered Ivy's hands. She cradled them against her chest. Ivy clenched her teeth together and breathed through her mouth, clearly trying to deal with what must have been immeasurable pain. Never, in my whole life, had I felt so helpless. The desire to heal was palpable. And yet I could not act on it. I'd *caused* Ivy's injury; I couldn't cure it.

Ivy needed a Mederi.

How I wished for Night's steady presence, but he was at least a hundred leagues to the south. Even my mother was across the Lethe. Ivy needed help *now*.

"Noon," Ivy said, panting against the pain, "call the medics."

"Hyrke medicine won't help you," I said, swallowing the lump in my throat and pushing all kinds of emotions out of the way for now. "You need a Mederi."

I rushed over to the room's wall mounted harmonic and turned the crank, nearly ripping it out of the box in my efforts to get an immediate connection. When the operator answered, I yelled Ari's name into the mouthpiece. After a few agonizing seconds, he answered, his voice thick with sleep.

"Ari," I said, brutally repressing the urge to burst into tears, "I need your help."

"What's wrong?" he asked, instantly alert.

"It's Ivy. She's hurt."

"Take her to the infirmary. I'll meet you there."

"She needs . . . I can't . . ." Even though we had no time,

I stopped speaking for a moment to regain control. Feeling all these emotions right now was selfish. Ivy needed help and the only way I knew how to get it for her was this call. It wouldn't help Ivy if I couldn't succinctly state what the problem was. "Ari, Ivy's been attacked by a demon. She needs a Mederi. Can you ask one of your . . . uh, friends to help us?"

"Attacked by a demon? Noon, did I hear you right? Is she alive?"

"Yes," I snapped, "but she's badly burned and she needs help *now*."

"I'm coming over," he said shortly and hung up. He was there in seconds, which made me wonder if he'd used some kind of magic trick to appear so quickly. He burst through the unlocked door, his eyes locking on mine. His gaze swept the room, taking in Ivy's burned hands, my uninjured state, and the slowly congealing mass of still-steaming demon flesh eating a hole through my bed.

In two strides he was by Ivy's side, lifting her gently into his arms. He looked at me again then, his expression different, unreadable. I forced myself not to look away. It wasn't defiance—not at all. I wanted him to know that I accepted whatever consequences came of this. I wanted Ari to know that I knew this whole situation was my fault and that, even though I couldn't fix it, I wasn't going to run away from it. I would do what I could, limited though my help would be.

"Come with me," he said and walked out. I followed, not bothering to shut our door and practically ran to keep up with him.

We crossed Timothy's Square in a blur of movement and Ari hailed one of the cabs running down Angel Street. We piled in the back, with Ari still assisting Ivy and my only contribution my useless presence.

"Eight Dauphine Street," Ari told the cabdriver and we sped off.

Ivy sat in the middle and I put my hand on her leg. The pain seemed to be getting worse. It would probably feel that way whether it was or not simply because Ivy's strength in keeping it at bay was likely ebbing with time. I tried not to squeeze her leg. She didn't need to deal with my stress on top of her injuries.

In the cab, Ari asked only one question.

"It was a demon familiar, wasn't it?"

I nodded and then turned to watch the passing row houses with their brick fronts and marble steps. I didn't want to look at Ari and see accusation or condescension in his eyes. It was all I could do to keep from breaking down. If I had to face Ari's judgment too, I knew I'd become a blubbering idiot, which wouldn't help Ivy and would only make me look worse. So I stared out the window, desperately trying not to think about the fact that I'd brought a demon into the room I shared with one of my closest friends here at St. Luck's. I'd endangered Ivy's life and caused her injury. And . . . I'd done something tonight that I'd never done. Something that made me even more of a monster than I'd thought I was before this. Something that was, if possible, even worse than killing trees or plants or gardens. I'd killed a living creature.

I'd killed Serafina.

Demon or no, she shouldn't have died. Tears welled. There was no stopping them. I didn't weep for me, but for Serafina. If I'd had more experience using my waning magic, this never would have happened. I would have been able to get her back into the ball before Ivy came home. Or, at the very least, I would have been able to control her enough during the encounter so that Ivy would not have been hurt and Serafina would not have died. That needle-sharp piece of magic I'd thrown in the end that had killed her was the work of an amateur. In my fear and panic I'd used the wrong weapon. I should have subdued her, not killed her. She was dead because of me. I wiped my tears away quickly and was glad when we pulled down Dauphine Street.

In the dark, number eight didn't appear much different than any of the other row houses attached to it. There were a few potted plants on the stairs that Ari didn't think twice about walking past as he stepped up the few stairs and rang the doorbell. I stood at the foot of the stairs with Ivy leaning heavily against me. I put my arm around her waist to support her, wishing I could do more.

The door opened and Beauty—Bryony—stood there. Of course it had to be her. Of all the Mederies Ari knew, apparently Bryony was the one he thought of first to call when there was trouble. And apparently she, with no explanation or forewarning, was happy to open her door for him at two hours past twelve. I knew I should be thinking only of Ivy, but I couldn't help wondering how deep their relationship had been.

Bryony was in her nightgown. She'd thrown a robe over the top of it but hadn't had time to belt it. Her lustrously wavy red curls fell loosely around her face as her azure blue eyes gazed adoringly at Ari. Beauty was no poker player.

"I didn't know you'd be back," she said, smiling as she motioned toward her now dead plants. But her face showed concern as she caught sight of Ivy and I huddled together at the foot of her stairs.

"Bryony, we need your help. One of my friends was attacked by a demon. Can you heal her?" Ari said, coming back down the steps and ushering us toward the door before she even answered. Bryony's face registered surprise, but she kept her questions to herself.

"Of course. Bring her inside," she said, stepping back, giving us room to enter. "Lay her on the couch," she said as Ari squeezed past her, already headed in that direction. He seemed all too clear about where to go.

Bryony's hallway was lit by one dim bulb. Ari had once again scooped Ivy into his arms. I followed him down the shadowy hallway. Odd angles of light fell across patches of torn wallpaper, showing crumbling plaster beneath. Bryony's living room was dark when we entered but she switched on a table lamp while Ari walked over to the couch. The room was small and the contents beyond worn, but it was neat as a pin.

Bryony had taken the natural Mederi's love for all things

flowering and run amok. Floral prints covered every conceivable surface of her living room. The couch was awash with a large orange poppy print. In the corner, a whitewashed secondhand folding table was draped with a pink and white azalea tablecloth. Even the hooked rug in front of the couch bore a faded rose motif.

Ari laid Ivy on the couch, careful not to touch her hands. Once Ivy was in position, Bryony, to her credit, did not even bother with us. She just got right to work. She knelt down in front of Ivy and placed her hands over, but not on, Ivy's own. Bryony closed her eyes and took a deep breath.

I'd seen a Mederi heal before. But it was still something to behold. Waxing magic was so different than the waning magic Maegesters used or the spells the Angels believed in. If waning magic was like the sucking sound of a black hole then waxing magic was the sound of wind blowing life back into the world. Waxing magic was the spark of life, whereas waning magic was the paroxysm of death.

Watching Mederies work always made me uncomfortable, as if my mere presence might taint the process. I glanced at Ari to see if he felt the same, but he was staring at Bryony as if transfixed. I was instantly envious, unaccountably angry. Ari's face changed as soon as I'd formed the thought and he turned to meet my gaze. I felt an answering swell of magic in him, a response to my sudden irrational anger. His signature suddenly felt like a great big ball of warmth. I wanted to crawl into it. I wanted to wrap it around my arms. I wanted to take solace and comfort inside of it. I bit the inside of my cheek, not wanting Ari to know how desperately I longed to have him look at me the way he'd just looked at Bryony.

Ari crossed the distance between us and took my arm by the elbow.

"Take her in the kitchen, Ari," Bryony said, without looking up from her work. Only the best Mederies could converse and heal at the same time. "There's some tea in there if you'd like and even some dried fruit and biscuits. Just don't open the icebox. I've got a lot of salad stuff in there."

"See?" Ari said softly to me. "Ivy will be fine. If Bryony is worried about her salad, then Ivy should be healed up in less than an hour."

I nodded miserably. Nothing about this situation was fine.

We entered the kitchen and Ari flipped a switch. The lights flickered for a moment and then steadied, illuminating a drab and hopelessly out-of-date kitchen. Well, really it was little more than a kitchenette. The entire space was only about twenty square feet. I thought the space might once have been a porch. It jutted out precariously past the end of the house. The floor sloped slightly and was laid with chipped tile. The appliances were old and the faucet dripped but, like the living room, it was clean and neat. Not a dish in the sink and not a trace of food on the counter.

Ari went to a cupboard and pulled down a blue tin—decorated with yellow daisies—from the top shelf. He grabbed a teakettle from beneath the sink and filled it with water. It galled me that he knew his way around this Mederi's kitchen so well. Ari put the water on to boil and turned to me, opening his arms wide. I didn't even think. I didn't care, for once, that Ari might think I was weak. I rushed into his embrace and clung to him fiercely.

I told him everything.

By the time I was finished, the front of his shirt was wet with my tears.

"If I hadn't been so eager to open the ball before I'd read the materials my father suggested—"

Ari pushed me away from him and gently shook my shoulders. "Your father shouldn't have sent a familiar to you in the first place." His touch was gentle but his look was hard. "If you're looking for someone to blame, blame your father for sending it. Or blame Seknecus for delivering it."

I was mildly shocked by the intensity of Ari's accusations. One didn't usually go around casting aspersions on the executive of the Demon Council and the dean of demon affairs as cavalierly as Ari just had.

"I still failed her, Ari. My inexperience killed Serafina as much as my eagerness or my magic."

"Serafina killed herself. Any demon who attacks, or attempts to attack, a Hyrke is to be executed. That's the law. The demons' rules are not to be broken."

"But did she know that? She was a familiar. They're known for their jealousy, not their intellect."

"Does it matter?"

I made an impatient, frustrated sound and tried to pull away, but Ari wouldn't let me. *No, it didn't matter. I knew that, as surely as I knew there were 899 other sins without sanction that would get you executed in Halja, whether you knew about them or not.* It was unfair. It was unjust. It was Halja.

"It matters to me," I finally said, looking down at the floor. "Demon or no, Serafina was a living thing. I didn't want to kill her, even if it was to protect a friend."

About an hour later, Bryony met us in the kitchen.

"She's sleeping. And she'll be fine," she added, after looking at me and correctly guessing what I most wanted to know. "So what happened? Was it . . ." Bryony's voice trailed off as her hands crept to her throat. Her earlier burns were nearly gone, only the faintest shadow of the two thumbprints remained.

"No," Ari said. "It wasn't the same demon that attacked you." He glanced at me. "This was . . . an accident."

Bryony's eyes widened, but then she gave Ari an affectionate smile. "I didn't think you had accidents. Is it safe to say the demon's no longer a threat?"

"It was my fault," I said quickly, before Ari could answer for me again. "I . . . Well, it was a demon familiar and I . . ."

What? I didn't bother to read the warning materials my father suggested before opening my "gift"? I thought it would be a good idea to cozy up with a deadly demon I couldn't control and then introduce her to my friend?

"The demon's no longer a threat," I said in a flat tone.

Bryony raised her eyebrows at me. "*You* took care of a demon threat? How'd you do that?"

I grimaced, recalling. "With waning magic. I'm a Maegester-in-Training with Ari at St. Luck's." I forced my tone and facial expression to stay neutral. Bryony was beautiful, and she was an old girlfriend of Ari's, *and* she had the one thing in the whole world I wanted: waxing magic. But the last thing she deserved from me were snide remarks or sneers. She'd healed Ivy when I couldn't.

She stared at me. I braced for the inevitable: revulsion, amusement, and pity were all things I was prepared to see in her returning gaze. Since *curiosity* wasn't one of them, she ended up surprising me almost as much as I did her. I realized she didn't even know my name.

"I'm Noon Onyx," I said. I didn't offer my hand. I wasn't sure she'd accept it.

"Oh," she said, "I know who you are. Your father was the one who saved me from the *rogare* demon who attacked me at the train station."

"I know." Thank Luck he had. Not just for Bryony's sake, but for Ivy's as well.

"I spoke with him earlier today."

"My father? What about?"

"I think Peony's missing." She'd answered my question, but was looking at Ari when she said it.

"Who's Peony?" I asked, confused by the sudden turn in the conversation.

"A friend of mine from the Gaia Tribe," Bryony said.

"When did you last see her?" Ari asked.

"The last time I saw you. At Marduk's." She looked at me again, this time more piercingly. I guessed she was remembering that she'd seen me before. And perhaps was realizing why Ari had broken it off. I wondered when *curiosity* would change to *antagonism*. Things suddenly clicked for me too. Peony must be the other Mederi that had been with them that night, the pretty brunette with the ash-colored eyes and the dimple in her chin.

Now she was missing too? That couldn't be good.

"Do you know if she was planning on returning to Farro anytime soon?" I asked.

Farro was the Gaia Tribe's southern outpost, just as Maize was Demeter's and Emmer was Hawthorn's.

"I don't know," Bryony said. "Why do you think it's important?"

"I'm not sure. But three Mederies have been attacked so far. Amaryllis Apatite, Laurel Scoria, and you. You and Laurel were attacked at or near the New Babylon Train Station and Amaryllis was last seen boarding the North-South Express at the southern terminal. I just wonder if the train station's the link."

"Why would the train station be the link?" Bryony asked. "It's a demon that's responsible. At least, it was a demon that attacked me."

"Exactly," I said. "I'm just wondering who the patron demon of the train station is and if anyone's checked in on *him* lately."

"There is no patron demon of the train station," Ari said. "No demon would watch over something built to house metal machines."

Oh. Right. Well, it had been stupid of me to think I might find a link that everyone else missed. If Bryony had already notified my father, there wasn't much more anyone could do. As estranged as my father and I were, even I had to admit that Karanos Onyx was the person best equipped to bring whichever *rogare* demon was responsible to justice.

On the way out, Ari embraced Bryony. I saw in her face that she'd hoped for more, but he released her quickly and headed straight for me. Ari's hand crept to the back of my neck and gently kneaded the knotted muscles there while we made our farewells. I gave the Mederi my honest gratitude as she looked first at me, then Ari, and back again. She seemed to come to some kind of understanding and accepted my thanks far more graciously than I would have in her circumstances. Ari's possessive gesture made no sense at all. Beautiful, talented Bryony could give him so much more than I could. I could offer him nothing more than he already had.

We brought Ivy home in a cab, heavily sedated with an herbal medicine. On the way, she slept curled up against the door and I sat in the middle, almost asleep myself. Just before we pulled up to Megiddo, Ari pulled me close and kissed the top of my head.

"I've never met anyone who is as strong as you—or as soft," he whispered. "I don't know what's more unbelievable, the fact that you were able to execute your first demon without getting hurt or the fact that it broke your heart."

Chapter 10

When we got up to our room, I laid Ivy down on her bed and pulled the covers up over her. She fell fast asleep. I wasn't so lucky. I cleaned up Serafina's remains, which was a nasty and pitiful job. Even if I'd been able to sleep in my bed after Serafina's death on top of it, it wouldn't have mattered. Her smoking corpse had left a gaping hole in my mattress. I pulled out some extra blankets from my closet and lay down on the floor. Ivy's steady breathing sounded reassuring, but sleep eluded me. I was plagued with guilt, grief, and worry.

Sunlight was sluicing through the cracks between shade and window when Ivy became fully conscious again. She moaned and I was instantly by her side.

"What happened?"

"You were attacked by a demon," I said. Her eyes grew wide, remembering.

"Why was it here in the first place?" Ivy's voice croaked like a frog's as she struggled to sit up. I rearranged her covers as she rose to a cross-legged sitting position and then opened the shades. Sunlight streamed through the room, temporarily blinding us. For once, it was a clear day.

"I let it in," I said, turning around and sitting on the bed next to Ivy. "I'm so sorry, Ivy. It was . . ." I searched for words to describe what I'd done but could think of none vile or repugnant enough. I settled on *terribly irresponsible* and *unbelievably stupid*, while acknowledging their inadequacy and interspersing my self-flagellation with further apologies. "I thought I'd be able to control her," I lamely concluded. "But instead I became enchanted by her. And then I had to kill her." My next words came out in a rush because I had no real desire to say them, just a sense that I ought to.

"You can request a new roommate if you'd like. I'm a danger to you and everyone else."

"*Demons* are dangerous," Ivy said fiercely. "Although, if you ever bring a demon into this room again, I *will* request reassignment."

She seemed to sense my misery then and she reached out to squeeze my hand. "Thank you for saving me," she said.

"Saving you? You were injured because of me."

She shrugged. "If you hadn't killed that familiar it would have killed me."

I nodded, still miserable.

A knock sounded on our door. "Probably Fitz," Ivy said. "He was supposed to meet us here before breakfast. Our original plan was to pry you away from Ari to pick your brain for the upcoming Sin and Sanction midterm."

I groaned. Ivy grinned at me and then winced. I guess there was still some residual pain.

"Don't worry," she said. "I don't feel like studying either."

I walked over to the door and opened it. Fitz stood there holding three steaming cups of coffee and a paper bag that smelled mouthwateringly good. If I had to guess, I would say cinnamon rolls. I threw my arms around him and kissed him on the cheek.

"Thanks—"

I cut off my welcoming cry when I saw who was standing

behind him. Ari, who raised an eyebrow at my unrestrained show of affection for Fitz. I detangled myself from Fitz and stepped aside to let them in.

I hastily scooped my blankets off the floor and piled them on my desk chair, still avoiding my ruined bed.

"I ran into Ari on the way up here," Fitz said. "He told me what happened last night. Ivy, are you okay?"

She nodded.

"Are *you* okay?" Fitz said, turning to me.

"I'm fine," I lied. I'd killed a demon, been the cause of Ivy's injury, and had gotten zero sleep last night. How fine could I be?

"Your dad's really something, you know," Fitz said. "Who gives someone a demon as a gift?"

I shrugged. "The same person who's married to the woman who thought giving me an evergreen was a good idea."

Fitz and Ivy looked puzzled, but Ari's face showed first surprise then anger. He shook his head and walked over to me.

"Don't drink that," he said, grabbing the coffee from my hands. He didn't look upset when he said it though so I was only mildly alarmed when he put his arm around my shoulders and started marching me to the door.

"You need sleep and you're not going to get it here," he said, looking at the rolled up blankets piled on my chair.

Fitz and Ivy looked at each other. Ivy tried to hide her smile.

"What about Ivy?" I said, trying to sneak out from under Ari's arm. "Someone has to stay with her."

"I'm fine, Noon," Ivy said. "Besides, Fitz is here. Go get some rest in a comfortable bed." She gave me a wicked grin as Ari squeezed the scruff of my neck and propelled me through the door.

I told Ari I didn't want to go back to Infernus.

"If you're worried about meeting anyone else right now, don't be. They're all gone. There's only five of us. Well, six now," he said, grinning at me. "Three of the MIT's stick

together—Sasha, Brunus, and Tosca. They left to get breakfast and study somewhere. They won't be back until much
later. And Mercator spends every weekend with his girlfriend."

I was out of excuses or just too tired to think of any more
so I let Ari lead me up to his room. Even after the door was
locked, I was too keyed up for sleep. I paced the room, picking up Ari's things, examining them, putting them back
down, barely remembering what I had touched. Ari sat on his
bed, leaning against the headboard, watching me, saying
nothing. Finally, I perched myself on the edge of his bed, as
far away from him as I could get.

I didn't know how to act around him. I'd never had a
boyfriend before, never wanted one—and I wasn't even sure
that's what he was. The only guy I'd ever fallen asleep beside had been my brother in our early years. With Peter,
sleepovers had been out of the question. And later, when I
was older and had lain with Hyrkes, I'd always snuck out
after to avoid any potential awkwardness. But I realized now
my escapes weren't made to avoid awkwardness. They were
made to avoid closeness. Sleep required a deep state of relaxation, an openness which made one vulnerable to deeper
connections. I didn't want that. I liked my emotional gates as
they were—high and impenetrable.

*What was with Ari? Did he mean to tear down my every
defense?*

As if he'd read my thoughts, Ari reached down for me
and scooted me up next to him, so that I was leaning against
him in the crook of his arm. He clasped his arms around me,
the gesture affectionate but also, I couldn't help thinking, a
means of deterring my escape. I leaned into him, half resis-
tant and stiff, closing my signature down as tightly as I could.
He seemed to sense my reservation and dampened down his
own signature so that all I could feel from him was a small
dose of balmy heat, like the steam coming off a teakettle.
But the lessening of magic made me more susceptible to
Ari's other, more physical, offerings. Suddenly I was intensely aware of how hard his chest felt beneath my back, the

strength of his arms around me, and the clean scent of his clothes, lightly laced with something pleasant I couldn't quite place. Vanilla or anise maybe. And beneath that was a musky, manly smell that made me want to bury my head in his neck and breathe deep.

I turned to look at him. I wanted to see his face, know what he was thinking. But when I turned my head, he brushed the hair away from my neck and kissed me there. His lips felt full and soft as they pressed into my skin. His mouth lingered and his tongue tasted as he worked his way up to the spot just behind my ear. His slow kisses sent shivers racing down my spine and I gripped his thigh without thinking.

"I'm sorry," he said, laughing softly. "I really do want you to sleep."

I thought about telling him I could never sleep there, that he made me so agitated I would never be able to relax enough to sleep in his presence. But I opted for a diversionary discussion so I wouldn't have to talk about how he made me feel.

"Tell me about the other Maegesters-in-Training," I said. "The MIT's."

Ari grunted. "You'll come to your own judgments, of course, but on the whole I find them to be very tedious. Mercator is a decent sort but the rest, honestly, Halja could do without. Sasha you already know," he said with a dismissive wave.

I made a face, which Ari couldn't see, but he must have sensed my magic flare up at mention of his name because he tightened his hold and then put his chin on my shoulder so that our cheeks were touching.

"Sending him to talk to you wasn't the best plan," he admitted. "But Mercator wasn't available and I knew Sasha was your cousin—"

"My second cousin, whom I'd never met—for good reason! And besides, nearly everyone in the Host is distantly related."

"I was desperate. You had shut me out, decided I was the enemy because I knew your secret."

Settled in Ari's arms, his cheek pressed against mine, this man felt like anything but an enemy.

"Would you have declared for me?" I asked.

After a while, he answered with a question of his own. "If Peter finds the Reversal Spell, will you let him cast it over you?"

He seemed to hold his breath, waiting for me to answer. But I couldn't. For the first time, I was unsure.

Ari sat behind me, absolutely still. Slowly I felt his hold on me lessen. The silence between us became a roar in my ears. The steamy teakettle heat I'd been feeling from him grew tepid and then cold. Ari's signature closed down to a trickle, like drops from the end of an icicle. It was as if he'd shut himself off from me. The thought left me frightened for some reason and the fact that I was suddenly afraid of him not being there bothered me intensely. I needed to stick to my own plan, my own goals.

"I should have been born with waxing magic," I said. "Nothing is going to stop me from reversing my magic if I'm given the means to do so."

Ari stood up, keeping his back to me. His signature felt frustrated and angry, but there was some other emotion in it. Conflict? Fear? I hugged my knees, my back to his headboard, and let Ari's magic wash over me. I threw up no answering shield or counterforce. I absorbed what he threw off, trying to better understand it. It hurt. I laid my head on my knees and turned away from him, feeling an intense loneliness and a panicked sense of having lost something precious. But the feeling receded. Ari came over and helped me to my feet. He wouldn't look at me. He pulled the covers of his bed down and tucked me in, pulling the blanket beneath my chin. He focused on it instead of me, and then turned toward the door.

"You were born with waning magic," he said. "You should learn how to use it." He opened his door and stepped out. "Get some sleep," he said gruffly. "You're going to need it."

* * *

I'd sworn I wouldn't sleep there but I did. I was too exhausted to do anything but. I'm not sure, but it's possible that Ari joined me at some point. I dreamed of someone strong. As strong as I was but unafraid. It was a nice dream. I smiled and sighed and threw my arm across the someone's chest, burying my face in their neck like I'd wanted to do earlier with Ari. The someone murmured something in my ear, low and sweet. I felt the rumble in his chest as he did so and then the someone hugged me close. Closer. But I was as close as I could get. *For now.*

Then I slept deeper still, in a place where there were no dreams, but my rest was fitful and torn. In that place I was alone, unaware of the future, and wary of what lay ahead. When I woke up, it was dark and Ari was gone. There was a note.

Noon—

> *You probably shouldn't spend the night. I'll see you in Manipulation class tomorrow morning. 4th floor of Rickard Building, last door on the right.*

Ari

I left Ari's room and walked back to Megiddo to check on Ivy. She was tired but fine, so I spent the rest of Sunday cramming at Corpus Justica for Manipulation. I intentionally sat where Ari had first kissed me, thinking maybe he'd show up. But he didn't. It was probably for the best since I had lots of work to do.

I knew (because I had finally read the Maegester part of the St. Luck's course catalog) that Manipulation class consisted of three parts: (1) a classroom component, where we would discuss our assigned demon law cases; (2) practice sessions, which would teach us how to shape our magic and use it as a method of control (i.e. a weapon—needless to say, I had mixed emotions about *that*); and (3) the application part, where we would apply our newfound knowledge and experience to a real case. Our final grade in Manipulation would be based upon how well we represented and/or controlled our assigned clients.

With that in mind, I selected three books (*Demon Law Fundamentals: Azazel's Legacy* by Ludovicopolis Diasporite, *Swords and Shields: Shaping Waning Magic into a Weapon of Peace* by Mediolanum Pyrophane, and *The Art of Appeasement: Representing Regulare Demons* by Eboracum Acerila) from the thousands that were available to students at Corpus Justica for just such cramming emergencies. I spent the rest of Sunday and into Sunday night reading them, leaving the library only once to grab some soup at the Black Onion. I drank it straight from the cup on my way back to campus, glancing over my shoulder only six or seven times as I passed the New Babylon train station. Nothing out of the ordinary happened however (besides me nearly choking when my footsteps startled a large alley cat out of hiding. My signature zinged, but luckily the only effect of the encounter was slightly overcooked chicken). I threw the paper cup into a trash can before reentering Corpus Justica and then proceeded to read hundreds of thousands of words that really could have been summed up in the three words of advice I'd already been given by Seknecus: *take great care*.

The bright sun was gone by the next morning. Halja saw very few sunny days between Yule and Bryde's Day, which was this Thursday. Already the preparations had begun. I'd seen workmen delivering boxes to Lekai and I'd heard there would be a service that day in the auditorium for any St. Luck or Joshua School student who wanted to attend. No doubt the whole place would be full of corn dolls and other Bryde idols representing the coming spring and the first flush of new life. No one with waning magic would be given a corn doll to hold, no matter how dead it was. It would be near sacrilege. And the last thing I wanted was to be invited to torch the place with the rest of the MIT's who would surely be given the "honor" of setting fire to the last remaining Yule greens. Nope, I would celebrate Bryde's Day my usual way. By throwing open my window and thanking Luck (not Bryde) that spring and warmer weather were coming.

But first I had to make it through my first Manipulation class. I scurried across Victory Street, huddled beneath the warmth of my cloak and ten tons of books. I'd brought all of the books Seknecus had given me, all of the books I'd gathered at the library last night, and each of my demon law language primers. I was determined to be prepared.

I entered Rickard Building, lowered my hood, and adjusted my bag of books. I tried to convince myself that I couldn't wait to get to Manipulation class so that I could put them all down. But I was filled with dread. I held my head high and forced myself to walk at a normal pace. My fingers started to curl inward and I realized I was hyperventilating. I slowed my breathing and stepped into the school's lone winder lift. The lift operator shut the metal gate and tried not to stare when I told him my destination: the fourth floor. Heading to the fourth floor of Rickard was like handing out a calling card. I imagined what mine might look like:

Noon Onyx, Maegester-in-Training

- † Spontaneous firestarting
- † Accidental demon killings
- † Sin and Sanction Expert
- † Hyrke Poser
- † Mederi Wannabe
- † Possibly in love with Ari Carmine

Would my card really include that last line?
Was I falling in love with Ari?
I swallowed. As if I needed *more* to worry about . . . but *yep*, it was true. Despite the fact that I still desperately wanted to reverse my magic, it was impossible for me not

to be the least little bit emotionally affected by Ari's unwavering acceptance of me and my magic, *as it was*. Not as I wanted it—or me—to be.

I'd expected the fourth floor of Rickard to be like the Rabbit Warren. But the hallway I stepped into was long and infinitely straight. At its far end was a small block of light, one tiny dirty window. The light from this single source was all that lit the narrow hallway. At one time, St. Luck's enrollment must have been larger. I passed several open doors to empty unused classrooms. The floor had a creepy, abandoned feeling and I wondered for a moment if I had read Ari's note wrong. Just then my eyes started watering furiously and the unbelievable stench of rotting onions assailed me. I covered my mouth and nose with my hand and stumbled, hoping feverishly that I wouldn't gag.

Someone bumped me from behind. Hard enough to knock my bag of books off my shoulder and onto the floor. He kept walking. I bent down to retrieve them, frowning at his back. Just before he stepped into the last door on the right, he glared at me. The young man was short and pudgy, with dull brown hair that looked like it had been cut with pinking shears. A blast of rotten stink like moldering cabbage struck me. I realized it was his signature, so I blasted back, but he'd already stepped into the room. Maybe someday I'd be good enough to reach someone through walls.

I gathered my books and repacked my bag. I walked to the end of the corridor and stepped into the room. Everyone stopped talking at once and six sets of eyes turned toward me. The largest man among them stepped forward. He was huge, in fact, and his signature felt just as big, like a marble pillar. It was patently obvious that should Quintus Rochester choose to throw his weight, either physical or magical, in my direction, he would crush me.

"Ah, Nouiomo Onyx," he said. "You're late."

I frowned. I'd come early on purpose.

"Where were you after Yule when the rest of the class showed up?"

I heard a low snicker and dared a surreptitious glance at the source—Sasha. He reached out with his magic to bump me, no doubt meaning to send me stumbling but I shoved it back at him, as easily as flicking a fly off my desk. His eyes widened and he sat back in his seat staring. He'd obviously expected the weak sputtering that he'd felt from me while Peter's cloaking spell was still intact.

"I heard Bryde's Day was the deadline for adding this class," I said, chin up, unblinking. I sensed immediately Rochester would have no time for shrinking violets.

"Brunus Olivine," he said, confirming my guess and launching into introductions without further preamble. He motioned to the man who'd knocked my books over in the hallway. Brunus leered at me and sent a rush of magic up my legs. This time there was no wall to block my return thrust. I sent a blast back at Brunus that I'd intended as no more than a magical slap on the cheek, but my lack of control turned the maneuver into a swift nose jab. Brunus cried out as a thin trickle of blood dripped from his nose. He threw no more magic at me but, instead, shot me a lethal look and left the room, presumably to find a tissue. Under ordinary circumstances I would have apologized profusely and walked him to the bathroom, but I instinctively knew, with this crowd, any apologies for defensive magic, no matter how poorly directed, would be a sign of weakness.

"Mercator Palladium," Rochester said, pointing to the Maegester who'd been sitting next to Brunus. Mercator looked like he might be as tall as Ari, but he was thinner, almost gaunt. His hair was nicely trimmed and he wore clothes that were more formal than the rest, a gray linen shirt, black leather vest, and a platinum pocket watch, complete with chain and a half-dozen charms in the sorts of shapes my mother would have approved of (bells, stars, arrows, hearts—but *no flowers*). His eyes were a striking light gray and he looked like he wanted to wink at me. Instead, he tapped me with his magic. I had no idea what the proper etiquette was, but the gesture appeared to be no more than a magical handshake. Mercator felt like silver—shiny and hard, but something I could probably bend if necessary.

"Sasha de Rocca," Rochester said, moving to the next table.

"We've met," I said, preparing for whatever blast Sasha decided to throw my way. But none came. He sat still, narrowing his ice blue eyes at me, no doubt furiously recalculating stronger means of bringing about my demise. I moved to the person sitting next to him.

"Tosca Kaolin," said Rochester. Tosca's signature was erratic, like the wind. A gale force struck me as if I were the broad side of a barn. I lifted one foot preparing to step back so I wouldn't fall, but then I sensed the gust was over, blown out. All that was left was the whistling sound of wind at the window. I slammed my shutters. Tosca sat in front of me with two bright spots of color forming on his cheeks. He hadn't been quick enough getting out and my magic had caught his, pinching it like fingers in a door.

Last was Ari. I'd been waiting. After all this magic muscle flexing I needed a dose of his warm, therapeutic signature. But when I stood in front of him, I felt almost nothing, just the same low-dose trickle I'd felt last night. Like drops of icy water. Ari looked up from his books as if just noticing me and nodded. What was going on? Was he still ticked off that I'd rather be down in southern Halja with the Mederies?

Then I remembered that signatures could change depending on what the sender was experiencing. Maybe Ari's signature felt cold to me because I'd been pushing him away. What was it he'd said the day I touched his demon mark? *You could never hide from me, any more than I could hide from you.*

What would happen if, instead of pushing him away, I tried to pull him closer?

I wasn't ready to find out. But Rochester was staring at me, as if expecting something. Ari was reviewing his notes, ignoring me. His indifference felt like a challenge. Was it feigned?

Did it matter? I nudged Ari with my magic. He brushed it off with no more effort than I had with Sasha. I was stronger than that, almost as strong as Ari. I narrowed my eyes, thinking. This class had nothing to do with academics. Rochester wasn't judging me on how I used my mind, only my magic.

I realigned my feelings and concentrated on sending out a strong dose of pure magic. I miscalculated. The blast singed Ari's books, cracked the crystal in his watch, and exploded his pen, splattering ink all over. A creaking sound preceded the shattering collapse of the table behind him. But Ari was unaffected. He made a great show of wiping down his books and then calmly reached into his pack for another pen.

Brunus returned from the bathroom and all eyes were on me. I knew the next few seconds would establish my rank in the class. Coming in at such a disadvantage, I could hardly afford to lose more ground. Did I dare try to really manipulate Ari? Was I brave enough to reach for him magically using the feelings that were between us?

Is that what he wanted?

Suddenly, I wanted to wring his neck. He made me angry. He got under my skin. He made me feel things I didn't want to feel and he made me afraid. Every time I was around him, I felt agitated and aroused. But I also felt invigorated and energized. Being around Ari, for me, was like lying in the sun. All that warmth and heat, I wanted to feel it on every part of my body. I closed my eyes imagining what it would be like—

"Stop!" Rochester's deep voice boomed. "What you're doing is dangerous. No more," he said, waving a flat palm through the air. It was unquestionably a gesture of cessation. Woe to any student who ignored it. I slid into the seat beside Ari and dared a quick look at him. My last little magic trick had finally gotten his attention. He stared at me. At once I felt like a rabbit caught in a snare. Had I gone too far? I swallowed and fought not to twitch my leg.

"Noon," Rochester said. My attention snapped to him. "You've developed bad habits as a result of insufficient training. You add emotion to your magic to make it stronger but that makes you vulnerable to enchantment. We will work on this." He walked to the center of the room and addressed the whole class.

"I have determined new pairings for this semester's client representation. Noon, you are *Secundus* now. You and Ari are in opposition. Mercator, you're *Tertius* now opposing Brunus. And then Sasha and Tosca." I gathered from everyone's reactions that these were the new rankings caused by my late entry. The only Maegester to take it magnanimously was Mercator, who nodded conciliatorily in my direction.

Beside me, Ari's signature felt like the smoldering coals of a banked fire. I made the mistake of looking at him again. His gaze captured mine, his eyes dark and unreadable. His hair fell in unruly waves, just past his ears, its color somewhere between burnt amber and black coffee. Under the weak, diffused light of the indoor classroom, Ari's skin looked like stone. But I knew he would be hot to the touch, like lit charcoal. He winked at me, his signature never changing, never giving Rochester a reason to look over at us. A sweet painful burst of something shot through me. My whole body suddenly felt like my jaw would have if I'd bitten down on a thousand lemon wedges. I fought to keep my signature steady and switched my gaze back to Rochester.

Rochester paced the front of the classroom, his massive bulk moving effortlessly back and forth from Brunus to me. He explained that, as of Bryde's Day, we would be assigned a real client.

For a moment I wondered how big a mistake I'd made by waiting to declare. I'd missed nearly a quarter of the class. But by not paying attention now I was only making matters worse so I diligently refocused on Rochester, who was assigning the first case to Brunus and Mercator. It was an Oathbreaking case. Rochester gave us the background.

"About a year ago," he said, "a young Hyrke couple, Temone and Finora Greenwald, purchased two annual passes from Western Myst Cruise Line to travel the upper Lethe. Under the terms of the contract, which was printed on the back of the passes and countersigned by the Greenwalds, a full price ticket entitled the pass holder to unlimited access to all outposts between New Babylon and Morkill Steppe, for a period of one year from the date of issuance.

"The Greenwalds are farmers. Their plan was to stake a claim using one of the Lethe outposts as a base for supplies. They bought their passes to explore the outposts and determine which area would be best to settle in. Because the Greenwalds have limited capital, they worked out an oral agreement with the owner of Western Myst, James Ashe. Instead of requiring full price up front, as the preprinted terms dictated, Mr. Ashe agreed to accept installment payments. The passes were issued, five installment payments were made, and six outposts reached when the level of the Lethe dropped so low further travel was impossible."

"Wait!" Brunus interrupted, raising his hand but shouting out anyway. "Where are the demons? I thought we'd be representing demons. This sounds like something for A and A."

"Not all of you will be representing demons. But that doesn't mean Maegester services aren't required. Listen, learn, *live*, Mr. Olivine," Rochester said, giving Brunus a look that would have gelled my insides if directed at me. Brunus swallowed and shut up.

"After a few months of living tethered off of the Blacken Ridge Outpost, the Greenwalds asked Mr. Ashe to reduce the amount they were paying for the passes that were taking them nowhere. An argument ensued. Ashe called upon Rictus, the Demon of Rules, insisting that the couple pay the full rate as agreed. When the couple threatened to call their hearth demon, Ashe reconsidered and agreed to a fee reduction."

Rochester paused, peering down at Mercator and Brunus, gauging their understanding. There was obviously more to the story, otherwise, why would this be a Manipulation case? Something must have happened to set off the demons or this would not be a matter for Mercator and Brunus to handle.

Mercator wore an expectant look that told me he was waiting for the rest of the story. Brunus just looked bored and impatient. Rochester continued.

"A few days later, Ashe introduced the Greenwalds to a seed merchant, who sold the Greenwalds some Mederi-blessed seeds for their future farm. The price of the seeds was exactly the difference between the old pass rate and the reduced pass rate."

Ah. The first wrinkle. I felt sorry for the poor Hyrke couple, who I suspected had been swindled. Most Hyrkes weren't as well-off as Ivy and Fitz and the rest at St. Luck's. Many were poor and could barely afford the services of a Mederi midwife when their children were born. This couple must have thought Mederi-blessed seeds would be the boon their new farm needed to make it a success.

"Another month went by, the seeds rotted, and still the Lethe level remained low. In a fit of frustration, the Greenwalds called their hearth demon. The hearth demon arrived, furious with Ashe for taking advantage of his clients, furious with his clients for not calling him sooner, and"—Rochester cleared his throat, alerting us to the real problem—"furious with Rictus."

The room fell silent. Brunus' bored look was gone, replaced by one of near rapture. He'd be one to watch if he enjoyed the idea of demons fighting. It was *exactly* what Maegesters were bound, by law and scripture, to prevent. Squabbling among demons, no matter how petty, had to be stopped at once. No one wanted a small feud to turn into a full-fledged war, which is what might happen if demons were allowed to work out their own differences. Demon dispositions being what they were, one minor argument might lead to demons gathering armies, making attacks, and laying siege, an eventuality that Halja could ill afford. Our world had already sacrificed its future for an uneasy peace. Two thousand years ago, we'd won the Apocalypse but in so doing had destroyed Heaven and, some believed, our own souls. Another war, therefore, was Halja's greatest fear. For these reasons, the Council had long ago established their "zero tolerance policy" for demon infighting. It was easier to stop the war that never got started.

Rochester looked around, satisfied that each of us understood the gravity of the situation. Though the matter was to be handled by Mercator and Brunus, it seemed that Rochester wanted us to learn from the others' assignments. So I assumed we could comment and raised my hand.

"Who brought the matter to St. Luck's for representation?" Mercator nodded. Brunus frowned at me.

"The Greenwalds," said Rochester. "They're still stuck at Blacken Ridge, but they wrote to request representation. It seems they were . . . worried . . . about the extent of their hearth demon's fury."

In spite of the seriousness of the situation, a few of us laughed. "Worried" was likely a euphemism for "horrified." Mercator picked up his pen and leaned forward in his seat, his signature heating up with interest.

"Has the hearth demon made any specific allegations about Rictus?" Mercator asked, "Or is he just blustering about, unhappy that his clients ignored him for too long?"

"Good question," Rochester said, his voice deep and rumbling, like an avalanche of boulders. "Specific allegations have been made. The hearth demon, whose name is Yul by the way, accused Rictus of hypocrisy."

Sasha gaped and Tosca made a grunting sound that seemed to indicate surprise or amusement. Maybe both. Hypocrisy was a severe accusation. It would have been taken badly by any demon but the fact that it was leveled at a demon such as Rictus, whose honor was bound up in being the strictest of the strict, made it that much worse.

"Yul claims that Ashe designed the seed trade to recoup what he'd lost when he agreed to reduce the Greenwalds' annual pass rate. Yul accused Rictus of encouraging, or at least tacitly agreeing to, the seed-trade scam. According to Yul, this means Rictus was involved in a deception designed to thwart an agreement. In other words, he broke the rules."

I saw how easily one small Hyrke disagreement could spin so out of control that Maegester services were required. One moment, a couple of Hyrkes are arguing about money and the next, one demon is accusing the other of hypocrisy and rule breaking.

"Was the seed trade really a scam?" Brunus asked. "Or is that just Yul's position?"

Rochester nodded, acknowledging another question well asked. Apparently even Brunus was capable.

"Interestingly, Rictus takes no position on the seed trade. But he is enraged about the hypocrisy claim and wants immediate restitution. Rictus' position is that his client, Ashe, scrupulously followed the rules. Per the contract, the full price of the ticket was to have been paid up front. It was not. Ashe considerately agreed to payment in installments per the Greenwalds' request. Later, the Greenwalds used seasonal fluctuations in the Lethe's level and the threat of their hearth demon to strong-arm Ashe into further price reductions. If anyone was guilty of breaking rules, Rictus claims, it's the Greenwalds, who ignored, thwarted, and breached their contract with Ashe at every opportunity."

What a mess. I considered how I might handle the matter if it were assigned to me. The seed trade was clearly a scam. No Mederi-blessed seeds would rot in a month. The legal solution was to argue fraud and make Ashe reimburse the Greenwalds for the cost of the seeds. The demon part of it, what we Maegesters were really paid to do, was a little less clear. I thought for a moment. What would appease the demons and make them back down? Yul was furious because he'd lost adoration from his clients. The couple had bought bogus seeds to start a new hearth instead of making a sacrifice to him. I would advise the couple to immediately make amends, appease their hearth demon, and pledge no further loyalty breaches. If I were forced to represent Ashe, I would chastise him soundly for the seed debacle, force him to honor the oral amendments he made with the Greenwalds, and advise a hasty sacrifice to Rictus for his troubles. But all of this would still leave the Hyrkes stranded at the dock.

"Are Maegesters able to summon other demons to assist in a matter like this?" I asked.

All went still and quiet. No shuffling of papers, no squeaking chairs, no coughs or scratches of pen on paper. How could there be when every eye was suddenly on me?

"Summon *another* demon? Are you crazy?" Tosca said. Brunus guffawed. Sasha looked at me, eyes agog, mouth agape.

"Well," I said, unable to prevent the spreading blush on my cheeks, "I just wondered what would happen to Ashe and the Greenwalds after their demons are appeased."

"Who cares?" Brunus shouted and then groaned. "You're still thinking like the Hyrke you've spent your whole life pretending to be. Stop wasting our time. We need to focus on how to put the demons back in their balls so to speak, not pull more of them out."

"Strong but stupid," I heard Tosca murmur under his breath.

"She has a point," Ari said. He'd been so quiet during the discussion of Mercator and Brunus' assignment, I'd wondered if he was paying any attention. "Which demon would you call?" he said, turning to me.

"Ari," Rochester said, his tone of voice a clear warning.

"I was thinking the patron demon of the Lethe might be helpful."

"Helpful?" Brunus echoed, his face pinched with scorn. "In what corner of Halja would summoning a demon ever prove *helpful*?"

"Even if you settle the current dispute," I said, racing to get my point across before I lost my nerve, "it will likely heat up again with everyone just sitting there tethered to the Blacken Ridge dock, going nowhere. It's obvious that Ashe hasn't been making his sacrifices to the river demon."

Obvious? Hardly. I'd been denied the education and experience that everyone in this room had been given since birth. I'd based my assessment only on the general knowledge that every resident of Halja had and common sense. But was that enough? Had I missed something crucial?

Rochester cleared his throat and folded his hands in front of him, contemplating me. He appeared to consider his next words carefully.

"You will be interesting to teach, Ms. Onyx," he said. "You dismissed appeasing the on-site demons, Rictus and Yul, as if it were a fait accompli. In practice, appeasing demons, even if you have a plan, is a grim and difficult job. Separating entangled demons often leaves Maegesters with little strength to tackle additional problems. Also, while summoning demons is not strictly forbidden, it is discouraged. Summoning the river demon for 'assistance' could backfire. Once the river demon's attention is focused on the matter, he may require more than just a sum of sacrifices to balance his truant client's account."

To my left, Sasha laughed. I looked down at my desk.

"Mr. Olivine," Rochester snapped, "you'll represent Ashe. Mr. Palladium, you'll represent the Greenwalds." They nodded, apparently satisfied with the sides they'd been given. "Opposing counsel shouldn't collaborate, and should avoid even the appearance of collaboration. This means you may not discuss your assignments outside of class.

"Okay, that's it for today. Tomorrow I'll hand out the rest of the clinic assignments. We'll discuss them in class again on Wednesday. By Bryde's Day on Thursday, you should have some thoughts on overall strategy and be prepared for your first client interview. Ms. Onyx, please see me after class."

Chapter 11

ぞ

Beneath my desk my fists clenched, echoing my stomach. Chairs scraped across the floor as the rest of the class gathered their books and prepared to leave. Beside me, Ari sat still. I didn't want to look at him. I didn't want him to see how stupid I felt for suggesting an additional demon might help with Brunus and Mercator's problem. I reached down to grab my backpack. I'd spent half the night reading the books that were in it and I'd barely scratched the surface of the material. I didn't have time to read more. We had a Sin and Sanction midterm coming up that everyone needed to pass, regardless of whether they were Host or Hyrke. I'd now missed more than a few study group sessions with Ivy and Fitz. I was behind in my Oathbreaking work. I'd never mastered remedies like I planned. By Thursday, I'd have a client to represent in a matter that was likely to have serious, real-life implications. And the one person who'd offered to help me catch up in Manipulation was now my opposing counsel. Further study sessions with Ari were now unadvisable.

Ari gave my shoulder a brief squeeze and walked out. I

slung my overweighted backpack over my shoulder and walked to the front of the classroom where Rochester waited for me.

He stood draped in a cloak of blue so dark it seemed to swallow light, like a new moon midnight sky. Rochester must have been in his early sixties, but I saw not a single strand of gray in his coarse, black hair. His eyes were a cold gray and he wore a neatly trimmed mustache. It was rumored that every Maegester had a drop of demon blood in them. Looking at Rochester, it was easy to imagine that the rumor was true.

"Most of my students wouldn't think of the Hyrkes' fate after the demon issues have been settled," Rochester said. "Your unique upbringing may have hidden benefits."

I still didn't understand why calling the river demon was such a bad idea. My Hyrke friends were forever calling upon their demons to help them out. I said as much to Rochester.

"Exactly," he said. "Calling, not summoning. There's a difference." He folded his hands across his bulging stomach and leaned back against his desk.

"Hyrkes have the privilege of calling their demons anytime they want. But that's because they can't control or manipulate them. Hyrkes beseech demons, they adore them, and make pleas to them, which the demons are free to answer or not, at the demon's discretion. Maegesters, however, *are* capable of controlling and manipulating demons. When a Maegester summons a demon, the demon feels bound. A Maegester's summoning can create feelings of animosity and ill will between the demon and the Maegester."

I nodded, and wondered what my life would be like if I survived my training. Everything about being a Maegester seemed counterintuitive.

"Thanks for the additional background," I said. "I realize I have a lot of catching up to do. I had thought to study with Ari Carmine, but if we're going to be opposing counsel . . . ?"

Staying away from Ari outside of class would be difficult. How broad was the prohibition on collaboration between opposing counsel? Unfortunately, I couldn't imagine studying with any of the others. Well, maybe Mercator, but Ari had said he spent most of his free time with his girlfriend.

"Your magic today was strong and effective," Rochester said. "That's why I ranked you second. But your methods are unorthodox. It's clear you've had no real training. Under ordinary circumstances, I would say Mr. Carmine would make a fine study partner, but . . ."

Rochester paused, peering intently at me. I could feel his signature creeping along the edges of mine. It was very subtle and I wondered if someone with less sensitivity than I had would have felt it. I fought an instinct to push it back. It would have been futile and I didn't want Rochester to think I had anything to hide. But what was he looking for? Did signatures carry residual magic from things previously experienced? Declaring had wiped clean any potential sin of denying my magic. Did Rochester sense some lingering emotion over Serafina in my signature? Guilt and grief had been my main reactions to the ordeal, but maybe fear would have been more appropriate. I shuddered and Rochester's look became more inquisitive. It was impossible to tell what he was picking up. But his next words surprised me.

"Are you romantically involved with Mr. Carmine?"

I blinked, not sure I'd heard him right. I wasn't sure what to say. Regardless of the fact that we were opposing counsel *now*, what we'd done outside of the classroom *before* was no one's business but our own.

"I only ask because your magic affected him, and there's no way it could have unless there was a connection between you. It also seemed as if he was taunting you into proving it. And you did, by tapping into some shared emotion. It's very dangerous stuff, for both of you."

Two spots of color formed on my cheeks. I could feel them. Sure, a part of me was embarrassed. But a part of me was livid.

"Do you plan on giving this lecture to Ari?" I asked, looking straight at Rochester, my back stiff. He could eat me in one gulp, but I refused to be bullied. His question was out of line.

"Mr. Carmine will get a slightly different version," Rochester said, returning my stare. But his posture remained relaxed. If he'd wanted to threaten me, I doubted he would be leaning against his desk while he did it. And his signature was far from fired up. Good thing. If Rochester ever lost it, I sensed it would be a seismic event.

"I heard your father sent you a familiar to work with before class," Rochester said, changing controversial subjects at dizzying speed. "How did that go?"

"I killed her," I said, thinking bluntness would be the best way to handle someone who seemed to know everything already.

Rochester grunted. "Did you read the books Dean Seknecus gave you before opening the ball?"

Slowly, I shook my head.

"It was a great gift that Seknecus bestowed on you, giving you his books. You should have read his margin notes." Rochester's massive physical presence and the bulk of his signature loomed over me. I forced myself not to look down.

"Pull out Skleros' *Lesser Demons* and open it to chapter nine," he said.

I did. A picture of a demon familiar covered the first page of the chapter. The demon looked eerily like Serafina, with a distended belly, beady black eyes, and grayish green skin. It appeared to leap off the page, claws extended, a malevolent, evil grin on its face. I wondered if the artist had been an Angel (many were) and had infused the page with a bit of magic. My throat tightened and my belly clenched. The chapter was titled "Demon Familiars." I started reading.

> Familiars are a subclass of the demon race. Like winged imps, they are physically small and psychologically immature. Like all members of the demon class (except ice breathers, see Chapter 23), familiars have the power to start fires and leech oxygen. Familiars have a moderate amount of magic and are capable of wreaking havoc and causing great pain. The single

most dangerous aspect of the familiar, however, is its power to enchant.

Enchantment occurs when a Maegester develops too close an attachment to a demon. Understanding enchantment is easiest when it is compared to adoration. Adoration is the Hyrke act of beseeching a demon. It is a healthy connection, voluntary on both sides. Enchantment, on the other hand, is a sickness. Once enchanted, a Maegester will be enslaved to the demon. The relationship is involuntary and forced. The demon becomes the sole focus of the enchanted Maegester's life, often with life threatening consequences . . .

I couldn't bear to read any more, but Seknecus' bold strokes in the margin were impossible to ignore.

Only way out—Death or Dementia

I slammed the book shut. "Great, so my dad sent me something that had the power to kill me or the potential to drive me insane."

"No. He sent you something that would teach you a valuable lesson. Demons enchant. Don't become enchanted."

I shoved Skleros' *Lesser Demons* into my bag, fighting to not cry. Did Rochester actually think I should be grateful for the gift I had to kill? Again I thought of the evergreen my mother had sent me. I would damn my parents, truly, if we weren't all damned already. I swiped at a tear that slipped free.

"Nouiomo," Rochester said softly, "If you were forced to kill the familiar to control her, that meant you'd become enchanted. It didn't take long. I suspect you have a soft spot for demons. And Hyrkes, but that's another discussion," he said, waving his hand through the air. "Familiars are the best enchanters the demon class has to offer, but they are not the only thing in Halja that can enchant. Maegesters can enchant too."

I frowned and shrugged. I hadn't known but why did it matter? I wasn't enchanting anybody.

"You and Ari Carmine are opposing counsel because I assign pairs based on rank. But there is another reason. I believe you are in danger of becoming enchanted by Mr. Carmine. The less time you spend with him the better."

I walked down the long hallway of the fourth floor of Rickard Building in a daze. I entered the winder lift and murmured "Lobby" to the operator. I don't know if anyone else rode down with me. Maybe someone spoke to me. Maybe not. When I stepped out of the lift onto the ground floor of Rickard, I only knew I had something new to fear. I honestly wasn't sure how many more things I could be afraid of without losing my mind.

In the lobby, St. Luck's students were clustered in groups, talking and laughing. It was so loud, it was impossible to pick up individual conversations. Everyone was waiting for their next class to start. I had Sin and Sanction with Copeland in fifteen minutes. I couldn't even remember what we were supposed to be discussing today. And I was supposed to be the Sin and Sanction expert.

I shoved and bumped my way through the crowd, thinking to find a quiet spot to sit before class. Somewhere that I could pull myself together and regroup. I could not think about the implications of my meeting with Rochester right now. If I did, I'd never make it through the rest of my day, since Ari was in all my classes.

Were my feelings for him the product of enchantment? If so, was Ari aware of his effect on me? Was he doing it on purpose? To what end?

I shook my head and sat down on the nearest bench, unable to go any farther. Around me, the din and buzz of conversations hummed along, with all oblivious to my distress.

I'd never thought the feelings between Ari and I would last, but I'd at least thought they were real. Now, I realized, they might not be. I was beyond feeling embarrassed by my infatuation for Ari. I was afraid. After the ordeal with Serafina, I knew where enchantment could lead and I wanted no part of it. Hands on my knees, I breathed deeply, trying to calm myself with the thought that, at least if we broke it off now, the hurt would still be manageable. But could I do it? Even now, I scanned the crowd looking for him, desperately hoping to find him, desperately hoping I wouldn't.

Luck below, was I already enchanted?

I felt him before I saw him, which ratcheted up my fear a notch. By the time he stepped into view, I was almost in full panic. I debated running off to Megiddo and skipping class, but that would only put off the inevitable. Ari stood in front of me, smiling. His hands were in his pockets and his backpack was casually slung over his shoulder.

"You did great today," he said.

I said nothing, only swallowed and tried to shut my signature down to nothing. Magically, I tried to make myself small so I would be less of a target. I had no idea what would work or how to stop what was happening to us. Even while trying to shut down, a part of me opened to accept Ari's signature. His warmth seeped into me unbidden. I bit the inside of my mouth to keep from crying out. Suddenly, Ari's presence felt like a violation.

"Noon," he said, dropping his pack to the floor and kneeling in front of me. "What's wrong?" He grabbed my hands and a few of the students closest to us glanced our way. I shook my hands free of his and stood up, shaking.

"Nothing. Everything," I said.

Realizing I was still capable of rejecting his touch made me less panicked. What I was feeling now didn't feel like what I'd felt when I was with Serafina. She'd made me feel fuzzy headed and sleepy. Ari made me feel hypersensitive, ultra aware. I supposed enchantment could feel different depending on who was doing the enchanting, but the difference was enough to calm me. Rochester had said I was in danger of becoming enchanted, not that I already was. I took a deep breath.

"We're going to be opposing counsel," I said. "We probably shouldn't talk outside of class until the semester is over."

"That's four months from now," Ari said, almost laughing. He seemed relieved now that I'd recovered from my fight-or-flight reaction to him. But when he realized I wasn't joking, his expression became serious. "I can't go four months only seeing you in class," he said matter-of-factly.

Again I cursed how he made me feel. Just that simple statement had my heart racing, from elation, and then from fear.

"I don't want to see you outside of class," I said. "I don't want to risk . . . things."

"What things?" he asked, narrowing his eyes.

"You heard Rochester," I said. "Collaboration between opposing counsel is prohibited."

"We're not planning on collaborating—or are we?" He gave me an impish grin. "Actually, I can think of several things I'd like to collaborate with you on." His gaze caused a supernova-like explosion in my stomach. The aftershocks moved to other parts of my body and I squirmed.

"Ari," I said, my tone a clear warning.

"Always so reluctant," he chided. "Seriously, Noon, you're not going to let Rochester's pairing stand in the way of us, are you?"

"I wasn't aware there was an 'us.'"

Ari just looked at me, with one eyebrow raised. I guess it was stupid to deny a connection since even Rochester had picked up on it. The question was the nature and extent of the connection. Best to sever it now, while I was feeling confident about my decision.

"We should follow the rules, Ari. *Praeceptum primum, praeceptum solum.* Scrupulous rule following is 'the first rule, the only rule,' right? Opposing counsel shouldn't collaborate and should avoid even the appearance of collaboration."

I hated that I sounded preachy. Like everyone else in Halja, I was a rule follower. But it didn't feel right to be giving Ari the wrong reason for not wanting to see him.

He studied me for a moment. I could feel his magic building.

"You'd better not," I said.

"Better not what?"

"Just keep your magic to yourself. I don't want any part of it." His signature folded in on itself. I wondered if any other Maegesters were around to pick up on the byplay between us. If Rochester found out Ari was the first person I'd talked to after his class, it would confirm his suspicions about my susceptibility. I glanced around, nervously biting my lip.

"What did Rochester say that scared you so much?" Ari asked. His voice was calm and his signature roiled just below full boil, but eddies and undercurrents abounded. I had to be careful not to get swept up and pulled under.

"He didn't," I said, unable to meet Ari's eyes.

"Noon," Ari said, his voice going hard. "Don't lie to me. I was only half-serious about not being able to wait four months to see you outside of class. I won't like it, but I'll wait if that's what you want. I'd wait any amount of time, if at the end of it you'd finally accept who you are and the feelings I have for you. But I cannot, and will not, let you hide things from me again. Ever." His voice shook with emotion.

His gaze stung. I felt immobilized, helpless to prevent the feelings that were spreading in me like venom. But meeting his eyes, I realized then that even the threat of death would not keep me from Ari Carmine. If I were enchanted, or to become enchanted, so be it. I wouldn't lie to him. And I wouldn't keep the truth from him.

I put my hand in his, pulling him through the crowd.

"Come on," I said. "We only have a few minutes before Copeland's class."

He followed me without reservation. We made our way through the crowd. More than a few people glanced our way. But it was the type of look I was beginning to get used to. They didn't stare because they thought we were conspiring, they stared because one day we would be Maegesters.

I led Ari through the front door of Rickard, around the

corner of the building, and into a narrow alley. The north side of Rickard was the edge of campus so there weren't any other students there. Across from Rickard was a warehouse. The tall walls of the two buildings blocked most of the sun and the area was dark and cold. Neither of us had our cloaks; they were hanging in our lockers. I was glad for the warmth of Ari's hand around mine as I pulled him farther into the alley. It would have been convenient to use enchantment as an excuse for what happened next, but I knew I wasn't that far gone.

Yet.

Halfway down the alley I stopped and looked around, seeing no one. I looked up at Ari and let my feelings run riot. No longer restrained, my magic heated up immediately. Rochester said I added emotion to my magic to make it stronger. I could feel that happening. Every emotion I had felt in the last hour got rolled up into a tight little ball in my chest. Trepidation over my first Manipulation class. Horror over Brunus' bloody nose. Pleasure at proving I could provoke Ari with my magic. Shame over realizing my methods were unorthodox and dangerous. Embarrassment, anger, guilt, grief, fear, and then finally abandonment, recklessness, and desire. The ball in my chest grew so dense, I could barely breathe. I grabbed Ari's hand and started untucking my shirt.

"What are you doing, Noon?" he asked, suddenly alarmed.

Instinctively, I knew that what I was about to do would cause something irreversible to happen. I remembered Ari's words the first time I'd met him at Infernus.

It's called a signare, *which is the magical equivalent of pressing your thumb into someone else's heart.*

But I could no more stop the building emotion within me than I could stop killing a garden as I walked through it. I brought Ari's hand up under my shirt and placed his bare palm over my demon mark, skin to skin.

The ball in my chest exploded. My knees buckled and I nearly dropped to the stone floor of the alley.

A searing wind, with us at its epicenter, raced through the narrow tunnel of the alley, burning trash and laying waste everything in its path. Fortunately, there wasn't much. Thank Luck there hadn't been any Hyrkes around. They would have been fried on the spot. But they were coming. I heard the doors of Rickard bang open as people shouted, no doubt wondering what had caused the echoing boom they'd heard. Ari stood rooted before me, his hand still on my chest. His expression was like none I'd ever seen before, rife with as many emotions as I'd just released. He looked up at the Hyrkes gathering at the far end of the alley. They were just far enough away for their faces to be unclear.

"Let's go," he said, grabbing my hand this time. He pulled me farther down the alley and back behind the warehouse. We were a block off campus now. With class starting in mere minutes, it was unlikely any student would follow us here. After all, strange things happened at St. Luck's and no one had been hurt.

When he was sure no one had followed us, he backed me up against the wall.

"Why now?" he asked roughly, touching his forehead to mine. "Why here? In the *alley*?" He laughed then, slightly breathless and almost giddy. He pressed one hand against the wall next to me while the other cupped my cheek. *Because I'm falling in love with you,* I thought. *And for one reckless moment, I wanted to feel what it was like to have you put your mark on my heart.* But there was no way I was going to say that. It was scary enough just to think it. So I told him the other thing I was almost as scared about.

"Rochester thinks you're enchanting me," I panted.

"*Me* enchanting *you*?" he said, his tone incredulous. "Try the other way around." He kissed me then, a long, deep, slow kiss that melted the edges of my magic and, despite the chilled air, made me feel soft and warm.

After a while Ari tilted his head back but kept both hands pressed to the wall behind me. He frowned.

"*Rochester* said that?"

For a moment it seemed as if Ari's magical strength rivaled Rochester's. I hoped Rochester wouldn't directly accuse Ari of anything. Who knew what might happen.

Despite what I'd just done, I still felt wildly confused. "We need to stay away from each other," I said.

"We need to spend more time together," Ari growled.

"Ari, I'm serious. I want you to promise me something. Your magic is stronger than mine. If you make a promise, I know you'll keep it."

"Don't underestimate yourself, Noon."

"You're changing the subject."

"My mark's not enough?" he teased. "You want an oath too?"

"Ari, I'm . . ."

Well, the fact was, I was scared. And, even though I'd had this big magic moment in the alley a moment ago when I'd decided I could no longer hide my feelings from him, it was still incredibly difficult to just say, "I'm afraid." And it was even more difficult to say, "I'm afraid Rochester is right and even though I don't care, I *should* care."

"I'm . . . concerned," I finally said.

Ari gave me a wry smile and pushed off the wall. He stepped back and looked away for a moment. The air was still and cold. I shivered. Ari returned his gaze to mine. He reached for my hands and clasped them between us.

"You know why I was able to put my *signare* on you, Noon?"

I shook my head.

"Because your feelings for me are *real*. Remember how I said not everyone can do it? It takes reciprocity, both magically and emotionally. If I'd enchanted you, I wouldn't have been able to mark you."

"Have I marked you then?"

He gave me a look that was mostly unbelieving, but just the least little bit hurt. "Yes."

"So your feelings for me . . . they're real?"

"Since the day you tried to make a five-foot jump to the moving boat you'd sworn you weren't boarding." I tried to pull my hands away from his. He wouldn't let me.

"What do you want me to promise?"

I bit my lip. It was for the best.

"Promise that this is it until the end of the semester. Promise we won't see each other outside of class until Manipulation is over."

"No," he said simply. "But I'll promise you something else."

He brought my hands to his mouth and tenderly kissed the back of each of them. He looked at me, his face a mask of ferocity.

"I will *never* enchant you. Should anyone, or *anything*, ever try to, I will kill them, if you don't first."

Chapter 12

჻

We went to Sin and Sanction late. I walked in first and Ari came in a few minutes later. Everyone probably knew we'd been together. Many of them had seen us in the lobby walking out, but Ari respected my wishes to at least try to be discreet. The class itself was hellish. Copeland strung me up for being late, calling on me an unmerciful eight times. I stumbled my way through my answers, glad Sin and Sanction was a subject that came naturally to me, because I couldn't remember a word of the assignment I'd skimmed just last night.

I hung out with Ivy and Fitz during the break between Sin and Sanction and Oathbreaking and assured them there would be no more study group lapses. Ivy was completely recovered from Serafina's attack. Her red hair was unbound and flew madly around her face, which was pink with color and curiosity. Both she and Fitz wanted the scoop on Manipulation.

"You're our entree into the madcap world of Maegesters," Fitz said, chortling.

"Let's get lunch at Marduk's," I said, suddenly missing it. I hadn't been there since the night before Peter had left. "I'll fill you in then."

Fitz and Ivy nodded enthusiastically and we shuffled into Oathbreaking. I had to admit, I found the cases somewhat dull compared to the one we'd discussed in Manipulation. But I did my best to pay attention, take notes, and participate.

By late afternoon, Ivy, Fitz, and I were installed in a back booth at Marduk's. I ordered the Innkeeper's Pie. Fitz ordered a cheeseburger with a loaded baked potato and Ivy chose the vegetarian chili. I hoped they weren't going fresh free because of me. While we waited for our food, I told them about the other MIT's.

"Most of them sound pretty horrible," Ivy said. "Too bad. I was hoping they might be more sympathetic."

I gave her a dubious look. "Who cares about them?" I said. "I've got you two, right?"

Fitz sat up straight, a look of surprise on his face. Members of the Host didn't usually go around telling Hyrkes how much they meant to them. His surprised look dissolved into an ear splitting grin and, I couldn't be sure—it could have been the heat from the fire—but I thought I saw two spots of color form on his cheeks. My declaration of friendship had made Fitz blush.

Ivy smiled at me and grabbed my hand from across the table, squeezing it. "I knew I would like you from the moment that nose-blowing, lozenge-sucking student affairs lady told me you were my roommate." She let go and leaned back in her chair.

"What about Ari? Where's he?"

"We're opposing counsel," I said.

"No!" Ivy said, slapping her hand down on the table for emphasis. A&A had the same restrictions regarding collaboration outside of class. She and Fitz knew immediately why Ari and I wouldn't be spending much time together during the rest of the semester.

"That's rough," Fitz said.

I nodded and tried to think of a way to change the subject.

"Ivy," I said, "does your family ever have trouble with the level of the Lethe?"

"No. Why?"

"We were discussing a case today in Manipulation and some of the parties had trouble traveling on the Lethe because the river was so low."

"Call Estes, the Lethe's demon patron," she said. She shrugged, indicating that this was a no-brainer. "The travelers need to make their sacrifices."

I smiled to myself. *Exactly.* A simple solution to a simple problem. It was thinking like a Maegester that complicated things.

When Ivy and I returned to Megiddo, I had two letters. The first one was from Peter.

Noon—

My parents were furious that I left Joshua School midterm. They made it clear I wasn't welcome back home until the semester ended. Sound familiar? I suppose they thought I would slink back to school, but I moved into an old abandoned gardening shed at the edge of our property. I've been breaking into my own house at night to search for the spell. I half hope I'll be caught just to see the look on my mother's face.

The spell continues to elude me. The Aster Archives are a dirty, disorganized, and dusty place. My dad's an Angel, but his faith is only a step above perfunctory and he's no historian. I doubt my mother has ever even seen the crypts. Our records have been ill served.

I've found very little on my ancestor, Jonathan Aster, the Angel's post-Apocalyptic scribe. I did find a previous version of his manuscript, Last Stand, *however, its pages were so rotted and its ink so faded, it was impossible to read. Interestingly, his remains are not here in the family crypt. He must have been buried elsewhere.*

*Do not lose hope, Noon. I'm not giving up and you
shouldn't either. I'll find the spell. I promise.*

Peter

I considered Peter's letter. It certainly showed a side of
him I'd never seen before. He'd always been so diligent, so
dutiful. I think the reason we'd never dated was because his
mother hated me so much. The Peter I knew would never
have defied her and I couldn't imagine him breaking into any
house, much less his own.

The second letter was even more unsettling. It was from
Night.

Noon—

*Maize is an amazing place, so full of life. I wish you
could see it. I never thought I would be comfortable with
who I am. I always wanted to be able to blow things up
and blast people on sight. I guess you're the one stuck
with that power now.*

*Seriously, though, I hope you've found at least half
the fulfillment in your new career as I have in mine. Can
you picture me delivering a baby? But I have. Three, in
fact. The one last night was a boy, born too early. He was
jaundiced, anemic, and had a small hole in his heart.
The touch of my hand on his chest healed him.*

*The only dark spot in Maize is worry over an-
other missing Mederi. Our monarch informed us tonight that Peony Copperfield from the Gaia Tribe is now
missing as well. Apparently, Gaia's monarch was expecting her back in Farro last week to consult about a patient but she never showed and no one's been able to find
her.*

*Please be careful, Noon. Who knows where the rogare
demon is hiding . . .*

Night

I slept like the dead that night. I think it was the atomic release of emotions earlier with Ari. Or maybe it was realizing that declaring hadn't changed everything. I still had Ivy and Fitz. We were still eating lunch at Marduk's.

And I still hated having to eat Innkeeper's Pie.

Tuesday dawned brighter and colder, reminding me that, though the Yule greens would be burned this week, winter was far from over. Ivy and I scarfed down stale pastries and coffee laced with sugar and headed to meet Fitz for a crack-of-dawn Sin and Sanction cram. Later, we suffered through Meginnis' meandering morning lecture on esoteric Evil Deed remedies like detinue, replevin, and trover and howled over Fitz's one-man skit about demon conflicts of interest in Council Procedure. I'd avoided looking in Ari's direction throughout the morning's classes, but couldn't help noticing that Fitz's antics made even him laugh. Dorio, never one to condemn a clown, gave Fitz extra class participation points. More than a few students were outraged. Neither Fitz nor Dorio cared. By late afternoon, it was time for Manipulation again.

Unlike A&A, Manipulation was held every day of the week. It was grossly unfair. If the demons didn't kill us, the workload would. As Fitz and Ivy headed home, I tromped up to the fourth floor of Rickard, bracing myself for another brutal round with Rochester.

When I entered the classroom, only Rochester, Ari, and Mercator were there. In contrast to the day before, the environment was almost welcoming. I nodded to Rochester and Mercator and slipped into my seat beside Ari.

"Hey," I said.

"Hey yourself."

It was kind of silly that I hadn't talked to him yet since we'd already shared two classes.

"Fitz will end up as a litigator," Ari said, chuckling. "And Ivy will become a lobbyist and represent the interests of the ferry owners on Satyr Hill."

I scoffed. "How do you know?"

"Just a guess," he said, smiling.

Rochester sat behind his desk, reading. His gaze flicked to us and, for the briefest moment, the edges of my signature shimmered as Rochester probed and prodded. He probably didn't even know I knew what he was doing. But after yesterday's release I couldn't imagine there was much buildup of anything to get me in trouble so I let him. Perverse bastard. I stayed open and easy, continuing the casual banter that Ari had helpfully started when I walked in. We appeared, I hoped, like two students who were no more than friends.

Tosca, Brunus, and Sasha arrived en masse, which blew my somewhat buoyant mood. I shut down immediately to lessen the corrosive effect of their combined signatures. Sasha's signature reminded me of rusted iron, which was interesting. I wondered what others felt when they encountered his magic. To me, it felt like he might once have been a strong magic user, but something had happened to him. Maybe he'd damaged his own magic through misuse or maybe he'd been attacked. Of course it was equally possible he'd been born that way.

In any case, he threw nothing my way, didn't even look at me. Tosca came in like a dust devil, but the edges of his swirling vortex never reached me. Brunus scowled at me and took his seat beside Mercator, who he didn't acknowledge at all.

Rochester carefully marked his place in the book he'd been reading, set it aside, and stood up to greet us. He reminded us that he'd be handing out the last of the clinic assignments and launched into an explanation of the case Tosca and Sasha would handle. It was an Evil Deeds claim. Last month, a Hyrke from Stafford had brought a suit for alienation of affection after his wife had an affair with their neighbor.

"Charles and Clara Verdigris had been married for less than six weeks when Clara took a lover," Rochester said, his tone dryly academic despite the titillating subject. "According to Mr. Verdigris, the couple had barely returned from their honeymoon when he noticed her waning interest in coital relations. Initially, he thought it was just that his young bride needed time to get used to her new living arrangements. But he came home from work early one day and found her in bed with the man who lives two doors down, Owen Amberworth."

Ouch.

I glanced at Sasha and Tosca to see how they were taking the news. Tosca grinned recklessly. Sasha scribbled furiously.

"Charles called Maahes, the demon who had blessed his marriage." Rochester said. "Maahes is a war demon. He isn't quite old enough to have fought in the battle of Armageddon, but almost. You've probably heard of him by his other name—Lord of the Slaughter."

Sasha pinched the bridge of his nose. Tosca paled.

"Despite his moniker," Rochester continued, "he is not known to be violent, *unless* he is called upon to protect the sanctity of the marital bed. Maahes has been known to inflict horrible punishments on those who break their wedding vows, and upon anyone who incites such a breach.

"Charles' love for his new bride trumped his sense of betrayal, however, and he asked Maahes to spare Clara. But he was not so forgiving of her lover. Maahes was more than happy to massacre Amberworth on Charles' behalf, but at the last second, Amberworth called Asmodai to defend him."

Rochester paused, giving everyone a chance to consider the case. "Who is Asmodai?" he asked. "Mr. de Rocca?"

"The Demon of Infidelity?"

"No. Mr. Kaolin?"

"Is he the 'Corruptor'?"

Rochester shook his head, disappointed. "Read and memorize the *Demon Register*," he snapped. "Mr. Carmine?"

I turned to Ari, along with the rest of the class. Ari leaned back in his chair, his long legs sprawled under the desk, his hands folded gently in his lap. He was the picture of unperturbed. *And yet . . .* Under the surface tension of our collective signatures, I felt an energetic hum. A thin cord of magic stretched between Rochester and Ari. Ari had said I was a good receiver, but I could barely sense the cord. It was like a shadow, a mere outline of whatever passed between Rochester and Ari.

"The Demon of Lust," Ari finally said.

Rochester nodded and continued lecturing.

Apparently, Asmodai was as adamant as Maahes that his follower's position was correct. Rochester snatched some papers off of his lectern and started reading.

"From Asmodai's statement," he said. "'Look at Clara. She is the embodiment of robust femininity, ripe and lush. Who wouldn't want to ravish her? To worship her—and *Me*—by engaging in sexual relations with her?'"

Rochester pulled a picture of Clara out of the file and held it up for the class. Clara was indeed ripe and lush.

I pleaded to Luck that my cheeks would stay pale. *Thank the absent lord I would not be assigned a client in this case!* Dealing with a woman like Clara, one who was so overtly sexual, so blithely fertile, would be difficult enough. But it would be doubly difficult to deal with Asmodai, who I suspected was a misogynist. I sighed to myself. These would be the peculiar challenges of being a female Maegester though and the sooner I got used to them the better. Halja's demons (and many of their followers) were randy beasts and it wouldn't serve to get pink cheeks every time there was a case involving bawdy behavior, buxom women, or behaviors that led to breeding and lots of it.

"Thoughts, anyone?" Rochester arched an eyebrow and looked around the room. No one volunteered. I was aware of Maahes' reputation. He was a powerful demon. Asmodai was a demon I wasn't familiar with, but based on his overly confident statement, he would likely be formidable. I didn't want to make yesterday's mistake of underestimating how difficult it would be to subdue quarreling demons.

Rochester paced in front of us.

"Ms. Onyx? You've been quiet today. Think this one can be resolved with sacrifices?"

I shook my head. Gut instinct told me no. Unlike the demons involved in the Lethe case, the demons here were in direct opposition to one another. Maahes was the protector of marriage vows; Asmodai the instigator of extramarital affairs. I thought I might start with thrashing the Hyrkes for being stupid but I could hardly say that.

"The demons would have to be forcefully controlled," I said reluctantly.

Rochester nodded. "Would *you* be able to control the Demon of Lust, Nouiomo?" His intimate tone and use of my birth name implied a deeper meaning. I supposed he was referring to his suspicions about Ari and me.

"I guess we'll find out," I said dryly.

Beside me, Ari cleared his throat and looked down at the desk. If class wasn't such a serious setting, I might have thought he was laughing.

Rochester grunted, but moved on.

"Mr. Kaolin, you'll represent the husband and Mr. de Rocca, the lover. I want a preliminary outline of how you're going to handle the client interview on my desk by tomorrow." Tosca nodded and Sasha scribbled a final note.

"I saved the last assignment for the *Primoris* and *Secundus* positions because these positions will be representing demons directly. There are no Hyrkes in this case. That may be to your benefit, Ms. Onyx," Rochester said sotto voce, "since you will be forced to focus exclusively on the demons' problems. On the other hand, it may be to your detriment, because this case will test every bit of your manipulative ability."

Disgruntled murmurs that Ari and I were representing demons sounded throughout the room, but no one complained outright. I supposed, at this point, those who had already been assigned a case were realizing how hard it would be. No one would have seriously considered trading assignments with us, had that option even been offered.

"Are you familiar with Nergal, Ms. Onyx?" Rochester asked.

I nodded. I was, but not because I had read the *Demon Register.*

"He's the Demon of Pestilence," I said, practically spitting the words out. Nergal was also the Demon of Brushfires, Locusts, and Drought. He was the Patron of Midsummer Death. His favorite dying time—nouiomo, or high noon.

I'd never liked Nergal. He seemed piggish. Why couldn't he leave the dying times to winter? Why did he have to come in and claim the height of a season that was otherwise known for its abundance of life? I erased my sour expression and refocused on Rochester's case explanation.

"Nergal is married. Has anyone read enough of the *Register* to know who to?"

To my surprise, Mercator raised his hand. He hadn't said much during the earlier discussions.

"Lamia," Mercator said quietly. "She's one of the oldest known demons. No one knows when she was born. Rumor has it she crawled out of a well. She herself propagates that myth. A few centuries ago, she circulated a rumor that her parents were Nethuns and Babilu."

"Nethuns?" Brunus interrupted. "The Patron Demon of Wells?"

"The Patron Demon of *Poisoned* Wells," Sasha clarified, looking smug.

"And Babilu?" Brunus asked. "Who's that?"

Rochester leaned on his desk, folded his arms across his chest, and let the discussion take its own course. Mercator took the lead.

"Long before the Apocalypse, there was a Babylon. It didn't look anything like it does today. It was mostly fields, some scattered homesteads, and a fort."

"How do you know?" Brunus asked.

"Because I read more than just what I'm assigned," Mercator said. Brunus rolled his eyes but shut up. Mercator continued.

"Babilu was Babylon's demoness protector. The story Lamia tells is that her mother succumbed to the advances of

Nethuns and, as a result, Babylon's well was poisoned. The price for her indiscretion was a weakened Host and the blood-bath of Armageddon. Lamia says Babilu died on the field beside Lucifer just after she was born."

"But demons are spawned from the ground," Tosca said. "They don't have parents."

"Of course not," Mercator said with exaggerated patience. "Lamia's birth story is a metaphor. Old Babylon was a virgin, spoiled by the ravages of war, her well—or womb—poisoned by invasion."

"Lamia's husband wants a divorce," Rochester said, bringing the discussion back around to the case.

"But demons don't divorce," Tosca said. "They mate for life." He seemed triply put out for having been doubly confused in the span of a single minute.

But I'd heard the same thing about the demons' marital practices. With *regulare* demons, it was always about the rules. A promise is a promise. There was no reneging. Unless both parties wanted out . . .

"Does Lamia want a divorce?" I asked.

"No," said Rochester. He stared grimly at me. "She was livid with Nergal for contacting the Council for representation. We had to send an upper year out to calm her down just so the matter could be assigned. But these types of cases are what you'll be expected to handle in the field, so if you can't do it . . ."

Rochester let his words hang, leaving his sentence unfinished. But I knew. If I couldn't control my client, I wouldn't pass Manipulation, and if I didn't pass Manipulation, I'd end up like those poor missing Mederies. The monstrously powerful, enormously old, and rarely seen demons who sat on the Demon Council wouldn't think twice about executing a young, ineffective Maegester for *everyone's* sake. The future of Halja depended on having Maegesters who could keep the peace. And if I couldn't, I would be considered just as rogue as the *rogare* demons.

"We can handle it," Ari said. I wasn't as sure but I wisely kept my mouth shut.

"Good," Rochester said crisply. "You'll represent Lamia and Ms. Onyx will represent Nergal."

Rochester walked back to his lectern and addressed his final comments to the entire class.

"Mr. Kaolin was correct. There is no divorce available for demons unless both sides unequivocally agree. There may be a separation, and that separation may be prolonged, but it cannot be permanent. And, as always, for all of these matters, there can be no lasting ill will or animosity between demons once your representation ends."

No lasting ill will between two creatures with vengeful natures and nothing but a mile of bad blood between them? As Darius Dorio would say: *Sunt facta verbis difficiliora. Easier said than done.*

Chapter 13

❧

They say Wednesday's child is full of woe. No kidding.
Wednesday was my third day of Manipulation. Ari
had warned me that, every Wednesday, Rochester took the
first year MIT's down to the basement in Rickard for magic
practice. To say I had conflicted emotions regarding these
practice sessions was as much of an understatement as saying
the Apocalypse had changed things. I still wanted no part of
my waning magic, but I knew it was probably best if I started
learning how to use it. So this morning, with equal parts
dread, anticipation, and curiosity, I found myself clamoring
down a narrow, rickety, metal staircase that felt like it was
going to come loose from its mountings at any minute.

The stairs were only wide enough for one person. Rochester took the lead, followed by us in the order of our class
rankings, which meant Ari was in front of me and Mercator
was behind me. I was thankful not to have to descend the
wobbly stairs with either Brunus, Sasha, or Tosca at my back
but it was the last break I'd get that morning.

When we reached the bottom we clustered around Roch-

ester, who was the only one with a light. He'd lit a fireball so
we could see in this Luck forsaken hellhole of a place. The
air felt cold, damp, and expectant, like a winter cloud teetering on the razor's edge between rain and snow. Even though
we were in a basement, there was nothing moldy or musty
feeling about this place. Stepping onto the floor had given me
a bracing jolt. Maybe it was hitting solid stone after descend-
ing what had seemed like an endless number of unsure steps;
maybe it was an echo of old magic finally finding a live (albeit unwilling) receiver in me.

I rubbed my arms for warmth and wondered why Ari
had told me to leave my cloak behind. We continued following Rochester as he made his way deeper into the basement.
The corridor turned and twisted so many times I couldn't
help thinking of it as an underground version of the Rabbit
Warren.

Finally, Rochester led us into what felt like a large room.
Sound reverberation lessened and echoes increased and the
edges of his circle of light no longer reflected off of walls.

Suddenly I felt his signature heat up, and then—*whoosh*—
fire raced through the room. But it landed in the most contained and controlled place I could have imagined: wall
torches.

We were in an area that was roughly two hundred feet
square and at least twenty feet high. On the far wall were
chains, enough for at least a half-dozen prisoners. On the
wall closest to us were weapons: swords, knives, daggers,
maces, pickaxes, and hammers. It looked like an old dungeon but I couldn't—or didn't want to—imagine why St.
Lucifer's Law School would have a dungeon in the basement
of its administrative building.

As ominous as the room was though, I had to admit it was
the perfect place to practice waning magic. No fire would
burn uncontrollably for long down here. And no Hyrke would
accidentally walk in on a training session and get himself
killed.

Whether I was equally at risk for accidentally getting myself killed was a question I didn't dare dwell on.

"A brief review," Rochester said, clearing his throat, "for those who added this class late."

The groans I would have expected from Sasha or Brunus upstairs were conspicuously absent. Instead, they stood tensely, expectantly. I felt the uptick in everyone's signature, like a cat's ears twitching at the first sound of movement. My body and magic followed the others' lead.

"A Mederi's oath is 'First do no harm.' With Maegesters, it's the opposite. You must learn how to harm a demon if you're going to be able to control them. *Rogare* demons, and even some *regulare* demons, will never respect you, listen to you, or be controlled by you, if you can't harm them.

"The type of cases you will be assigned when you graduate—*ahem*, if you graduate," Rochester looked straight at me, "will depend on many things. Among them are how strong your magic is, how well you can manipulate it, how well you can use it to control demons, and how strong the demons are that you can control."

Okay . . . all that seemed pretty straightforward, except for the part that I didn't want to do any of it.

"Ms. Onyx," Rochester called. I snapped to attention.

"What is one of the easiest ways to control something?"

"Overpower it," I said without hesitation. Every kid knew that one. Might makes right and all that. I didn't believe it, but it was the answer Rochester was looking for.

"And how exactly do you overpower a demon?"

I had no idea. Wasn't this class supposed to teach me that?

"Use a weapon?" I said, taking inspiration from the completely unsubtle array of weapons on the wall closest to us.

"And which weapon would you choose?" Rochester motioned to the wall behind him.

Beside me, Ari stiffened. Was the question a trap? I considered the weapons on the wall carefully.

I'd never studied Apocalypse-era weapons before. I had no idea what sort of damage they could do, how to wield them, or which one I would choose if I were to go up against a demon. In fact, as bad as I was at controlling it, there was only one thing I'd use.

"My magic," I said.

Rochester's mouth quirked. "Perhaps . . . Mr. Olivine, choose your weapon and take the south position."

I felt Brunus' signature swell. He turned to me and smiled. It was the most chilling smile I'd ever seen. Suddenly I knew he'd pay me back for the bloody nose—and more.

"A reminder to the rest of the class . . ." This time Rochester looked directly at Ari, "No interference during a sparring match."

Brunus selected something that looked like a cross between a hammer and a pick. Rochester called it a nadziak. When Brunus pulled it off the wall, Ari's signature ticked up a notch. Why was Rochester having us pick out actual weapons if our magic was the best weapon we had? How would using real weapons help us to learn how to control our magic? But class wasn't optional. I couldn't just sit out or pass.

Again I studied the weapons debating which to choose.

"Go for the bullwhip and for Luck's sake, Noon," Ari said, "don't let him get near you."

"Mr. Carmine," Rochester's voice boomed in the cavernous space. "There will be no more warnings. Any further tips for Ms. Onyx and you will be asked to wait outside."

Ari didn't even acknowledge Rochester. He squeezed my arm as I walked past, his face tight, his body tense. I pulled the bullwhip off the wall (thank Luck I knew what it looked like . . . if Ari had suggested I choose the nadziak before I'd heard Rochester call it that, I would have had no idea what he was talking about). I placed the handle in my right hand and turned toward Rochester.

"Begin," he said.

Wha—? Really? I looked down at the bullwhip in my hand and almost laughed. I couldn't even *imagine* using this thing. But when I looked up and saw Brunus' face, I knew he suffered from no such qualms. A second later his magic hit me. A blast that seemed hard enough to string my teeth and tie them around my neck. It knocked me off of my feet and onto the floor. I shook my head and felt my jaw to make sure it was still attached. Toward my left, someone laughed. Sasha

probably, but my ears seemed clogged so I couldn't be sure.
I raised my torso and leaned on my elbows, looking for
Brunus. His blast had blurred my eyesight as well.

I felt Brunus' next blast before it hit me. I realized he
was shaping his magic like the weapon he'd chosen. His last
blast must have hit me with the hammer end. This time, his
nadziak-shaped magic came slashing through the air toward me pick end first. The impact would have been scarily
effective—if my magic wasn't naturally stronger than his.
Instinctively, I threw up a shield. It kept his magic from
reaching me, but not him. He towered over me, the real nadziak raised in one hand. I scurried back across the floor like
a crab beetle. I would have thought it belittling but for the fact
that I was starting to think Rochester really would just let this
play out. And one look at Brunus told me he really wanted to
use that nadziak on me. Suddenly, a sliver of bright shiny fear
pierced through me. Until now, I'd been thinking of this practice session as I'd had all my other classes. But it couldn't be
more different. I realized then that Maegesters-in-Training
had likely died in this room. Maybe many of them.

If I couldn't prove I could hold my own against Brunus,
who had less waning magic than me, then how would I fare
against a demon?

I blasted Brunus with a magic jolt that was about as
shaped as a mushy ball of pie dough. He crashed to the floor,
hitting his head and losing his hold on the nadziak. It clattered to the ground a few feet away from where he fell. I had
to resist the urge to run over to him. I truly despised him, but
I hadn't wanted to hurt him. I'd just wanted to stop him from
hurting me. He picked himself up off the floor and stood up.
His badly cropped, matte brown hair stood on end. He
rubbed the back of his head and when he removed his hand,
it was covered in blood.

This was way worse than the bloody nose. *Way worse.*
Because everyone in the room had sensed how little effort it
had taken me to press Brunus back. It was only my lack of
desire to harm him that saved him from me. It dawned on me

that, if I wished it, Rochester might also let this sparring match play out the other way.

It was dawning on Brunus too. He realized that he might be in real danger from me, and he *hated* it—hated *me*—hated my very existence. He walked over to the nadziak and picked it up. He was going to charge. I saw it in his eyes.

"Stop!" Rochester bellowed. Brunus lowered his weapon. He looked neither defeated nor relieved. Instead, he looked *expectant*, as he had when he'd first entered the room. He glared malevolently at me and swung the nadziak around in an arc. He brought the hammer end down in the bloody palm of his other fist and then pointed it straight at me and grinned. He knew Rochester's teaching methods. He must know what was coming next. That sliver of bright shiny fear inside me multiplied. My limbs felt cold and my fingers stiff.

"Ms. Onyx, you said you would control demons by overpowering them and that your weapon of choice was your magic, yes?"

I nodded warily.

"You certainly overpowered Mr. Olivine, didn't you?"

This time Brunus didn't grin. His look of hatred nearly gnawed a hole through my stomach. If I didn't know any better, I would have said Rochester was provoking Brunus. But why? Why torture us? Why have us even spar in the first place? We all knew how this fight would end if it continued.

But it soon became clear that I had no idea how it would end.

"Most demons you encounter in the field cannot be overpowered. The strength of their magic will either be greater than yours or, if you throw a large uncontrolled blast at them, they will simply absorb it and add it to their own."

Curiosity won out over the wisdom of silence. "So how do you control them?"

"By throwing something that's controlled. Something that is shaped like a weapon. Something that is shaped like the weapon that is most likely to hurt them."

It sounded repulsive to me. I had to remind myself he was

talking about controlling demons who had broken laws and hurt others. Demons like the ones who were attacking and abducting Mederies. What if Night were the one being attacked? Wouldn't I want to know how to defend him?

"I've taught this course for many, many years," Rochester said. "I've found the most effective way for students to learn how to shape their magic like weapons . . . is to have them fight with actual weapons. So for this round, magic use is not permitted.

"Begin."

Brunus wasted no time advancing on me. A part of my brain couldn't believe this was happening. We lived in a civilized society. How could a classmate be advancing on me with a pickax? Would my professor really allow him to use it? But a quick glance around the room told me all I needed to know: Halja was only civilized because its peacekeepers were not.

Brunus was halfway to me by the time I decided to use the bullwhip. Ari had said I shouldn't let Brunus get near me. Rochester had said I couldn't use my magic.

I snapped the bullwhip. But there was no snap. It uncoiled in a lazy, limp extension and then fell to the floor again. Brunus was taking his time. The metal tipped point of the nadziak gleamed in the torchlight.

I snapped the bullwhip again. This time, at least, there was a snap. The sound was about as threatening as the snap of a clean sheet being readied for the laundry line.

I wielded it with more force, trying to learn the feel of its length and recoil. Each time, my efforts to convincingly and threateningly use the bullwhip were as ineffective as the last. My right arm ached and I hadn't even managed to hit Brunus yet. His laugh echoed off the stone walls and made it sound as if there were an army of Brunuses advancing on me.

And then he was in front of me. His mud-colored eyes met mine and I knew he wanted to kill me. For what? Just because I was stronger than him? Rochester had made it clear during this round that I was weaker too. Couldn't we just call it a draw and go have a beer?

Brunus smashed the hammer end of the nadziak into my nose.

The entire room seemed to light up and my face felt instantly hot. I fell backward and looked up at Brunus with blood dripping down my face. My eyes watered from pain but I refused to give Brunus the satisfaction of seeing me whimper. I also refused to crawl backward.

Pride or suicide?

Brunus brought the nadziak down toward me slowly. I didn't want a repeat of the nose smashing so I jumped to my feet, landing an arm's length away from him. He lunged and raked the pick part of the nadziak across my torso, shredding the front of my sweater and tunic and nicking the right side of my chest. Bright red blood bloomed on my now exposed white cotton camisole like some obscene red flower pin.

My signature expanded. I couldn't help it. Rochester called my name as a warning reminder. I wasn't sure if I'd be able to hold back . . . Magical control—as we all knew—was not a strength of mine.

"Get away, Brunus," I said.

"Or what? You're going to make me? With what? Your magic? You may be strong, but you don't know how to throw anything that works." Spittle was flying from his lips as he said it and a blackness far more poisonous than mold was growing in his rotten stink patch of a signature. He slashed the left strap of my camisole with the point of his pickax and squinted at my bared demon mark.

"Disgusting." He spit the word out like it was venom he'd just sucked from a cut.

I looked down at my ruined clothes. What did he want from me?

"I don't like it either!" I shouted, finally losing it. "I *hate* this mark, I *hate* this class, and I hate . . ." Luckily, I stopped myself before I said anything truly unretractable.

"Then this will be a relief," Brunus said.

He stepped forward and swung the nadziak in an arc behind him. Out of the corner of my eye I saw Ari push his way toward me and Mercator hold him back. Ari's signature expanded as Serafina's had the moment before she attacked Ivy. I knew Ari was going to throw something deadly at Brunus despite Rochester's warning. I didn't want him fighting my battles for me. I hated using my magic, but I wasn't about to let Ari break the rules for me when I could do it for myself.

I threw a blast at Brunus hoping to knock him off his feet as I had earlier, but whether it was nerves or just inconsistency, the blast missed Brunus and exploded at the far end of the room in a shower of sparks. Brunus looked incredulously at me. He glanced at Rochester, who was looking at me with narrowed eyes.

The nadziak swung toward me. This time, I *blasted* the damned thing, hoping I'd used enough power to completely obliterate it. But no fireball appeared, not even a spark. Instead, the blast knocked the nadziak out of Brunus' hands and sent it flipping, end over end, toward the rest of my classmates. They ducked and the nadziak clattered to the floor behind them.

Rochester did not look pleased. *Would he really have let Brunus kill me?*

"Enough," Rochester said to Brunus, waving a flat palm through the air. He turned to me, scrutinizing me for a few seconds before speaking.

"You hate waning magic, Ms. Onyx, and *that* is the reason you have trouble manipulating it."

My nose ran and I swiped at it with my hand. Bright red gobs of blood dripped off my knuckles.

"What I hate," I said advancing on Rochester, "is blood on my hands." Without thinking, I flicked my fingers toward him. Drops of my blood splattered on his face and clothes.

For the first time, I felt Rochester's signature heat in anger. I was afraid if I stayed, he would crawl inside me and just keep expanding, until I was nothing more than a quivering mound of red jelly on the stone-cold floor of this hideous place. So I walked out without being dismissed.

At least I didn't run.

Ari found me later in the bathroom at Megiddo cleaning my face.

"Do you want me to take you to Bryony?"

"No," I said, not even meeting his eyes in the mirror. A Mederi was the last thing I wanted to see.

Chapter 14

ৼ

I woke up Thursday with mixed emotions. For twenty-one years I had dreaded this day. Every year, I'd marked Bryde's Day's passing with as much interest as my own birthday, though neither had been much celebrated in our house. My declaration last week meant I would survive the day, but it couldn't erase a lifetime of unpleasant memories. Bryde's Day celebrated young women, small animals, and children. In other words, life and those who make it. Bryde was the patron of weddings, of course, but she was also the patron of any fertility union and was generally associated with all things regenerative and abundant. She was the ploughed ground pregnant with seed, she was the swelling bud ready to burst, and she was the first flow of milk, from ewe to lamb, from cow to calf, from mother to child. She breathed life into the dead mouth of winter and resurrected it.

It was said Bryde had been wet nurse to Lucifer himself. That she had suckled him as an infant, cured his fevers, and tended his scrapes and sores. It was said she tended him even now, wherever he was, willing him to heal and return.

Bryde had been Halja's most powerful Mederi. So Bryde's Day was, obviously, a major holiday.

Classes had been cancelled today and we were on a modified schedule. This morning was our first midterm, Sin and Sanction. Later today, there would be a big festival at Lekai and then tonight, all students would have their first client interviews. Even the Hyrke A&A students would be meeting at various places around campus to discuss cases and strategies and lay the initial groundwork for hopeful settlements. None of it would be easy. Nothing at St. Lucifer's ever was.

Ivy, Fitz, and I had stayed up as late as we dared, comparing outlines, drafting practice answers, and drilling each other on the difference between *actus reus* and *mens rea*, causation and complicity, mayhem and malfeasance. We memorized all the Latin names for Halja's numerous sins as well as the demons who protected their practice. Fitz and Ivy were thrilled to have my Manipulation books to supplement our Sin and Sanction materials, but I was afraid we might have overstudied that. It was unlikely the midterm fact pattern would have Host or demon deviants.

We entered Copeland's class bleary-eyed and anxious, strung up on too much coffee and not enough sleep. My eyes had deep, dark circles under them and I carried a pack of tissues for my still swollen nose. The three of us took our seats near the middle of the classroom, about halfway up the rise. On the way, I passed Ari, who looked irritatingly calm and well rested.

"Good luck," he said, giving me an encouraging smile. Thick dark waves of his hair fell to the collar of his shirt, which was a bright white buttoned affair, open at his throat.

"Luck be with you too," I mumbled, rushing past him. He was too distracting.

The exam was a toilsome, laborious, perspiration-inducing mess. Three hours of reading fact patterns, code sections, outlining, drafting, and sweating. I broke five pencils, chewed off three fingernails, and wrote enough to fill two and a half sheaves of paper. Afterward, fellow students' reactions varied. Some wanted to debrief endlessly by discussing and comparing answers. Some didn't want to talk about the exam at all. A few were clearly relieved, while others cried.

I chatted briefly with Ivy and Fitz, as we dumped books into our lockers and grabbed our cloaks. Fitz was in hand-wringing mode. He nearly freaked when I told him how many sheaves I'd gone through.

"I have large handwriting," I tried to assure him. Fitz looked strained. His face was red and his coppery hair was standing up in places where he'd obviously been pulling at it.

"It's time to celebrate," Ivy said, putting her arm through Fitz's. "I'm sure you passed. And now it's over. Let's head over to Lekai for the festival. Lunch won't cost anything but the calories. It's Bryde's Day so everything will be loaded with cheese or smothered in cream sauce." Ivy smacked her lips in mock anticipation, looking increasingly vexed at my lack of enthusiasm. "Vanilla ice cream with *real* butter-scotch? Come on!"

"No thanks," I said, slamming my locker door. I jumped when I saw Ari leaning against the lockers behind it. I'd been so focused on shutting him out for the exam I didn't feel him sneaking up on me. I noticed his signature was on stealth mode. He'd ratcheted down to low hum. I glared at him.

"How'd you do on the test?" he said.

"Fine."

He raised an eyebrow. "You two?" he said to Ivy and Fitz. Ivy gave him the so-so sign, which was Ivy's way of being modest. I was sure she'd end up in the top 10 percent of our class. Fitz, on the other hand, grimaced. Ari laughed.

"It can't have been that bad," Ari said to him. "Besides, they usually fail no more than three students per section."

The red in Fitz's face disappeared, replaced with a deathly white pallor. His skin shined with sweat. The effect was awful. For a moment, I thought Fitz would be sick. But then Ivy propelled him toward the door.

"We'll save you a seat if you change your mind," she called over her shoulder. The hall door swung shut behind them. A few other students milled about.

"You're not going over to Lekai?" Ari asked.

I shrugged on my cloak.

"I don't celebrate Bryde's Day," I said.

"Why not?" Ari looked genuinely puzzled.

What could I say? That I hated corn dolls? I didn't. I just hated the fact that I couldn't hold one. What's more, I dreaded the thought of being asked to burn Yule greens in front of an audience. It was something I'd never even done in the privacy of my own home.

"Because I don't like setting things on fire."

"It's much easier to control your magic if you're not sparring with someone who's trying to hurt you. And I'll be there. I won't let your magic burn anything it's not supposed to."

"Ari, I don't want to burn the Yule greens, or anything else."

He leaned in toward me so that his face was only inches from mine. His closeness in such a public space, when we weren't supposed to be seen together, made me nervous.

"Have you ever seen a Bryde's Day ceremony, Noon?" His voice was quiet, almost tender. I stubbornly refused to answer.

"Burning the Yule greens isn't meant to be destructive," Ari said, his words making it clear he understood me all too well. "It's meant to represent the flame of life. When the Yule greens are burned on Bryde's Day it symbolizes the destruction of winter. But by destroying winter, we destroy death. Sometimes destructive powers give rise to new life. Just look at Nergal's forest fires."

I frowned, not following.

"The burnoff created by a forest fire allows new growth afterward that wouldn't have been possible before. The fire burns away old brush and other dead matter, preparing the ground for new life." Ari reached out and clasped my shoulders, gently shaking them to emphasize his words. "Come celebrate Bryde's Day with me. Come feel what it's like to burn something so that it can be reborn."

We hadn't embraced since I'd let him touch my demon mark in the alley on Monday. That had been four days ago. I was ready to agree to almost anything he said. But Rochester's warning about not collaborating with Ari outside of class and the fact that I was already on shaky ground with Rochester firmed my resolve.

"Speaking of Nergal," I said, stepping back. "I'm going home to prepare for our meeting tonight. You said it yourself, I'm behind. I need the time to catch up."

I ignored Ari's disappointed look and broke free of his hold. I could feel him staring at my back. His signature flickered, some flare-up of emotion that was too fast to define. Then I was around the corner and racing to Megiddo, half-afraid I might change my mind and decide to voluntarily burn something (or involuntarily burn someone) in front of all of St. Luck's and the Joshua School too.

The rest of the afternoon passed quickly. I was determined to be as prepared as possible for my first interview with Nergal. I pushed away all thoughts of Yule greens, corn dolls, and dairy products. Instead, I reread the section of the *Demon Register* devoted to Nergal and Lamia, I studied chapters thirteen through fifteen of Dymas Painbourne's *Demons, Deities, and Devotional Practices*, and I reviewed the *Barrister's Guide to Separation Agreements*. I dug out my Manipulation books and read all of Seknecus' margin notes on first encounters, meeting protocol, and establishing the upper hand with recalcitrant clients.

Almost as an afterthought, I decided to test my magic control. I wadded up a piece of paper and placed it on the linoleum floor. I sent a whiplike surge of magic in its direction and it instantly went up in flames. Unfortunately so did everything in my trash can, which was over a foot away. My hands shook as I leeched oxygen from around the fires. They hissed and went out, leaving black ashes and the burning smell of shame. I grabbed my cloak and a notebook and headed for the door, my thoughts as dark as the ashes in the can.

Outside of Megiddo the sun set in chalky reds and yellows, glazed with streaks of white from low lying clouds. The night was cool, but not cold. My hood hung down my back along with my hair, which I'd left loose and long. I'd traded my usual high-necked sweater and canvas trousers for a heavy black sheath dress. I belted it with a waistband of thick black leather and paired it with black leggings and boots. The dress had a raccoon fur collar that completely covered my demon mark. The demons would know I had waning magic, and everyone else did now too, but it was hard to break a lifetime habit of covering it up.

Around me, the cement paths were full of students walking back from Lekai. Nearly to a person, they carried small lit candles. I gritted my teeth. Would this day ever end? Most years I holed up inside to avoid spectacles such as this. Everyone smiled and laughed, some couples even embraced. I stood there in the dark with my dark clothes and dark mood, solitary and unlit, wondering why I felt left out when all I'd wanted was to be left alone.

I was on the verge of scowling when I felt Ari's signature touch the edges of mine and slowly melt into it, the way the sun melted into the horizon at dusk. He was the only one who could soften my edges like that. He rounded a corner and stood before me. I swallowed. He seriously tested my resolve to stay away from him.

His crisp white shirt, still open at the collar, was now smudged with black soot. In the semi-dark of sunset and the glow of passing candles, Ari's skin looked golden. His eyes shone like black glass, reflecting the myriad flames around him. He stared at me solemnly, his face a mixture of desire and determination. A single candle burned bright in his hand. He held it out to me.

"I saved one for you," he said.

I shook my head. "No, thanks."

"You can't know this," he said, "since you've never celebrated Bryde's Day, but the custom is that you find someone you . . . care about, and you give them a lit candle."

"Why?"

"It's a gift," he said.

"You're giving *me* the gift of fire?"

"No, I'm giving you the gift of life. That's what it means today."

Oh.

I reached for the tiny flame, speechless. My hand grazed Ari's just as he stepped forward to embrace me. I clasped my hand around his as he pulled me close, cradling my head with his other hand. He tipped me back, touching his lips to mine. You would have thought four days was forty years from the urgency I felt in him. But he kept his kiss light, his lips barely skimming mine. He held me for a moment, his eyes locked to mine, and, for once, I felt absolutely calm in his presence. I laid my head on his shoulder and stared into the flame.

"Thank you," I said.

We would be meeting with our clients separately first, in the old abandoned classrooms on the fourth floor of Rickard Building. It was a place the demons would be comfortable in and it was less risky for the Hyrkes if we confined our interview to places they were less likely to be. The other MIT's, who had Hyrke clients, were meeting elsewhere on campus. After the introductions and initial assessment, Ari and I were to take our clients to the Manipulation classroom where we would make our first settlement attempt. Both Ari and I thought it prudent to go up to the fourth floor alone, although Ari seemed far less concerned about what Rochester might think than the clients.

The lift ride up was slow, creepy, and quiet. The operator seemed nervous. *Had Nergal and Lamia taken the lift to the fourth floor?* It would be unusual since demons had the ability to shift into forms of things that traveled far faster than those of us with only two feet.

When I stepped out on the fourth floor, the experience was anticlimactic. I knew walls and physical barriers interfered with my ability to perceive signatures, but somehow I'd thought that I'd be able to feel them immediately. Instead, all I saw were two lit rooms farther down the hall. Ari had told me Lamia would be on the left. So that meant Nergal was waiting for me in the room on the right. I squared my shoulders and walked in.

Two people stood to greet me. The first was a robust-looking young man dressed somewhat similarly to me in a black suit with a white shirt. His shirt was fully buttoned but had soot marks like the ones I'd seen on Ari earlier. The second was a large, almost beefy man, somewhere in his midforties with sunburned skin and blond hair that was so long, thick, and curly, his hair reminded me of petals on a giant yellow chrysanthemum. Their signatures hit me at once, the young man's black and dense as coal, sure fuel for any fire he chose to use it for, and the older man's the equivalent of a radiation blast from a solar explosion. I knew, both from my reading, and from my first day of Manipulation class, that touching signatures was kind of like shaking hands. They were introducing themselves to me. And I thought the old man, who must be Nergal, was also testing me, similar to the way someone squeezes your hand too hard to see if you flinch.

I didn't.

I carefully avoided directing any magic toward Nergal and concentrated on the younger man, obviously the upper level Maegester-in-Training who'd been sent to make the formal introductions. I pushed a thick flat slab of magic at him, which he was unable to disperse. We tussled for a moment, my magic seeking to smother his. His magic flared, first red, then blue, as he turned up the heat in an attempt to throw me off. My magic shimmied and swayed with the effort of trying to extinguish his. When it became clear neither of us would win, he backed off.

"I'm Clarence Diamond," he said, clearly annoyed with my bungled efforts to "shake hands" gracefully.

Clarence turned his magic off as easily as turning a knob on the stove. My cessation wasn't quite as adroit. I realized I didn't know how to retract magic. After an agonizingly slow few seconds, I managed to disperse what I'd thrown without setting anything on fire. To my chagrin, it burst in the air like a bubble full of firecrackers. Nergal appeared appallingly delighted.

Clarence's expression soured. "Nergal," he said in a dry

voice, "this is Nouiomo Onyx of Etincelle, first year Maegester-in-Training here at St. Lucifer's Law School, daughter of Karanos Onyx, executive of the Demon Council, and daughter of Aurelia Onyx nee Ferrum of the Hawthorn Tribe. She is sister to Nocturo Onyx, a Mederi who goes by the name of Nightshade."

Nergal raised an eyebrow at this last sentence and then Clarence turned to me.

"Nouiomo, this is Nergal, Prince of Drought and Patron of Midsummer Death." He gave Nergal a short bow and whispered in my ear on his way out.

"Fare well, Noon." I couldn't tell if he was wishing me luck or saying good-bye.

I turned to Nergal, whose signature was still blisteringly hot. I was in danger of being melted on the spot but I didn't dare try to tussle with Nergal the way I had with Clarence. I raised my hand, gesturing like I was shielding myself from the noon-day sun.

"Do you mind?" I said.

Nergal cut the heat in half as his gaze swept over me. His eyes were a light grayish blue, the color startlingly vivid against his sun-darkened skin. His gaze lingered longer than it needed to on my hips, lips, and breasts. He chuckled, the sound raspy and rough.

"A Host female with waning magic, how delightful," he said. "They didn't tell me."

"Why should they?" I said, masking my annoyance. "There'll be no difference in the representation I give you."

"Hmm . . . we'll see," he said. His throat sounded dry, like he hadn't had a drink in days. He walked around me, looking me up and down. He was so close I could feel his breath. It felt like a dry summer wind, the kind that blows and brings no relief. I stood still, hiding my offense and irritation. He stopped behind me and I fought the urge to turn around. It would be a sign of weakness. Keeping my back to him showed I wasn't afraid.

But it was a lie.

Sweat began to pool in my armpits and I wondered if he

could smell my fear. His breath, hot on my neck, itched like an insect bite. I don't know if it was my subconscious or his magic, but I suddenly heard a great swarm of bugs behind me. *Locusts,* I thought. *No.* My skin prickled as a thin film of sweat broke out over my entire body. *Yellow jackets.* I bit my lip to stop from screaming and reached out to steady myself. But we were standing in the middle of the room so there was nothing to hold on to.

"Nouiomo," Nergal said harshly, gutturally, putting his hands on my shoulders to stop me from falling forward. I steadied myself and tried to shake free of Nergal's unwanted embrace. His touch felt like fire ants crawling over my skin.

"You're shaking," he said, his voice crackling in my ear.

"Enough," I said, humiliated that my voice shook too.

"You can't just say enough, you have to show me enough. Didn't your parents ever warn you about demons?"

My cheeks flushed. They hadn't. But I knew what he was referring to. The demons' reputation in the pre-Apocalyptic world had been well deserved. They were lustful creatures with base natures and poor control over their sexual appetites.

"You excite me, Nouiomo," Nergal said, turning me around. He disgusted me. I shook off his hold and stepped back. "Just look at you," he said. "Your hair is like the cool dark waters of a mountain spring at midnight, your skin as white as the milky sap of a dandelion, and your lips . . . ah, your lips are as red and full and quivering as a beating heart. With your lack of experience and control, you are virgin material, ready to be taken, as ripe and luscious as any demon might want—if you weren't already marked by another."

A small fissure of alarm shot up my spine, this one having nothing to do with my fear of plague or pestilence.

If he could sense Ari's mark on my heart, could anyone with waning magic? Rochester? Seknecus? Or were demons the only ones who could sense a signare?

"Interesting that you do not deny it," Nergal said. "He must share your feelings. Ah, to be young and in love again."

"No one's in love," I said, with far more conviction than I felt.

"I was once in love," Nergal said, finally backing off. His voice was clearer and his stance less threatening. It felt like we'd crossed some sort of threshold. The introduction was over, I thought. The interview was starting.

"How did you meet?" I asked. There was no doubt about who I was referring to. Demons mate for life, as Ari had pointed out.

"Centuries ago, when New Babylon was smaller, I was setting fire to the eastern fields one summer. The grasslands were withered and the wheat fields were ripe and ready for burning. As wildfire, I tore up and down the hillsides, destroying crops and fallow fields alike. In time, I came to a spot that would not burn. Enraged, I took human form."

Nergal sat down, choosing a large wooden chair with armrests and a worn cushion. He motioned for me to sit opposite him. I did, somewhat uncomfortably, since the only other choices were bare benches and stools.

"The heat was immeasurable," he continued, "and the smoke disorienting, but it was my doing and I was proud. I must have walked for miles, determined to find the obstinate spot of land that had refused my touch. Finally, hours after sunset, I came upon a well. A young woman was drawing water from it. She was the most beautiful thing I had ever seen. Her hair was like black rainwater and her skin like liquid pearls.

"Not unlike you, Nouiomo," Nergal murmured, sounding like wind on a wheat field. I motioned impatiently for him to get on with it. I figured if my client were going to strike me with wildfire he would have done so by now.

"Her breasts and hips were wonderfully round and full and her skin was cool to the touch—and moist, like dew in the morning. Imagine. I'd never felt anything like it in my life. I began to imagine what it would be like to lie with her. How I might place my parched and peeling self inside certain places of hers. What blessed relief she would be to my burning need, my never ending thirst."

I wanted to roll my eyes but didn't dare.

"I imagined how wet, how lush, how succulent she would be. She was so full of blood, so engorged, so *swollen*.

"We married and built a house right there at the well. At the time, it was a beautiful place, endless fields and fruit trees. I never lost my urge to burn it all down but the spot was impervious to my touch. But she wasn't. She loved me, did my Lamia. But, with time, whatever she gorged on to make her so sweet turned on her and poisoned her. And the land around her well died. The trees grew old and twisted. The house fell into disrepair. We stopped spending time there, preferring to spend more and more time in our true forms— me as midsummer heat, crackling, dusty, and stiflingly hot, and she as the cold hours after midnight, damp, dank, and dark.

"Nouiomo," Nergal said, putting a hand on my knee. This time it only felt like a rock warmed in the sun. "I can't bear to be connected to her anymore. I want us to be put asunder."

"You know you can't have a divorce, Nergal, absent her consent," I said. "It's against demon law."

"Demon law?" Nergal practically spat out the words. "What is the law with no sovereign to enforce it? Lucifer is too weak to return, so demon law is enforced by Maegesters, descendants of his old warlords ruling as regents who still believe in the application of thousand-year-old precedents. Do you really believe in the anachronistic rules you are asked to enforce?"

"Promises are timeless."

Nergal scoffed at me.

"Only the young can make such a statement and believe it. Lamia changed and that change was a brutal betrayal. All that she was is gone now, replaced by a vile creature I don't know. I miss her, my old Lamia, even still. And I would have her back if what happened to her was reversible. But instead I am filled with rage at the thing she has become. I hate the thing in the next room for stealing my young bride away. Lamia no longer loves me, nor I her. She is as old and twisted as the trees around our well. I should have burned them,

Nouiomo, even when they were young and green. I should have found a way."

Pain, bitterness, and loss enveloped him the way heat hovered over the ground after a burning. I stood at the edge, as a survivor might stand at the edge of a field after a battle, surveying the broken, the burned, and the bloody. The end is always easy to spot. The wreckage and desolation of a thing torn apart is unmistakable. What is more difficult to determine is the cause. Why had Nergal stopped loving Lamia? Why had my father stopped loving my mother? If life and youth were not immune to the corrosive effects of time, why should love be any different?

Nergal had painted a story that vividly portrayed him as the victim. But I rather thought it might be the other way around. Our interview had been conducted without the use of magic, neither with me trying to control him, nor him trying to enchant me. But that didn't mean that manipulation hadn't been attempted. Good old-fashioned emotional manipulation was still practiced by every resident in Halja. I had a hunch that Nergal's loss of love was caused by something extraordinarily common—Lamia had aged and Nergal's attraction to her had dried up along with her youth and vitality.

When Nergal and I entered the Manipulation classroom to meet with Lamia and try our first settlement attempt, Ari rose to greet us, covering the distance in a few long strides. In my mind, I'd always compared Ari to the sun, but as he stood facing Nergal, I realized it wasn't the sun so much as *sunlight* that he reminded me of. The two squared off and something passed between them. A flash of recognition, I thought.

Nergal narrowed his eyes at Ari and glanced at me, frowning. Ari ignored him and took my arm, turning me away from Nergal and toward a hunched creature who was sitting in the corner. Ari's touch instantly heated me, shielding me against the cold I felt radiating from Lamia. Her signature was the worst I'd ever felt. It wasn't full of malevolence. It was full of madness.

Evil, gray, cold unhappiness wafted around her like disease on still air. She felt like black ice, frozen in odd patches, a danger unseen until it was too late. Physically, she was pitiable. The hair that Nergal had compared to black rainwater now lay flat and lackluster down her back. Bare patches of scalp peeked through thin spots on a head now covered with warts and lumps. Her skin, which had once reminded Nergal of liquid pearls, now looked like the outside of an oyster shell, wrinkled and calloused with a sick bluish gray undertone.

"Lamia," Ari said, "this is Nouiomo Onyx. She's assisting Nergal."

She raised her head in my direction, her gaze focused somewhere past my face. *She can't see me,* I thought. *She's blind.* But she could feel me.

Lamia's signature wrapped around mine like a snake, squeezing and constricting. Breathing became more difficult. To fight my growing panic, I reminded myself that touching signatures was standard. Lamia would let go any minute and I'd be winded but fine.

But she didn't let go.

"Lamia," Ari warned, and I could hear the anger in his voice. But, if anything, the squeezing got worse. Surely ribs would crack and lungs would be punctured. My vision blurred at the edges. I wanted to scream, but couldn't because I couldn't take a single breath. As consciousness faded, I felt Ari blast Lamia—a sharp, concentrated burst. She rocked back in her chair as if slapped and suddenly I was free. I slumped against Ari, heaving.

"Threatening Nergal's counsel is counterproductive, Lamia," Ari said. His signature was still hot but his voice was soft, as if he were speaking to a child. "Ms. Onyx is here to help. Try anything like that again and I'll send over something that hurts."

Lamia cackled and rocked in her chair. I glanced back at

Nergal, but he seemed to be paying more attention to Ari's arm around my waist than his wife. I disengaged from Ari and walked over to sit with Nergal. I reflexively rubbed my throat, ignoring an impulse to shoot Lamia through with the kind of magic I'd used to kill Serafina. With a demon like Lamia, it would probably be like stabbing a wild boar with a needle. And with my luck, I'd probably aim for the eye and get the rump.

I sighed. It was going to be a long negotiating session.

Ari got the ball rolling by explaining, as if they didn't already know, what their positions were. Nergal wanted a divorce but his only legal option, absent Lamia's consent, was a separation. In short, under demon law, Nergal was stuck with Lamia until she said otherwise. Her debts were his debts; her sins were his sins. Demon lovers who married were bound by magic. They lived—and died—together, unless both agreed to end the marriage.

For over an hour we tried to reason with Lamia as Nergal became more and more agitated.

What if, in return for her consent, Nergal built her more wells to the west and north of New Babylon?

She didn't want more wells.

What if Nergal built Lamia a new subterranean vault in New Babylon to hold her non-viable urban offerings?

She didn't want a new vault.

What if Nergal helped Lamia to establish a devotion cult centered around Blacken Ridge, Morkill Steppe, and some of the other western outposts?

She didn't want more devotees.

What did she want?

When I finally thought to ask her, her answer was so unexpected, it left me breathless, like I'd been hit in the gut with the lance that had unhorsed Lucifer.

"I want a child."

"What you want is impossible," Nergal said, his voice laced with bitter magic. It hurt to hear it.

Lamia smiled sweetly at him, revealing a disgustingly sharklike double row of razor-sharp canines. An image of her smiling down at her infant—a second before she ate him—assaulted my imagination. *How unfair,* I thought. *Were my desires that different from hers? Was I any better just because I had only a drop of demon blood whereas she was one?*

Nergal fished in his pocket and threw a handful of something at Lamia. Two small objects hit the floor and broke apart. Husks of corn and strands of wheat shattered around her feet.

"Waxing magic can't help you!" Nergal shouted. "Mederies can't help you!" Suddenly, the room felt like a closed cab during summer solstice. "I want to be free of you, you mad, fat cow!" Nergal threw two more. One bounced off Lamia's shoulder and fell to the floor; the other flew over her head and landed somewhere in the back of the room. Lamia cackled like a crow. I had a feeling Nergal's next move would be to start throwing magic. I was afraid he would go apoplectic and spew his demon rage in one great big solar flare. I readied myself to leech massive amounts of oxygen from the room, thinking that would be the only way to control a sun demon like him. But before I could, Lamia's cackling turned to coughing and the coughing to retching.

She pitched over in her chair and vomited on the floor.

I stared at the steaming mass of blood, tissue, hair, and half-digested grain products that Lamia had just disgorged from her innards. A cold, hard knot of fear formed in my belly and spread outward, drying my mouth and stiffening my limbs. Ari picked up one of the objects Nergal had thrown at Lamia. He studied it for a moment, his signature dimming, and then he started picking up the other ones. I beat him to the last one and clutched the tiny thing in my hand.

It was a Bryde idol. A corn doll. And Lamia had been eating them.

II

*Confusion heard his voice, and wild uproar
Stood ruled, stood vast infinitude confined;
Till at his second bidding darkness fled,
Light shone, and order from disorder sprung.*

—JOHN MILTON

Chapter 15

ೆ

Spring rescued us from the clutches of winter. The snow melted, leaving the ground soggy and the sidewalks wet. I packed up my high-necked sweaters and heavy cloak. I moved my boots to the back of my closet. I started wearing sandals and even traded in my usual assortment of bulky black and charcoal gray wraps for a few body-skimming, above-the-knee tunics in burnt orange and deep purple. But I refused to go so far as to wear pastels for Eostre.

Once, after our initial client interview, Ari tried to talk to me about it. But I cut him off. For reasons both personal and professional, I told him if he ever raised the subject outside of class, I'd stop seeing him. He didn't. But he did often wander into the secluded area of Corpus Justica where we'd first kissed.

Our amorous encounters there always left me feeling shaky. Like I'd reaffirmed some treacherous vow or risked an even deeper level of enchantment. Or, at the very least, fallen several more feet toward the simple act of falling in love.

But I never said the words. No further declarations were made. Clothes stayed on. Demon marks—and other places—remained frustratingly untouched.

I met with Nergal several times to discuss his case. He wanted me to pursue an insanity exception to the mutual consent requirement for divorce. There was no such thing. When I told him that, he started threatening. Threatening is a demon's bread and butter, but his threats had a degree of candor and credibility that often turned my blood to ice.

I lived in fear that Nergal would come to me in the night, while I was asleep and defenseless. His agitation since our first meeting tripled, which tripled my worry. *Did Nergal have another demon lover waiting? Why else would he be gnashing his teeth over six weeks of strategy sessions when he had another six hundred years to live?* Then it dawned on me that the demon lover might visit too, to serve her own version of a Motion to Compel. And if Lamia was any indication of the type of demon Nergal favored, I didn't want to meet Nergal's next bride. In the weeks following Bryde's Day, I bit my fingernails to the quick, bought three new deadbolts (knowing they were useless), and sometimes made Ivy sleep at Fitz's because I was convinced room 112 of Megiddo would see another demon attack.

My life continued in a tense, stagnant sort of way. I was terrified of Nergal and the potentially lethal "what ifs" and "don'ts" we discussed in the classroom part of Manipulation. I wanted to discuss it all with Ari, but he was the last person I could really confide in. Every time Ari "accidentally" ran into me in the library, Rochester's voice boomed in my head: *Avoid collaboration. Avoid even the appearance of collaboration.*

Meanwhile, I made some headway in the Manipulation dungeon, which was what I'd started calling the basement of Rickard Building. I learned how to distinguish a war hammer from a hatchet, a battle-ax from a broadax, and a claymore from a rapier. A few times I was even able to shape my magic into something that vaguely resembled one of them. But most times the training sessions were as tortuous as that first one. I threw off large uncontrolled magic blasts when cornered, still inadvertently set things on fire from time to time, and had yet to master the technique of retracting my magic without a big fireworks show. My hand-to-hand fighting strategies improved only incrementally. Bloody noses became such a usual occurrence for me on Wednesday mornings that I started packing a med kit so I could dope and doll myself up before Copeland's class at 9:00 a.m.

To his credit, Ari did the best he could to try and soften Wednesday's blows, both literal and figural. When we weren't reading, studying cases, or engaging in other nonacademic activities at Corpus Justica, he helped me with my magic. He still murmured advice or words of encouragement during training sessions in the basement. And he always walked me to the bathroom afterward and waited outside for me to clean up and pretend I was okay when I wasn't.

Every Wednesday afternoon, I rang the Aster house hoping to reach Peter. But each time Mrs. Aster told me (in increasingly irritated tones) that she hadn't heard from him either. Some Wednesdays, the only thing that got me through was knowing Peter was still in the Asters' garden shed searching for the spell that would finally put an end to my misery.

One Sunday afternoon in Rign, Halja's fourth month, Peter finally returned. Fitz had gone to see his mother and Ivy had gone shopping. I'd finished my morning reading on quit claims, quiet titles, and equitable conversion and was heading to Marduk's, thinking I'd have the clam chowder with a side of asparagus. I was debating the merits of grilled versus roasted, when someone yelled my name from across Angel Street. I turned toward the voice and almost didn't recognize the man waving at me.

Peter's hair had grown longer than Ari's, but, unlike Ari's dark mane, Peter's hair was so light it was almost white. He wore it gathered behind his head, tied with a simple black band. His canvas trousers were frayed at the bottom and his shirt, collared though it was, looked slightly wrinkled. He wore a bone-colored leather jacket that fell past his waist. I stared at him, my thoughts piling up on one another like a ferry collision at dawn.

Did his appearance here mean that he'd found the spell? Living in the garden shed seemed to have freed Peter from more than just Mrs. Aster's thumb. Wrinkled shirts? Leather? Long hair? And then . . .

Peter looked pretty good as a scruffy rebel.

We embraced, which was still a bit awkward, and stared at each other. We each spoke at the same time.

"Did you—"

"How are—"

I laughed and Peter smiled. He grabbed my hand—that was a first—and pulled me toward the Joshua School. In seconds we were sitting side by side on a firm white couch facing a huge glass window that overlooked Angel Street. Behind us was the boyish-faced man who guarded the Angels and their wall of cubbies. He'd been utterly expressionless and silent when Peter and I had walked in.

Peter sank down into the couch, his arm resting casually along the back of the sofa behind me. I perched on its edge, unusually uncomfortable about leaning back into Peter. He didn't seem to sense my unease. Using his foot to gently push aside a fluted glass bowl, Peter stretched out his legs and rested them on the glass table in front of us.

"The Etincelle search went well, Noon."

"It did?" My heart beat faster.

Now that we were four months into the semester, the stakes for casting the Reversal Spell were getting exponentially higher. For one, I'd declared my magic and started training to be a Maegester. Attempting to reverse my magic now, absent the Demon Council's permission, would be risky for both caster and castee. For another, Ari had made his thoughts on the Reversal Spell clear. He didn't think I should let Peter cast it over me—ever. I was determined not to live my life making decisions based on what a guy would want me to do, but Ari had become a lot more than just "a guy" to me. Ari reminded me time and again that there was nothing wrong with me, that my waning magic was unique instead of abhorrent, that Manipulation would get easier. He reminded me that Mederies were the weak ones. There had been no attacks or abductions since Bryde's Day (Seknecus had even removed the alert he had posted at the beginning of the semester), but the sins were unsolved. The *rogare* demon who'd burned Bryony, attacked Laurel Scoria at the train station, and likely abducted Amaryllis Apatite and Peony Copperfield was still at large. Ari often asked me, if I were ever to encounter the *rogare* demon who'd committed the unsolved sins against the Mederies, would I rather have waxing magic or waning?

Six days of the week I leaned toward waning. But every Wednesday I changed my mind.

Peter was explaining how he had searched every inch of the Aster archives. He'd found no further copies of *Last Stand* and no mention anywhere of the Reversal Spell either directly or indirectly.

"But I know where Jonathan Aster might be buried," he said. "I found a copy of his Last Will and Testament, including a codicil indicating his burial wishes. If he died in battle, he wanted to be buried on the field."

I scoffed. "That's hardly helpful. Armageddon's battlefield was the whole of New Babylon. If he died in battle, he could be buried anywhere. He could be buried right out there under Angel Street for all we know," I said, motioning toward the street.

"Yes," Peter said patiently, "and if we had nothing more to go on, I might agree that continuing to search for the spell by attempting to locate Jonathan Aster's remains might be futile. But . . ."

He leaned forward and pulled a slim leather case out of his jacket pocket. He flipped it open. Inside was a folded piece of parchment paper, obviously very old.

"What's that?"

"I found it in the archives, in a cabinet marked 'Correspondence—First 100 Years.'" He laid the case on the table and looked expectantly at me.

"May I?" I asked, reaching for the paper.

"Of course," Peter said. "I brought it here for you."

I picked up the paper and gently unfolded it. Scrawling lines of script blurred and blotched their way across a page faded and stained with time. I squinted, straining to make out the uneven writing.

Dearest Cousin—

It has been difficult settling among the Host. They are not cruel, but the memories of war are not soon forgotten.

The baby will come soon. Next month, the Host midwives (or Mederies as they call them here) say. I fear, however, that my rash actions this morning may have dangerously hastened what was to have been a natural and uncomplicated birth.

Grief and loneliness compelled me to visit Jonathan's grave one last time before I became housebound with an infant. I woke early, dragged a skiff to the river's edge, and rowed to the north shore. From there I walked east, around the abandoned fort, to the battle site.

I wasn't the only mourner on the field. Nor am I the only one still grieving over what was lost. Hundreds walked the field placing small markers where loved ones died. Servants cried or sang. Angels prayed and Lucifer's warlords wept. In my madness, I threw Jonathan's Prayer Book into Lucifer's tomb and crept away.

It is my child's only inheritance. Should you retrieve it, cousin, I would be most grateful. With love and affection,

Mary Aster

I frowned, not following what clues this letter provided or why this information should be important. From a schol-

arly perspective, it was fascinating. I found myself wishing
Mary Aster had written more letters, or that Peter might have
found a personal journal of some kind. This young woman
had lived during the single most important event in our history, the Apocalypse. Few personal accounts of the days following Armageddon had survived.

"What happened to her?"

"Other records indicate that she died in childbirth."

"Oh," I said, inexplicably saddened by this woman's death
though she was a stranger. Then something occurred to me.
"Why is her letter still in the Aster Archives?"

"Because it was never sent. The baby must have come
prematurely as she'd anticipated. She must have died shortly
after writing the letter."

"So, if the letter was never sent . . ."

"Then Mary's cousin never knew to search for the Prayer
Book."

"Right."

"Noon, do you know what a Prayer Book is?"

"A book of prayers," I said, trying not to sound sarcastic.
I may not have been given an Angel education like Peter but
I wasn't stupid.

"Yes," Peter said, his smile a little too patronizing for
my taste. "But no one calls them that anymore. 'Prayer' is an
antiquated term from the pre-Apocalyptic days. In modern
day, *prayers* are called *spells*."

So Jonathan Aster's spell book was in Lucifer's tomb. If
his spell book contained the Reversal Spell, no wonder no
one had cast it in thousands of years. The location of Lucifer's tomb was one of the greatest mysteries of all time.

The Joshua School's equivalent to Marduk's was Empyr.
But comparing Empyr to Marduk's was like comparing
blown glass to the forge it was fired in. Empyr was located
thirty-three floors above New Babylon on the top floor of the
Joshua School. All of the walls were floor to ceiling windows
and, rumor had it, the views were majestic and splendid. Cer-

tainly the Angels had Heaven in mind when they built it. It was all lightness and glass, the décor modern and gleaming, the staff exceptionally courteous yet reserved, attentive but unobtrusive. The tables were covered with crisp white linens, fine china, and real silver. Empyr served wine in crystal goblets and the only fire was the tiny flame at the top of their myriad beeswax candles. Any wood burning fireplace would have generated far too much smoke. In Empyr, what wasn't glass was covered in white.

Sometime during our discussion on Jonathan Aster's spell book, Peter had asked if I wanted to go to dinner. Fitz was having dinner with his mother, and Ivy was likely still shopping, so I agreed and mentioned that I'd been headed to Marduk's just before I ran into Peter. But Peter balked at Marduk's. It could have been the uninspiring menu but I suspected Peter didn't relish another run in with Ari. I didn't either, at least not with Peter in tow. So Peter suggested Empyr and, I have to admit, I was excited not to have to eat clam chowder or, Luck forbid, another Innkeeper's Pie.

Empyr was a private club. The Joshua students ate there, just as the St. Luck's students ate at Marduk's, and all Joshua School alums were lifelong members (so long as they paid their fees). But the real reason Empyr was such an exclusive, privileged club was that most of the Divinity were members there too. It would be like eating a minced ham sandwich at Marduk's with a demon from the Demon Council. I couldn't even imagine it. But for one night, I thought glamming it up would be a welcome change from the everyday slumming I did at Marduk's. The only problem was that I wasn't dressed for the occasion.

Still seated on the white couch looking out across Angel Street, I glanced down at my outfit. My trousers were less worn than Peter's, but they were still made of canvas. I'd never been to Empyr, but if the dress code was anything like my mother's, pants for dinner would be a mistake.

"Should I change?" I asked Peter.

"What for?" he said. He got up and offered me his hand. I raised an eyebrow. The old Peter would have suggested we both change. I linked arms with him. He led me across the lobby, nodding at the boyish-faced man behind the counter. The man nodded back, his eyes resting briefly on me before turning his attention back to his duties.

As we walked into the lift, Peter slid his arm down so that he was holding my hand. We rode up to Empyr in silence. Peter held my hand loosely between us and I tried not to feel uncomfortable about that, neither squeezing back, nor letting go. In seconds, the lift door opened and we stepped into Empyr's waiting area.

The place smelled divine. Like warm bread fresh out of the oven, with hints of honey, almond, and peaches. My stomach growled in response. I smiled at the tall, regal woman who greeted us. She had hair that was a shade darker than mine, almost pitch-black. She wore it straight, long and loose, but not a piece of it was out of place. Her clingy floor-length dress was absolutely spotless and bright white. She gave us a smile that was as white and bright as her dress and I knew instantly that any member of Empyr would be welcomed regardless of whether they were dressed in flawlessly draped silk or fraying canvas.

"Two for dinner, Mr. Aster?" she said expectantly, grabbing menus for us. I used the moment to look around.

Empyr was every bit as grand as I'd heard it was. Stepping out of the lift, one faced directly south. New Babylon spread out beneath Empyr like small blocks on a grid. In front of me the grayish blue length of the Lethe ran a serpentine course at the southern edge of the city. Beyond it, Etincelle sparkled in the distance, its faint, yellow glow like a lightning bug's next to the nearer white starlight bright of New Babylon at dusk. To my right, the sun set over the western part of the city, its fiery colors melting behind the buildings of St. Luck's into a viscous mix of red, orange, and yellow that made it seem as if the whole world was on fire.

I stared, stunned for a moment, by the beauty of it. But then, at Peter's request, we were led into the section of the restaurant facing east. It was the least crowded section. Only a few other tables were occupied. It had a quiet feel to it;

even the view was subdued. Instead of the brilliance of the western sunset or the sparkle of the Lethe and Etincelle, the eastern section of Empyr looked out over mostly fields and farms. It seemed an odd choice for Peter, who, like most Angels, preferred urban, modern aesthetics to scenes of pastoral tranquility.

We were given menus and a wine list and left to ourselves. I reached for the wine list before Peter could. Empyr's wine was as legendary as the restaurant itself. All of the wine was made in-house by Angels selected as much for their wine making abilities as their spell casting skills. All of the wines were made from apples (Angels were obsessed with apples) and each was paired with a beneficial spell. Empyr's menu changed every few days; its wine list changed every night.

Curious about the night's offerings, I took a look at the list:

EMPYR

~Wine List~

CALVILLE BLANC D'HIVER: *Pale green with swirls of red. Sweet & tart. Temporarily relieves aches and pains. Aids in healing.*

SPRING PEARMAIN: *Greenish yellow. Served chilled. Refreshing & crisp. Enhances positive outlook.*

VANDEVERE (OR GRINDSTONE): *Golden bronze. Sweet & salty with a buttery texture. Increases powers of observation.*

SWEET WINESAP: *Rosy pink. Sugary and thick. Strengthens romantic attachment.*

ORANGE PIPPIN: *Layers of red, orange, and dark yellow. Fruity with a hint of spice. Creates feelings of warmth and relaxation.*

The Spring Pearmain would have done me good but I wasn't in the mood for a cold drink. And I didn't need the Sweet Winesap to strengthen my romantic attachment. I was feeling far too attached to Ari already. The whole purpose of this meal was to forget about my current anxieties, both academic and romantic. So I ordered the Orange Pippin and tried to hide my smile when Peter ordered the Grindstone. Some things *hadn't* changed. Peter might look different but his intellectual core was still intact.

Over drinks, the easy camaraderie Peter and I had always shared came back as if the last four months and my declaration had never happened. We were at it again, plotting my way out of being a death dealer. Surely, I convinced myself (the Pippin contributing greatly to this line of thinking), if we found the Reversal Spell and Peter successfully cast it, the demons on the Demon Council would not take offense. Peter's value as a spellcaster would only increase and I could do more good for Halja as a Mederi than as a Maegester. My newly acquired knowledge of our potential sins should we cast the spell without permission (for Peter, Unauthorized Spellcasting; for me, Waste, to name the first two that sprang to mind) were easily pushed aside as I sipped my second Pippin.

After much mulling of the menu, I selected broiled whitefish with tomatoes, olives, and capers while Peter picked pine nut–encrusted sea bass served with potatoes. Our food arrived sometime later, smelling rich and flavorful. For a few moments I merely inhaled and consumed, happily aglow with the buzz of my Pippins and the company of my long-lost friend. Peter continued the discussion we'd started earlier, telling me how he—*we*—were going to search for Lucifer's tomb. His usual unassailable confidence, combined with the effect of my drinks, had me nodding along with him.

"But what really happened to Lucifer after the battle of Armageddon?" I asked, picking at my fish with a fork. As delicious as it was, I was getting full.

"That's the biggest mystery of all time," Peter said. "Some say he transmuted on the field and turned into his true form before he died. Others say he's off somewhere gathering his strength so he can return to claim his throne. Others say he was buried where he fell in battle and that he rose again the next day as the Morning Star."

Peter drank the last of his wine and looked out the window. The sun had set and the world below was mostly dark. Gas streetlights in the foreground gave way to yellowy glows behind farmers' shades and shutters. Beyond that was the blackness of the unpopulated fields at night.

"The star legends are the most interesting," Peter continued, "because they are unusually factual about the time and place of Lucifer's death. According to those legends, Babylon was no more than a small fort at the time of Armageddon. Lucifer, his warlords, and the fallen demon legions were buried six leagues due east of the old fort."

"Mary's letter mentioned an abandoned fort," I mused, getting caught up in the ancient mystery. "Too bad we don't know where the old fort was. That would make looking for the tomb remarkably easy."

Peter smiled knowingly at me. Despite the Pippin, I shivered. My voice dropped to an awe-inspired whisper. "You know where the fort is."

"Maybe," he said. "Take a look at these." He pulled the slim leather case out of his pocket again and opened it. Inside, tucked down behind Mary's letter, were two small pieces of paper I'd missed. He unfolded one of them and spread it out on the table.

"What is it?" I asked, reaching for it. I picked up the small piece of paper and examined it. It was tiny, no more than six inches square. It seemed to be some kind of architectural drawing.

"Some kind of building plan?"

Peter nodded just as I saw what was printed beneath it: *Fort Babylon*. The drawing showed the outline of the fort, complete with administrative buildings, a magazine, and parade grounds.

"Where did you get this?"

"Some old map store near Northbrook," Peter said, waving his hand to show the location of the clue had nothing to do with its significance. He laid down the other piece of paper. It was new, printed in color with a glossy finish. I recognized it immediately. Peter had torn out the first page of my Student Handbook. I pinched my brow, not understanding, and then suddenly, something clicked. My mouth went dry. I couldn't speak. My hand shook as I moved the old Fort Babylon drawing over the top of the new student's map of St. Luck's.

They were the same.

Lekai had been built where the magazine used to be and the administrative buildings were in the same place, although the Rabbit Warren had expanded. I realized, breathlessly, that the parade grounds could still be used for the same purpose today, if someone were to remove the benches from Timothy's Square.

Suddenly, I felt like running over to Empyr's western windows to press my nose up against the glass. But Peter sat still, gazing east. I knew now why he had wanted to sit here with a view to the east. How much had the Grindstone increased his powers of observation? Enough to see in the dark? Enough to see into the past?

"Do you see the tomb?" I whispered.

Chapter 16

౽

Peter hadn't actually seen the tomb, but with what he'd discovered so far we had a pretty good idea of where to look. The Pippins' effect had largely disappeared but Peter's enthusiasm had me agreeing to accompany him with shocking alacrity.

After penning a quick note to be delivered to Ivy to let her know I was with Peter, we caught a cabriolet on Angel Street. Peter told the driver to take us as far as Sheol, a cluster of about a half-dozen homes at the far eastern edge of the city. Beyond that were only woods and uncultivated fields. The driver grumbled a lot about going so far out. He'd never pick up a return fare, but Peter shushed him with a wad of cash and we rode the rest of the way in silence. I wasn't having second thoughts exactly. But the farther away from the city we drove, the louder Ari's voice became in my head.

If Peter finds the Reversal Spell, will you let him cast it over you?

If I answered honestly, only fear would make me hesitate. Fear of the exact effects of the spell. Fear that Peter, skilled though he was, might not be a match for a spell as powerful as the Reversal Spell. Fear of demon reprisal. Waste was a serious crime, as Copeland had made me realize during Sin and Sanction the day after I'd declared. Possibly even, although I didn't want to admit it, fear of what Ari would say, although I still didn't understand why he was so averse to me reversing my magic. If he liked me with waning magic, wouldn't he like me even better with waxing magic?

I knew full well that fear wasn't a good basis for making decisions. Fear might keep soldiers one step ahead of the blade during battle but woe the warlord who used it to chart the course of war. And woe the woman who used it to chart the course of her own life. Fear had not kept me from declaring. So fear would not keep me from allowing Peter to cast the spell should we find it.

The high stone, iron, and glass buildings at the city's core quickly gave way to the shorter, squatter shape of suburban sprawl. In minutes that disappeared, replaced by the older, more dilapidated homes, barns, and sheds of Sheol.

The cab slowed and came to a stop, its headlamps illuminating a makeshift barricade of rough timber at the end of the street. Peter exchanged a few words with the driver—I hoped they were working out the arrangements for our return trip. We were at least fifteen miles out and had more to walk if we were going to search six leagues east of St. Luck's tonight. I was already bleary-eyed thinking about classes tomorrow morning.

The cab drove off and we were left alone. In front of us was an old farmhouse. Its windows were completely dark; its inhabitants likely asleep for the night. We walked over to the barricade, scrambled over it, and dropped down onto a narrow dirt path that snaked its way through tall grass on either side. I glanced nervously at all the greenery around me, envisioning a blackened path of scorched earth that would take the land months to heal, but Peter quickly cast a protective spell over the path's grass edges and then took the lead in crossing the field.

He walked fast and, since he was taller and his strides

longer, I almost had to run to keep up with him. Around us, the night wind blew sporadically as if in prestorm mode. I glanced up at the sky, thinking how stupid it was that we hadn't even considered the weather before setting off. We'd been too caught up in the momentousness of it all. Who worried about umbrellas and slickers when they were searching for the greatest archeological and ecclesiastical find of all time?

With each whip of wind the wild grass crackled as if an unseen army was moving through it. It made my hair stand up on end. I scurried after Peter, ignoring the impulse to stop and turn around. My feet scuffed through the dirt and I was thankful I'd chosen to wear low boots this morning instead of sandals.

Ahead of us were the eastern woodlands. At night, their rough edge loomed before us like an ancient medieval wall. By the time we reached them I was perspiring so much my linen shirt was damp beneath the armpits. We stopped to rest before entering the woods. I was thirsty but we'd brought no water so I made do with taking big gulps of air. Peter apologized for the pace and insisted I wear his jacket. The night had grown chillier and, now that we'd stopped, the sweaty film I'd worked up on the hike over here made me shiver. Peter finished buttoning his jacket around me but left his hands on the buttons, holding me close. The moonlight shone harshly on his face, making its planes and angles appear sharper than they were.

"Whatever happened to . . . the other St. Luck's student from Marduk's?"

I knew he meant Ari. It was interesting that Peter didn't want to say his name. I knew he remembered. Peter remembered everything.

"He's still around."

"He seemed overly fond of you, Noon. Are you . . . fond of him?"

"Yes," I said. I ignored the brief look of distaste that crossed Peter's face and tried to step back, but Peter kept hold of the buttons of his jacket, preventing me from going too far. He refocused on me, in that eerie, overly intense Angel way.

"Do you know why I never kissed you, Noon?" he asked and I stiffened. "When I was eight, my mother forbid it." Peter laughed, a harsh guttural sound that sent goose bumps up my spine. "But I am through listening to her."

He bent his head toward me so that his face almost touched mine.

"Ever since we were kids, I knew you were the one for me, despite the fact that you were born with waning magic. In fact, that's how I knew. A woman who looks like you is meant to create things.

"With your hands," he said, grabbing one of mine. "With your heart," he said, placing his other hand on my chest. Beneath his palm, my heart beat but my demon mark stayed cool. Apparently Ari was the only one who had the power to truly touch me there.

"I knew a birth such as yours would not occur without a reason. From the moment I met you, I knew my destiny would be to reverse what happened to you. I knew if I could cure you, I could have you." He squeezed me hard. "I want to give you your life's dream, Noon. And then I want to live that life with you."

Before I could react, he kissed me. I was so shocked, for an instant, I did nothing. His lips were firm, almost hard, and his embrace was crushing. When we were teenagers, I'd constantly dreamed of Peter holding me like this, touching me like this, tenderly kissing me. But his kisses weren't sweet; they were savage. After a few shocked seconds, I stiffened. But Peter didn't seem to notice.

"I hope I'm not too late," he whispered roughly, releasing me.

"For what?" I asked breathlessly, wondering how—*if*—this would change things. My thoughts scattered in a thousand different directions.

"Just promise me, if I find the spell and cast it, that you'll be mine—*my* Mederi, *my* wife."

I opened my mouth. I didn't know what to say. "Peter . . ."

But he laughed and released me. "I'm getting ahead of myself. First, let's find the spell. Come on."

He grabbed my hand and led me into the forest.

We walked for what seemed like hours, although I knew it couldn't have been longer than half an hour. Sweat pooled under my armpits again and I gave Peter's jacket back. Somewhere in the distance a low roll of thunder sounded. It rumbled toward us, reverberating through the trees and the ground. I felt it in my feet and teeth, which did nothing to ease my anxiety. The forest had been pitch-black when we'd first entered. The dark, dense canopy of trees had completely obscured the stars and moonlight. But Peter had cast a light spell and we now walked by its solid bluish white light. Its steady illumination made the trees look dead. For the first time in my life I almost wished for fire. Its flickering warm glow would have at least added the illusion of movement and life.

I stepped on a stick, cracking it in half, and bit my lip to keep from crying out. What had sounded like a good idea while sitting in the opulent comfort of Empyr, buzzed from two Pippins, now felt like the height of lunacy. Here we were in the middle of an ancient forest, two hours to midnight and no one knew where we were. We lived in a world full of demons and one demon in particular (if not more) was already ticked off at me. What if Nergal or his lover chose this moment to find me and start harassing me?

And everything Peter had said earlier . . . It was a lot to think about.

It's not as if I'd never wondered what a life with Peter would be like. I'd spent years of my adolescence thinking about it. We'd grown up together; we could grow old together. Our families' estates bordered each other. Night could raise his family on the Onyx estate and Peter and I could live in the Aster house. Peter and I were roughly the same age and, in modern times at least, it wasn't uncommon for Angels and members of the Host to marry.

I supposed my life would be near perfect with Peter as

my husband. There would be no end to my mother's gratitude if Peter found a way to reverse my magic. Even my father would likely give Peter anything in his power to give (which was substantial). Despite Peter's recent leave of absence, he was well respected at the Joshua School. One day there might even be a place for him on the Divinity Council. Our children would grow up in Etincelle. They could climb trees, swim in Cocytus Creek, run races in Elysian Fields . . . My mind positively raced with the possibilities.

Peter could give me all of that. *But did I want all of that with Peter?*

Four months ago I would not have thought twice. He was my oldest friend. He had understood what I wanted and needed better than anyone. But now . . . I rubbed my demon mark furiously, trying to ignore my conflicted feelings. A sense of unease so profound I almost couldn't breathe enveloped me.

We stepped into a clearing.

There were still trees but they were spindly and short, spread out and thin on the ground, all of them diseased or dying. With a crack, a bolt of lightning struck not half a mile from where we stood. Instantly, thunder boomed and the firmament of Halja broke loose. Rain fell in sheets as if the whole Lethe was being poured on our heads. Peter's light spell wavered as he concentrated on moving forward. I wondered how much distance we'd traveled. Were we six leagues due east of St. Lucifer's yet?

With the next blast of lightning, I knew. There was no mistaking a graveyard no matter how old it was. Small mounds covered the ground. Row upon row of them, too straight and evenly spaced to have been anything but manmade. And more than half of them still had headstones, or what was left of them. Jagged slabs of rock jutted vertically out from most of the mounds. I was suddenly struck by an image of what the field must have looked like after Armageddon, covered in the gory remains of what death had left behind. The place reminded me uncomfortably of Lamia's double row of rotting, decayed shark teeth.

How much blood had been swallowed by this ground?

Peter consulted something, a pocket pedometer or compass, and kept looking around. Rain splashed off his head and face, dripping from his nose and cheeks. My linen shirt clung to me, feeling as heavy as Peter's leather jacket had.

"What now?" I shouted, spitting a mouthful of rainwater out. It tasted off here, like water from a contaminated well.

"Look for the tomb," Peter yelled, fighting to be heard over the roar of the storm. He motioned for me to go east while he went north. I wasn't happy about splitting up, but figured the sooner we found the tomb the better. I stumbled along, hugging my arms close to my side, shivering.

It wasn't long before I lost sight of Peter. The rain was relentless. I kept my head down and wound my way through the mounds. The rain soaked my hair and dripped into my shirt collar and down my back. I shielded my eyes with my hand and searched for the tomb, or anything we could use as shelter from the storm. Peter had taken his light with him and I quickly realized I would find nothing on my own in the dark and the rain. I picked up a large stick from the ground and considered it. I was capable of making light and heat on my own. I didn't have to search in the dark and the cold. Thinking to make a torch, I tried to light the end of the stick with magic.

Nothing happened.

I tried again. Still nothing. It was puzzling and frustrating. What was I doing wrong? With my power, it shouldn't have mattered how wet the wood was. Yes, my magic control and consistency left much to be desired. Sure, I still inadvertently set things on fire from time to time. That was why this situation was twice as infuriating. *Now that I actually wanted a fire, I couldn't light one.*

I threw the stick to the ground and smothered the area around it with a light spray of highly combustible magic. I flicked my wrist toward it for focus and then spread my palm flat across the area hoping to ignite it, half expecting the whole area to ferociously explode in a blast of heat and light.

I was even prepared to leech oxygen, so great did I think the conflagration might be, but no containment measures were necessary. The ground remained wet as a bog and my frustration level ratcheted up another notch.

I continued navigating the mounds, swiping my sopping wet hair away from my face, and squishing through what was now inches of mud. Every moment, I half expected something to reach up out of the ground to catch my ankle and haul me to a place darker than Halja itself.

Finally, I spotted a structure buried back in the rotten tangle of tree trunks and decaying vines surrounding the mounds. As I approached I realized it was an abandoned house. Half of it had collapsed. The other half, while still standing, bore gaping holes where windows should have been. The front door hung unsteadily by one hinge, banging against the side of the house in the wind. It was old, centuries old perhaps, but not as old as the Apocalypse. It was doubtful Lucifer's final resting place was housed in this derelict shack. The feeling of the place settled over me like frozen mist. Ari hadn't mentioned that places had signatures, but this one seemed to.

The place felt like too much magic of too many sorts. Like waning magic, waxing magic, even spells, were bound up in the mist, trying to break free. I supposed that made sense. More demons and Angels, Host and Hyrke had died here together than anywhere else in Halja. It was as if the ground had gorged on magic as well as blood, become sick on its grisly feast, and then died before it could retch up the overabundance.

Maybe I'd be able to light a fire inside, out of the rain. I strode purposefully toward the decaying house and entered, shutting the door behind me to stop the wind and constant banging. But the relative silence of the house unnerved me further. I squeezed the water out of my hair and let my eyes adjust to the dark interior. The house felt like an icebox, cold and still. I rubbed my hands together and blew into them for warmth, wishing desperately I'd brought gloves. How could it be this cold this late into spring? Slowly, I made my way down the hall, thinking to find the kitchen. My best chance of starting a fire would be in there.

My desire to produce heat and light was almost palpable, and I had to focus on controlling my magic for fear I would burn the house down with me in it. But I found no kitchen, or any area of the house that might have been used for cooking. Maybe it was in the section that had collapsed, I thought. I continued searching for any safe area within which I might try to light a fire and, finally, at the end of the hallway, I found a room with a fireplace.

But this fireplace was unlike any fireplace I had ever seen. For one, it was huge, taking up the entire back wall of the house. Second, it appeared as if it had been here first, with the house being constructed around it. It was also the wettest firebox I had ever seen. *Everything* about it felt wrong. I hugged my shoulders as I glanced around the room searching for something to burn. The room was littered with all sorts of stuff, but in the darkness I couldn't tell what. Likely it was the abandoned domestic trash from several generations' worth of grave keepers. I navigated the rubble and crept toward the fireplace with equal parts dread and anticipation.

Through a gaping window, frequent lightning strikes provided unsteady light. A massive burst illuminated the room and I clapped my hands over my ears, preparing for the intense and immediate crack of thunder. Another splash of brightness highlighted ancient graffiti cut into the stones rimming the hearth. Deep swirls and slashes decorated every inch of stone, an uncanny silent cacophony of ciphers, glyphs, and symbols. The largest looked like a rudimentary drawing of the sun with triple-tined forked rays shooting out from it.

In the center of the inner hearth, on the floor, was a circular stone door with a large iron ring on the top. I supposed a fireplace as large as this needed a huge ash pit, but there was something about the door that made me afraid. Maybe because it covered a hole big enough to fall into. I wondered how deep the ash pit went. I stepped closer, morbidly fascinated despite my growing sense of unease. In the flickering light of the storm, the hole seemed to breathe. Wetness seeped into the dirt around its edges and then disappeared again, like puffs of breath in the cold night air.

Sometimes magic had a smell, like the way Brunus smelled of rotten onions. I smelled nothing now, but as I grew closer, I sensed something in the air. Something beneath that covered hole. Something deadly and poisonous. Hyrke miners often talked of air that was so old and so ancient that merely breathing it would kill you. I backed away then, stumbling over a pile of unseen rubble. I turned around to run, my desire for a fire completely gone. I just wanted to run, to get as far away from this place as possible. But before I could take two steps, someone grabbed me from behind. I opened my mouth to scream but a hand clamped over it first. I struggled, trying to shake loose my captor. I stepped back, stomped on their foot, and unleashed a bolt of magic. A voice cried out. I recognized it—and the protective spell—instantly.

It was Peter.

Luckily, he had blocked my magic, but unluckily, we were still standing in this vile place.

"Let's get out of here," I said, no longer caring about the rain. Better wet from above, than wet with whatever was seeping out from below.

But Peter didn't move and he didn't let go of me. His fingers dug painfully into my arms.

"Noon," he said, his voice pitched low, "do you see that center stone there? The one that's slightly larger than all the others?"

I shook my head. Still holding onto me so that I wouldn't bolt from the room, Peter cast a light spell and pointed toward the hearth. In the blue light of Peter's spell, the inky shapes of the glyphs seemed to leap from the surface of the stones. It was as if they were shouting. But, after so many millennia, only an Angel could hear them. And only one as educated as Peter could have guessed their meaning.

"That symbol there," he said, "the dark circle with six staves coming out of it . . . It's the ancient symbol for Lucifer.

Historians used to believe the circle represented the sun, but it represents another star—the Morning Star. And the six staves are really lances. Remember the legends? Lucifer's lance was triple tipped?" Peter's voice rose with his excitement. "You did it, Noon! This is it. You found the tomb!"

At once, everything clicked into place. No wonder this fireplace was so unusual. No fire had ever been lit here. Suddenly the size, depth, and dampness of the area made sense. These stones didn't mark an area to be used for light, warmth, and comfort. They marked an area reserved for death. And that meant the ash pit wasn't really an ash pit. It was the entrance to Lucifer's crypt.

A feeling of dread washed over me. If Jonathan Aster's spell book had been thrown into that hole, I wanted no part of going after it. But Peter released me and, instead of walking toward the tomb, he looked around the room with awe. I saw now that the room wasn't crowded with the detritus of former grave keepers; it was crowded with votive offerings. In former times, the location of Lucifer's tomb had been far from a mystery. Piles and piles of books—not just spell books, but anti-war treatises, genealogies, and personal journals—lined the room. Pieces of cloth and hair, dirty old ribbons, scribbled notes, dead flowers, corn dolls, and even rice littered the floor. There were life-sized cradles and miniature carvings, tarnished bells, rusty blades, and bowls full of what looked like dried blood. It was all very macabre and very disgusting, but it was also very much the way Halja grieved—by offering the grave anything and everything that represented life.

Peter gave a whoop of laughter that sent chills racing up my spine. It was so out of place here. He bent to the task of searching with glee, oblivious to my lack of shared enthusiasm. I stood mute, watching as he sifted through what must be centuries of offerings. Despite his marked show of enthusiasm, Peter handled each relic with respect. Angels were the archeologists of Halja. Even in his search for the greatest spell of all time, he took care to disturb as little as possible.

I couldn't shake the feeling I'd had since we first discovered the graveyard outside, that the sooner we found the spell book and left, the better. So I too started sifting through the rubble. I wasn't quite as careful as Peter though, and not nearly as interested in what I was sifting through. The rotted top of a large coffin leaned against the wall in one of the room's corners. I shifted it a few inches so that I could peek around behind it. There, protected by the coffin lid from the layer of dust and grime covering everything else in the room, was a stack of a dozen books or so. It didn't take long to scan the titles.

Somehow I knew I would be the one to find it and not Peter. I suddenly had the urge to push the coffin top back into place. Peter would assume I'd checked this corner and the spell could stay hidden forever. But I couldn't. I'd spent all night—well, really my whole life—searching for this spell. The letters on the spine of the book were old and faded, some half-missing, but I knew what it was: *Prayers of Deliverance* by Jonathan Aster.

I reached for it.

Chapter 17

❦

Monday dawned bright and hot, promising all the light and heat I'd sought last night. We'd discovered within minutes of finding it that Jonathan Aster's spell book was written in Anglentine, an ancient scholarly text favored by Angels in the first and second centuries following Armageddon. Peter wasn't fluent in Anglentine, but it wouldn't take him long to translate the book and identify the correct spell. He'd left for the Joshua School last night with the book tucked safely under his arm and I'd trudged back to Megiddo and crawled gratefully into bed.

When my alarm bell went off at the Luck forsaken hour of seven in the morning, I considered trying to melt it but didn't want to frighten Ivy. So instead I practiced my magic control by trying to boil water for tea. The fact that the water boiled, and nothing else burned, was a significant victory for me, especially considering last night's failure to light even a single spark.

I sat on my unmade bed, clutching my tea, willing my eyelids to feel less like sandpaper, trying to remember the

Sin and Sanction cases for this morning. We'd been discussing murder, a crime consisting of only two elements but one which had dozens of defenses and an unlimited means by which it could be committed.

"How was shopping yesterday?" I asked Ivy, expecting her to launch into a solo shoe debate concerning the merits of jeweled slip-ons versus ribboned platforms that would take my mind off of the bludgeoning, garroting, and staking cases we'd be discussing later today. But Ivy gave me a guarded smile and walked over to her closet. She rummaged around for a few moments and then pulled out a dramatically low-cut, deep emerald evening gown made of silk, organza, and chiffon. If I'd been looking for a fashion distraction from all the gore, this dress was it.

"It's beautiful," I said. "But a bit dressy for class, don't you think?"

She barked out a mock laugh to let me know she didn't think I was very funny. "It's for the Barrister's Ball."

"The Barrister's what?"

"The Barrister's Ball," she repeated. "Every year, just before the Beltane break, the Joshua School hosts a ball for the St. Luck's students over at Empyr. It's a really big deal. Have you ever been to Empyr, Noon?" She didn't pause long enough to let me answer, but instead continued in a rush of words. "They make apple wines and infuse them with magic. Fitz said the sommelier has been working on the spells for this year's ball batch since the summer solstice."

I could understand the appeal of Empyr. I'd felt the same way not twenty-four hours ago. But then I considered the significance of everything that had occurred post-Pippins last night—wandering around an ancient graveyard in the wind, rain, mud, and muck, possibly defiling Lucifer's lost tomb by removing one of the offerings, Peter kissing me and his declarations.

One bite of the apple seemed like one too many the morning after. But Ivy walked over to her closet and pulled out another gown, a real showstopper. It was made of taffeta and had a laced brocade bodice decorated in a swirling pattern that could evoke flames or flowers. Like the emerald dress, it was full length, but this one had a small train of cascading silk. The color, however—a blazing orange shot with red and gold—was all wrong for Ivy.

"Definitely the green one," I said, draining the last of my tea. I placed the empty cup on my desk and started to get up to shower.

Ivy's face fell. "You like the green one better?"

"The orange dress is spectacular, but with your hair . . . I just think the green will set that off best." I grabbed my soap bucket and prepared to walk down the hall.

"Oh, good," Ivy said laughing. "I thought you meant you liked the green one better for you. I agree. I bought the green one for me and the orange one for you."

I paused, soap bucket in hand. I didn't know what to say. I was extremely grateful and touched that Ivy would think to buy me a gown. It was extraordinarily generous. And I'd never been to a formal dance. For one thing, I'd never dated anyone seriously enough to get invited. Second, and most importantly, it was an impossible wardrobe challenge. This dress proved why.

"Um," I started, not wanting to hurt Ivy's feelings, but also not knowing how to explain my discomfort in baring my décolletage. "It's very revealing."

"That's the point," Ivy said, making an emphatic gesture. "Can you imagine Ari's face when he sees you in this? It's perfect!"

"I can't. Look, I don't want to . . . I don't celebrate Beltane," I finished lamely.

But Ivy just snorted. "You don't celebrate anything."

"And besides," I continued as if I hadn't heard her. "I can't go with Ari. Remember? He's opposing counsel."

Ivy gave me a look that told me she thought all bets were off at Beltane. That the usual rules didn't apply.

"You can go with me then. Come on, I can't go with just Fitz. He's my cousin."

"I don't know, Ivy," I said, torn. The dress was amazing and a part of me wondered what it would be like to wear something so provocative. There would be nowhere to hide in that dress. Its color meant all eyes would be on me and its cut meant my demon mark would be front and center, for all the world to see. I wasn't sure I was ready for that. I shook my head and hung the dress back in Ivy's closet.

"I hope you still have the receipt," I said turning back to Ivy.

She stared at my chest. I realized I'd been self-consciously rubbing my demon mark through my pajama top. As if I could rub it off.

"We all know you have waning magic and the mark to prove it, Noon."

"Yeah," I lowered my hand, feigning confusion. "So?"

"So," Ivy said, exasperated, "you don't have to hide anymore. You're out. You declared. It's time to show off." She walked over to her closet and took the dress out again. "You're beautiful. You're strong." She walked over and firmly placed the dress on my bed. "This dress is perfect for you."

I swallowed. With everything else I had to be afraid of, was this dress really something to fear?

I didn't try it on, but when I put it away, I put it in my closet.

H ow was dinner last night?" Ari asked.

I was standing on the second floor of Corpus Justica, next to the study carrel I used on the nights when I met Ari. This area of the library was far from the main door and students didn't usually come back here unless they were looking for something in particular. An unlikely event on any given night since we were in the tithing and tax section. People usually put off a visit here for as long as possible.

Tonight's quiet was the rule rather than the exception and, in fact, there was an almost complete lack of sound coming from the floor below because most students had packed up and left for the night. It was twenty minutes to close. I'd been packing up and preparing to go when Ari had appeared from behind one of the stacks.

His signature had hit me full force. It seemed stronger than usual and I'd suddenly felt like I'd been scrubbed with sand and doused with salt water. A tingly, burning sensation had raced across me, finally settling densely within the inch square spot of my demon-marked skin.

Skin that was safely covered for now.

"Fine," I said, my voice higher than it ought to have been. *How did Ari know about my dinner with Peter?*

Ari strode over to me, his face expressionless. He had on dark canvas pants and a white cotton shirt. Sometime in early spring he had abandoned the collared shirts he'd worn during winter in favor of short-sleeved shirts like this one. It had made paying attention in class even harder. He reached me and, despite his lack of expression, I could tell he was upset. The tenseness of his muscles and the strength of his signature gave him away.

His lips quirked in a smile, but it offered little true humor. "You were late getting back."

I shrugged, torn between guilt about the dinner (and what it had led to) and irritation that Ari thought he had any right to comment. I fiddled with my backpack, not wanting to meet his eyes. Irritation turned to resentment. I shouldn't have to feel guilty about the fact that I only wanted what I should have had in the first place.

Ari caught the bottom of my chin with his finger and tilted my head up. We stood like that for a few moments, his face inches from mine, his gaze peering into mine, his signature circling mine. And that's when I noticed. He wasn't letting his signature meld into mine the way he usually did. I knew then that he wasn't going to kiss me.

Did he somehow know about Peter's kiss as well as the dinner? How could he? And so what if he did? It wasn't as if Ari and I had ever made any promises of exclusivity to one another . . . Right?

"Anything you want to tell me, Noon?"

"Like what?" I said, turning my head and stepping back.

"Like where you and Peter went after dinner."

"How do you know I even went to dinner? Or that I went somewhere after? Are you *spying* on me, Ari?"

For a moment, I thought my words might have hurt him, but then his expression darkened.

"I rang your room last night. Ivy told me that you were with Peter. Considering the semester started with two demon attacks, one in your room and one right outside this library, can you blame me for wanting to make sure you made it back safely?"

I blew out my breath. No, of course I couldn't blame him for that.

"I'm sorry," I said. "I didn't mean to imply . . . well"—I cleared my throat. "I know you've been looking out for me this semester, Ari, and I appreciate it."

Ari's eyes widened. "'Looking out for you,'" he repeated, shaking his head in disbelief. "Is that what you call it? Noon, I'm not just looking out for you. I'm in—"

He shook his head harder and clenched his fist. "And what do you mean, 'this semester'? As if I'll feel differently next semester." He snorted. "Is that what you're afraid of?"

Luck, what wasn't I afraid of? I shook my head quickly, but I could tell he didn't believe me.

"Noon, you're so skittish sometimes. I don't want to scare you away." He reached for me. "But you should know . . ." One of his hands wrapped around my waist, pressing me close, while the other tucked a stray piece of my hair behind my ear.

"I want you to stay," he said in a soft, heartfelt voice. "With me."

He lowered his mouth to mine and gently bit my bottom lip. "Always." I gasped and he slid his tongue in, its course slow and wistful. His signature slipped into mine as his hand wound its way through my hair, pulling lightly but firmly, until I was nearly bent back over his arm, with no choice but to yield to him more completely.

After a minute, he raised his head and rested his forehead against mine.

"You know demons choose their mates by marking them with a *signare*."

I frowned in confusion. "Demons mate for life," I said, laughing. "Are you telling me we're married?" I was half-joking, half-terrified.

"Would it be so bad to be married to me, Noon?" he whispered.

I scooted out from under his embrace and backed away. I couldn't help it. With Peter, I could imagine what marriage would be like—children, Etincelle, endless gardens. With Ari . . . ?

"Doesn't a *signare* fade with time?"

"Do you want it to?"

"Why can't you just answer my questions?"

"I'm sorry. It's just that knowing you had dinner with Peter last night, and then knowing you left with him after . . . I don't like it. I wish you hadn't gone."

For a moment, I was speechless. Then I shook my head and sputtered, my anger growing by the second. I didn't even understand my own emotions. One minute I lived in fear of Ari tiring of me, the next I chafed at his possessive streak. I knew I couldn't have it both ways but, honestly, I couldn't tell which would destroy me faster—allowing myself to fall completely and irrevocably in love with him or walking away because I thought I still could.

"What right do you have not to like it?" I demanded. "I don't owe you anything."

Ari just stared at me, arms crossed, eyes narrowed. My cheeks got hot. The fact was, I owed Ari more than I could ever repay. I lowered my gaze and shuffled my feet. A sure sign of guilt.

"Do you have feelings for Peter?" His voice was harsher. I think he feared my answer. For my part, I couldn't believe how fast this conversation had led to places I didn't want to go. Of course I had feelings for Peter. Maybe not the same kind of feelings I had for Ari, but Peter could give me what I wanted.

Ever since we were kids, I knew you were the one for

*me . . . I want to give you your life's dream, Noon . . . Prom-
ise me, if I find the spell and cast it, that you'll be mine . . .*

Ari was watching my face closely. What emotions was he
picking up in my signature? Guilt? Conflict? Love? Betrayal?
I tried to press my magic into a tight, tiny ball but Ari was
doing what he did best, getting through my defenses. Without wanting to, I remembered Peter's face in the moonlight
as he bent to kiss me. I remembered wondering what it would
be like . . .

I felt Ari's magic rush in on me, a searing heat that swirled
around and into me, pouring into every crack and crevice.
His magic seemed to fill me to the point of bursting. He put
his hands on my shoulders and shook me. The look on his
face was frightening. It was the first time I had ever seen Ari
Carmine fight for control.

"Why Peter?" he said, his voice tortured. "I love you for
who you are. He wants to turn you into something you're
not."

"Something I was meant to be," I said quickly, turning
away. It hurt to see Ari this upset. I removed his hands from
my shoulders. "We found the spell." We both knew what
spell I meant.

In the shadows of the library, the lines of Ari's face appeared deeper and more angular than ever. His eyes glowed
like two bits of blown black glass, eerily reflecting the lamp-
lights. He stood still for so long I thought he might have
turned to stone. But finally he stepped back, seeming all the
more dangerous for the distance. Then he walked out and I
let him go, too conflicted to do anything else.

It wasn't until I was back at Megiddo that I realized he'd
said he loved me.

On Tuesday, I was so worked up about what Ari had said
that I actually skipped Evil Deeds and Council Procedure. I couldn't bear to face him. And because I couldn't bear
to tell either Ivy or Fitz what I was really upset about, I
feigned a sore throat and lay in bed all morning. I knew,

however, that I couldn't skip Manipulation. I wasn't nearly as confident in my ability to pass that class as I was with the others. I had made some strides in learning how to shape my magic, but I still lacked the finesse and control of the other Maegesters-in-Training. And my client was proving to be the most difficult. Despite the futility of it, Nergal was still insisting that I spend copious amounts of time researching ways to obtain a divorce, even though I knew none were available absent Lamia's consent. It made me all the more eager for Peter to finish translating Jonathan Aster's spell book so I could ditch Manipulation and any further Maegester classes forever.

Despite my serious predicament, I spent an inordinate amount of time getting ready for class. I shaved my legs, gave myself a facial, and even lacquered my nails. It was ridiculous considering the other things I should have been spending my time on. But I couldn't stop myself. The soothing and scraping, the sloughing and smoothing, all seemed to act as a counterweight to my riotous thoughts. My mind bounced between annulment ideas for Nergal (Would the Demon Council accept some sort of *void ab initio* argument? But, if so, on what grounds?), translation worries (How long would it take Peter to translate Anglentine into the common tongue? How could he be sure the translated spells would work the way they were supposed to?), and Ari's declaration (He *loved* me?).

By midafternoon I had never looked so well coiffed, so well put together on the outside, nor had I ever been so disastrously frazzled on the inside. My day's musings had left me a shaking, writhing, twisted mess. I started to doubt my memory. Maybe Ari really hadn't said he loved me. Maybe I'd just heard him wrong. Or, if he had said it, maybe he didn't mean it. Or maybe he already regretted it.

I grabbed my backpack and an umbrella. Outside Megiddo, the campus walks were wet with the light drizzle that often fell in Halja before Beltane. Holding the glass door open with my hip, I snapped my umbrella up before leaving, thinking not to ruin my morning's efforts. Shallow though they were, they served a purpose. Chin up, I strode down the path toward Rickard Building. I focused on the orderliness of my appearance. Girls with silver coated fingernails and shiny metallic tops didn't panic when a man said they loved them. Women with glossy hair and rouged lips never felt fear. Halfway to Rickard I lowered my umbrella and let the rain drip over me. It was easier to pretend Ari had never said it then it was to bolster my confidence. I might look beautiful outside but I was still the same inside, a weird gender bender with some seriously nasty, seriously lethal powers. One who could never be given roses for Sweet's Day. One who could never take a bite of fresh fruit. One who could never go too near a pregnant woman, much less give birth to a child of her own. I chucked the umbrella in a trash can and stomped toward Rickard, not caring that my hair now felt like matted plaster and my rouge was likely gone.

Because it was the end of the day, not many students were still around at Rickard. After classes, students cleared out pretty quick, anxious to get home to the two to three more hours work awaiting them. I rode up in the lift with only the operator for company, dabbing under my eyes with the ends of my sleeves, hoping the rain's damage wasn't too extensive. I wrung my hair out and tried to fluff it up as best I could. I desperately wished I had worn another top. The silver now seemed entirely too bright.

When I arrived at the Manipulation classroom, Rochester, Ari, and Tosca were already there. Tosca stared grimly as I walked in the room. Rochester nodded. Ari sat up straighter, his face bearing a look of brief surprise, which settled quickly into a look of general wariness. His signature echoed his outward expressions. His magic had briefly sparked, causing my cheeks to flush, and then his output diminished almost immediately. Now all I could sense from him was weak heat, like the sun during the coldest months of winter. My flushed cheeks turned cold and clammy and I imagined my skin looked quite gray in the pale indoor light of the classroom.

I slid into the chair beside Ari and wondered why Luck

had arranged it so that we were sharing a table for Manipulation. I took my journal and an ink pen out of my bag. I shuffled through my backpack ostensibly searching for other materials I might need. Where were Sasha and Brunus? Mercator had never been late before. Would Rochester ever start class? I glanced at my watch. Ten minutes. I didn't think I could sit beside Ari for ten minutes not talking or even looking at him. I wasn't sure how to act. Ari saved me by making the first move.

"You don't look sick," he said.

I turned toward him, almost involuntarily. His dark eyes were sunken. Deep half-moon crescents shadowed the area underneath his lower lashes. His beard had grown in coarse and thick. Unlike some men whose hair had reddish highlights, Ari's beard was jet-black. His hair fell in uncombed waves, spilling over his collar and into his eyes. By all rights Ari should have looked unprofessional and unkempt. But to me his tousled look just made him more appealing. His animalistic appearance made me want to spar with him, both physically and magically. I was struck with a sudden desire to lash out, not in fear or anger but for fun, the way a cat would swipe at a piece of string. Ari's eyes dilated and I suddenly wondered if I could shape my magic like a claw. I'd shaped it like knives and needles, so why not? But the thought of hurting Ari with my claws held me back. Tosca was too weak to notice the byplay but Rochester looked over and frowned. He threw a blast of cold, neutral energy and I suddenly felt like a cat that'd had water thrown on it. My magic sputtered and went out, doused by the cooling shock of Rochester's reminder to control myself. I smiled sheepishly at Ari and mumbled something about feeling better.

"You could never hurt me, you know," he said, his voice pitched low enough so that only I could hear it. It was uncanny the way he seemed to read my mind. "At least not with your magic," he added. "I was worried you'd left. Let Peter cast that blasted spell over you. I would have come looking for you, you know."

I stared at him, willing my jaw to stay closed. He was

always saying stuff like that. Making outlandish claims. I was saved from figuring out how best to reply by the arrival of Brunus and Sasha. Mercator trailed in behind them and Rochester rose to start class. I forced my attention up front.

"Angels," Rochester said preemptively. "Does anyone know why, at least in modern times, we Maegesters have such a close association with the Angels?"

Rochester must have seen mostly blank faces because he kept prodding. "Does anyone know why we share a square with the Joshua School and celebrate most of the major holidays with them?"

I didn't dare look at Ari now. Was it Luck's hand again that we were discussing the very thing that had come between us?

"Does anyone know why the Demon Council works so closely with the Divinity? Why the Joshua School would go to the trouble of hosting a Barrister's Ball at Empyr?"

Sasha raised his hand. Rochester nodded at him. "Mr. de Rocca?"

"Angels are often called as expert witnesses at trial," he said as if reciting a passage direct from the text. "They are renowned historians and excellent linguists. Angels are often called upon to give opinions on matters concerning early post-Apocalyptic knowledge, including changing demon worship practices and the interpretation of ancient laws originally codified in Vandalic, Venetic, or Vestinian."

"Correct. But Angels are useful even before the trial period."

Sasha slumped. It was clear his Angel knowledge font was dry. I didn't dare raise my hand, although I knew only too well how useful Angels could be.

"Angels can be particularly valuable in the field," Rochester encouraged, trying to entice someone else to volunteer further information. I remained mute and no one else seemed to have anything useful to say so Rochester launched into lecture mode.

Apparently, among Barristers, the pretrial discovery phase was a relatively straightforward process involving paper exchanges, legal Q and A, and evidence gathering. For MIT's, however, the discovery stage is fraught with peril. Demons were notoriously secretive and deceptive. They hid everything. So instead of using the more traditional depositions and interrogatories to gain information, MIT's often gathered the facts they needed directly. They conducted their own investigation into the other side's business.

This news was greeted with varying degrees of enthusiasm. We were all having difficulties with our assignments. It was almost impossible to imagine going out and spying on the demons too.

"Most Maegesters engage the help of a Guardian Angel when conducting the investigation," he said, wandering slowly throughout the room. He moved liked a glacier, his immense signature grinding and pressing down upon those around him. I could almost hear the cracking and popping as his signature rubbed up against the others, always pushing, always testing.

"Powerful Angels can mask a Maegester's signature in the field, cast useful protective spells, or serve as an interpreter for any demon who doesn't speak the common tongue. Have any of you thought about who you might ask to be your Guardian Angel?"

Well, I certainly had. And even though choosing Peter would wreak havoc on my relationship with Ari, I didn't think I'd be able to work with anyone else. For starters, Peter and I were already working together. Rochester, the Demon Council, and the Divinity may not know of our clandestine investigation, but we were already conducting one. And it was near to completion, with as big a payoff as I could hope for—the end of classes like this one. Second, I didn't know any other Angels, which brought me to my last and final reason. I trusted Peter. He was my oldest and (except perhaps for Ivy) closest friend.

But before I could declare my intentions, Ari's hand shot up.

"Yes, Mr. Carmine? You have thoughts on a possible candidate?"

Ari nodded. "I'd like to work with Peter Aster."

I blinked. Slowly. Like an owl. And then turned toward Ari, afraid if I moved any faster, my motions might turn frenetic, like when a Lethe river shark smells blood and attacks or when a wolf viciously shakes its prey to break its neck. For a moment, I almost wanted to do that to Ari. *What was he thinking?* He no more wanted to work with Peter than a Mederi wanted fire in her garden. Then I saw his mouth twitch up at the corners and my jaw dropped. I stared at Ari as he and Rochester calmly discussed his shocking, traitorous, thieving suggestion.

"An unusual choice," Rochester said. "You know he dropped out of school recently, although I hear he's back. His father's not very prominent either. But he has a strong reputation at the Joshua School. I hear he's brilliant, astute, and driven. And his specialty is an interesting and ambitious new field of study—power polarities, the *reversal* of power and negation."

Ari clenched his jaw and pressed his lips together in a firm line. It must have been hard for him to hear Rochester sing Peter's praises.

"I've also heard he's an amateur archeologist, as interested in the history of spellcasting as its future," Rochester said, "All things considered, he's a fine candidate. Have you approached him yet?"

Ari shook his head.

"No? Well, despite Mr. Aster's patchy record, I agree. He has great potential as a Guardian. Don't wait to speak with him."

Rochester turned to me.

"Ms. Onyx, any thoughts on who you'd like to work with over at the Joshua School?"

After class, Ari quickly packed up his books and left. I sprinted to catch up with him but didn't reach him until he was in Timothy's Square. He was just about to turn the corner and walk down Victory Street when I called his name, causing him to abruptly stop, but not turn around. A light, steady drizzle dribbled down from the sky, making me regret my earlier umbrella toss. I reached Ari and walked around to face him.

"What are you doing?" I cried.

"What do you mean?" Laudably, his tone wasn't the least bit facetious. He sounded serious. I made a derisive sound that was a combination of disgust and disbelief.

"You know what I mean. Telling Rochester you want to work with Peter."

"I do."

"No you don't," I said, shaking my head.

He smiled then, but without warmth or humor. "I do," he said simply, "because I don't want you working with him."

"Peter won't work with you."

Ari shrugged. "It'll buy me time," he said.

"Time for what?"

Suddenly I was too aware of the fact that we were alone for the first time since he'd said he loved me. And we hadn't even talked about it. We were only talking around it. He stared at me. I swallowed, standing my ground.

"Time to convince you," Ari said, glancing around to see if anyone was watching us. It was late in the day and the temperature was dropping, but it was still pretty warm for spring. The slight heat and light rain produced a misty shroud that shielded us from prying eyes. Those few students who were still out and about weren't recognizable. They were just gray shapes walking in the rain, anonymous drifters floating around campus.

"I want you to come to the Barrister's Ball," Ari said. His voice had an odd catch to it that I wasn't used to hearing.

"I'm already going," I said. "I promised Ivy I'd go with her."

Ari shook his head. "I want you to promise *me*. I want you to go as my date. Before you make irreversible choices, I deserve a chance to show you what one night of a life with me would be like. I deserve a real date."

I stared at him incredulously. I don't know what I'd been

expecting after that stunt he'd just pulled in Manipulation but I definitely hadn't expected this. And I certainly didn't expect what came next.

"And I want you to come home with me for Beltane Break. Meet my family. I think you'll like them. They're Hyrkes, you know. We live in Bradbury, not Etincelle. You won't have to talk about St. Lucifer's unless you want to. We could just hang out and do Hyrke stuff. You'd like that, right? Matt finally decided to go to Gaillard and you and he could talk."

He seemed to realize he sounded like Fitz and closed his mouth. He cleared his throat and looked away. But he remained silent when he looked back at me, apparently deciding whatever he had been about to say was ten things too many. His uncharacteristic rush of words had the most profound effect on me. He was nervous. Luck below, Ari Carmine, the man who was ranked *Primoris* in Manipulation class, the man who had formerly been a demon executioner for my father, the man who turned me into a melted puddle of pleading desire nearly every night in the stacks of Corpus Justica, was nervous about asking *me* on a date.

I had qualms, to be sure. It wouldn't be a good idea to show up on Ari's arm. For so many reasons. First, there was the fact that he was opposing counsel and we'd been warned many times to avoid even the appearance of collaboration. Certainly, appearing arm in arm at the Barrister's Ball might be reasonable grounds for thinking we were in cahoots. Second, Rochester had warned me that he thought I was in danger of being enchanted by Ari. Swooning in Ari's arms, as I was sure to do at some point if I went with him to the ball, would lend credence to that theory. Third, since the ball was being held at Empyr, it was inevitable that Peter would be there. If I arrived with Ari, would Peter refuse to cast the Reversal Spell over me? We were so close, was one dance worth throwing away my dream?

But I could have had a hundred qualms and I still would have agreed. Because the one thing, *the only thing*, that convinced me, was that one moment of vulnerability I'd glimpsed before Ari had clamped his mouth shut. If Ari had tried to bribe me (by agreeing to rescind his request to work with Peter, for instance) or if he'd tried to coerce me (by attempting to assert some sort of *signare* right) or if he'd tried to threaten me (the threats he could make were limitless), I would have flatly rejected him. But he so obviously wanted me to go with him, and for such a normal reason, that I couldn't bear the thought of saying no.

Besides, hadn't I been incensed by Rochester's completely inappropriate interest in my love life? Had I ever felt sick or poisoned when in Ari's presence? Confused and muddled—yes. At times, undeniably rattled, but the feelings Ari aroused in me were as different from those I'd experienced with Serafina as a Gaillard street party was likely to be from the Barrister's Ball. Lastly, did I really care what Peter thought of my relationship with Ari? Did I care if, in the end, Peter refused to help me?

Well . . . that was the million dollar question. But not one I had to answer now. Truth is, I *was* a little nervous about how Peter might react, but Ari was watching my face carefully. I knew how keenly he could sense my feelings and I wanted him to know that I wanted to go with him.

"You convinced me," I said, reaching up and lowering his head to mine. "I'll go to the ball with you." I kissed him then, slow and sweet and then moved my hand lower until my fingertips rested lightly on the soft linen of his shirt just above his demon mark. Beneath my hand, he tensed. Suddenly, I knew what I wanted—at least with Ari.

"Where can we go where no one else will bother us?" I asked him. "Somewhere with no librarians, desk clerks, or classmates?"

His bold gaze met mine.

"Somewhere we could walk to right now?" I asked, reaching for his hands.

Ari's face beamed with an emotion I hardly recognized on him—*happiness*. In fact, I was pretty sure I had just made him grin.

He grabbed my hand with his and said one word before bolting from the spot with me in tow, "Lekai."

If I was doubtful that Lekai Auditorium would provide the privacy we needed for what I had in mind, I needn't have worried. All lectures, classes, and events were over for the day. In fact, when we got there, the interior was so dark, I half expected the doors to be locked. Thankfully, they weren't and we went right in.

Like all of the buildings on St. Luck's campus, Lekai was grand. Its lobby was large, almost majestic, with rich embellishments. Front and center was an ornately carved wooden counter where students and guests could check their cloaks. On either side of the counter were twin staircases rising to the mezzanine level. Ari lit a small, glowing fireball and led me upstairs.

"Where are we going?" I whispered.

"Somewhere I've wanted to take you all semester." At the top of the stairs, he led me around the corner and into a small room. There were no exterior windows in this room. It was even darker than the lobby had been. In the flickering light of his magic, I got a glimpse of a large, dust-covered desk; a terra-cotta oil lamp; a wall of cubbies stuffed with yellowing letters, crumbling scrolls, and fraying scarves; and an old settee. *The manager's office,* I thought.

"How did you know about this place?" I asked, worried for a moment that I wasn't the first girl he'd brought here. But his signature was still radiating what I'd seen on his face earlier—*happiness*—so I had no reason to doubt his answer.

"Mercator. Lekai hasn't had a manager since before Seknecus became the dean of demon affairs."

With easy control I couldn't help but envy, Ari directed the fire from his hand onto the wick of the lamp. We stood facing one another, the warm, orange glow of the wick echoing our signatures. I swiped at the rain that had beaded on my cheek while we were still outside.

The care that I had taken with my appearance earlier today was laughable now, the effect totally ruined. My hair hung in drippy threads, my makeup was surely smeared, and my silver top clung tightly to me, heavy and wet. Ari looked at me with smoky, unreadable eyes. He must have sensed my need because he clasped me to him and raked his hands up under my shirt. He skimmed his fingers across my back, bringing delicious heat to skin left slick and damp from my rain-soaked shirt. He lowered his head to my neck and breathed deep. His breath tickled my ear and I gripped his shoulders. He caught my earlobe between his teeth and nibbled, carefully kneading muscles tense with the stress of an unbearable workload, two questionable futures, and countless crises of confidence.

His tongue began a slow exploration of the sensitive outer edge of my ear. I shivered and he brought his hands around to my abdomen. I knew he wanted to raise them higher and I tensed, thinking of the last time he'd touched my demon mark. But he moved his hands to my hips and squeezed me tighter to him. My breasts were crushed against his hard chest and the air left my lungs, making me breathless.

Ari captured my mouth in a scalding kiss before I had time to breathe. My hands raked through his hair, but then, as I started to feel light-headed, I moved them down and started pressing against Ari's shoulders, urging him to release me. He did, but only for a moment. His kisses became fierce and possessive. Finally, he nipped my lip and relented, holding me close.

Ari seemed delighted with my response to him. And I have to admit, he made me feel so desirable I was willing to let him do almost anything to me. I caught my breath and he started again, this time nipping at my neck. His hands worked their way underneath my shirt again and he moved them around back, dipping his fingers below my waistband. Slowly, he traced the top of my pants. His fingers stopped at the front pewter button. I knew what he wanted. I knew why he paused there, his fingers stiff, his mouth hovering, his breath hot on my skin. I knew what he was asking.

"Noon—*Nouiomo*," he begged, wrapping his hands in my

hair. He brushed his lips down my nose and across my cheekbone. "Let me love you."

I would have said yes even if he hadn't asked so nicely. This is what I'd come here to do after all. In answer, I threw my arms around his neck.

His warm, soft, full lips closed on mine as he scooped me up into his arms. He laid me down on the settee, oblivious to everything but us. I could tell by his signature that he was lost in his arousal. His signature felt red and hazy, thick and viscous, enlarged. It bumped up against mine but instead of the popping and grinding sensation I sometimes experienced when rubbing up against a signature that was stronger than mine, there was only a slow gooey feeling as the edge of Ari's magic met mine. Without waiting for further permission, Ari stripped off my top. I lay beneath him, my breasts heaving beneath my lacy brassiere, my eyes likely dilated to full black, my breath hitching convulsively, thinking if all there was to love was a physical reaction then I had been in love with Ari Carmine since the day we'd first met.

"You are amazing," Ari said, his voice husky and warm. His eyes fastened on my demon mark and I marvelled that he could see its pale shape in the dim light from the lamp.

His hand moved up and unclasped my brassiere. My breasts sprang free, jiggling a bit. They'd always been more than ample and I tried to compensate by buying a brassiere two sizes too small. Ari grunted in surprise and, seeming unable to help himself, immediately lowered his mouth to one, sucking roughly on the nipple. I mewled in protest as the other one puckered, awaiting his touch. It was embarrassing how my body betrayed me, showing Ari the feelings I didn't want to acknowledge.

He lifted his head and smiled at me, his eyes half-closed with desire. "Your body and your magic are always in sync, Noon. You are put together so well, both inside and out." He gazed reverently up and down the length of me. "You are the most beautiful creature I have ever seen." I swallowed, my throat dry.

Ari splayed his hand across my stomach and moved it lower, over my thin gabardine trousers to the heat between my legs. He cupped the area as he kissed me, his tongue exploring my mouth, slow and deep. I pressed against him, wanting more. The cool wet cotton of his shirt rubbed against my bared nipples, causing an unbearable friction. I sat up suddenly, and tore the brassiere from my shoulders. I yanked Ari's shirt off. I glanced at his face, expecting to see a wolfish grin, but instead I saw a look of fierce longing.

He pushed me back onto the settee but instead of kissing me, he started licking me, slowly, with the tip of his tongue. He traced the line of my jaw and the pulse in my throat. He nibbled at my collarbone, and then, taking great care to avoid my demon mark, he trailed his tongue lower, between my breasts, and then in lazy circles around an areola, getting closer and closer to the center, where I most wanted to be touched. But he was agonizingly slow about it. He seemed to take great pleasure in teasing me.

He was still circling with his tongue when he popped the front button on my trousers and slid his hand underneath the slip of silk that served as panties. I gasped, knowing where his fingers were headed. Still it was a shock when he plunged in, taking my nipple in his mouth at the same time. I bucked beneath him and he shushed me, murmuring my name.

He haltingly tugged my pants off. When they were finally bunched around my ankles, I hastily kicked them off the rest of the way. He stood up to remove his as I lay splayed on the settee, nearly naked and waiting. For one tense moment, I second-guessed myself. How could I ignore his wishes after this? What promises might he demand? But I couldn't stop the wanting and I probably would have offered him anything right then if he would just finish what we started. Ari's signature radiated *happiness* and *arousal*. I remembered how anxious he'd been about asking me to the ball. How much he had wanted me to say yes. This man cared about me. He *loved* me. More than I ever thought possible.

The sound of the rain on the roof above us stopped and all was silent. There were no footsteps or voices. I couldn't even hear the sounds of the cabriolets splashing on the still-wet streets outside. The entire world seemed far off and distant. There was only us.

Ari stood above me, hands fisted on his hips, filling himself with the sight of me—as far from nervous now as any man could be. His gaze lingered on the tiny strip of lace covering the only part of me that was still hidden from him. He arched an eyebrow, clearly contemplating the artful but impractical design.

"You better have worn those for me," he said gruffly. I blushed, remembering how I'd spent the earlier part of my day, and wondered again at Luck's hand in all this. How much of my destiny was really mine to direct?

I drank in the sight of Ari hulking above me. In the long shadows he looked almost demonlike. But I wasn't afraid. He knelt before me, hunched and ready, his muscles bunched, his eyes gleaming. I shook with anticipation.

"I want you, Nouiomo." He bowed his head as though making an offering and then looked up at me, his eyes full of longing. "Do you want me?"

It was so unexpected. No one had ever asked me before. But then I'd never given myself to anyone the way I was giving myself to Ari. Every part of me—body, mind, and magic, was open to receive him. I wanted nothing else but to be full of Ari.

I slid off my panties. Any barriers between us now seemed ludicrous. Ari growled, a sound so real, so animal-like, I twitched in response.

"Yes," I said, opening my arms wide. My voice was throaty and rough with desire.

Ari lowered himself down on top of me and nudged my legs apart with his knees. He dipped his head to kiss me, but I knew the kiss wouldn't last long. It was time. He wanted something more and so did I. He lowered his mouth to my demon mark and kissed me there. I cried out, forgetting the sting of his touch there, and arched my back. My hips rose to meet his. Ari's magic swirled around mine, the edges between our signatures blurring. He entered me, a slow thrusting motion that filled every part of me. I wriggled and twisted under him, wanting to get closer, wanting him deeper, just wanting *more*.

He plunged in and out in rhythmic strokes designed to send me over the edge. Just when I was on the verge of peaking, he would slow until I begged him *faster, Ari* or *please, Ari!* or just simply cried out his name. Finally, when I had been reduced to such a whimpering, pleading state I wasn't sure how I could ever hold my head up again, he bit my demon mark, drawing blood, and plunged himself so deep inside me I thought I'd be skewered in half. He shuddered convulsively and I felt the world slip away. I came with such explosive force I feared we'd be singed to ashes. Who knew I would respond so pleasurably to such a rough touch?

Afterward, it seemed as if Ari didn't want to let me go. We lay on the settee, naked in each other's arms. Ari's signature wrapped around and inside of mine as surely as his body had. It felt like someone had poured honey all over me. The sensation of *Ari* was everywhere on me, in my hair, on my skin—

The sound of one of Lekai's outer doors opening dissolved the honey feeling as surely as a bucket of vinegar would have. I leapt up and grabbed my clothes. Ari was right behind me. We heard footsteps echo on the marble floor of the lobby below us. We dressed in a frantic rush, leaning against one another to pull on pants and shirts, fumbling with buttons and brassiere clasps, tying laces and tucking in shirttails. Finally, when we were both fully clothed, we collapsed on top of one another in a heap of quiet laughter. Ari scooped me up, settled me in his lap, and waited for the footsteps in the lobby to recede. A moment later, I heard the sound of a lock turning in Lekai's outer door and wondered if we were locked in for the night. Beneath me, Ari shifted into a more comfortable position. The muscles in his thighs hardened and I grinned.

Maybe being locked in wasn't such a bad thing after all.

Chapter 18

ॐ

The week passed in a blur. The semester was winding down. After the Beltane Break, we'd return to school to start prepping for finals. There was an aura of celebration around campus, which was at odds with my feelings. My relationship with Ari entered a new phase.

That night at Lekai had been unlike anything I'd ever experienced before. It shouldn't have been shocking to me, since I'd only ever dated Hyrkes and had never, *ever* either lost control or given over control during sex (Luck forbid the potentially disastrous results for my poor unsuspecting past lovers). But the encounter with Ari had surprised me, wholly because I had not known, until now, what I'd been missing. And now that I knew, I couldn't wait to experience it all again (and again and again and again). But Ari became stubborn. He refused to meet me anywhere in secret and instead asked me a dozen times daily to accompany him (in plain sight) back to his room at Infernus. But caution compelled me to avoid such a public display of my affection. So I always shook my head, or pulled my hand away, or turned my cheek when he sought my lips.

I wavered, caught between agonized yearning and debilitating indecision. Ari simply wasn't going to hide how he felt anymore, no matter what arguments I made about impropriety. As he pointed out frequently, sometimes with humor, but mostly just with an increasing mix of belligerence and incredulity, if I was considering allowing a nonmatriculated Angel to cast an unfathomably powerful, dangerous, unauthorized spell over me, then I couldn't possibly be worried about what the St. Luck's faculty would think of us dating.

Thursday night of that week, Night rang room 112 of Megiddo. For once, I was there instead of at Corpus Justica (since Ari never met me at the library anymore, studying in the stacks had lost all appeal). The connection between Maize and New Babylon was incredibly patchy. Though every dorm room at St. Luck's now had an electro-harmonic, I knew the tribes (who eschewed modern aesthetics as much as the Angels adored it) still had only one each. Night was likely calling from his Monarch's office. After some initial pleasantries, made difficult by the bad connection, Night got right to the point.

"Noon —meter recently received a request for assis— from . . . families in Sheol . . . wife of . . . the residents there is due . . . trouble delivering in the past . . ." Night's voice became even more difficult to hear. ". . . Neighbors took up a collection for midwife . . . Heather Alumen . . . coming up . . . North-South Express . . ."

Night's voice trailed off. I was surprised I hadn't set the damn harmonic on fire yet. I resisted the almost overwhelming urge to smash the receiver on my desk and crack it in half. Honestly, carrier doves or scrying in a mirror would be preferable to the pain of communicating via Halja's harmonics.

"One of Demeter's Mederies is coming up to New Babylon by train?" I shouted.

"Yes!"

"Okay . . ." Why was Night calling? Did he believe the Mederi was in danger? Had she already left?

Over the next few painstaking minutes I was able to piece together what Night's concern was and how he hoped I might help. Apparently, one of Demeter's Mederies, Heather Alumen, was coming up to New Babylon tomorrow to help a woman in Sheol. She'd be riding up on the North-South Express. Demeter was worried about her traveling alone but couldn't spare anyone to go with her. No one at the Council (including Karanos) believed Heather would be in any danger. After all, no Mederies had been attacked or abducted since before Bryde's Day.

Night was hoping I might meet Heather at the train station tomorrow, just to set her mind at ease. I was a Maegester-in-Training, right? And wasn't the train station right next to St. Luck's campus? I jotted down Heather's arrival time, my heart racing just the least little bit. The last abduction had occurred months ago. Alerts had been taken down and the Council's attention had turned to other cases. Our campus had long ago resumed its usual, albeit crazed, rhythm. So how likely was it that I would encounter demon trouble at the train station tomorrow?

I told Ari about my plan to meet Heather. He insisted on coming, which was fine with me. If I were going to run into a demon at dusk at the creepy, century-old New Babylon train station, I couldn't think of who I would want with me more than him. After a round of uneventful classes and a quick bite at Marduk's, Ari and I walked over.

Despite Ari's steady presence, I grew jumpy. Rochester had shown me time and again every Wednesday morning that I lacked control. I had immense difficulty shaping my magic into anything that could be used as a weapon. I also had trouble throwing fire. My magic tended to either sputter or explode in the unlikeliest of places. Neither effect would be very helpful if we ran into a demon tonight. I reminded myself there was no reason to think we would. No Mederi had been threatened in months.

The New Babylon train station had been built over a century ago. Clearly inspired by the metal beasts that would be stopping, docking, and disgorging passengers in it, the building's architects had designed it as a huge, boxy, black structure with a giant, belching smokestack rising up out of its roof. We entered and quickly found track three, where the North-South Express would be arriving. A few Hyrkes milled about, likely waiting to board an outgoing train or looking for arriving passengers, as we were. I didn't sense any waning magic except for Ari's. His signature was gauzy and loose.

We took a seat on a metal bench that overlooked the track Heather would be arriving on. I had no idea what she looked like. But she'd be wearing a green Mederi traveling cloak, so I figured we'd be able to pick her out without too much trouble. Ari's signature settled over me like shimmering light—slightly warm, slightly electric, infinitely bright. It occurred to me then, that were I to allow Peter to cast the Reversal Spell over me, I wouldn't be able to feel Ari like this anymore. And *that* would certainly change our relationship, even more than what had happened at Lekai.

"What do you think happened to the Mederies who went missing at the start of the semester?"

Ari's grim expression was answer enough. But it soon became apparent he didn't want to talk about anything that had occurred months ago. In fact, he didn't want to talk at all.

He reached for my hand and flipped it over so that it was palm side up. Ever so lightly he pushed the sleeve of my shirt up past my elbow. With the barest touch of his fingertips on my skin, he traced the lines in my palm, across and down, up and over, swirling, curling, moving to the tip of one of my fingers and then back down again. Then to the next. The tips of his fingers tingled against my skin as he drew invisible sigils with his magic. My palm itched and I longed to scratch it, but we both knew that wouldn't release the tension he had created in other, deeper parts of my body. He leaned toward me, his face blocking the light, and then dipped his head so that his mouth hovered near my ear.

"Stay with me tonight," he said, his voice low and rumbling.

Oh, how I longed to. But it was a horrible idea, for so many reasons.

"I said I'd go to the ball with you," I said, turning my face toward him, thinking he would kiss me then. I wanted him to, as much as I wanted to return to Infernus with him later. But while I couldn't have the latter, I could use this secluded spot and the remaining minutes until the train arrived for the former. But when I leaned toward him, he backed away smiling. He moved his mouth toward my ear again as if he were going to share some deep dark secret.

"Stay." He blew gently into my ear. I shivered and repressed an uncharacteristic giggle. "With." With a featherweight touch, Ari traced the veins in my wrist with the tips of his fingers, all the way to my elbow. His fingers hovered there as his mouth had hovered behind my ear, and then they moved with shocking swiftness to my armpit—"Me!"— where he tickled me mercilessly until I shrieked so loudly everyone would have come running, but for the fact that, at that very moment the train pulled up, all whistles and wind.

My hair blew madly about my face and Ari lowered my sleeve. I rubbed my cheeks, not wanting to meet this Mederi blushing like a schoolgirl, but Ari laughed at my efforts.

"You'll just make it worse," he said, smiling. "Come on." He stood up and so did I.

Heather stepped off the train a moment later. There was no mistaking who she was. Even if it weren't for the traveling cloak, I would have recognized her from the overly anxious look on her face. She was short and squat, with a round face and wide eyes that darted every which way. *Looking for us? Looking for demons? Probably both . . .*

I put an end to at least half her worries by stepping forward and introducing Ari and myself.

"I'm Heather Alumen," the Mederi said, without extending her hand. Instead, she clutched a small handbag in front

of her as if it were a shield and demons were already directing
fire at her midsection. She glanced back over her shoulder
toward the train. "You're Nightshade's sister?" she asked. I
nodded and she craned her neck to peek over my left shoulder. "I hadn't expected you to be so . . ." But then her voice
trailed off and I was left to wonder what she could have
meant. *Hadn't expected me to be so—what? Feminine?
What had she expected a woman with waning magic to look
like?* "Tall," she said finally, standing up on the tips of her
toes to squint at another passenger deboarding behind me.

After a few more furtive glances, she told us her ride up
had been nerve-racking. Every minute of it she'd been convinced she'd be attacked or abducted. Her fear bordered on
hysteria, so completely out of proportion to her experience,
that even I found myself thinking we might have all overesti-
mated the risk. I found myself reassuring her repeatedly that
we'd neither seen nor felt a demon presence here at the train
station. It was likely she was in no danger at all. Still, just to
fulfill our chaperoning duties, we accompanied her in the cab
to Sheol.

We pulled up to the house at the address Heather had been
given. All the lights were out so we trudged up to the door
and rang the bell. An older, forty-something farmer's wife
answered. She was thin and frail looking—and clearly not
pregnant.

She'd never heard of Demeter and certainly hadn't sent for
any Mederi.

"What in Luck's name would I pay you with?" she said
with a laugh and then she'd said good night and gently but
firmly shut the door in my face. I couldn't see Ari's expression in the dark, but I could feel his signature. It bubbled with
unease.

"Do you think I wrote the address down wrong?" Heather
asked. *Doubtful,* I thought. But we had the cabdriver take us
to the three closest houses just in case. At each, the story was
the same. No one had called for a Mederi. Not only had they
not called for a Mederi, but they weren't aware of any of their

neighbors having done so. And no one they knew in Sheol was pregnant.

The cab ride back to the train station was silent. Heather had completely clammed up. She sat, nervously twisting her cloak, looking out the window. I think she was realizing just how much danger she'd been in—what might have happened to her if Ari and I had not met her at the train station.

For my part, I was wondering who had lured her up here. Because I was sure, even if I had no direct proof, that it was the same demon who was responsible for the earlier attacks and abductions.

I knew Ari had said the train station had no patron, but what if, like St. Lucifer's, the train station had once been something else? What if the patron demon of whatever had once been there returned to find his devotion center paved over, his followers gone, and himself forgotten? Would that be enough to turn an adoration-loving, rule-following *regulare* demon into a vengeful, murderous *rogare*? Unfortunately, I believed the answer was going to be yes.

A ri and I arranged for Heather to ride back to Maize in the front of the train with the conductor. She was grateful, but her gaze never once settled on mine. Instead she constantly scanned the train station. She reminded me of a rabbit. The moment before the fox got it. I pushed that thought to the back of my mind and bade her farewell. She seemed to relax a bit once the conductor shut the door and soon the train pulled out of the station.

Ari and I waited a few minutes, watching it go. We stood side by side, not touching, but as the train departed, I felt Ari's signature slip easily into mine. A moment later, however, I sensed an interloper. The stinging sensation of someone else's unwelcome waning magic reached the edge of mine. The stinging turned into an angry buzzing and I suddenly knew exactly which demon was standing behind me. I turned around.

Sure enough, Nergal stood there. Instantly, I was glad he hadn't caught me in a compromising physical position with Ari; it was bad enough he'd just sensed our signatures melding together. That alone could be academically disastrous.

"Hello, Nergal," I said, keeping my voice neutral. I wasn't happy to see him outside of our regularly scheduled meetings, but there weren't any pluses to picking a fight with him either. Ari nodded politely to him. Nergal ignored him and spoke directly to me.

"My, what interesting company you keep for your Friday night dates, Ms. Onyx. Opposing counsel? Wonder what Seknecus would say about that, hmm?"

"It's not a date."

Nergal gave me a look of exaggerated surprise. "No? You sure look cozy together, although"—he dropped his voice as if Ari couldn't hear him—"I heard that Mr. Carmine's preferences leaned toward women with, well . . . a different sort of magic."

"What are you doing here, Nergal?" I snapped, finally losing patience.

"I was just about to ask you that, Nouiomo. Shouldn't you be in the library, researching ways to grant me my divorce?"

"Actually, I'm headed there right now."

Nergal brightened, literally. The wattage of his signature became radioactive and I worried that all my skin had suddenly turned to dust—that one puff from the Prince of Drought would send it flaking off into the cool night air.

"Then you won't mind if I walk with you. Make sure you get there safely. You know, someone's bound to report that they saw a demon here tonight." He grinned malevolently. "And I wouldn't want anything to happen to you *before* you find a solution to my problem."

Thankfully, the walk from the train station to Corpus Justica was short. Researching the train station's history, however, took forever.

Three hours later, I finally found what I was looking for in the *Demon Register*:

VIGILIA *(C. 1300-1900), Patron Demon of Traveling Women, Particularly Traveling Mederies.*

Vigilia was spawned in the early fourteenth century. Hyrke mothers began pleading to her for safe journeys sometime in the midfifteenth century. During the seventeenth century, Mederies began to adore her. The tribes established a devotion center on a fallow field, north of Victory Street.

Vigilia's following reached its peak during the late eighteenth century. The makeshift tents and traveling fairs that had previously been sited on the Victory Street field were torn down and an elaborate stone shrine was constructed in its place. Inside the shrine, a group of Mederies kept constant vigil over an eternal flame to honor their patron, Vigilia.

Vigilia left New Babylon circa 1900. Reports vary as to why. Some say she fell in love with ***CHRISTOS*** and the two left to travel the lands far beyond Halja. Some say she fought with ***ADEONA*** and ***ABEONA*** over followers and that the two sisters overpowered Vigilia and killed her. Some say, after 600 years, she simply died of old age. Regardless of the reason, her followers diminished and finally disappeared altogether. The Victory Street shrine was torn down in 1911 to make room for the New Babylon Train Station.

Chapter 19

ॡ

When I awoke the next morning, I felt like the strings of a violin whose pegs had been wound too tight. Edgy, anxious . . . jittery, fidgety . . . rattled, ruffled . . . pick an adjective, they *all* applied. I spilled my coffee twice, knocked over a bottle of nail lacquer, and, for the first time in weeks, accidentally set something on fire. As I tossed the smoldering remains of my slippers in the trash can, I wondered if I'd be able to pull it together by evening. Because tonight was the much anticipated, long awaited, social event of the semester—the Barrister's Ball.

Much as the food at Empyr was worth waiting for, we couldn't go the whole day without eating, so Ivy and I decided to grab lunch at Marduk's before getting into any serious primping. I ordered a prosciutto and provolone sandwich. I debated adding a cappuccino to my order but didn't think my nerves could take it, so I ordered chamomile tea instead. Its taste was weak but the effects of the mild, warm drink, combined with the cozy, unpretentious atmosphere of Marduk's, finally allowed me a moment's respite from my agitated thoughts.

Fitz was off handling some domestic matter for the Seknecai estate. (Ivy and I had wondered who he was trying to curry more favor with, Seknecus or his mother, and decided it didn't much matter, since it probably amounted to the same thing.) Once Fitz found out Ivy would have me for company at the ball, he'd wasted no time in asking Babette Sanders.

Babette wasn't very motivated in the classroom, but she was extraordinarily pretty and she knew how to have fun. No surprise then that Fitz had been keen on her for months and she'd accepted his invite with unrestrained zeal. Though Fitz was hopeless at Evil Deeds, he was Darius Dorio's darling in Council Procedure. His performances in that class were almost as electrifying as Dorio's. In addition to his budding theatrical skills (which boded well for him if he chose to become a litigator), Fitz was equally attractive to the opposite sex, if in a ruddy, street urchin sort of way. I could understand their mutual appeal and envied them their cavalier attitude toward lust. There was no pretension about where their night would lead. Asking either of them would have gotten the same response: a toss in bed at the Stirling, a super chic Hyrke hotel where Fitz had rented a room for the night.

I was gazing into my teacup half-hopeful, half-fearful that maybe Ari had done the same when Ivy kicked my chair and said, "Who is *that*?" and pointed at the door. I looked up and then grinned. I got up from the table so quickly I knocked my chair over and I raced through the crowded pub, bumping table corners, upsetting drinks, and thumping the backs of heads in an effort to embrace the tall, sinister-looking man who had just entered the room.

"Night!" I shouted, hugging him fiercely. His eyes twinkled and his mouth twitched. For Night, this was the equivalent of my grin.

Luck, how I'd *missed* him. Over the past four months he'd written a letter or two, and there was that horribly hard to hear call from two nights ago, but I hadn't really *talked* to

Night since midwinter and letters and harmonic connections were never as good as seeing someone in person. Circumstances had forced Night and I on such divergent paths, paths each of us would have chosen for the other, but we'd started from the same beginnings. We'd shared everything (first a womb, then distant parents, Hyrke schools, a best friend, and a shameful secret) all our lives. Only recently had our experiences started differing.

"You're not here because something happened to Heather on the way back to Maize, are you? She arrived safely, right?"

"Yes, she's fine. Thanks to you. I'll tell you all about what's going on down in Maize once I sit down. I'm starving. You know there's no diner car on the North-South Express?"

Night laughed in disbelief and I led him over to the table where Ivy was sitting, anxious to introduce someone important from my old life to someone important from my new life.

"Ivy," I said, with my arm still around Night's towering frame, "this is my brother, Night."

"Nightshade," he clarified, extending his hand to her. She clasped it, saying simply, "Ivana." They regarded each other for a moment and then Night pulled out a chair for me and sat down in another.

"So how's the tribe?" I asked, unable to resist prodding Night. He had to know how anxious I was to hear *any* news, not just about Heather and Demeter's reaction to what had happened last night, but anything about Demeter and how the tribe was treating him and what life was like for him now that he was living down in southern Halja.

"The seasons are different down there, for one thing," said Night. He pulled off the black traveling cloak he'd been wearing and draped it over the back of his chair. By all rights, Night should have been the one on the Maegester's path. He certainly looked the part. His hair was jet-black and glossy, worn long and parted severely down the middle. His teeth and skin were as blindingly white as mine, his eyes as dark, but that's where our similarities ended. I was by no means a frail or petite woman, but Night dwarfed me. Even sitting in his chair, he appeared to loom over Ivy and me.

"The snow at Yule was unlike anything I've ever seen. Things just started thawing out down there recently. We had snow for Eostre. Can you imagine?" he said, shaking his head. He accepted a menu from the server and glanced over it, choosing the Innkeeper's Pie. I made a face.

"Ugh! Why do you eat that stuff when you don't have to?"

"Because I'm sick to death of grazing like a cow," he said. "You're not getting anything else?"

I shook my head and Night turned toward Ivy. "Ivana?"

Ivy order another espresso, although I thought that might have been a mistake. She seemed as jumpy as me, and Night continued his tale.

"Finding my place within Demeter took a while. It was a huge adjustment just getting used to how Mederies live. Aside from the fact that they're all women," he winked at Ivy and me, "there's the fact that they're absolutely obsessed with flowers. Luck granted me a boon though. My talent thins out at the blooming end of the Mederies' power spectrum. Thankfully, I've managed to avoid most of the greenhouse and potting shed duties to focus on the area I like best."

"Which is?" I asked.

"Infectious disease."

It was an unusual answer for a Mederi. Most were more delicate and would have answered, "healing people" or "curing illness," preferring to focus on their patients, rather than the silent, faceless, often deadly enemies they fought. But Night and I had not been raised to be delicate. Subtle, yes. Delicate, no.

Ivy frowned and looked uncomfortable. I tried to figure out why. Night might be embracing his unchosen career more easily than I (he practically oozed confidence now), but it wasn't that long ago that I'd seen him as miserable with shame and confusion as I often still was.

The server brought over Night's meat pie and, despite my having said I hated them, I had to admit Marduk's made the best: inside, minced beef and onions; on top, a golden brown, buttery, flaky crust. I stole a sip of the red wine Night had ordered and listened as he told us more about the tribe he'd chosen to join.

"Demeter's Monarch is Linnaea Saphir," Night said, tucking hungrily into the pie. "She's young, only twenty-six, but she's been at the helm for almost two years now. When I first appeared, Demeter didn't know what to do with me. They tried me in one area after another, passing me around like a hot coal. Everyone thought I'd chosen them as a default.

"But even if Hawthorn or Gaia *had* wanted me, I wanted Demeter," he said chuckling, and I knew why. Hawthorn was our mother's tribe. They likely viewed Night's birth with as much shame as our mother, and Gaia, the strict traditionalists, never would have accepted him. "Demeter has a liberal reputation. They're more accepting of the unconventional. I knew they'd be more open to training a male Mederi, and I also wanted to learn some of their newer healing techniques, especially the ones having to do with communicable diseases. Too many tribes shun Hyrke healing methods. Demeter has had success combining ancient Mederi and modern Hyrke practices. Think what that might mean for some of the river settlements."

Ivy perked up. Maybe I'd misread her earlier expression. Of course, anything concerning the river settlements concerned Ivy. The Jayneses made their living off of the Lethe and those who lived along its banks.

"Yes," she jumped in, "the farmers at Bloodshot Downs are often plagued with disease. They're too near the sea so their wells go brackish and they can't seem to get any of their crop rotations right so they're malnourished too."

Night nodded, his face grave. Failed crops and bad wells often meant death for settlers. They usually couldn't afford to pay for a full-time Mederi to live among them and a settlement like Bloodshot Downs was too far east to ship a Mederi back and forth easily or affordably.

"You would know all about the settlers' problems," Night said, turning toward Ivy. She looked uncomfortable under the full weight of Night's stare. "I'd heard of your family—

the enterprising Jayneses and their fleet of ferries—but Noon also filled me in on some of your background. Have you really been to each and every settlement?"

Now that Ivy had Night's full attention, she looked reluctant to speak. Not one for false modesty, Ivy often touted her family's successful river ventures. So it was odd that she answered Night with a simple nod. He held her stare for a moment longer than necessary, but then shifted his gaze and continued.

"So Demeter was my choice, mostly because they're nontraditionalists. Once I met their Monarch, I understood why they're so unorthodox. Linnaea's talent makes my gender seem unremarkable."

Ivy and I processed this for a moment. Ivy bit first. "So, what makes this Linnaea so special?"

"She can heal the mind. Psychosis, neurosis, even grief and depression. All Mederies can heal, but not every Mederi can help a Hyrke want to stay well."

Well, she'd obviously had an effect on my brother. I wondered if he'd been a patient as well as a student of hers. I'd have to meet this Linnaea someday. Night's clear self-acceptance made me as much envious as hopeful.

It was getting late though, and even if one part of me wanted to hang out at Marduk's all day catching up with Night, another part of me was anxiously turning my attention to the night ahead. But before I could ask Night how long he was in town for or where he was staying, he told me why he'd come up.

"Linnaea gave me a pass on my weekend duties in return for your looking after Heather last night. I can't tell you how grateful I am—as is Linnaea and all of Demeter. No one knows what might have happened if you and your friend hadn't met her at the train station. The truth is, you may have saved her life."

I gave Night a dubious look. He made me sound heroic, which is not at all how I viewed myself. If it weren't for the fact that I too unfortunately felt that Heather had been in real danger, I would have argued. But there was little point since we both believed the same thing: a demon was stalking Mederies again. But this time, I thought I might know which one. In a quiet voice (it never paid to say a demon's name too loud), I told Night and Ivy about Vigilia.

"You think she's the one who's been attacking and abducting Mederies?" Ivy whispered. "How could she do that? You said she died."

"No, I said no one knew where she was. Big difference."

Night considered my information. "Well, it's an interesting theory. And one I'll bring up with Karanos." He laughed at my surprised look. "Okay. Here's why I'm really up here. Linnaea *is* grateful to you for keeping Heather out of harm's way. But gratitude isn't the only reason she gave me a pass this weekend. She wants me to talk to Karanos about what's happening. Press him to put more Council Maegesters on the case. The three Mederies who disappeared earlier this year haven't been heard from. The Council needs to do more."

"Four," I said.

"Four what?" Night asked.

"Four Mederies have been attacked or abducted."

I told Night about Bryony.

"How'd she get away?"

I half grunted, half laughed. That was the same question I'd asked.

"Luck. And our father. Karanos happened to be crossing through the train station on his way from St. Lucifer's to the Council offices when Bryony was attacked. The demon left as soon as she sensed Karanos coming. That's why Bryony Ijolite's still with us."

The three of us sat quietly for a few moments, digesting the magnitude of the situation the Mederies were facing. I finally broke the silence.

"When are you talking to Karanos?"

Night shrugged. "I haven't been able to reach him yet. You know how busy he is. But I'm hoping to talk to him tomorrow."

I nodded. I didn't want to offend Night but concern compelled me to make my next comment.

"You took a big risk coming up here alone, you know."

But typical of Night, he just snorted. "You think I look like a Mederi?" Well, I couldn't argue with him about that. His cloak wasn't even green. Still . . . it bothered me intensely that Vigilia—if she was the offending *rogare*—was out there somewhere, watching . . . waiting . . .

"So where are you staying tonight?"

"With Peter. He said the Joshua School was hosting some big event for the St. Luck's students tonight. I assume you're both going." He spared me a glance but then looked at Ivy, awaiting her response. Red splotches suddenly bloomed on her cheeks. The mild tension that I'd sensed between them suddenly came into sharp focus. Aha! I grinned.

"We're going," I said.

"Great," Night said, grabbing his cloak from the back of his chair and heading out. "Then we'll see you in your lobby at seven."

My grin faded, replaced by the same anxious, edgy feeling I'd been trying to get rid of all morning. *We* meant him and Peter.

"What time did you say Ari was coming over?" Ivy said, looking at me with eyebrows raised.

"Seven," I said weakly.

All dolled up, dresses donned, hair coiffed, we looked pretty good. Actually, Ivy and I had never looked better in our whole lives. I, for one, had never worn a dress like this. It made me more than a little uncomfortable to bare my demon mark. I felt scandalously naked with my shoulders and upper chest uncovered. But my feelings fit the mood of the holiday.

The Patron of Bryde's Day was Bryde, of course, who'd been Halja's most powerful Mederi and who was still worshipped as a mother figure by Haljans everywhere, but Beltane's patron was Flora, a lesser demon whose favorite followers had been maidens. Flora's followers didn't need to be fertile; they just needed to be sensual and desired. They weren't trying to get pregnant. They only wanted to have fun.

According to legend, Flora had been a young demoness, beautiful in her corporeal form, and named after her one true unrequited love—flowers. Legends say one spring she took to the hills, unable to keep her hands away from the flowering buds and bursting blooms. Needless to say, her touch was deadly and caused her no small amount of remorse. In her frustration, grief, and madness, she torched the hills with a series of great bonfires. The flames rose high into the night, drawing Hyrkes from their homes, who danced and sang and drank with delight by the light of them.

Due to these beginnings, the holiday has the air of an impromptu celebration, even when it is meticulously planned. Its mood is often frivolous and playful. Unlike Bryde's Day, where the focus is so overtly on mothers, babies, and fertility, Beltane is a festival of flowers, fire, and sexuality— sometimes with your partner, sometimes not. But while Beltane's *anything goes* attitude was appealing to me, Flora's story was just a tad too close to my own for comfort. So I'd never really embraced the holiday. Of course, we Onyxes had never really embraced any holiday.

Until now.

In keeping with the spirit of the holiday and my promise to Ari, I'd elected to go all out with my appearance. I'd applied shimmering champagne, gold, and bronze eye shadow all around my eyes, all the way to my brows and even underneath my lower lashes and then heavily lined them in charcoal. The effect was dramatic and almost otherworldly. The dress was even more spectacular on me than it had been on the hanger. The bright yet burnt, fiery orange color suited me and the swishy sound of the silk taffeta train pleased me. I stood before the mirror, hands on hips, swishing back and forth, assessing.

"Do you think the flower's too much?" I asked Ivy.

"No!"

It wasn't the first time I'd asked. The silk flower in my hair had been a last minute addition. I'd styled my hair in a large, carefully sculpted messy updo. The entirety of it had been teased, then some parts straightened, and some curled.

I then artfully arranged it in a great mass on the top of my head. A few strands were left to trail down the back of my neck and around my face. I'd found the huge orange silk flower in Ivy's hairpin box and had tucked it up into the side of my elaborate updo, just above my right ear.

I stuck my tongue out at my reflection, laughing at the flower on one side, demon mark on the other. The tight fit of my dress molded to my every curve. To me, it looked like my breasts were in danger of spilling out of the top. They weren't, Ivy assured me, but there would be no question of my femininity tonight.

Ivy looked radiant. The soft drape of yards of emerald green silk combined with her tall, ethereal figure only enhanced her natural grace. The front cut of her dress was low, but the back was the most dramatic part. It dipped almost (but not quite) to the top of Ivy's buttocks, baring a wide expanse of naked back.

Ivy's golden red hair was braided with deep green ribbons, and adorned with freshwater pearls from the mouth of the Lethe. She'd chosen to make a statement with her makeup. I hadn't realized what an artist Ivy was until she painted her face. She'd covered cheeks, nose, forehead, and chin with a mix of sparkling, iridescent light and dark green paints. Then she'd drawn flowing swirls and whorls in black, accented with white. She looked fantastic. She grinned and we decided to wait for everyone downstairs, in the lobby of Megiddo.

Megiddo probably didn't go all the way back to the days when St. Luck's had been Fort Babylon, but it was easily hundreds of years old. The lobby was cavernous, with a high beamed ceiling and rows of two-story arched windows on the east and west sides. The floor was inlaid parquet, topped with wool rugs in muted colors. Scattered around the great space were small seating areas with expensive but uncomfortable-looking couches and chairs. An eclectic mix of artwork, from the tasteful to the moderately profane (this was the dormitory lobby of a demon law school in Halja after all), adorned the walls.

The excitement I'd felt while getting ready with Ivy upstairs faded and the anxious, edgy, jittery feeling I'd started
the day with returned. I wandered around Megiddo's lobby,
adrift, looking for a piece of artwork or furniture to anchor
myself with. My teeth chattered, my palms were sweaty, and
my throat was dry. I was a Maegester-in-Training with a class
position of *Secundus*. I had killed a demon (albeit a small
familiar I still felt grief-ridden about) and I was doing an
adequate job of controlling my client so far (in fact, he'd
been chivalrous enough to walk me to the library the other
night, right?). And I was more than holding my own in my
Hyrke law classes. I should not have been this nervous.

But, tonight, it seemed, there was no end of things to get
worked up about: my provocative appearance, fear and longing of greater intimacy with Ari, wonder and worry over
Peter and the Reversal Spell, my earlier discussion with
Night and Ivy about Vigilia, and the overall unsettling feeling of upcoming Beltane and the *anything goes* mentality
that came with it.

Hung above a massive, beautifully ornate stone and tile
fireplace in our lobby was a large, evocative oil portrait of
Flora. Her swelling breasts and generous hips beckoned, her
luxuriantly rich, deep, dark tresses flowed like the water in
the river she walked along. She was lovely, youthful, and
strong. She was *happy*, traipsing through those blooming
fields, her long skirts swirling, hand poised to pick a single
flower. Behold, Flora, surrounded by life and its never ending colors: lilies of the purest white, trees a verdant green,
the river a bright blue, and the sky the lightest pink. In the
picture, it was sunset, the moment before it all turned to dust.
In the time it took Flora to pluck one stem, everything in the
picture would be gone. The artist had captured the last moment of Flora's joy so clearly it pained me just to look at it.

I could not have said why I did it. It was a reaction, an
instinct. I just wanted to burn away that brief burst of inde-
scribable pain. I wanted to be comforted by something I
could touch, something I could look at without wanting to
weep. My magic swirled around me, a whirling vortex of

energy that began in my core and then radiated outward, spinning furiously until I finally flung it into the hearth, setting the unlit wood on fire. The roaring flames danced and moved. They were real. They were warm. And they were oddly purifying.

I heard a low whistle. I turned from my fiery creation to see Fitz and Babette slowly approaching. Ivy was some distance away, mouth agape. *Great,* I thought, *now I've gone and done it.*

Fitz came within a few feet of me and gave me a courtly bow. Babette made a similar move, but while Fitz was clearly enjoying himself, Babette looked terrified.

"What are you doing, Fitz?"

"You look like the demoness herself, a deity to be worshipped."

"Hardly," I said, laughing self-consciously.

"Beltane is near, is it not? This is the time of year when the veil between past and present is lifted. Who's to say you are not—just for tonight—our patron personified?"

"Don't be ridiculous!" I protested and then added, "But thank you," as humbly as I could after a compliment like that.

"Hello, Babette," I said, turning to Fitz's date, hoping for a more normal conversation. "You look terrific." And she did. She wore a simple gray tunic dress with white embroidery that Mrs. Aster would have loved. But her understated appearance set my teeth chattering again. Would Ivy and I be the lone standouts among a sea of serviceable gray, black, and white?

Night and Peter arrived next. I could tell from Peter's face that he had seen me light the fire, and was not best pleased about it. His gaze raked over me, zeroing in on exactly those parts I was most anxious about, my demon mark and the flower in my hair. I introduced him to Ivy. He shook her hand unenthusiastically. Night's eyes, however, widened in delight when he saw Ivy.

"Ivana," he said, taking both of her hands in his and gently squeezing them. Ivy's face paint hid any telltale blush.

She smiled, her grin wide and white against the green paint. Night himself had cleaned up well. He had borrowed a fawn-colored silk frock coat and matching pants from Peter. Underneath he wore a plain white tunic. He'd opted to leave the bronze buttons undone and had left his hair unbound.

Further introductions and amicable greetings were made. A few minutes later, Night offered Ivy his elbow and she took it. Fitz and Babette started making their way toward the door. Peter stayed back with me, leaning in close and whispering in my ear.

"You are an inspiration, Noon," he said smiling. He was dressed in pure white; everything he wore—pants, shirt, even his brocade vest—all were as colorless as the lilies in the portrait above the mantel. "I have a surprise for you later," he said, offering me his elbow.

I didn't accept it. But I could tell when Ari walked in, he didn't like what he saw. His signature smarted like a sunburn. I wanted to assure Ari that I wasn't breaking my promise to go with him to the ball. That, nervous though I was, I'd been waiting for him.

In the time it took my heart to contract, Ari was through the doors of Megiddo and beside me. He brushed Peter's arm away and placed his hands on my shoulders. His hands felt hot and fiery and my skin seemed to glow beneath them like windblown embers. His gaze swept over me, taking in every detail. His hands slid slowly down my sides until they were resting on my hips. I was now oblivious to everyone else in the room. I could not have said where they stood, or what they thought, whether they watched or had left. Buried under the onslaught of Ari's passion and possession, I was only aware of him. He bent his head to my neck and kissed me there, briefly and chastely. He raised his head and smiled.

"A flower, Noon?" he said playfully. "I wouldn't have thought of it. But it suits you. You look stunning." He managed to pack a considerable amount of meaning into that one little word. It was clear that, though he'd asked for a real date, it would take little convincing on my part for him to agree to skip the ball and move immediately to *after*. I swayed and Ari kept tight hold of me as he turned to face the now gawking crowd of my friends.

Peter was openly scowling and Night didn't look very happy either. That was my fault, I realized, because I'd never even told Night about Ari. I'd never been sure how to explain him. *What place in my life was Ari supposed to occupy?* But his role for tonight, at least was clear.

"Ari, this is my brother, Nightshade," I said motioning to Night, who stepped forward. "Night, this is Ari Carmine, my date for tonight."

If Ari was unhappy about my stated limitation on the duration of our involvement, he didn't show it. Night, however, frowned and glanced at Peter, whose jaw was clenched with naked animosity.

"Carmine?" Night said dubiously. Mederies couldn't sense Maegesters magically, but Night's other five senses worked perfectly well, along with his common sense.

Ari shrugged, but smiled to soften it. "Carmine's no more an accurate surname for me than Nocturo is an appropriate praenomen for you."

I stiffened and tried to pull away. Regardless of my feelings for Ari, I wasn't going to let him pick a fight with my brother. I was regretting how I'd handled this introduction, that I hadn't told Night about Ari earlier. But Ari held me close, his grip tight.

"Carmine is a name that was generously given to me by my adoptive parents—Hyrke parents from Bradbury," Ari explained, his tone light. "Noon and I are classmates."

"You mean you're both training to be Maegesters," said Night. But, like Ari, his tone was casual. Night was just calling it like it was. "You're the one who went with Noon to meet Heather at the train station last night."

Out of the corner of my eye, I saw Peter's eyes widen and then narrow. But Ari nodded, looking almost pleased. Night looked at me, carefully studying my face. Finally, he nodded and stuck his hand out to Ari, who accepted it, shaking it steadily. Night was a Mederi, who Ari could easily burn into small dry bits of bone and tissue. But Night wasn't cowed and I knew Ari respected that.

Ari grinned and called out to Fitz, "You'd better watch out, Dorio's going to want to trade suits with you." Fitz was wearing an outlandishly long purple brocade jacket with green silk pants, a canary yellow vest with brass buttons, and a gold pocket watch. *Only at Beltane*, I thought, rolling my eyes. All of the St. Luck's students laughed, even Babette. Ari complimented Ivy's body art and her warm response was a further clue to Night that Ari was no stranger to the friends I'd made since I'd left home. He seemed a bit crestfallen to be so ignorant of my current life and times and I vowed to try to make it up to him. I didn't know what to do about Peter. I smiled tenuously at him, but he just scowled and looked away. I started to go to him, but Ari's hand tightened around my waist and he pulled me closer as we exited Megiddo.

"Do you know what Flora's true form was, Noon?" he asked.

I shook my head.

"Fire," he said. "Her true form was breathtaking."

Breathtaking, indeed. As in *life taking*. But I didn't say it. I really did want to try to have a good time tonight.

Chapter 20

ઠ

When we arrived at Empyr there was a long line to get in. At first I worried there might be some sort of ticket requirement, but then I saw the Angels had posted two Seraphim by the door to greet their guests. The Seraphim appeared in high spirits, making ribald jokes, mocking some people's costumes and enthusiastically praising others. I was relieved to see that the crowd was almost equally divided between polished and professional (black robes, gray gowns) and dramatic and decadent (bright iridescent fabrics, shimmering face paints, masks, ribbons, trains . . .).

Peter refused to even look at me while I was at Ari's side and Ari made it clear he wouldn't be letting go of me anytime soon. Not that I minded. For the ball, Ari had donned a two button, black frock coat with matching pants. He wore a deep mahogany vest of the same material and a coordinating striped silk ascot. His chin and cheeks were now free of stubble but, like Night, he'd left his hair unbound. It fell in unruly waves, almost reaching his starched white collar. His appearance was a drool inducing combination of debonair and devil-may-care. I could hardly believe he was *my* date for the night.

Fellow students' reactions to me were mixed. A few complimented me on my dress or on my choice to use Flora as my muse (I hadn't, but in deference to the demon, I didn't correct them). Some women even showed signs of envy, until they remembered who or what I was. I gathered none would have wanted the beauty if it meant having to live with the mark. Others, like Babette, just seemed awed to be in my presence. They were almost as hard to take as the ones who reacted to me as if I were an insect skittering across the floor. Apparently seeing really is believing. My mark seemed to grow darker with my mood. I knew I was being oversensitive (and likely seeing devils where they did not exist), but I couldn't help it. By the time it was our turn to enter Empyr even Ari's rock-solid presence by my side couldn't steady my skittish nerves.

The two Seraphim at the door were passing something out as guests entered. I froze when I saw what they were.

Flowers. Morningstar lilies, of course. Flora's favorite. Legend had it they hadn't even existed prior to the Apocalypse. According to the story, they'd first grown from the ground where Lilith had shed her tears over Lucifer's death. Since every lily was supposed to represent a tear, and Lilith's tears had been endless, lilies now dot every field and valley of Halja. Their blooming time: early spring, or Beltane. There were some who believed Flora had been a religious zealot, or at least a good patriot, and that her motivation for scooping up the lilies she eventually killed was purely altruistic, instead of vain and destructive. Those who told that version of the story believed Flora had meant only to collect her lady's tears, and in so doing somehow reverse what had happened to her lord. But when the lilies died, Flora knew the land wasn't yet ready for his rebirth so she lit the bonfires, not in outrage, but instead as an act of holy purification.

I didn't know which version to believe so I took my lesson from the common element in both, the one which was most likely to mirror reality. My touch would kill a flower as surely as Flora's had. And despite how brave I'd been to bare my demon mark, there was no way I was going to willingly kill something, even if it was only a clipped piece of green-ery that only had days more to live.

Luck, let me pass by unnoticed.

It was possible. The hallway was a crush of people, the interior of Empyr was a cacophony of sound, and the last few minutes had felt like a pell-mell rush to get into the biggest event in New Babylon. I figured I had it made when Ari waved off the Seraph to our left but a second before I entered the Seraph to the right spied the flower in my hair and thrust one of the lilies in my direction. I stopped, almost unwill-ingly, mesmerized by its perfection. Like the apple wines, were they enhanced with a spell? The lily was flawless: its top large, smooth, and white as milk, its leaves and stem thick, stiff, and dark green with robust health. It smelled amazing and I nearly reached out to take it so that I could bury my nose in its top and breathe deep the smell of life. But sanity prevailed and instead I turned toward the Seraph so he couldn't miss the demon mark on my chest. I inclined my head ever so slightly.

"I'd best not," I said, my voice hoarse with emotion. The Seraph stared at me, knowing he'd made the gravest of social faux pas, something any Angel was loathe to do—even a Seraphim, the equivalent of their court jesters. Myriad emo-tions splashed across the Seraph's face—disbelief, revulsion, interest, and then . . . inspiration.

"Tonight, you are Flora, our patron," he said. "Accept this. Let your touch start the celebration."

Once again he pushed the flower toward me. I stepped back to avoid contact and stepped on someone's toes, which made me feel angry and self-conscious. It seemed wrong to force someone with waning magic to blacken something she didn't want to. I felt my magic thicken inside me and had to consciously work to control it. This would be no time to ac-cidentally set something on fire. I'd worked hard this year. I wasn't going to embarrass myself in front of my classmates or, Luck forbid, the faculty. I shooed the Seraph away with an impatient motion.

"Flora's first touch may have been a flower," I said, "but her next step was to burn everything in sight. Is that what you want, Angel? I was under the impression Empyr was at its limit with candlewicks. Do you really want me to burn Empyr down to the ground?"

Everyone in the hallway went completely silent. The Seraph stood before me, his eyes wide, his mouth opening and closing like a hooked trout. I swept past him without a further glance and headed straight for the bar. I needed a drink.

Ari was right by my side, grinning foolishly.

"What?" I snapped.

"I enjoy seeing you embrace your dark side, Noon."

"Well, I don't," I said, my resolve to enjoy myself tonight faltering. Ari grabbed my hand and pulled me back toward him. Since I'd been walking at a near frenetic pace my reversed momentum propelled me straight into him before I could stop myself. He was as immovable as a mountain, his chest beneath his coat as solid as Corpus Justica's cornerstone. I tilted my head up, slightly dazed by the impact. Ari put his hands on my shoulders and gently rubbed my arms. His gaze held mine and suddenly it was just us again. By all rights I should have felt breathless and unstable. Wobbly and rickety. That's usually the sensation I felt when Ari held me close and looked at me that way. But instead I felt calm again. Since the day we first met, Ari's actions had made it clear that he wanted me to stand on my own two feet, but he wouldn't let me fall.

My temper subsided and I glanced around the room, curious as to how the straightlaced Angels would celebrate the debauched holiday of Beltane. To my surprise and pleasure, Empyr had been transformed into a high-class carnival. Awash in white, silver, gold, and glass, everything gleamed. There was fire, but it was limited to hundreds of tiny candles. High in the ceiling, and likely protected further by powerful spellcasting, were bowers of fresh flowers and leaf garlands. Their smell was intoxicating. Ari wrinkled his nose in distaste.

"You don't like them," I said, smiling.

"I like that you like them," he said, kissing the tip of my nose and releasing me.

Our voices were almost lost in the din of hundreds of people talking, laughing, and clinking glasses in toast or greeting. Far off, set against the sparkling outline of Etincelle in the darkened southern windows, a band played. The music was a curious combination of heavy beats and light ethereal notes, an eclectic mix of beautifully harmonized sounds coming from an unusual array of instruments: cellos, harps, and violins, dozens of woodwinds, and a small battery of drums. The singer was another Seraph, a slender woman who was dressed in what appeared to be only undergarments. But, if so, they were the most expensive underclothes I'd ever seen. The Seraph's bejeweled skimpy top and tight satin knickers flashed brilliantly against skin covered in white reflective body paint as she danced under colored lights magically timed with the music she sang to. Her voice was throaty and deep, completely at odds with the body it came from, but enthralling. Since she was an Angel, I was sure she'd cast a fair amount of magic into her song. But no one here looked ensorcelled. She didn't look powerful enough to pull that off.

I eyed the spinning couples on the dance floor with envy. I had a vague notion of how to dance. As a sophomore at Gaillard I'd taken a class to fulfill a history requirement. Dance steps hadn't changed in centuries. But I hadn't had much practice. The class had lasted only one semester.

Ari and I made it to the bar with Fitz and Babette still in tow. Night had led Ivy to the dance floor and Peter had disappeared soon after my scene at the door. I sighed and grabbed a drink menu, interested to see what the night's offerings would be.

EMPYR

~Wine List~

NONPAREIL: *Pale orange with streaks of brown. Light & crisp. Provides a temporary body glamour.*

GOLDEN RUSSET: *Yellow with a bronze top layer. Served flaming. Sweet & sugary. Experiment with fire breathing, hold a fireball in your hand, play with fire nail tips or flaming hair. (Illusory only.)*

SUMMER QUEEN: *Pink blush. Sharp & tart. Explore the sensual connections between music, magic & the mind. Increases rhythm & coordination.*

NORTHERN SPICE (AKA THE "RED SPY"): *Dark purplish-red. Rich raspberry & blackberry notes. Served as a deuce. Provides deep empathetic connection with partner.*

BLACK GILLIFLOWER (AKA "VERACITY"): *Reddish black. Dry powdery consistency. Pepper-like smell and taste. Compels honesty. Removes surface glamours.*

My eyebrows arched as I read through the menu. The Angels had spared no spell or expense. I looked around the crowded room, considering my choices. By far, the most popular drink seemed to be the Nonpareil. Nearly every woman had bought one, and a few of the men too. But the Golden Russet's effects could certainly be seen. Throughout the crowd I spied a number of Hyrkes convincingly using fire as an accessory. I knew they were likely living it up, taking advantage of this one night of "free magic," but I couldn't imagine why anyone would willingly set themselves on fire, illusory or no. Veracity was a dud. What a buzzkill. Perhaps it might be useful at the end of the night though, when it was time to go home. Without a Black Gilliflower chaser, the Golden Russet's effects might prevent some Hyrkes from catching cabs or checking into hotel rooms for the night. This might be Halja, but cabbies and hotel clerks had their limits.

Predictably, Babette ordered the Nonpareil and Fitz the

Golden Russet. Fitz's first attempt at a fireball was so clumsy he would have set my dress on fire had it been real. I gave him a mock glare as he howled with mirth. Babette dragged him away from me, looking mildly terrified that I might lash out with the real thing. Ari asked what I'd like, and I told him to surprise me. He picked the Summer Queen.

"No Northern Spice?" I asked teasingly, glancing at the canoodling couples out on the western balcony.

"That's like offering me an eye dropper full of water when I'm drowning in the Lethe."

Oh. Damn, Ari. Now my cheeks were the color of my drink.

I sipped demurely, trying to rid myself of images of Ari. Things he'd done to me. Things I wanted him to do to me. All the while aware of his gaze on me, and the fact that he likely guessed my thoughts, and without a doubt knew my feelings. I drained my drink, feeling deliciously woozy. My limbs suddenly felt supple and strong; my feet nimble and quick. The heavy beats of the music resonated within my chest wall. Wildly, impossibly, I felt my heart rhythm change to the beat of the music. My body became an elastic drum as the beats pounded against me and through me. The high ethereal notes I'd heard before now tinkled like bells along my skin. It was the lightest touch, like a lover's caress. I shivered as the music made its way up my arms, across the swelling tops of my breasts, over my cheekbones with the barest feather light touch. Into my ears, where it tickled and teased, confusing my senses. I knew it was magic, but my body could no longer distinguish between sound and touch. It was an amazingly erotic feeling.

Had anyone else ordered the Summer Queen?

The bartender smiled at me, a little too lasciviously for Ari's tastes. Ari offered me his hand, growling, "Let's dance."

He led me out onto the dance floor and twirled me around for an opening presentation. I let Ari and the music lead me. It didn't surprise me that Ari was a great dancer even without the drink. I had yet to find something he *wasn't* good at. As Ari held me, I felt his signature change into that tingly electric feeling Ari called *arousal*. I sensed that he'd exercised the utmost restraint since Lekai. That he'd honored my wishes to act appropriately in public and stay apart at great cost to his self-control. Caught up in the moment, I lost track of how many times Ari set me free, spinning me endlessly like a flaming silk taffeta top. Always, he caught me, his strong hand reaching for mine or his firm grip encircling my waist. Each time my heart skipped like a flat rock thrown across still water. But my feet never faltered. I gave myself over to the man and the music, knowing that tonight there would be no holding back.

We dipped and swayed and I thoroughly enjoyed myself, nearly forgetting about the myriad things in my life there were to worry about. I was bent back over Ari's arm, my head nearly upside down, when I felt him stiffen. I came back up suddenly, the first clumsy move I'd made all night thanks to the Summer Queen, and skittered to a stop in Ari's arms. Despite the music, he'd gone still. I turned around abruptly to see what had caused his reaction.

I suppose I should have known. This annual Barrister's Ball really *was* the biggest event in New Babylon tonight. Sure, the St. Luck's and Joshua School people were present. But that would have made it of no more importance than the book fair they held down in Timothy's Square every year. No, the real reason this event was so important was that important people came to it. Members of the Divinity. Members of the Council. Sometimes, even the executive.

"F-Father," I stammered, unconsciously backing into Ari. It wasn't that I was afraid of my father. Not exactly.

But even if you were related to Karanos Onyx, it was still unnerving to have the single most powerful person in Halja standing not two feet in front of you, giving *you* their undivided attention. My father radiated power. He was well over six feet tall and substantially built. His suit hung impeccably from his imposing frame, in a color blacker than blindness. Its custom cut, the cloth it was made from, even the gold and sapphire buttons spoke of the wealth and influence he held.

His eyes were as dark as mine but, eerily, when I looked at him, the brightness that should have been reflected from the dance floor lights or the myriad candles, wasn't there. Neither was his signature. I'd never remembered him having one. But I thought I'd just forgotten what it had felt like because of inadequate exposure.

"Enjoying yourself, Nouiomo?" he said. I couldn't be sure, Karanos wasn't one to broadcast something as petty as emotions, but I thought he might have been amused. Or scornful.

Ari's hands rested lightly on my shoulders. He had powered his signature down to the lowest hum. The electric jolt I'd been receiving while we danced was completely gone, replaced by a signature so weak it felt like the winter sun through three inches of leaded glass. I, on the other hand, had a difficult time ratcheting down my signature. I gritted my teeth and tried to suck my magic back inside me, but it was a trick that still eluded me. I started sweating, desperately wanting to avoid the usual unintentional fireworks display when this sort of thing happened. But seconds later my fear was realized and the air in front of us exploded in a bouquet of bright lights accompanied by popping sounds and the acrid, bitter smell of dampened waning magic. My father frowned, but otherwise chose to ignore my lack of control.

"Aristos," he said, inclining his head slightly toward Ari. Ari's fingers on my arm tightened almost imperceptibly.

"Karanos," Ari said, and I felt his return nod behind me, deeper than my father's had been.

"I didn't realize you two knew each other," Karanos said, pointedly eyeing Ari's hands on my arms. Ari's hands slipped from my shoulders, but he didn't move away. "I suppose your meeting was inevitable," Karanos continued, "but I can't imagine that you two have much in common. Nouiomo, you've always been rather squeamish about killing things and, Aristos, well . . . you are not."

My father's voice dropped meaningfully at the end. I'd always assumed that Ari had performed his work for my father out of a sense of duty or, at worst, because he needed the money. My father implied otherwise.

Had Ari actually enjoyed being a demon executioner?

"If you're available over the break," Karanos said to Ari, "I could use you out at Rockthorn Gorge. There've been some . . . incidences there over the past few weeks."

Beside me, Ari stilled. I sensed some inner conflict. The barest uptick in his signature. Karanos must have sensed it too. He pressed further. "I'm headed over to the train station later tonight. You could accompany me. Catch the Midland Express. Meet up with Opiter and Septimus?"

It was clear from the way he said their names that my father thought highly of Opiter and Septimus, whoever they were. Executioners, I guessed. Karanos' eagerness to send Ari north as if he were a hunter's hound just waiting to be unleashed was off-putting to say the least.

I glanced up at Ari. I was appalled to see that he looked genuinely torn.

"I appreciate the offer," Ari said slowly, "but I have other plans." I suddenly remembered Ari had asked me to go to Bradbury with him next week and I hadn't yet given him an answer.

"What about you, Nouiomo?" my father said. "Are you going back to Etincelle for the break?"

I paused. When I didn't immediately answer Karanos' question, a curious tension developed among the three of us. Ari finally broke it by taking my hand in his. "I've invited Noon to come home with me next week," he said.

"Home?" My father said, his eyes narrowing at Ari. There was a peculiar tone in his voice.

"Bradbury, to meet my adoptive family."

Karanos seemed to digest this information for a moment. I wondered if he wanted to protest, but having had almost nothing to do with my life for twenty-one years, it was a little late for him to start sifting through my suitors now (not that there had ever been that many to begin with). Finally, abruptly, he ended our discussion with a slight, curt bow and no good-bye. I looked at his back as he left, filled with all manner of emotion. *Damn, crying would absolutely ruin my eye makeup.*

The dance floor was nearly empty and, despite the Summer Queen, the last thing I felt like doing was dancing. Ari led me out to the western balcony. The night air was cool, quiet, and dark. Our appearance caused a few couples to scurry back inside, which made me feel positively plague-ridden. I walked over to the waist-high iron railing framing the edge of the balcony and leaned over the edge. Beneath us Halja went about the business of a busy Saturday night. Ari stood beside me.

"You should go to Rockthorn Gorge," I said.

Ari looked surprised for a minute, but then scooted closer to me. Our elbows touched as we leaned against the railing and looked out across the twinkling lights of the city below.

"Do you want me to?"

"I know you want to go."

"Is that what you think? That I'd prefer to spend next week tracking down *rogares* and hoping I don't get myself killed rather than hang out with you?"

"Ari, I'm being serious. If you want to go, *go*," I said just a little too vehemently. "If someone up there needs help . . . you should go."

"Opiter and Septimus can handle it."

There was a long moment of silence between us. I don't know what Ari was thinking. His signature felt like it did in the Manipulation dungeon. *Expectant.* Was he expecting a fight? Finally, I gathered enough courage to ask my next question.

"How many demons have you killed?" It came out as a whisper. I hadn't meant it to. I'd meant it to come out conversationally. But the answer mattered too much.

Ari blew out his breath and stepped away from the rail. Along with *expectancy*, I now felt *agitation* and *aggravation* in his signature.

"How many is too many for you, Noon? What number has any real meaning? Is a few too many? How about ten? *Twenty?* A hundred?" His voice rose with each number. He seemed as scared of his answer as I did. "I don't know," he said finally.

"You're lying!"

Ari stepped behind me and turned me around. My outburst had cleared the last of the people off of the patio. Ari leaned toward me, his gaze intense.

"I know what you're doing, Noon," he said quietly. "I know why you want to know and I know why you're afraid. You think you'll be forced to become someone like me. But you couldn't be more different. Just because our magic is the same, doesn't mean *we're* the same."

"Does that mean you *love* killing, Ari?" I said angrily, my eyes tearing at the corners. "Because I *hate* it," I snapped. "I don't want to have the power to kill things." My voice sounded defeated. My dreams, at this point, sounded all but impossible. "I don't want to have magic that hurts or harms . . ."

"I know," Ari said, reaching for my hands. "You'd rather be a healer." He tried to pry me off the railing and into his arms. But I wouldn't let him. Stubbornly, I clasped my hands behind my back and leaned away from him.

"How many?"

"I'm not going to tell you."

"Ari," I said icily, "you told *me* not to hide things from *you*. Your favorite thing to do is break down *my* defenses. You can't pick and choose which parts of your past you want me to see. Tell me or there's no way I'm going to Bradbury."

He laughed, like he couldn't believe I'd make such a childish threat.

"Oh, you're going to Bradbury. I deserve a chance to be seen in a light other than the one your father shines on me."

I started sputtering. "You can't just tell me what to do. Luck, Ari, you could not be more pushy!" I pushed on his shoulders to demonstrate what I meant. My shoving had no effect. He stood before me, as immovable as a stone wall. "You're always pushing me," I said, thrusting my finger into his shoulder with each subsequent point I made. "Pushing me to declare, pushing me to study, to practice, to accept my abhorrent magic and the life you lead."

"The life you were born to lead," he said. "With me, if I have anything to say about it."

My jaw dropped.

"Ari, what are you saying? You think just because we had sex—"

"Sex? Is that all you think is between us?"

"I knew it!" I cried. "I knew you would try to assert some sort of claim on me."

"I do have a claim on you," he said matter-of-factly, pointing to my mark.

I tried to step back, but my heel just banged into the railing. I felt like a doe caught between a tree and a wolf. Before I could scoot sideways, Ari placed his hands on either side of the railing, effectively trapping me between him and a thirty-three-story plunge to my death. He bent toward me, his lips nearly touching mine. He smelled spicy, like cloves, and his breath tickled my upper lip. I didn't want to fight anymore.

I tilted my chin up so that my lips brushed against his, but he pulled back. I'm ashamed to say I leaned forward a bit until I realized what he was doing. I scowled.

"Always an irresistible combination of eager and reluctant," he said softly. He clasped my chin in his hand and gently shook it. Then he pulled me away from the rail, put his arm around my shoulders, and gave me a light squeeze. The gesture felt so affectionate, so natural and unrestrained. There was absolutely nothing sexual or possessive about it. He led me back inside. Despite myself, I grinned, although somewhat lopsidedly. Both my eagerness and my reluctance were due to the same problem: falling thirty-three stories wasn't nearly as frightening as falling in love.

Chapter 21

ॐ

When we walked back inside, the band was taking a break and people were finding seats for dinner. True to the impromptu mood of Beltane, there were no assigned seats. Guests were allowed to choose any seating arrangement that suited. I glanced around, hoping Fitz and Babette had thought to save us seats at their table. But when I spied them at the bar, I wondered if they would be joining anyone for dinner. It looked like they'd traded in the Nonpareils and Golden Russets for Northern Spice and were happily oblivious to the world around them. I spotted Night and Ivy across the room talking with my father and Peter. I hoped Night was confiding my suspicions regarding Vigilia to Karanos. Obviously, since Karanos had walked off after learning that Ari had invited me to go to Bradbury with him over the break, I hadn't had a chance to say anything to him about my theory.

I figured now was as good a time as any to freshen up so I left Ari at the bar and went to look for the ladies' lounge. Someone with a jewel- and feather-encrusted peacock mask helpfully pointed out the way. I lifted my skirts slightly to make walking easier and hoped there would be a water closet big enough to accommodate me and my dress. As I rounded the corner into a more deserted area of Empyr, I felt a collective group of signatures I'd rather have avoided.

Tosca's signature struck me like a high altitude mountain pass blast, full of gale forces and stinging icy pinpricks. Instinctively I blasted back, my hotter and stronger signature completely melting his. He stared aggressively at me. Brunus' signature always made me want to gag and tonight was no exception. His magic hit me like a vat of fresh squeezed onions. My eyes watered as his lecherous gaze swept across my bared upper chest. He zeroed in on my mark and his lip curled in disgust. Sasha leered at me and lewdly waggled his tongue. From the corroded feel of his magic, I half expected to see half of his teeth missing.

"My, don't we look pretty tonight," Brunus sneered, stepping in front of me. "How can a woman bear to bare that thing?" he said contemptuously, reaching toward my demon mark with his finger. It was the one thing he'd never tried to do in the dungeon. Countless times he'd tried to rake me with his magic—or a metal weapon. But he'd never tried to touch me. The attempt unbalanced me, literally, and I stumbled backward . . . into Sasha, who'd moved behind me. It unnerved me that I'd been so focused on Brunus I hadn't felt Sasha moving. I twisted, but Brunus stepped on the hem of my dress with his foot to hold me in place. My choices were to stay put, try to wrench myself free with potentially disastrous and humiliating consequences to my dress and me, or . . . fight them with magic. *Here.* In the hallway of Empyr.

My signature flexed involuntarily, like a fist, and the three of them smiled. Their signatures expanded and became exponentially *expectant.*

Brunus reached toward my mark again, just to see what I would do, and that's when Night stepped into the hallway.

"What's going on?" he said sharply, striding over to us. He either didn't know or didn't care that this trio of bullies could burn him alive. He shoved Brunus away from me and took my arm. I thought we were going to get out—no harm, no foul, right?—but as we turned, Brunus stomped on my train. I heard the fabric rip just as a flash of metal appeared at Brunus' throat.

"I heard they teach you Maegesters-in-Training how to use real weapons," Night said. "Recognize this?"

Whatever it was, it wasn't one of the ones from the wall in the dungeon. It was a small knife, but from the way Night held it, it looked deadly sharp.

"Apologize, or spend the rest of your life wondering if I'm going to sneak into your room one night to finish what I started here."

"You're the one who should be wearing the skirt, Nocturo. I heard you're practicing medicine down in southern Halja with the rest of the women with waxing magic. Maybe you can use your stitching skills to sew up your sister's dress."

Brunus snorted, even with Night's knife pressed to his neck. He wasn't going to apologize. Night had to know that. Night finally lowered his hand and pushed Brunus off my dress.

I felt Brunus' return thrust before he threw it. He shaped his magic like his beloved nadziak and swung it toward Night's head. But I was faster. I shaped my magic like a rapier and shield. I blocked the nadziak with the shield and thrust the rapier toward Brunus, intending only to cut a lock of his hair—just to show him I was serious and that he shouldn't mess with us. But my magic control wasn't quite up to the job I'd assigned it. My magic nicked Brunus' cheek, instantly burning and cauterizing it. The putrefying smell made me sick—but worse, way worse—was the instinctive feeling that rose up in me. I suddenly wanted to *kill* Brunus.

I shook myself and concentrated on dissolving my power. That's where the feeling was coming from and it terrified me. Thankfully, my magic disappeared in a shower of sparks. No firecrackers this time; it was more like falling glitter.

Brunus' eyes glowed hatred at me as he, Sasha, and Tosca retreated. But they knew better than to turn their backs before they rounded the corner. I slumped against the wall for a moment as Night eyed me worriedly. I mumbled something about needing to use the bathroom and walked into the ladies' lounge. I found an empty corner stall and locked the door. I stood there shaking for five full minutes.

I wasn't scared of Brunus and the others. I was scared of me. Of what I was becoming.

E ventually, I came out of the bathroom stall and tidied myself up. The ripping sound I'd heard when Brunus stomped on my dress turned out to be only a few threads. When I came out of the ladies' lounge, Night was still waiting for me. I smiled at the concerned look on his face.

"I'm sorry."

"*You're* sorry? I'm sorry you have to put up with people like those three. I guess I always thought training to be a Maegester would be fun."

I barked out a laugh. "Is training to be a Mederi fun?"

Night paused, thinking. "No, but it is fulfilling."

"Fulfilling enough to keep doing it if you had a choice?"

"What are you talking about, Noon? Is this about Peter and his spell again? I told you, I don't think that's a good idea." Maybe it was, maybe it wasn't. But after tonight, I was more determined than ever to try.

I told Night that Peter and I had found the spell.

"You found the spell?" It was like a repeat of the discussion I'd had with Ari.

"Yes."

"And you're going to let Peter cast it over you?" Night said, frowning.

This time I gave the unequivocal answer I should have given Ari.

"Yes."

N ight walked me back to the ballroom. On the way, we ran into Peter, who held a tumbler full of something from the bar that smelled like it might spontaneously combust. I knew that Empyr only ensorcelled its apple wines, so it was only alcohol, but Peter looked as if he was on his third or fourth of the night. Night deposited us both at a table along the wall and went looking for Ivy.

Fitz and Babette spotted us and came over bringing loaded plates of food. Apparently hunger had driven them to seek out sustenance for the night ahead. They were both grinning like idiots and I envied them. Beside me, Peter stared morosely into his glass. I spied Ari across the room talking to Karanos. Likely discussing whatever it was that Opiter and Septimus were handling in Rockthorn Gorge. I didn't feel left out.

I wanted out.

Peter turned to me, his eyes bloodshot but fully focused. "Do you still love flowers like you used to?"

His question annoyed me. Of course I still loved flowers. I just didn't like what happened when I touched them. I pointed to the silk flower in my hair to illustrate how silly Peter's question was and sighed miserably. Peter reached out to touch my cheek. I turned my head away and he let his hand drop.

"Noon," he said, "I only have one more spell to interpret. *The* spell. It has to be it. It's the longest, most complicated spell I've ever seen."

The excitement in his voice was contagious. A spot of tingly anticipation formed in my belly.

"I spoke to your father tonight," Peter said, straightening and looking more sober by the minute. "I told him everything. He gave his permission on one condition. He wants a Show of Faith."

"Permission for what exactly?" I said warily, remembering Peter's words from the night we located the spell. *Just promise me, if I find the spell and cast it, that you'll be mine . . .*

"Permission to cast the spell, although what happens after that is up to you," Peter said, scooting closer so that his knee now touched mine. "Your father's aware of my feelings for you."

I clutched my stomach and bit my lip, scanning the crowd for Ari. He was still talking with my father. Peter followed my gaze.

"I despise Carmine," he said vehemently. "I have no idea what you see in him. He's everything you don't want to be."

"Just because he has waning magic?" I said, suddenly defensive.

"Yes— No!" Peter fumed. I'd never seen him stumble over his words before. "I did some checking, Noon, asked around. Did you know he's your dad's number one hit man?"

"You did what?" I sputtered, barely able to form words myself now. "You've been investigating my boyfriend behind my back?"

The words slipped out. In my anger, I hadn't really thought about what I was saying, or what effect it would have on Peter. He clenched his jaw so tightly; I thought he might crack a molar.

"Your boyfriend, huh?" he said in a quiet voice that pierced my ear like a skewer. "How well do you really know Ari, Noon? Do you know that in the year before he came to St. Luck's he killed three times as many *rogares* as your dad's former favorite? Rumor has it Karanos can't wait to get him back in the field." My heart dropped to my stomach. "Did you think Ari was going to graduate from here and start representing *regulares* with their divorce cases?" Peter laughed derisively. "He's going to go back to what he does best. What he loves. Tracking down *rogares*. Do you really want to be with someone like that? You claim you want to be a healer? Well, you're dating a professional killer."

"How many?" I croaked, my voice nearly breaking.

Peter looked at me in confusion. "How many what?"

"How many demons?"

Peter shrugged. "I don't know. Hundreds. Does the number really matter?"

No. It didn't.

"What Show of Faith does my father want?" I asked Peter in a rush. I didn't want to think too hard about what I was doing and change my mind.

"He wants to know that you're in agreement and he wants proof that I can capably cast the spell. Oh, and the spell book. To secure the Council's consent, your father wants me to give them the spell book as compensation for the loss of one of their future Maegesters. The Divinity's not going to be happy about it, but it's mine to give.

"And the trade is more than worth it," he said, grabbing my hand and pulling me to my feet. "I told you I had a surprise for you tonight. I do. Jonathan Aster's spell book was full of arcane spells I'd never heard of before. There's one in particular, you'll *love*. It would be a perfect Show of Faith." He gave me a winsome smile, his first of the night, and although it did nothing to make me feel better, I squeezed his hand, willing to cling to anything right now that might give me relief from what I was feeling.

Peter led me to the dance floor. On the way we passed closer to Ari than I would have liked. The emotions played on his face like lightning. Confusion, anger, and then, realization. He may not have known exactly what we were doing, but he was smart enough to figure out that if I was with Peter, it had something to do with the Reversal Spell. And, by the look on his face and the feel of his signature, he also correctly guessed that whatever I was about to do would lessen his hold on me.

Peter led me out onto the empty dance floor. Still holding my hand, he walked over to the band who had been playing light instrumental background music for dinner. They broke off midsong at Peter's approach, which caused most of the guests to turn toward us. Peter stepped up to the standing microphone and turned toward the crowd. He gestured dramatically to me, riveting the crowd's attention on me. I'd known our Show of Faith would be public, but I hated being a spectacle. I felt Ari's penetrating gaze but kept my eyes on Peter.

"Behold Flora," Peter said, lacing his voice with the soft sugary magic Angels used when putting on a show. "What if, instead of flowers, Flora's first love had been an Angel?"

At those words, Ari started walking toward the dance floor. But Karanos held him back, leaning in close to say something in his ear. Ari's only response was to switch his gaze to me. His stare was magnetic, as if he were daring me to look at him. But I was too scared. Scared of what I was becoming. Scared I'd change my mind about what I was about to do. Scared whatever it was Peter was planning wouldn't work. Scared of Ari, the man I was falling in love with. The man I might have already fallen in love with. Because I didn't want Aristos Carmine to have a claim on me. I didn't want him to have a mark on my heart if it meant he could tell me what to do. This choice was about *me*. And the life I wanted to lead. And the man I might eventually choose to lead it with. Who wasn't someone who'd killed hundreds of demons. No matter what the demons may have done to deserve it. Killing was killing.

Right?

I wanted no part of it.

Peter asked the band to play "First Blush." The first high slow notes of the song sounded as the violinists drew their bows across their strings. Peter raised my hand with his and brought it down again, leading me into an opening bow for the crowd.

"A posse ad esse," Peter bellowed in my direction, *"corpus agito." I drive to constant motion the body from being able to being.* It was a balletic spell. Suddenly, I felt as if I'd drank an entire carafe of Summer Queen.

The traditional couple's dance for "First Blush" was a love story. I don't know if Peter had cast a spell over himself as well, but he was a beautiful dancer. I supposed, being an Angel, he would have to have been. After all, dance was a form of expression and we were, in fact, telling a story. So it made sense that his movements were as elegant and articulate as his speech. For my part, I felt like a marionette. The spell Peter had cast granted me balletic grace but its source was Peter, not me, and we could never share or swap magic the way Ari and I had. I knew, to the crowd, we likely looked dazzling, with me in my fiery orange swirling skirts and Peter dressed head to toe in blinding white. Both of us executed the technical, complicated dance moves of "First Blush" flawlessly, but to me, the dance felt cold.

I started having second thoughts about what I was doing. *Damn Luck and his warlords too, why couldn't I just stick to a decision and stop second-guessing myself?* I looked over at Ari, still scared, but unable to just turn off my feelings. Apparently I had the same problem with my feelings as I did with my magic. At that moment, I would gladly have illuminated the entire room in a great big magical fireworks display if it would have burned off and cauterized the outpouring of feelings I still had for Ari Carmine.

He was a killer.

But then so was I, right? But I didn't want to be. That was what this whole Show of Faith was about. Proving something to my father so that he would secure the Council's consent and allow Peter to cast the Reversal Spell over me. Then I could become what I'd wanted to be my entire life: a warm, nurturing, life-affirming Mederi healer.

As if cued by my thoughts, the next dance move separated Peter and me so that we were each on opposite sides of the dance floor with our backs to one another. When I turned around, Peter had closed the distance between us. He stood before me holding a bouquet of white lilies, live ones. I froze as he offered them to me.

Peter had repeatedly warned me that *no* spell could protect plants from my direct touch. No waning magic user had *ever* held live greenery for more than a second. Casting a spell that would allow me to accept this bouquet without killing it would be just the thing to convince my father that Peter was powerful and erudite enough to pull off grand arcane spells. I reached for it with a shaking hand, my fingers closing briefly around Peter's before pulling the ribbon wrapped stems toward me. I expected them to turn black before my eyes. I waited, clutching them in front of me with both hands. I realized from the lights and music that this was the closing act of our story. The audience was deadly quiet, believing my natural hesitation to be a well-rehearsed dramatic conclusion. When it became clear that my touch was not going to kill the flowers, I raised them to my nose and breathed deep.

The audience erupted. People were shouting, standing, and clapping. No one noticed my grimace before I lowered the flowers from my face. Up close, they smelled horrible. All my life I'd dreamed of burying my nose in a bouquet, but when the moment came, it had not been nearly as satisfying as I'd expected. I knew then with a certainty I'd never possessed before that I'd feel the same about any spell cast to change the way Luck had made me. The feeling was amazingly liberating and I beamed with joy. I looked up in time to catch the expression on Ari's face.

He was stunned. Then his eyes met mine and I held his gaze. He'd always accepted me for what I was. Wasn't I strong enough to do the same for him? Ari's stare pierced my heart and then he turned abruptly and pushed his way through the crowd. Just before he left the room, I felt the radioactive blast of his magic. It was as if he'd held it together for as long as he could, but hadn't had quite enough time to make his escape before he went supernova. That brief burst was so full of rage and despair that I swayed from its impact. Clearly, my Show of Faith in Peter had hurt Ari deeply.

I thrust the bouquet back at Peter. He frowned and looked confused.

"You can't let go," he hissed quietly, pushing the bouquet back at me.

"I don't want it," I said. I thumped the bouquet against his chest and when he didn't take it, I let the bouquet fall to the floor.

Peter stared at me, aghast.

"I'm sorry," I said, knowing the words were completely inadequate. Peter had spent a lifetime searching for a spell that would help me and now I was throwing it all away. I strode across the dance floor, looking back only once.

On the ground at Peter's feet lay a blackened, charred,
twisted mass tied with white ribbon. The spell had changed
nothing, and yet, it had changed everything.

P ushing through the crowd took time. Everyone wanted to
   congratulate me on my performance. Those who might
have been reluctant to approach me before had now clearly
lost all reserve. Peter Aster's name was on everyone's lips.
His spell had made my touch less deadly. They had no idea,
of course. It had only been an unusually powerful stasis
spell, affecting the flowers, rather than me. Remarkable simply because it had been forgotten for millennia. Eventually I
made my way out of Empyr and into the hallway. There was
no sign of Ari. I ran to the lift and frantically pressed the
button. I was out on the sidewalk of Angel Street in no time.
   I darted across Angel Street and turned toward Infernus.
I wasn't sure what I would say to Ari once I found him. He
would just have to realize that I'd needed to be sure. That I
hadn't wanted to spend my whole life wondering *what if.*
   What if . . . Ari never wanted to speak to me again?
   I reached Infernus and raced up the stairs to Ari's floor.
When I stepped into the hall, it was deserted. I imagined
anyone who wasn't at Empyr for the ball had already left St.
Luck's for Beltane Break. Ari's room was also empty. I
paused in the doorway, unsure of where to go next.
   Had he left for Rockthorn Gorge? Karanos had mentioned
meeting at the train station. Had Ari left to catch the Midland Express? Would he leave just like that? No packing? No
preparations? No good-byes? It couldn't be good practice to
hunt *rogares* in the state of mind he was in when he'd left the
ball. That would be more than catastrophic, it would be sui-
cidal. I gnawed the inside of my cheek. I couldn't decide
whether I was more fearful *of* Ari or *for* Ari. Was this what
love did to a person?
   Suddenly I thought of the Stirling, the hotel where Fitz
had rented a room for the night. *What if, indeed . . .*

I rocketed down the hall and burst out of Infernus, desperate to find a cabriolet. I felt twisted up inside, turned inside out. I still had no idea what I would say to Ari if and when I found him. I wasn't even sure I should be looking for him. I understood for the first time how love could destroy, why people like Nergal might want to put an end to their suffering. But I could no more stop my search than I could stop breathing.

I found a cab on Victory Street. The driver's eyes went wide when he saw my demon mark, but my intended destination seemed to calm him. Throughout the trip, I impatiently tapped my fingers on the door handle, which made the driver nervous again. When we finally arrived at the Stirling, I sat in the backseat, unmoving, while the driver held the door open for me.

"Miss?" he inquired timidly. I thought about what Ari had said, about me always being both eager and reluctant. Never had I felt either emotion as strongly as I did just then. I accepted the driver's offered hand and lit from the cab like a dove flushed off the ground. I paid him, smoothed my skirts, and might have lost my nerve entirely had not one of the Stirling's uniformed bellmen rushed to my side. He offered me an elbow and whisked me inside.

Inside, the Stirling was as tasteful and understatedly elegant as the outside, but I gave my surroundings little notice. The decor barely registered as I swished to the front desk, my throat tight, my hands shaking.

"Is Aristos Carmine staying here tonight?" I asked. The woman behind the reservations desk blinked at me. I saw her hesitate—I'm sure it wasn't her practice to give out guest room numbers to strangers—but then she spotted my mark.

She nodded, her head bobbing up and down almost unwillingly. "Penthouse Suite." I'd like to think some feeling of female solidarity convinced her to give me Ari's location but it was probably fear if my face was showing even a quarter of the emotion I was feeling.

In less than a minute, I was standing outside the door,

knocking. No one answered. I pounded louder, grateful to have something to do with my hands. If it weren't for the pounding, they'd be shaking.

"Ari, it's me. Open the door," I called, feeling ridiculous. "Come on, I know the woman at the front desk called up. You can't just ignore me."

Still, that's exactly what he did. Every second that I stood outside his door begging for entry made me angrier until finally, in a great blast of frustration, I singed the lock and burst through. The room was completely dark. Instantly, I was pinned to the wall by something large and unmovable.

"Are you mad? Breaking into my room? I could have killed you." Ari's voice rumbled in my ear. His tone was incredulous and angry, but there was something else to it, something more difficult to define.

"Is it that easy for you to kill?" I spat out, my words unintentionally harsh.

"Is anything?" He pressed his forehead against mine, still keeping my hands locked in an iron grip at my sides.

I struggled futilely, more from a sense of frustration than an actual desire to get away. Ari looked at me, the way a pinscher might look at a rabbit caught in a snare. He raised my arms above my head, holding both of my hands effortlessly in one of his. I was acutely aware of how cool the wall felt on my back and how hot Ari's breath felt on my neck. I squirmed. Without warning, Ari pressed a finger against my demon mark. It was no quick touch. He left it there long enough to burn. In the dark, the orange glow of my skin's response was easy to see. I gritted my teeth and refused to protest.

"I should tell you to go home, Noon."

"You mean back to Megiddo?"

"No, I mean home. To Etincelle." His words were little more than a rough whisper in my ear. My heart pumped erratically as he pressed his lips to the soft pulsing spot on my throat. Slowly, as if he were positioning himself for attack, he moved his hand from my demon mark to the top of my dress. For one wild second I wondered if he would simply rip it from my body. But instead his hand slipped around my back, causing me to arch against him.

"I should tell you to go home to Peter." He untied the ribbons at the back of my bodice and then he started unlacing it. He pulled the ends of the ribbons through each and every eyelet with excruciating slowness, giving me time to stop him. I said nothing. Did nothing. Finally, he wrenched the now loose bodice free from my skin and let the dress drop. It fell to the floor, pooling around my ankles. "Peter can give you what you want."

I shook my head. I was having trouble swallowing, let alone speaking.

"No?" Ari asked, his voice slightly mocking. He plucked the flower from my hair. In a parody of my earlier performance, he brought the flower to his nose and breathed deep, then tipped it toward me in offering. I shook my head again, this time more violently. My body quivered, half-fearful, half-desirous of his touch. He reached for the light switch and suddenly a soft yellow glow lit the entire room. I expected him to let me go then but his grip never wavered. Instead his gaze raked over every inch of me. I realized he'd turned the lights on just so that he could see me better. The blood rushed to my face. Ari stood before me almost fully clothed. He had removed only his tie, whereas I was now pressed up against the wall clad only in the thinnest strip of silk panties and ribboned ballet shoes.

I had never stood naked in a lit room with a lover before. On the contrary, all of my experiences before Ari had been conducted in the dark, with me in whatever shirt I happened to have been wearing. This was sorely testing the degree to which I was willing to expose myself. And Ari seemed to know it.

"I can still feel his spell on you," he said. His gaze was steady, daring me to flinch or look away. He hooked his thumb in the thin strip of silk at my hips and pulled. A second later the delicate fabric tore, leaving me finally and completely exposed. Ari moved his hand from my hip to between my legs. I bit my lip, not wanting to cry out. I didn't want to give Ari the satisfaction of knowing how easily he could affect me. *I'd come here, hadn't I? I'd do anything for him, forgive anything. Wasn't that enough?*

Below he played with me, teasing me, drawing his fingers in and out, slowly, shallowly, never reaching any of the places I really wanted to be touched. His lips came down on mine, first soft and slow, then harder and more demanding. When he finally withdrew his hand, I was shaking with need but he broke off the kiss and leaned back from me. I tipped my head forward attempting to capture his mouth in another kiss but he resisted. A tiny spark of anger flared. There was only so much teasing I could take. My arms were getting sore.

"Aristos," I said softly. "Let me go."

He shook his head slowly, as if coming to a terrible realization. "I never expected to fall in love with you so completely, Noon." Once again he rested his forehead against mine. "I knew you were different, of course. Different from any other woman I'd ever been with. I knew my feelings for you would be stronger. But I didn't know you would make me feel so . . . *powerless*. So unable to do what must be done. I should tell you to go home. Tell you to let Peter reverse your magic so you can live life as a Mederi. That's what you want, isn't it? That's what you've always wanted."

That was what I *had* wanted. I opened my mouth to tell him, but one look at his face made me shut it again. I'd never seen Ari look as vulnerable, or as determined. I was afraid if I interrupted, he'd never say what he wanted to say, what he *needed* to say.

"I should tell you that a life with me will be full of bad and difficult things. Tell you that there will be blood and death and evil. I should want to protect you from all that, right? *If I loved you* . . ." His voice broke in anguish and he raked his hand through my hair, pulling it free from its pins, almost yanking on it in his desperation. Clumsily he pawed at me, raining feverish kisses across my eyes, my cheeks, my nose. He wound his hand through my hair to the base of my neck and pressed me toward him, flattening his body against mine. He kissed me fiercely, hungrily, and then broke off abruptly.

"But I can't tell you those things. And I won't apologize for wanting you in my life. There is nothing, *nothing* I wouldn't do for you, except for the one thing I really should do for you. Let you go."

And yet, he did. He released his hold on me and my arms dropped to my sides. I rubbed them, trying to massage the ache out of them. Ari turned his back on me and walked over to a far corner of the room. His stance, and the unbelievable chaos of his signature, told me how hard he was struggling to do the right thing.

"Oh no you don't," I said, extricating myself from the enormous pile of ruffles at my feet. I wanted to kick off my shoes too; I must have looked ridiculous, but the ribbons were long and twisted and there was no way I was going to let Ari suffer for one moment longer than he had to. "You can't turn your back on me," I said. I strode purposefully over to him and put my hand on his shoulder. He tensed.

"Ari, I came here tonight because . . . because I love you too. I realize how tonight must have looked to you."

I saw the last few minutes of the ball as Ari must have seen it. Me, reaching achingly, longingly for Peter and the live bouquet of greenery he offered. Me, reaching for Peter and the life he offered. Me, clutching the bouquet to my breast, burying my face deep within its folds, and then lowering the bouquet so the entire world . . . and Ari . . . could see the uncontained zeal on my face, the unbridled glory, the rapturous joy.

But it hadn't really happened that way. I struggled to find the right words to tell Ari how I felt.

"You say I'm equal parts eager and reluctant," I said to his back. He still refused to look at me. "It's true, but not for the reasons you think. From the moment I saw you, I was attracted to you, wanted you. But I thought there was no possible way you'd ever want me, being what I was. Even when you indicated an interest, I thought for certain your feelings would dwindle or die out. I figured all I'd be left with were dashed hopes and a whole lot of hurt. I never dreamed your feelings would intensify. But as that intensity became more real, more believable, it terrified me. I've never felt this way about anyone before either. Not even close. You're not *powerless* around me. You're the most powerful force in my life."

I put my other hand on his shoulder and tried to make him turn around, to see the truth of my words. His signature was a choppy, sloppy, roiling mess.

"You scare me, Ari. But not because your magic is stronger than mine or because you've killed demons. I've killed a demon too," I said softly, my voice trailing off. Ari turned around then and clasped me to him.

"Nouiomo," he said tenderly, crushing me against his chest.

"You scare me, Ari," I said, my voice muffled against his suit coat, "because loving you means loving myself. It means admitting that someone with waning magic—death magic— is worth being loved. Your love makes me feel unbelievably strong, but also immeasurably vulnerable. Because it means you have a claim on me, a say in what I do. You have an enormous effect on me. I never wanted anyone to have that kind of power. But it's yours. I didn't give it to you, it just happened. *It just is.* You helped me to love who I am. I guess it's only fitting that you have the right to destroy me too."

I didn't think it was possible for Ari to squeeze me tighter. "I will be annihilated before I ever let anything happen to you," he said fiercely.

He scooped me up into his arms and carried me into the bedroom. It was an immense space with high ceilings and huge windows. He laid me on the massive bed as if I were as fragile as a butterfly. In seconds he shucked his suit. He sat down gingerly beside me. It was as if he couldn't believe I was real, or that I was *his*. He acted as if one sudden move might pop me like a bubble and make me disappear.

But I was his.

And he was mine.

"I'm not going anywhere," I said.

"Dressed like that? I hope not."

"There's still one thing that's between us."

Ari narrowed his eyes. "What's that?"

"These," I said, raising one leg. I pointed my toe and wriggled my slipper-clad foot, grinning at him.

Chapter 22

Sometime during the night I had promised Ari I would go to Bradbury with him. At the time, sequestered away in the opulent comfort of the Stirling's penthouse suite, cradled in Ari's strong arms, and magically surrounded by his rock-solid and intensely warm and soothing signature, it had seemed that nothing further would ever hurt or harm me. But as day broke and the sun streamed across our rumpled satin sheets, a small fissure of doubt began to creep back into my mind. What, in all of Luck's scorched Hell, would Ari's family think of me? But I kept my fears to myself, figuring Ari had had enough of my self-doubt for a while.

Sunday morning, we parted ways in the back of a cab at the edge of Timothy's Square. Ari claimed my mouth in a last bruising kiss, sneaking his hand beneath the coat he'd lent me. His hand slipped across my demon mark with the lightest feather touch, but it was enough to show that his effect on me was as strong as ever. I squeaked in protest and the sound was swallowed by Ari's full, soft mouth on mine. The driver cleared his throat impatiently and Ari reluctantly broke off the kiss. We each set off for our respective dorm rooms to pack.

The campus had an abandoned feel. Almost everyone had left for the break. I returned to Megiddo to find two letters. The first was really a note, from Ivy, indicating she and Fitz had left. They were staying at the Seknecai estate over the break. Personally, I couldn't imagine spending Beltane with Waldron Seknecus, but I supposed they were used to it.

The second letter was from Night, telling me that he'd talked to Karanos at the ball. He'd shared Linnaea's renewed concerns about the Mederies and their safety while traveling, as well as my suspicions regarding Vigilia. Karanos had given Night the name of the Maegester who'd been working the case and they were all going to meet. He was taking Peter with him so I wasn't to worry. I smiled at that last part, but then bit my lip, concerned about Night's increased involvement in the investigation. He might have stood up to a bunch of Host thugs in the hallway of Empyr last night, but putting a lancet (or whatever my brother's blade had been) to a demon's neck would only result in him getting his arm gnawed off. But there was nothing I could do to stop them so I tucked that letter, along with Ivy's, into my desk drawer.

I changed into a pink silk cami and lace mini bloomers and contemplated my closet, dithering. What did one wear when meeting one's boyfriend's parents for the first time? I had no idea, not ever having had a boyfriend before. I couldn't imagine meeting the parents of anyone I'd ever been romantically involved with. Ari had mentioned a Beltane bonfire too. I hope he didn't expect me to participate in any way. I was just getting used to the idea of *attending* these sorts of celebrations. I rubbed my arms nervously, trying to decide whether I could fit my boots in my backpack, or whether I'd have to carry them separately, when I felt a signature that was hot and blistery but the opposite of Ari's in every other way.

Nergal.

I'd almost, but not quite, forgotten about him. Really, what I had decided to do was not think about him, at least over the break. I still hadn't found a solution to his problem. He still hated Lamia as much, if not more, than when I'd first been assigned to represent him. And Lamia still refused to release Nergal from his marital vows, which were as strict as any demon obsessed with rules could make them.

I shall take you as mate, for here and ever after, to live and die by your side. Your debts are my debts, your sins are my sins, your life is my life . . .

Demons were nothing if not serious about promises.

My skin itched as if infected with a rash. Apparently Nergal was shifting into human form with an emphasis on the pestilence part of his personality instead of the drought and midsummer death part. He appeared before me in full fiery glory. On previous occasions such as this, I had always shielded my eyes with my arm and requested that he turn down his wattage. Today I wasted no time with such niceties. I threw up a magic shield that could have stopped a ten-ton radiation blast. His magic hit mine with enough force to knock my teeth together. Suddenly, my temples throbbed and my vision doubled. Nergal's magic bounced off my shield and reverberated back to him. But instead of reabsorbing it, he easily turned it away, uncaring of where else it might land. My armoire burst into flames.

"No!" I cried, watching my collection of high-necked tunics, sweater shawls, and wool wraps go up in smoke.

"You've been avoiding me," he said, leaving me to leech oxygen and put out the fire. By the time I was finished, an entire quarter of our room had been destroyed. I stood in front of Nergal, sweating, sooty, and panting.

"Small wonder," I said, irritated, and gestured back toward my ruined wardrobe. I walked over to Ivy's closet and pulled an old sweater out, glaring furiously at Nergal the whole time. Though I itched sorely to do it, I refrained from throwing any more magic.

"What do you want?"

"I want to discuss my options. You may be looking forward to a leisurely Beltane break lounging on a blanket in front of a bonfire, but I'm looking forward to another week with a curse worse than death. What do you think I want?" he snarled, advancing on me. "I want out." I pulled Ivy's sweater tighter around my shoulders, but refused to shrink back. Nergal loomed over me, his voice as harsh as his crusty, weathered features.

"I want you to act like my counsel and advise me." His words were clipped, his temper barely restrained. Nergal had been threatening me for months, had caused me countless sleepless nights, but I hadn't realized until now that he'd been merely impatient. Now he was angry. And I wasn't at all sure I could control him.

"I have, Nergal," I said quickly, hating the fact that I sounded desperate. "There are no options absent Lamia's consent."

"She will never consent."

I nodded, miserably chewing the inside of my lip.

"I want you to see what she has become."

"I've met her, Nergal. I know what she's like."

"Do you?" he said scornfully. "You have no idea."

He grabbed my arm and I glanced down, wishing I hadn't. My entire arm appeared shredded and riddled with maggots. I knew it wasn't real, but the pain and shock of seeing it made my pulse rate skyrocket. Bits of grisly, pulpy bicep tissue hung from my exposed humerus bone, all of it teeming with small, ricelike insects. I stifled a shriek, barely remembering that demons were like dogs. Showing fear only invited further attack.

I tried to jerk my arm away, but Nergal only squeezed tighter. "Come with me," he said, and we were instantly *gone*.

I knew demons could shift in and out of physical form but I hadn't known that they could carry someone with them when they left the corporeal world. I felt like a rag doll flushed down the toilet. My body twisted and turned and whirled around so violently that I wretched upon reentry. I knelt on a familiar looking wooden floor, clutching my stomach and heaving. The contents of my stomach were replaced with a small, cold knot of fear. My belly burned as I wiped my mouth and stood up.

Nergal had brought me to the Manipulation classroom. Lamia was there too.

In the last three months, she had grown infinitely more vile. She sat in the corner as she had the night of Bryde's Day when we'd first met, cackling at me. The sound sent shivers up my spine. Her signature felt raw and poisonous, like meat left to thaw on the counter for too long. But it was worse than that. Behind the overall nauseous feeling she gave off were pinpricks of pain, as if someone had slipped razor blades in the meat.

I tried to collect myself, but everything about me was in tatters: my dignity, my magic, even Ivy's sweater had somehow been torn by Nergal's forcing me to come here this way. Lamia's magic hit me then, squeezing me as she had before. My breathing became labored and I fought not to panic. Ari wasn't here this time to control her. Would Nergal allow her to squeeze the life out of me? How angry was he that I had failed him?

I glanced over at him. He looked back at me contemptuously. I could almost feel his disdain for me, his revulsion to my current unkempt state. My hair was tangled, my lips were dry, and I knew my skin likely looked green and sallow. Worse, Nergal now looked at me as if I was of no further use to him. I hadn't helped him the way a Maegester should, and I was too weak to control either him or his vile, repulsive wife, who he was still saddled with thanks to me. And then I realized that's why he'd brought me here. To give me a taste of the medicine my failure forced him to drink.

Only when I lay on the floor, gasping like a fish, thinking I was seconds away from dying of asphyxiation, did Nergal finally walk over to Lamia and whisper in her ear. His manner looked affectionate. He even chuckled softly as Lamia gave him a lopsided smile, showing all two rows of her pointed shark teeth. Her magic withdrew. But when Nergal turned back toward me, his face was a mask of hatred. For her or me, I couldn't tell. I raised myself up on two arms, panting. I didn't have the strength to stand. In the corner, Lamia turned her attention to something she was cradling in her lap. A fetid, rotten corn doll. She started rocking it back and forth, singing softly.

"Let's discuss my options," Nergal said calmly. He dragged a chair over to me, turned it around and straddled it so that his beefy, sun-darkened arms rested on the top of the seat back. He didn't bother to help me up. "How can I get out of my marital contract, Noon?" He looked at me with pity, the way one might look at a mangled insect before stepping on it to put it out of its misery.

I struggled to my feet and leaned against Rochester's desk, gripping its edge for support. For a moment, I craved Rochester's massive presence. *He* would not have been brought so low by these squabbling demons. But then I realized if he were here, he'd likely let this situation play out. If I couldn't control my client, I was of no use to the Council and I would be an embarrassment to the St. Luck's faculty.

We'd been over this, but I had nothing to fall back on but my training. "Duress," I said, glad to hear my voice sounded stronger than I felt, "forcing someone to do something against their will, can be one way of getting out of a contract."

Nergal waved a hand in the air, dismissing the idea. "No one was forced to do anything, then or now." I bit back a nasty retort and decided my best bet would be to play the professional.

"Fraud," I said. "If Lamia claimed to be something she wasn't and you married her relying on her lie then maybe we could argue that your marriage vows are void because of this misrepresentation."

Nergal looked contemplative, even though it wasn't a new idea. "The fact that she changed after your marriage doesn't count," I said. In the corner, Lamia sang a macabre lullaby. She was lost in her madness, completely unaware or uncaring of what was going on around her.

"Then what?" Nergal asked. He stood up and walked over

to me, intentionally ratcheting up his signature. Waiting for him was like waiting for a swarm of bees to settle on me. My instinct to run was so strong, I twitched.

"Rescission," I said, now almost frantic. A thin film of sweat broke out all over my body. "Were either of you married to another when you made your vows?"

Nergal shook his head, looking disappointed. "I grow weary of waiting for you to find an answer for me." He reached for me. I backed away, but not fast enough. He pressed his finger into the muscle of my shoulder. When he let go, it felt as if he'd just pressed a revolver against my arm and pulled the trigger. Instantly, a shooting pain burst forth from the area, pain worse than any sting Serafina had given me by a thousandfold. I shrieked in agony. Tears welled in my eyes and dripped out, wetting my cheeks. I had no shame, no further reserve of professional detachment left. Nergal had finally stripped all of that away, leaving only icy fear and an increasing physical numbness.

Nergal had infected me, as surely as if he'd filled a syringe with deadly plague and plunged it deep into my arm. I could feel death creeping under my skin and into my veins, sinking slowly into my muscles, curling around my innards, twisting through my bowels. I was powerless to prevent it. It was far too late for magical shields, defensive countermeasures, or useless attempts at controlling or manipulating him. I had failed, utterly and horribly. And, as I'd always thought, I would die for my failure.

I was on the verge of losing consciousness when Ari stepped into the room. He snarled so ferociously, for a second, he looked almost demonlike himself. He shot Nergal with a blast of magic so powerful Nergal sailed through the air and smashed into the back of the classroom wall. Old lithographs and framed etchings crashed to the floor in a shower of glass. My legs collapsed and I slumped to the floor, propped up by the side of Rochester's desk.

"Stop," I tried to yell, worried Nergal's counterattack would kill Ari. But the word came out slurred and thick, almost unrecognizable. My thoughts fractured. My brain felt swollen. "You can't . . . control my client," I tried to tell Ari, clutching the desk leg. I dug my nails into it, trying to stand. "Rule three . . . three thirty-one *C* . . . prohibits—"

Ari looked down at me, his face unreadable. "Stop talking," he said quietly. "Don't move." He turned to Nergal, who had picked himself up, brushed himself off, and looked ready to kill Ari next.

"This meeting is in violation of Professional Code of Conduct Rule 24-A and Ethical Cannon VII, both of which expressly forbid any communication with a party represented by counsel unless their counsel is present. Did *you* call this meeting?" Ari said to Nergal. "*My* client is present and yet I wasn't informed." Ari's expression was one of mild annoyance. But I could feel the underlying tension in his signature and I thought Nergal could probably feel it too.

Nergal narrowed his eyes at Ari and, for a moment, all our lives hung in the balance. Demons and Maegesters both used waning magic, but it was the way they used it that made all the difference. Demons were like war tanks. They'd been *the* Legion for Luck's sake. They were brute strength, practically unstoppable. But Maegesters were the warlords who had ruled the Legion. Why? Because, though the demons might have been the five hundred pound grappling infantry troops, Maegesters were the lance tip of the cavalry, the ranged precision of the artillery, and the single-minded command of the general. Battles, and certainly a war, could only be won with Maegesters calling the shots. But that martial advantage mattered less in hand-to-hand combat. I struggled furiously to sit up. If we were going to die, I wanted to be standing when the deathblow struck.

Nergal appeared to weigh his options. He glanced over at Lamia, who was still crooning softly. She squeezed the corn doll's neck as she stared at us fixedly, her eyes unfocused. Nergal clenched his hands into fists, clearly frustrated, enraged, and almost apoplectic. He shifted, before our eyes, into a huge, looming mantis. He scrabbled forward toward Ari, his long spiked forelegs scratching the floor and sweeping up desks as he went. His mandibles clicked rapidly back and forth and I suddenly remembered, even in my fever-induced fugue state, that mantes were not majestic, graceful creatures but rather predatory and cannibalistic.

Somehow I managed to grip the edge of the desk and push myself up at the same time. The effort nearly did me in. My whole body burned. Inside, it was as if fire ants crawled through my veins. Outside, it was as if the skin had been flayed from my body. The mantis Nergal raised one foreleg in the air, its long spiky front pointed directly at Ari's heart.

"Nergal," I shouted. "Stop!" But my words were little more than a barking croak. I tried to remember all of the things Rochester had taught me this year, but all I could re-member was how much I'd hated Manipulation and the dun-geon and Rochester and the weapons and Wednesdays . . . I poured all of those memories into my magic and threw it at Nergal in the form of the weapon I despised the most: Brunus' beloved nadziak. Once forged, my fiery war ham-mer was a thing of fierce beauty. I threw it straight at Nergal. Problem was, half of me went with it. That last blast of fiery war-hammer hatred tore through my gut, ripping it out. I felt a hollow, liquid feeling, as if my bones had turned to dust, and then I felt no more. I sank to the floor, my vision blacken-ing. My last thought was not very repentant.

I hoped Nergal was dead. And I hoped Ari lived.

I woke up in a room I'd never seen before. Much in the room was white: the walls, the sheets on the bed, and the gauzy curtains flapping at the open window. I squinted against the brightness, figuring it was near to midday. All that sun splashing against the clean bright white nearly blinded me. I raised my hand to block the light and felt how sore my arm was. Suddenly I remembered Nergal pressing his finger to my arm. I remembered the excruciating pain, the spreading numbness, and the sight of Nergal's horrifying spiky foreleg aimed straight at Ari's heart. For one awful second I considered whether I might be in Nergal's house. But it felt too safe and comfortable to be the home of my lethal, possibly adulterous, oathbreaking demon client. And I remembered Nergal saying something about how the land around his home had died and that his house had fallen into disrepair. This house was hardly in disrepair, although it was clear that most of the room's furnishings were recycled hand-me-downs.

The wooden dressers were mismatched. Sometime in the not too distant past, they'd been stripped and painted white. Colorful glass knobs had been added. On the floor was a braided wool rug in a swirl of reds, pinks, and blues, and on the bed was a pinwheel patterned quilt sewn together from boldly colored, multi-textured fabric swatches. Somehow, the mash up of colors seemed cheerful, like the fractured brilliance of sunlight caught in a prism.

I threw back the covers and got out of bed, thinking two things simultaneously. First, how unbelievably sore I was. Everywhere hurt, even places that made no sense—the backs of my knees, the spaces between my toes, my scalp and tongue. Whatever pestilence Nergal had visited upon me had been thorough. Second, where had these clothes come from? I stared down at a large Gaillard sweater and men's smalls.

I crept from my room and padded barefoot down the worn, polished wood of the hallway floor, wincing. It felt like I was walking on a bed of nails. Feeling a bit woozy, I steadied myself with a hand on the wall. I heard only my breathing and the beating of my own heart.

Where was I?

Suddenly, I smelled something familiar. I followed the smell into a large, airy kitchen dominated by a heavy oak table with benches instead of chairs. A cast-iron stove took up one whole corner of the room and the area above it was cluttered with hanging copper pots in every imaginable size. The countertops were crammed with ceramic crocks, bottles of what looked like wine or vinegar, and various spice jars. Every inch of available wall space was lined with pegs upon which saucepans, measuring cups, ladles, spoons, whisks, and all other manner of kitchen equipment could be seen. A desk had been built into the corner opposite the stove. The shelves above it were loaded with recipe books, their colorful spines cheerfully coordinating with a stripped table runner and braided wool rug similar to the one in the bedroom I'd come from.

Sitting at the desk was a woman. Her back was to me so that all I could see was her hair. It was as white as the walls. I cleared my throat, not wanting to sneak up on her, although I couldn't imagine she was a threat. This was the homiest house I'd ever been in. She turned to look at me and I inhaled sharply.

Her eyes were light pink and her skin was so white, it was almost translucent. Her features were as delicate as a doll's. She had high cheekbones, a cupid bow mouth, and white eyebrows that swept upward from her face giving her a regal, almost imperious look. Her gaze was preternatural in its intensity. I openly stared at her, not having seen anything like her before.

She perceptively guessed at my confusion. "I am *hveit*," she said, in answer to my unspoken question. "Like you, my birth was unusual among my people. Ari told me you didn't have much occult training. People who are *hveit* are Hyrkes. We don't have any magic, but sometimes . . . we *see* things."

I nodded, as if I understood. But I was as confused as ever. "Did you heal me? Is that why I'm here?"

She smiled and I could see she had the beginning lines of age in her face. She wore a long indigo skirt, brown leather sandals, and a vibrantly hued cotton batik shirt. Her nails were tipped with cherry red and chunky stones of red coral and turquoise dangled from her ears. She laughed and the sound was like bells tinkling.

"No, you were attacked by a demon, I was told. Your own client." Her tone was incredulous. I couldn't tell if she was amazed I'd survived, shocked that I should have to deal with such danger, or surprised I hadn't handled the situation better. She walked over to me and raised her hands to my face. I flinched and her features softened immediately.

"I'm sorry," she said, lowering her hands. "I was just going to see if your fever broke. I imagine you're still pretty jumpy. Here," she said, motioning me over to the table. Before I could sit down, however, the back kitchen door burst open. Of all the people I might have expected, she was the last. It was Bryony, followed immediately by Ari. My heart slipped and skid, righted itself with a wobble and then started beating again, only slightly less regularly than before.

The stubble on Ari's chin was at least two days old and his eyes were sunken with bluish black circles beneath them. I wondered how long I'd been sleeping, and how long Ari had gone without. Despite his apparent exhaustion, he smiled at Bryony as he held the door open for her. Seeing them together like that, I couldn't help remembering my old nickname for her, Beauty. She looked every inch the part, with her long dark red tresses, her aquamarine eyes, and her flawless cream-colored skin. Suddenly, my scalp itched and I stared down at my spindly legs poking out of someone else's light gray smalls. I bit the inside of my cheek, vainly wishing for a shower and my own clothes.

"Noon!" Bryony cried, "You're up." She rushed over and did what the *hveit* woman had tried to do, bringing her hands up to my cheeks and then moving her palm to my forehead. Her skin was cool and smooth. My eyes flickered back to Ari, standing behind her. He was tense with emotion. When Bryony finished, he stood rigidly in front of me for a moment. Then he reached out and crushed me to him. His hands stayed clamped to my arms like vises while his lips pressed against my hair.

I heard banging and the scraping of metal as Ari finally released me. I glanced over and saw the white-haired woman take something out of the oven. The smell of buttered crust, beef, and baked onions filled the room. I inhaled deeply, suddenly famished. At the look on my face, some of Ari's tenseness disappeared.

"Hungry?" he said. "My mom called Marduk's to get their recipe. She thought it would make you feel better to eat something that was familiar to you."

His mom?

I looked around the kitchen, realizing where I was. I tried

to imagine Ari scooting around this floor as a baby, or playing with toy cars here as a toddler, or even sitting at the table doing homework as a teen. I couldn't. But mostly because it all seemed so normal. And that's not what *my* childhood had been like.

"So you're . . ."

"Joy Carmine," Ari's mother said, slipping off her hot mitts and offering me a hand.

I looked over at Ari, who had a funny expression on his face. I clasped her hand and mumbled something like "Nice to meet you," and other words of thanks, wondering what sort of social etiquette standards applied to situations such as this. I tried to be as gracious as an unshowered girl in boy's underpants could be. Bryony sat down at the table and patted the bench beside her. I was still feeling pretty gross about myself though, so I chose to sit opposite her. She leaned across the table and spoke to me in low tones while Ari grabbed plates, glasses, and utensils from a nearby cupboard.

"I've never seen Ari so worried . . . or so angry."

"I'm pretty ticked off at Nergal myself," I said, thinking that was a vast understatement. I really wished I could rip his head off and then I wondered when I had become so bloodthirsty. Where was the girl with the soft spot for demons?

"The demon just acted like a demon," Bryony said. "It was *you* he was angry with."

"Me?"

"Your biggest injury was self-inflicted. Which is saying a lot because your other injury was a nasty plague that might have killed you if left untreated. But at least I knew how to help you with that. It was the damage you did to yourself that I almost couldn't fix. Ari said you threw out some uncontrolled, super charge. It ripped you up inside. Look, I only know enough about waning magic to heal its users. But I do know you can't try to throw more than you've got." She paused, glancing over toward Ari to see if he could hear. "You almost died," she whispered.

"I know," I said matter-of-factly. "But my client was trying to kill Ari. I'd do it again if I had to."

"No, you won't," Ari said softly, stepping up behind me. His voice was as hard as iron. He put his hands on my shoulders and squeezed, almost too hard. "We'll talk about what happened later."

Bryony gave me a look that seemed to say, *See?* but she let the conversation drop. Ari sat down next to me. Joy brought her baked dish over to the table and started cutting it. Everyone received a huge slice, but mine was the biggest. I stared at my plate, happy.

Happy to be alive. And happy, for once, to be eating Innkeeper's Pie.

After lunch, I was so tired I could barely keep my face off my plate. After thanking Joy for such a thoughtful menu I staggered back to my room. Ari wasn't far behind. I walked in and collapsed on the bed immediately. Ari shut the door behind him and leaned against it.

"I hope you haven't come in here to lecture me," I said. "I'm too tired to fight." I slid my legs under the covers and gratefully rested my head on the pillow. I guess closing my eyes finally convinced Ari I was serious about sleeping because he came over and climbed under the covers with me.

"Um," I said, thinking how my mother would react if I tried to crawl into bed with a boy I'd brought home. I might have grown to adulthood but, in her eyes, I would always be a child. "What will Joy say?"

"I spent two days sleeping outside your door."

"I don't know, Ari. This isn't exactly how I wanted to meet your mom."

He was quiet for a moment. Then he squeezed me to him. "Me neither. But you lived. I deserve this for what you put me through. She'll live too."

I was too tired to argue. I fell asleep in Ari's arms.

When I woke up, I was less sore and the woozy feeling I'd had earlier was entirely gone.

"I can't stand it," I said, jumping out of bed and startling Ari, who had fallen asleep next to me.

"Can't stand what?" he said, looking like he could have slept straight through till tomorrow.

"I need a shower and some real clothes. Do you think I could borrow something so we can go shopping? I forgot to mention . . . before Nergal kidnapped me, infected me with a deadly virus, and tried to kill you, he did something *really* unforgivable."

Ari looked confused. "Those things weren't unforgivable enough?"

"Oh no," I said, "the thing that really makes me want to fire him as my client is that he burned all my clothes, *every single stitch of them*. Nergal burned down my entire closet!" I started laughing. And then all the fear and the pain that I'd rolled up into a tight little ball and shoved deep down inside me somewhere suddenly exploded and I started bawling uncontrollably as I sank down onto the rug. Ari scooped me up and held me until I finished.

"I'm sorry," I said, hiccupping. "I'm sorry I couldn't control him better. I did everything I could think of."

"I know," Ari said, his hold tightening. "That's why I was angry. Rochester ranked us *Primoris* and *Secundus* for a reason. You don't have to protect me, even from your own client."

"You're the one who kept telling me to embrace my inner Maegester, Ari. If I'm going to spend my life as a Maegester instead of a Mederi, the last thing I'm going to do is let someone else get hurt when I can do something about it. Especially someone I care about."

"But that's the problem. You care too much. You almost killed yourself to save me. Remember that day in Manipulation when Rochester said you add emotion to your magic to make it stronger?" I nodded. "That's what you did. You almost gutted yourself. Which would have had the same effect on me. Promise me you'll never do it again."

"No," I said, getting up from his lap. "You said it yourself. Promises shouldn't be made lightly."

We argued a bit more, Ari pressed, I refused. We called it a temporary draw. Ari showed me where the bathroom was and got me all the towels and soap and shampoo I might need to put myself back together again. I stayed beneath the spray for a long time, scrubbing the soot, sweat, and tears away.

When I emerged, I wasn't yet 100 percent, but I was getting there. I padded down the hallway and back into the room I was staying in. On the bed was a new pair of pants and a high-necked short-sleeved blouse, both in my size. Ari came into the room holding a small glossy pink shopping bag by the finger.

"Here are a few other things you might need," he said with a knowing grin. "I took a guess, based on previous choices of yours."

I peeked in the bag and blushed. "Did you pick out the clothes too?"

"No, Bryony did. That's where we were today."

"Oh," I said, still not liking the idea of them shopping together even if it was for me and even if I did owe the well-meaning Mederi two major favors now. I picked at a loose thread on the quilt. "Bryony's nice."

"Very," Ari said, stepping closer. "But she's not you."

Sometimes I still didn't get why Ari was with me.

"What do you see in me?" I murmured, only half-joking.

"Everything," he whispered.

Chapter 23

ॐ

Bradbury was a neighborhood in the southwest of New Babylon proper. If one imagined New Babylon and its suburbs as a large boot standing on the northern shoreline of the Lethe, Bradbury was the toe that pointed west. Dockworkers, longshoremen, stevedores, and their families had slowly settled along the shore they worked and, over the years, the toe of the boot had grown quite large. Due to its geographical separation from the rest of New Babylon (fields and forest surrounded Bradbury to the north and west and the Lethe shoreline ran along its southern edge), and the nature of the work shared by most of its inhabitants, it had a closed-in, self-contained feel. Most people never left, and hardly anyone ever moved in. The same families had been living in the same houses for generations, loading and unloading all of the cargo ships that arrived and departed every week for the settlements and outposts along the Lethe.

The neighborhood was like Etincelle in a way. Everyone knew everyone else and the place had its own culture, its own customs. But where Etincelle was old money, old magic, large estates, and manicured lawns, Bradbury was street after street of row houses crammed twelve to a block. No one had more than a patch of grass for a yard (which suited me fine) and most had already paved over that to make room for a cabriolet, repair shop, or broken boat. The place of my birth was full of pedigreed people who lived in the past, but the Bradbury folk lived in the *now*. Their concerns were things like ship schedules and load lifts, not spells and magic. I doubted anyone in Bradbury had ever even seen a demon in person. Well, except Ari.

Ari and I decided to walk down to the riverfront before dinner. He wanted to show me the docks and I was curious about the bonfire site. There were no fields in Bradbury and it was difficult to imagine how the neighborhood would re-create Flora's famous tale. The sun had started its descent, but the shadows were still short. The air had cooled and I borrowed a light wrap from Joy before leaving. Ari wore a hooded cloak. He pulled my hand into one of the pockets and we set off.

The road outside of the Carmine residence was an amalgamation of old cobblestones, brick, and concrete. It was cracked and uneven with sand and grit tucked in every crevice. Tiny row houses crowded both sides of their street, each one with a different color, trim, or surface. Some were red-brick, others were faded grayish green clapboard, a few were bright yellow stucco. As we walked toward the dock, I noticed the most crowded blocks were the most colorful. The closer the houses stood together, the louder the colors, like siblings trying to shout over one another.

The oldest street in Bradbury ran along the riverfront. Ari told me people rarely drove along it anymore. It was too packed with cranes, cargo containers, and other equipment. But there were still some sections reserved for pedestrians. Every few blocks or so there were a group of benches and a large stone chalice.

"Who are the chalices for?" I asked.

"Estes," Ari said. That made sense, I thought. Estes was the Lethe's patron demon. Of course a community of long-

shoremen and dockworkers would revere and adore him. I
walked over to the chalice, searching for the knife I knew
would be there. Sure enough, I found a clean, sharp six inch
blade with a plain wooden handle tucked into a side niche of
the chalice's pedestal. I held my hand over the chalice bowl
and made a shallow cut along my left palm. The knife edge
stung when it cut, but I'd done this before and was used to it.
Apparently, Ari wasn't.

"What are you doing?" He leapt onto the base of the pedestal and grabbed my hand.

"Stop," I said, gently jerking my hand away from his. I let
the blood bleed into the bowl until it stopped on its own.
"Look on the other side of the pedestal. There should be a
pack of gauze or something to bind my hand with."

"I know where to look," he said tightly. He found a pack-
age of gauze tape, opened it, and started wrapping my hand
in silence.

"What?" I said. "You've never made an offering before?"

"No. I've never cut my hand and bled on the altar of a
potential client before." He ripped the tape with his teeth and
tied it tightly. "Our *lives* are sacrifice enough."

"Huh. Well, aren't we a pair?" I said, chortling merrily.
"You, raised as a Host child in a Hyrke neighborhood and
me, raised as a Hyrke child in a Host neighborhood."

Ari glared at me.

"Come on," I said. "Show me where they're going to light
the bonfire tomorrow."

Ari snorted. "If you'd been raised as Host you'd know . . .
we light the bonfire tomorrow."

I hoped *we* meant the Host in general and not Ari and me
in particular. I had never, in all my life, deliberately set
something on fire in front of an audience. And the few times
I'd inadvertently burned something in front of someone, it
had not been cause for celebration.

The bonfire sight was a few blocks down. The towering
frame of the structure was visible well before we reached it.
It was massive, rising almost forty feet into the air, like a
darkened lighthouse against the late afternoon sun. As we

neared, I could see that it was a very tall, narrow, six-sided pyramid made out of timber logs lashed at the top with rope. A small hole was cut in the bottom and people were lined up in front of it. It looked like they were taking turns stuffing kindling into the hole.

As we neared the group, Ari stopped and stood back, watching. Toward the back of the line, a pregnant woman waited to stuff the bonfire frame. I stiffened. Just a casual touch from someone with waning magic could make her miscarry. I pulled on Ari's sleeve.

"We should leave."

"Why? I thought you wanted to see the bonfire site." He turned to me. "Nouiomo," he said softly. "You're shaking. What's wrong?"

Before I could answer, the pregnant woman stepped out of the line with a young man who was holding her hand. I was petrified they would walk right over to us but they stopped a few yards away. Arm in arm they gave us a little bow.

"Welcome home, Aristos," the man said.

"Thanks, John. I see you and Grace are expecting. Congratulations."

The woman beamed and held up a bundle. "Baby clothes," she said. Then she glanced at me, her eyes resting briefly on the bandage around my hand.

"If you'd like to make an offering, as a guest, you're welcome to walk to the front of the line."

"Grace, this is Noon Onyx," Ari said. "We go to school together at St. Luck's. She's training to be a Maegester too."

The couple's eyes grew wide and I felt the blood rush to my cheeks. But their next words surprised me.

"So there's two of you to light the bonfire this year," John said. "That's wonderful, a double blessing for the baby." I frowned in open confusion now.

"What are you going to do with those baby clothes?" I blurted out.

"Burn them," Grace said, "or rather you will." She smiled. I was absolutely horrified but she looked enthusiastic.

"What do baby clothes have to do with Flora?" I asked,

irrationally upset that baby bunting would somehow be involved in a ceremony celebrating Flora. She was supposed to be the demon of sensuality, not fertility. I had to put up with enough of this sort of thing at Bryde's Day. Now Beltane too?

"They don't," Ari said quickly. "In Bradbury, all offerings are to Estes. In Etincelle, and most of the rest of New Babylon, the bonfires celebrate Flora, but Bradbury bonfires are lit in honor of Estes." He spoke to me then in a low whisper. "Hyrkes here make sacrifices by placing what is most valuable to them in the bonfire frame. If the offering is true, Estes will regift it three times over."

"So they're not all stuffing baby clothes in the bonfire?"

"No," Ari said, laughing. I think he heard the relief in my voice. Still, this poor couple was. And it was clear they were poor. Looking at their clothing, I couldn't believe they could afford to burn *any* clothes for their unborn child. They would need everything they had. But I knew such thoughts were blasphemous. Estes was supposed to provide for his adorers. And hadn't I just given the mighty patron demon my blood?

"Baby clothes is a very generous offering, John," Ari said.

John looked pleased and the couple both bowed again and made their way back to the line. In time, others came over. Most came no closer than the first couple had come. After a while, I began to see that they weren't afraid as much as keeping a respectful distance. The myriad offerings were fascinating: diaries, photographs, pieces of cloth, locks of hair tied with ribbon, letters . . . For a moment I was reminded of the mound of grave offerings left outside of Lucifer's tomb. But those offerings had been left to molder and decay, whereas these would be burned tomorrow.

The walk back home was slow and silent. I don't know what Ari was thinking, but his signature was drowsy and warm. When we stepped back inside the Carmine house, I heard men's voices coming from the kitchen. They were loud, boisterous and deep, arguing about something, but in a good-natured way, as if by ingrained habit.

"My dad and Matt are back," Ari said, grinning. He took my hand and led me down the hallway. I knew from what Ari had told me earlier that they'd both been out working the docks today.

When we stepped into the kitchen, the voices stopped abruptly. Joy was standing at the counter, rolling dough. She turned her head briefly and nodded in greeting. Two men were seated at the table, each holding a mug of beer. They stood at the same time, the wooden benches making a loud scraping sound against the stone floor of the kitchen. The younger man was the spitting image of his father. And he was huge, average height, but completely muscled. He had the build of a wrestler or a heavyweight boxer.

"You're Ari's *little* brother?" I said in disbelief, laughing. They looked at each other in surprise and then laughed too. I couldn't help wondering what they'd expected. Had they ever even met another member of the Host?

"Steve Carmine," Ari's father said, thumping his chest. He stuck his hand out awkwardly and I took it, my small hand completely disappearing in his large beefy paw. He pulled me into a fierce hug then, and though the gesture was rougher, I could tell it was more comfortable for him. He released me, but held on to my shoulders and gently shook me.

"You gave us quite a scare," he said. "I'm glad you've recovered." Although this man had no magic, his manner was compelling. In this neighborhood, where demons only existed as deities, he would be a force to be reckoned with.

Glancing around Joy's kitchen, after meeting so many of Ari's other neighbors, gave me a different perspective on how the Carmines lived. I'd been comparing them to Etincelle families and had thought them poor. I now realized the Carmines were rich by Bradbury standards. Steve Carmine obviously occupied a position of prominence here. I wondered how much of that position was due to the fact that he'd raised the only Host child these people had ever seen, the fact that he was married to a woman who was *hveit*, or just his imposing personality. Likely a combination of all three.

"So Estes gets a boon tonight?" Steve said, pointing at my

bandaged hand. "Onyx blood, huh?" He grinned. "The Lethe's current should stay swift and strong for weeks."

Joy turned around from her rolling and looked at my hand, her expression undecipherable. "There's some ointment in the bathroom," she said.

"It's okay, really," I said, but Ari left to get it anyway.

By the time he returned, Steve had put out two more huge frothy mugs of beer. Mine was so heavy I needed two hands to lift it. Ari cleaned and disinfected my cut without another word. The fact that he did this at the kitchen table told me the Carmines were far from squeamish. My guess was a lot of injuries had been sewn up at this table. Joy assured me she needed no help preparing dinner. When I'd heard she was making Lethe prawns with shallots, I'd voiced a mild protest, saying we could have just ordered takeout. Matt laughed and explained that there were no restaurants in Bradbury.

"Besides, my mom's prawns are the best," he said. "Even better than at Erasmus. My dad took a skiff out earlier and checked all our traps."

Erasmus was a Gaillard gastropub.

"So how's it going there?" I asked Matt. "You're home for the break, right? Are they still doing the Friday night pub crawls down Reed Street? The quad parties outside of Fallon?"

Matt nodded enthusiastically to my questions and then gave me a full rundown on campus goings-on. When that was through, he unloaded several freshman tales of woe. Mixed-up class schedules, mumbling professors, fights with the bursar. I'd had them all. I commiserated, offered advice, or just laughed out loud. Matt's stories made me nostalgic. I wouldn't have said I was blissfully happy lying about who and what I was, but hanging out as a Hyrke undergrad had been some of the most carefree years of my life. It was great to swap stories with Matt about the who, what, where, and when of Gaillard campus life.

Almost at the same time, Matt and I noticed that no one else was participating in the conversation. We stopped, dismayed at our mutual rudeness. But no one seemed to mind.

Steve was looking at me with a frank expression of wonder on his face. Perhaps he hadn't really believed I'd gone to Gaillard. He gazed at me like I was a tiger who'd just jumped through three hoops and was now balancing on a barrel. Joy gazed contentedly at all of us. Despite her chilly pink eyes and preternatural look, she looked like any other mom would under the circumstances—happy to have her whole family home and together.

I glanced over at Ari. He'd chosen to sit opposite me while he'd doctored my hand and he hadn't moved. He leaned forward on the table, one hand gripping his beer mug, the other resting comfortably beside it. His dark hair, windblown and riotous from our walk along the riverfront, brushed the hooded collar of his shirt. His expression was soft and his signature was like his heartbeat, steady and strong. My desire to touch him just then was so strong, my hand twitched. I forgot what I was saying and my voice trailed off. It was ridiculous really, how he could make me feel. I hadn't given him this power over me, it had just happened, organically. But I wouldn't have had it any other way.

After dinner, Ari, Steve, and Matt wandered down to the bonfire site. I stayed behind to help Joy clean up. We stood at the sink, with her washing dishes and me drying. Although we worked in silence, it wasn't uncomfortable. After a while, my thoughts drifted back to the pregnant couple I'd met earlier. Why had Luck made it so that some could conceive so easily and others never?

The window above Joy's sink looked out onto a small backyard, which had been paved over long ago. The cement was cracked and, scattered haphazardly around the area, were the rusty frames of various backyard items no longer in use: an old charcoal grill, a bent snow shovel, and toward the back, a swing set. How many years had it been since Joy had pushed her children on those swings? I snuck a glance at her. There was no denying that she looked *different*. Had I not seen her in this warm, nurturing environment, I might have misjudged her. With her pale white skin and bright pink eyes, she looked like a creature of the night. Yet I knew she had raised her sons with goodness and light. Perhaps I'd misjudged Lamia. Maybe the answer to my problem, and Nergal's, was as simple as giving Lamia what she wanted—a child.

"Where do demons come from, anyway?" I said. I gave the dish in my hand a final wipe and carefully placed it in the cupboard. "I heard they were spawned from the ground, with no parents, but someone has to raise them."

Beside me, Joy was completely still. I realized I'd just blurted out my question, with no context or explanation of the thoughts that had led me to it.

"Why do you want to know?"

"I'm sorry," I said. "It's just that, earlier, you said you see things. Well, I've never heard of anyone knowing where or when a demon child would be born. But then I'd never heard of anyone being *hveit* until I met you . . . I thought maybe, if you could see . . . Anyway, we have an assignment, Ari and I . . . It's been difficult," I finished lamely.

Joy grunted. I couldn't tell if she thought I was grossly understating the situation or if she thought I shouldn't waste words stating the obvious. How much had Ari told her about St. Luck's?

How much had she seen on her own?

"The woman involved wants a child," I said. "I was just wondering whether giving her one would help."

"'The woman'? Aren't you talking about a demon?" Joy looked at me curiously.

"Yes, but not the one that attacked me. That was my client." I laughed self-consciously. Most Host would believe the attack my fault since I'd failed to control the situation.

"Is this . . . woman capable of raising a child?"

"I'm not sure," I said, hesitantly, "but possibly a demon child. Who raises demon children anyway? Or are they spawned as adults?" Of course, if that were the case, I needn't spend even two more seconds considering what was already a fairly preposterous solution.

Joy stared out the window, silent. She waited for so long

to answer I thought the conversation might be over—that she didn't have any answers for me or that she felt the subject matter too uncomfortable to continue discussing. She peered out of the darkening window as if looking back through time. What memory was she recalling? Her pushing Matt in the swing? Her helping Ari down the slide? Finally, she spoke.

"Ari's told me a bit about your background. It's curious that Karanos never sent you and your brother to an occult school. He must have had his reasons. I took a different approach raising Ari. I'm Hyrke and so are Steve and Matt. But I didn't want Ari to grow up ignorant of Host ways." She turned off the water and leaned against the counter, crossing her arms in front of her.

"No, demon children aren't spawned as adults. And many are raised by others. But regardless of whether a child is demon, Host, or Hyrke, shouldn't the parent who is raising them be capable? Demons respond to a strong hand, to rules, boundaries, and discipline, do they not? The parent of *any* child should be able to teach their child how to follow the rules."

"Yes, I know. *Praeceptum primum, praeceptum solum.* Even I know that."

"If this demon isn't capable of following rules, the last thing she should be doing is raising a child."

"She hasn't broken any rules. It's *my* client who wants to renege on his promise. He's the one who wants a divorce. I feel sorry for her."

"Because her husband wants to leave her?"

"No, because . . . because she can't have a child." I looked away quickly.

Joy put her hand on mine. It was still warm from the water.

"Are we talking about the demon or you, Noon?" I fixed my expression and stared back at her, snatching my hand away. I didn't want her to *see*.

"You can always adopt," Joy said quietly.

"You had a son, birthed a child. Is it really the same?"

The words slipped out before I could even think about

them. Only after I heard them did I realize how horrible they sounded. Joy stared at me with those big pink preternatural eyes. Magic or no, she could be pretty intimidating.

"I have two sons, Noon."

I swallowed over the hard lump in my throat and nodded.

"You know, I cherish every day of my life spent with them." She reached into the soapy water and let the plug out of the drain. The water gurgled and swirled in the sink. "I wasn't sure what to think of you at first."

"I know. You would have been happier with Bryony."

"No," she said simply. "It's only that it's not every day you meet the woman your son is willing to die for."

The words to downplay our feelings were on the tip of my tongue. I wanted to assure her that things had not gone that far. But then I wondered. Had she *seen* something? I froze, speechless for a moment. She couldn't have meant her words literally.

"That's just an expression, right?" People said things like that when they really just meant a person had strong feelings for someone. "I mean, he wouldn't . . . he can't . . ." I gripped the counter, absolutely unwilling to contemplate a reality where those words were actually true. "Ari doesn't . . ." I made a choking sound, no longer able to speak. I wished now I'd never even brought up Lamia and children, or me and my stupid unobtainable desires. I wished I'd never opened the door to serious discussion with this woman. She scared me.

"You don't mean it," I whispered.

"There are worse fates than dying for someone you love."

"No! That'll never happen. Things would never get that bad. He has to know I wouldn't want that, couldn't . . . How could I go on living after something like that?"

She smiled, but it was a sad smile. She reached out and touched a lock of my hair. She twirled it for a moment and then tucked it behind my ear. Her next words were solemn.

"As I said, there are worse fates than dying for someone you love."

* * *

A ri came into the bathroom later that night after I finished brushing my teeth. I had on a pair of pink silk shorts and a white camisole.

"Can your mom see the future?" I asked.

"What? No," he said so matter-of-factly it instantly calmed me. "Whatever gave you that idea?"

"She said she could see things. I just wondered what she meant."

Ari paused, choosing his next words carefully. "She's good at reading people and how they'll react in certain situations, but she's a Hyrke, Noon. She doesn't have magic like us. Her ability to see the future isn't much more than Hyrke intuition." The tone of his voice indicated there was nothing further to discuss, or just that he had other things on his mind. He shut the door behind him and quietly turned the lock. He crept over to me.

"What are you doing?"

"What I've wanted to do all day."

He picked me up and sat me on the bathroom sink. I teetered on the edge and put my arms around his waist for support. He cupped my lower jaw, his long fingers touching at the base of my neck. When he had me just where he wanted me, he brushed my lips with his.

"Ari," I breathed, my lips parting. My signature flared as if I were a kiln that had just been lit. He pressed his lips to mine again, his mouth softly insistent. He smelled of sweat, wood, and work.

"We built you something," he murmured into my hair, pressing me close. I tensed. "Nouiomo, you've got to get over your fear."

"I'm not afraid of fire," I scoffed, leaning back. I almost tumbled into the sink though and Ari reached out to grab me.

"Yourself," he said, holding tight to my arms. "You're afraid of yourself. You have trouble controlling Nergal because your magic has two speeds, timid and berserk. In order to control a demon, you'll need to throw magic that is consistently strong and well shaped, not magic that is thrown in sputtering bursts or big, unshaped blasts. You need to stop adding emotion to it. That's what's making it so capricious and ineffective. You're going to have to lose your self-consciousness and your fear of waning magic if you want to manipulate it and use it to control a demon. You're going to have to learn to use waning magic like it's a toothbrush or a hairbrush. It's a tool, Noon. Nothing else."

Many of the things Ari said were true. I was afraid of myself, especially my magic and what it could do. And maybe my magic did have only two speeds: cautious and crazed. And it was true that I added emotion to my magic to make it stronger. But was that always wrong? Rochester and Ari seemed to think so. But maybe that was because waning magic users instinctively threw magic using destructive emotions like fear, anger, and hate and *those* emotions made magic capricious and unstable. I couldn't help wondering what might happen if I intentionally threw magic using other emotions. More positive, life-affirming ones.

Was I brave enough to test my theory at tomorrow night's bonfire?

The next day was the sort of day I'd dreamed about during school, after I'd read 180 pages of Oathbreaking cases, drafted a dozen case briefs, memorized the elements of sixteen evil deeds, reviewed eight sacrifice offers, and wrote (yet another) futile letter of advice to Nergal, all on less than five hours of sleep with barely more than coffee and a chocolate bar to keep me going. We slept in, woke to a breakfast of whole wheat pancakes with bacon and pan-seared potatoes and then lounged around on the couch playing mancala and looking through old photo albums.

One picture, in particular, fascinated me. A young Joy stood in front of the Lethe with an infant in her arms. Bright sunlight glinted off her hair and she squinted, one hand raised over her brow to block the sun. She grinned and gazed adoringly up at the camera obscura. I knew Steve had taken the picture. At her feet was a small reed basket.

"What's with the basket?"

"Joy found me at the riverfront one morning, floating around in that basket." He took the picture from me, staring at it more closely. But the only emotion in his voice was amazement. "If she hadn't come along, I would have drowned." He put the picture back in the album and turned to me. At first, I was unable to speak. It was unthinkable that a mother would have floated her newborn out into the Lethe to drown.

"Why?"

Ari shrugged. "Who knows? At first, my parents thought it was someone from Bradbury who couldn't afford a child. Even then Joy was known for taking things in, shining them up, and making them useful again. But then, when it became clear I was no ordinary Hyrke child, they looked to Etincelle. There are a few Host families in New Babylon, but not many, and the current flows in the opposite direction. It was pretty clear that basket had come from your side of the river."

"Then who are your real parents?"

Ari laughed. "Steve and Joy Carmine."

"But . . . don't you want to know?"

"No. As far as I'm concerned, I was born in that basket."

Ari tucked the picture back into the album and turned the page, chuckling over some other recalled memory. His signature was flat and steady as a board. I marvelled that he could be so cavalier about the circumstances surrounding his birth. I remembered the conversation we'd had in my dorm room on the first day of school, when Ari had confronted me about my birth and my angry, resentful feelings over it. What had he said?

Why do you waste one second on what might have been? What is, is. That's the only thing that matters.

He hadn't just been saying it; he'd been living it.

Dusk came quicker than I would have liked. I knew Ari was expecting me to participate in the bonfire lighting, but the whole idea of willingly burning something in front of an audience, no matter how celebratory the occasion might be, made me heart-poundingly nervous. I hemmed and hawed about getting ready. I took an unbelievable amount of time to shower and get dressed. Ari knew I was stalling but he didn't say anything. I think he knew I had to work through my fears on my own.

The day had been humid and hot. Some of the heat lingered so I chose to wear the only dress I had, a white cotton sheath that just skimmed the tops of my knees. I left my hair long and loose and, thinking of the uneven cobblestone walk down to the riverfront, slipped on a pair of low sandals.

When I emerged from my room everyone was at the door. Instantly I felt horrible about making everyone wait. The trepidation I was feeling must have shown on my face.

"Are you okay?" Matt asked, looking concerned. "You look like you're going to be sick."

Steve glared at his youngest son.

My anxiety only increased as we made our way down to the riverfront. As we walked, more and more people joined us. Soon, we were caught up in the crowd the way a leaf gets swept away on the surface of swiftly flowing water. The crowd streamed down to the docks with us riding the crest of the wave. This was all new to me. I'd never participated in any of Etincelle's bonfires.

"Then who lights them on the Onyx estate?" Matt had asked.

"We don't have them," I'd told him.

"Your Hyrkes have to go elsewhere? They can't celebrate at home?" He'd seemed aghast, put out on behalf of his southern shore brethren. I hadn't understood why until now. These Hyrkes had no signatures, but it was impossible not to feel their excitement.

Children were propped up on shoulders, shouting to one another, dogs barked and chased their owners, young men yelled and jostled each other, each one trying to muscle their way closer for a better look. We came to a stop not far from the river's edge. The crowd was so thick; I could only see the very top of the bonfire frame. In front of us were two large wooden boxes. Ari climbed up on one.

There were easily a thousand people down by the docks,

all facing Ari. He spoke to them as if he were addressing Copeland in Sin and Sanction, strong and confident, respectful but somewhat informal. He spoke in a clear oratory tone that carried well above the crowd, despite the rumblings of the mass and the blowing wind coming in off the Lethe.

"Pax vobiscum," Ari said to the crowd. *Peace be with you all.*

Almost as one, they responded back.

"Pax tecum, Aristos*!" Peace be with you.* A few of the young men whooped and cheered after that and then it got quiet again.

"We've come here to celebrate Beltane—the Bradbury way," Ari shouted. This time the crowd broke out in a contained riot. Their community pride was evident. When they calmed down again, Ari continued. "Tonight, we honor Estes, Patron Demon of the Lethe, protector of Bradbury's lifeblood."

I looked down at my bandaged hand. So Estes *was* more than a potential client to Ari. He had acted like Host didn't need to make offerings and show thanks. But I rather thought the opposite. I hadn't offered enough. Ari had said, as far as he was concerned, he'd been born on the Lethe. Estes had been his first protector, his first provider. Because of the demon's beneficence, Ari was alive now for me.

Ari turned around and reached out his hand to me. I took it and stepped up on the block. For one moment, it was as if the crowd was frozen in time. I knew I would remember this moment forever. Like the moment I'd written my name on The List, or the moment I'd let go of the lilies Peter had given me, some moments have the power to redefine a person, to redirect a life. I knew this moment was such a moment.

"I've brought a guest here tonight," Ari said, still holding my hand, but addressing the crowd. "Another Maegester-in-Training, from Etincelle. Nouiomo Onyx."

I tried to smile, but it likely looked like a grimace. I gripped Ari's hand hard enough to crack the bones. He didn't flinch. I remembered all the times my magic had gone awry. The times I'd tried to light something on fire and something else next to it had gone up instead. There were a thousand people here. Did Ari really have any idea what he was doing when he asked me to join him in lighting this bonfire? I wanted to do right by Estes. I owed the demon that much and more. But what if I failed?

A woman stepped forward from the crowd. She was young and pretty, but shabbily dressed. She waddled a little, her large, round belly making her gait uneven. She walked up to the boxes solemnly and stopped a few yards in front of us. It was Grace. She bowed her head and then, to my surprise, she addressed me.

"Nouiomo," she said, her voice higher than Ari's but just as clear. "Welcome." Some cheered after that but most were subdued. Their faces were expectant, however, not wary. They didn't know me as they knew Ari.

"Yesterday," Grace said, "you gave our hearth demon your blood. Today, we wanted to offer something to yours." The crowd parted to reveal a second, smaller bonfire frame some distance away from Estes' massive tower. "We built this bonfire frame to honor Flora. Will you light it?"

I nodded. Speaking was out of the question. I tried to swallow and couldn't. My stomach flipped and my hands shook. We Onyxes had no hearth demon, at least not that I knew of. But I wasn't about to insult these good people, or Flora, by saying that now. Ari let go of my hand and stepped back from me. All attention turned solely to me. It was the strangest sensation. All my life I'd avoided lighting fires in front of people. Now, the whole of a neighborhood looked to me to start one.

"Remember what I said," Ari said quietly, "strong and controlled."

"Sunt facta verbis difficiliora," I croaked. Easy for him to say. He wasn't the one who might accidentally set the crowd on fire.

He smiled. "You can do this."

I focused my attention on the small frame and felt my magic surge. For a single instant, I was full of heat and light. *Could a waning magic user throw magic mixed with any-*

thing but fear, fury, or hate? I had only a moment, but I tried to remember a time when I'd successfully thrown magic mixed with a warmer, softer emotion. I couldn't. The closest memories to what I had in mind were the times I'd used infatuation, arousal, or recklessness to provoke Ari. Instinct and past experience told me *those* emotions weren't going to make my magic less capricious. So instead I drew inspiration from the beaming faces of the people in the crowd. I knew I wouldn't be able to feel their emotions with my magic because they were Hyrkes, but I opened up my signature as if I could.

Then, feeling only hope and joy, I released my magic and directed it in a tightly controlled blast right into the heart of the little bonfire frame. To my delight and everyone else's, it sprang to life immediately, all fiery red and crackling. There were oo's and ah's, sounds of wonder, but no sounds of outright amazement. This was what they'd expected me to do, what they'd *wanted* me to do. I was the one who was amazed.

I turned to Ari and saw the light from my bonfire reflected back in his eyes. "Let's light the big one together," he said, looking eager. For once, so was I.

We faced the tower together, clasping hands. The crowd turned with us as one. I felt Ari's large, strong hand close around mine and it echoed the embrace of his signature. I tingled with the hum of gathered waning magic. Knowing there was a safe repository for all the chaos I was collecting and knowing that my fire was wanted, allowed me to feel my magic as I never had before. A molten, viscous heat developed at my core. I felt the edges of my signature blur into Ari's. For a moment, all that magic was too much. I felt myself bursting apart, losing control, but then I remembered to be hopeful, joyful, even giddy. In a heady rush, I abandoned my fear, opening myself as wide in offering as I had the first time I'd given myself to Ari. Only it wasn't just Ari I was giving myself to. It was Estes and his people, the living, breathing beings surrounding me who needed to know there was still magic in the world.

I heard Ari's sharp intake of breath beside me. I glanced

down at our clasped hands and saw a wisp of flame licking at his fingertips. Fire danced across my skin. I felt as if I'd immersed myself in a hot bath. The heat wrapped around me, seeped into my pores, and filled every open crevice until I couldn't stand it any longer. There was an elastic moment when everything seemed to expand and contract simultaneously. Then I felt the heat sluice off me and rush toward the bonfire frame as if it were Lethe water surging out to sea. The bonfire tower erupted. Every piece of the timber frame ignited at once, producing an explosion of heat and light. The crowd stepped back, shielding their eyes from the blast. One by one they lowered their hands and turned to us. Then they erupted as the tower had, their arms waving like flickering fire, their whoops and cheers competing with the roar of the flames.

Ari grinned and pulled me close, murmuring in my ear, *"Lucem in tenebras ferimus." Into the darkness, we bring light.*

Chapter 24

*

Despite the success of the bonfires, my sleep that night was uneasy. I woke up feeling heavy and thick. My limbs were sore. Ari said it was the aftereffect of the bonfire magic but it felt like tiredness and plain old worry to me. If I hadn't known that it had been hundreds of years since a real demon had actually been seen in Bradbury, I might have thought one was sitting on my shoulder (either Fraitan or Worghen, the demons of fret and worry respectively, to be sure). I even slumped from the imaginary weight of them while I sat at Joy's kitchen table, clutching my mug of coffee like a ward against the thoughts that plagued me.

For starters, I hadn't heard from either Night or Peter since the Barrister's Ball. Considering Peter's expression as he stood glowering over the blackened lily bouquet I'd ungratefully shoved back at him immediately before dashing off to find Ari, I couldn't blame him. But it was unlike Night not to at least send a brief note of assurance when he had to have known I was worried. But I reminded myself that it had taken him almost six weeks to write after he'd left to join the Demeter Tribe. And it certainly wasn't that I didn't have anything else to worry about.

Aside from my biggest academic concern, passing Manipulation when my client was homicidal, I also had my Barrister classes to worry about. Now that I wasn't *quite* as preoccupied with my love life and self-acceptance issues, I realized how behind I really was.

Three months ago I'd declared my intention to master oathbreaking remedies. I had yet to do so. Specific performance was the go-to remedy for nearly every conceivable breach (the demons and their unholy obsession with enforcing promises!) but there were dozens of others I needed to know, all of them bewilderingly alike. In my mind, compensatory damages blurred with consequential damages, incidental with nominal, treble with *terribilis* (the demons' second favorite remedy, predicated, as were many things in Halja, on the ancient "Rule of Three"). In Evil Deeds, I still struggled with *volenti non fit injuria*. Did Hyrke adorers willingly consent to harm just because demons were inherently dangerous? And the confusingly similar terms in Council Procedure that I needed to keep straight were almost too numerous to mention: impleader, interpleader, intervention, default judgment, summary judgment, judgment as a matter of law, judgment notwithstanding the verdict—

The Carmine's harmonic jangled, announcing that the operator was trying to put a call through. I jumped, spilling half my coffee across Joy's old oak table. I scowled and wondered if I should answer. Ari was in the shower. Steve and Matt had left for the docks and Joy had wandered down to the market. The tin ring set my teeth on edge. I picked it up before it could ring a third time.

"Carmine residence," I answered.

For a moment I thought that the person on the other end of the line had given up. Just as I was about to replace the receiver on its hook, I heard a voice I recognized.

"Noon?"

"Mom?"

She sighed. Like she'd found her cat in the neighbor's yard.

"So it's true," she said.

That my client tried to kill me? That I'd given up my one shot at becoming a Mederi? That I was now dating someone who killed demons for a living? That I might be forced to go that route myself one day? Nope, I knew what she meant.

"Yeah, it's true. I came to Bradbury for Beltane."

"Why?"

"When I left, you said good-bye with a one-way ticket to New Babylon. I didn't have a return ticket to Etincelle."

Wow. I don't think I'd ever been this blunt with my mother. Before, I would have um'ed and ah'ed and settled on something sufficiently unantagonistic like, "I thought you'd have other plans."

"Noon, you're always welcome here."

As if I were a guest. I mopped up my spilled coffee with one of Joy's kitchen rags. Typical of Joy, she'd knotted together dozens of old fabric scraps to make this one little rag. Had she ever thrown anything away? Or forced anyone out of her house? There was more to feeling welcome than words.

"How did you know where I was?"

"Your father told me."

"He's there?" I said, surprised.

"No. I have no idea where he is."

I did. Rockthorn Gorge. Although the only reason I knew that was because he'd asked Ari to go with him, not because he'd told me himself. I wondered what my mother would think if she knew what her husband was doing. Would she be worried? I felt the most peculiar emotion for her just then— sympathy. But her next words put us even farther into uncharted emotional territory.

"Noon . . . I'd like to see you. Are you able to fit in a visit before classes start again?"

I took a swig of coffee, stalling for time, and almost spit it out. It was stone-cold. What self-respecting Maegester lets coffee grow cold in her hands?

What self-respecting Mederi burns her garden to the ground?

"I'd have to bring Ari," I said.

There was a moment of uncomfortable silence.

"Bring Mr. Carmine," she said finally. "I'd like to meet him."

A ri took the news that we were leaving early easily. Joy admirably tried to hide her disappointment and both Steve and Matt gave me great big hugs that left me gasping for breath. Matt invited me to Gaillard for a future visit. I said I'd consider it. It would be odd going back there as a Maegester, but I supposed no one returned to their alma mater unchanged.

Ari and I boarded an afternoon ferry. Its name— *Apprehension*—did little to relieve my anxiety. There was no amiable chitchat this time. Ari grabbed a corner seat for us inside the cabin and I spent the entire crossing poring over my Oathbreaking hornbook. When we disembarked, the sun was setting, its warm reddish glow settling across the south bank like a blanket.

"What, no cab?" Ari joked when no one met us at the dock.

I laughed, my dour mood momentarily lightened. "Come on, it's only a mile or so down the Lemiscus." Ari grabbed my backpack before I could and we started walking. Despite the comfort of Ari's hand around mine, tension crept back into my muscles with each passing step.

"We're the first estate on the right," I blurted out after the silence grew too long. Ari squeezed my hand.

"Who's on the left?"

I swallowed. "The Asters."

We crunched along the gravelly lane, our boots kicking up dust that was almost invisible in the darkening light. When the umber lane lights came on in the Asters' stone wall I nearly jumped. Ari stopped and I was forced to stop with him.

"Noon," he said slowly, as if choosing his next words carefully, "I don't care if your mother doesn't like me."

I let out a puff of air I hadn't realized I'd been holding. "It's not you. It's me. I'm afraid she won't like *me*."

"Because you're a declared Maegester-in-Training now?"

I nodded.

"Quod me nutrit, me destruit," I mumbled. *That which nourishes me, destroys me.*

To my surprise, Ari laughed. "Mothers and fire," he said, shaking his head. "Maybe you two have more in common than you think."

At last we came to a brick walkway. Cutting across the grass had been out of the question, of course. We turned toward my house and I glanced over at Ari, wondering what his reaction would be. The Onyx estate could easily house scores of Bradbury families. The immense manor house rose up out of the landscape like a miniature skyline, with no less than seventeen spires, three huge towers, countless turrets, and several sprawling wings. But Ari's step was light and his signature solid. His only reaction was a low whistle of appreciation.

"Anything less and I'd have doubted your father actually lived here," he said, smirking.

His gaze shifted to the surrounding landscape. There wasn't much to see. You'd never know a Mederi lived here. It was the height of spring and not one flower rose from the ground. Not one tulip or daffodil, not one crocus or hyacinth. Flowering bushes and deciduous trees were also absent. Across the Lemiscus, the Asters' garden was probably bursting with lilac and forsythia blooms right about now. Their cherry trees would be vibrant and white, the petals blowing in the wind like celebratory confetti. Here, there was only grass and endless evergreens. Symbols of everlasting life.

Or were they?

When I'd last seen them, our evergreens had been covered with snow, but otherwise, they were exactly the same now as

they had been then. They would always be the same—never
changing, ever green. Changing seasons, passing years,
nothing would affect them. They would never shed their
leaves in the fall, never bloom in the spring. Bees didn't buzz
here; hummingbirds flew elsewhere. The ebb and flow of life
avoided this place because nothing ever died here. The Onyx
estate seemed stuck. I wondered what it would look like if it
ever got unstuck. Would it burst into bloom or would it
blacken like the bouquet of lilies I'd dropped at Peter's feet?

We stepped into the entryway, a grand but dark space, and
I wondered where everyone was. The place was so quiet I
heard the echo of our packs as we dropped them on the floor.
Just then my mother's housekeeper, Estelle, came in, wiping
her hands on a large linen apron. The apron bore the stains
and wrinkles of a full day's work. No starched white, frilly
aprons for any servant in Aurelia's employ. Unlike Mrs.
Aster, my mother frowned on anything ornamental.

Estelle gave me a warm embrace. As our housekeeper
she'd always known the true nature of my magic, but, respect-
ing my parents' wishes, she'd never directly mentioned it. She
must have assumed my declaration meant all such restrictions
had been lifted. She positively gushed with praise and congratulations. I tried to explain that such statements were not
only unnecessary but also inappropriate. I'd achieved nothing, accomplished nothing. But she was having none of it.
Ari's introduction, with his Hyrke surname, caused some
confusion, but when we finally got it all sorted out Estelle
gave him a big hug too. *Of course* she knew him (who didn't?)
from his Aunt Judy who worked over at the Decemai estate.
So Estelle and Ari spent a few minutes chatting about Judy
and her doings while I stood nodding politely.

At some point during the discussion we realized we
weren't alone. I don't know what it was exactly that alerted
us to my mother's presence at the top of the room's sweeping
staircase. She'd made no noise or movement. But suddenly
we were aware of her at the top of the staircase's swirl, looking down on us. Estelle made her excuses (she had dinner to
check on) and left. I stared up at my mother, unable to swal-

low or speak. She crept slowly toward us, her eyes never leaving mine. She didn't even acknowledge Ari's presence.

She wasn't smiling. On the contrary, her face seemed frozen and I realized she was struggling with emotions almost too vast to be contained. For a moment, I thought her inner struggle would tear her small frame apart, but then she stepped forward and clasped me to her in a fierce embrace, squeezing her arms around my neck and pressing her cheek against mine. I just stood there, not squeezing back.

How could I? How could I ever forgive her for the evergreen in my locker? For enrolling me at St. Luck's in the first place? She'd raised me to ignore and abhor my magic and then she'd thrown me to the demons.

She released me as abruptly as she'd embraced me, as if she knew her affection made me uncomfortable. She swiped at the corners of her eyes and then turned to Ari.

"Mr. Carmine," she said, her voice as steady as a spellcaster's, "thank you for bringing my daughter home."

D inner that night was not as unpleasant as I thought it would be. Once we were over the initial hurdle of awkwardly expressed emotions, conversation ran more smoothly. Estelle had prepared a late meal of *risotto alla pittoca*, which was immeasurably satisfying since we'd skipped lunch to study. She served roasted garlic and a loaf of braided bread with it and my mother opened a nice, unensorcelled bottle of *Vitis labrusca* wine.

"Leave the apples to the Angels," she said, raising her glass, "and the grapes to us."

It was a traditional, if somewhat somber, toast for an all-Host gathering. To the Host, apples symbolized infatuation, flirtation, and sometimes death, but if so, only because of accident, ignorance, or overabundance. Grapes, on the other hand, were the real deal. They symbolized blood sacrifice, a willful death so that loved ones might live. Ari and I murmured our assent and drank.

Our family dining room, a cavernous space three stories

high with a vaulted ceiling, arched windows, and stone walls, was about as formal as one could be. A massive fireplace with three hearths dominated one side of the room. A frieze depicting Lucifer's last battle cry at Armageddon ran atop all three fireboxes. Carved beneath were the words: *ADURO VELUM! Burn the veil.* It was said Lucifer's final strategy was to pierce the enemy's front line with fire, but he was struck with a lance before he could marshal adequate demon forces to do so.

The three of us sat at the end of a mahogany table that could have comfortably sat thirty. My mother regaled us with stories of Seknecus and Rochester in their youth. Aurelia had attended Holly and Oak with the two of them and my father, before leaving to join the Hawthorn Tribe. In her opinion, Seknecus had always been destined for the ivory tower, but Rochester's choice to become a professor was a surprise. She'd always pegged him, not my father, as the one who'd go for the executive position. She became quiet then and I feared the conversation would stall, but then Ari asked some purposely generic question about Etincelle's history and the discussion turned to less personal areas.

We finished off the meal with a piece of berry cobbler (minus the fresh fruit or mint garnishes that might have adorned the plates elsewhere) and my mother walked us upstairs. Ari was installed in Night's old room. I chewed my lip inconspicuously, wondering when we'd hear from him and Peter.

As it turned out, I didn't have to wait long.

When Peter and I were kids there was no way to prearrange play dates. Mrs. Aster hated me and my own parents did nothing to encourage the friendship. Peter's spellcasting ability manifested at an early age. At four, he learned how to cast a sweet spell. He spent weeks turning all manner of things into sugary, syrupy, edible confections. At six, he learned how to cast a spell of agility. It was the first time he successfully climbed the Aster wall and made it to my house. By the age of twelve, Peter wanted to find a more sophisticated way of contacting me than pebbles thrown against my window. He found it in scrying. At first, Peter only saw an image of me when he attempted to contact me. But through painstaking practice, Peter later learned to use any reflective surface—water, glass, mirrors—to send me a message.

Like all kids who pass forbidden notes, we had a favored "drop spot"—a gilded floor-length mirror in the corner of my bedroom. I hadn't checked the drop spot since I was fourteen so I didn't give it a second's thought as I climbed into bed that night. But when I turned out the lights, fear ripped through my gut. There, on my mirror, was a glowing red message from Peter.

Oh, merciful Luck, how long had the message been there? Peter hadn't known I was going to Bradbury for the break. He'd thought I'd come here . . . I rushed out of my bed and flipped on the lights. The message disappeared and I almost screamed. Frantic, I plunged my room into darkness again. The letters reappeared, scrawled backward across the mirror as if Peter were inside it. Of course he wasn't. He'd written the words from wherever he was, with a stick, his finger, a pen, if he'd had one. I bit my lip. The only reason Peter would have tried to contact me this way is if he'd had no other choice. *Where was he? Was Night still with him? I should have gone with them . . .* My thoughts tripped over one another as I tried to reverse the message. I scrambled in my pack for paper and a pencil to make translating easier. At last, I knew where they were and what they'd found. The answer made me wish I didn't. His message said:

Noon—

Missing Mederies were a demon's offering to Lucifer. We're being held at the tomb. Send help.

—Peter

What? I didn't understand. If the *rogare* was Vigilia as I suspected, why would she be making offerings to Lucifer? Was that how she planned on getting her followers back? By killing a few and then hoping Luck would return her sacrifice to her three times over? It didn't make sense. First off, I doubted any of the Mederies that she'd attacked or abducted were her followers. My understanding from the research I'd done was that no one followed her anymore. Second, how did she even know where Lucifer's tomb was? Peter and I had just found it last week.

My heart thundered and I could barely string enough coherent thoughts together to make a plan. In the dark, I fumbled for my clothes and then went to go wake Ari.

"Night and Peter are in trouble," I said, shaking him awake a few minutes later. I dragged him down to my room to look at the mirror message. To save time, I thrust the piece of paper with the deciphered note at him, but he waved it away.

"I know what it says. I just don't understand it. What tomb does he mean?"

"Lucifer's."

Ari shook his head in confusion. "That's impossible. No one knows where it is."

"I do," I said softly. "Peter and I found it. The night we went looking for the spell."

Ari stared at me. "The night you had dinner together at Empyr."

I nodded, two guilty red spots forming on my cheeks.

Ari had always suspected, correctly, that something had happened between Peter and me that night, but I'd never told him anything other than we'd found the spell. From the look on his face, learning about other discoveries we'd made, other secrets we'd been keeping, obviously didn't sit well with him.

"You can't possibly be jealous now," I said incredulously.

Ari shrugged and then his expression turned feral. "All I know is that I'd leave Peter Aster to the demons if it weren't for the fact that your brother is there with him."

His threat was so real, my stomach turned to ice water. *He meant it.*

"Well, thankfully, it's not your choice to make," I said and turned toward the door.

"You should stay here."

I stopped in my tracks, the red stain of guilt on my face turning to anger. "No."

"Peter said 'send help,' not come yourself. You think he wants you walking into the lair of a psychotic demon?"

"I don't care. I'm going. Besides, you don't even know where the tomb is."

"Noon, this demon has to know that if it's caught, it'll be killed. I don't want to bring you."

"Why? Because I'm inexperienced? Or because you're being overprotective?"

"Both."

"That's not good enough. You can't have it both ways, Ari. You can't convince me to keep training as a Maegester and then ask me to run for cover every time there's demon trouble."

"This is more than trouble. 'Trouble' is what the Greenwalds got at Blacken Ridge when Rictus appeared insisting they follow a strict interpretation of the contract they'd signed. 'Trouble' is what's brewing between the two demons squabbling over Clara Verdigris' tumble with Owen Amberworth.

"*This* may be a demon abducting members of the Host and possibly murdering them. If even half of what Peter's message says is true, my services as an executioner would be required. This demon will have to be put down—*killed, Noon*—and you don't like killing."

"You're right, Ari. I hate killing. But you know what I hate even more? The thought of Night and Peter needing help and me just standing by doing nothing when, for once, my magic is the kind of magic that might actually help someone. So I'm going, whether you like it or not."

We stood facing each other, our signatures stretched like

two balloons about to burst. I honestly don't know what I would have said to him next. Possibly something unforgivable. But my mother's presence in the doorway redirected my attention. She could have been standing there the whole time. There was no way to know when she'd arrived and how much she'd heard. But I was pretty sure from the look on her face that she'd heard enough.

With a muffled sob, she tore from the doorway and ran down the hall. I gave chase, at first not knowing why. We had to get out of here *now*! Even if my mother had heard everything, how could she help? She hadn't practiced the Mederi arts for over twenty years. But, as I chased her, I thought about what Ari had said. He was right. Killing might be required. And that meant I might be killed. Tonight's journey might be a one-way ticket I bought for myself. I didn't want to leave without saying good-bye. Despite everything, I didn't want to leave with any bitterness between us.

I found her in the most unlikely of places—her old garden.

"Why did you come here?" Out of all the things I could have opened with, *I love you . . . I forgive you . . . I'm sorry*—it was the first thing I blurted out.

Ari arrived a few seconds later. "Noon! You chased her into the garden?" He looked around at all the blackened, twisted wreckage. If it were daylight, he might have realized his mistake. But the silvery milk wash of the moon's light made the black look shiny and new. My mother started laughing, but the sound was half-hysterical, half-hiccup.

"I did this," she said, almost proudly, gesturing to an acre's worth of dead plants and charred debris. She slipped to her knees and knelt in the ashes. "I came here," she said, answering my earlier question, "because this is where I ran the first time Luck tried to take you and your brother from me.

"When I married your father, I was barely twenty. A little young for marriage, but we were so in love." She looked up at me; I suppose to gauge my reaction. The idea of my parents ever having been in love was pretty hard to believe.

"We were impatient to start our lives together," she continued, her voice low with recollection. "I moved in here and planted my first garden. *Edhen* they called it, because, even at twenty, I could create a paradise. Nothing was impervious to my touch. My fingers had only to graze the length of a stem and it would burst into bloom. I had only to press my palms against the bare bark of a tree to flush it. I could stroke my fingertip down the belly of mother earth and new seedlings would shoot from the ground. But from my womb? Nothing. Finally, after a year of despair, my monthly courses stopped and I dared to hope."

She pressed the heels of her hands to her eyes and rubbed. Despite my impatience to get to the tomb, I sank down beside her. Somehow, I knew that brief moment of hope she'd just described had been the apex of her life.

"I started to cramp and bleed," she said next, confirming my guess. "The blood was awful. Just a few little brown spots, no bigger than seeds. But they were the seeds of death and I was petrified. And then those little brown seeds burst into bright red bloom and I thought I would lose you. Pulling my hair out, scratching my face, I ran to my garden and knelt—*right here*—and I prayed."

"Prayed?" I said, confused. She had to have meant pleaded. Members of the Host didn't pray. *Ever.*

But my mother nodded. "I pleaded to Luck. And then I prayed to Him." I heard Ari's sharp intake of breath.

"But you're Host!" I cried.

"I didn't care! I still don't!" She practically bared her teeth. "I pleaded to Luck to save you. I prayed to Him to hear me. I wanted you to live and I called on them both to help." She lowered her head and looked at her hands, which were now clasped in front of her. "I don't know who answered," she said softly. "One of them did, because suddenly I felt the two of you alive and strong, kicking inside me."

For a moment, I froze. I couldn't move. I couldn't speak. I didn't know what to say. My whole life I'd questioned my mother's affection and now she'd just revealed that she'd sold her soul so that I might live. I swallowed, nearly choking, and looked over at Ari. He was staring down at my mother's clasped hands.

"Did your prayer include a promise?" he said flatly. I was surprised by the lack of compassion in his voice. My mother laughed unpleasantly and looked him square in the eye.

"I promised Him that if he saved my children, I wouldn't raise them to be a part of Lucifer's Host."

Of course, I thought. *What god would answer a prayer for someone in the enemy's army?*

Every odd, cold act my mother had ever done suddenly became clear. Her actions had seemed almost cruel at times, but they made sense now. Enrolling me in the Barrister program at St. Luck's and then putting the evergreen in my locker was her way of pushing me toward declaring without breaking her promise to the one who may have saved me. All along Aurelia had been motivated by one simple goal: she'd wanted her children to live.

And now, one or both of us might die.

W̱e left my mother in the garden. It had been naive of me to think we'd have a tidy good-bye. Despite her revelation, I still had the impression she blamed me for being what I was. That somehow, even *in utero,* I'd rebelled against His touch and that's the reason Night and I had been born the way we were. But it was now clear that my mother loved us ferociously. My mother was a lioness, with claws of her own. And the lengths she would go to in order to protect her cubs was truly frightening. Even now I wondered if she was offering up a moonlit prayer for our safe return.

I sighed.

"When we get to the north bank," I said to Ari, "call Bryony."

"Bryony?"

"Yes. Night and Peter are being held by a demon. How likely is it that they're unhurt?" *It'd been five days. How likely was it that they were still alive?* But I shoved that thought down deep and refused to think about it.

"Tell her to meet us at the tomb. It's six leagues due east of St. Lucifer's. Tell her to take a cab to Sheol and then walk into the woods. She'll see our path."

Breadcrumbs were for kids in fairytales. Maegesters like us scorched the earth.

Chapter 25

❧

When we arrived at the Etincelle dock, no one was there. A few ferries were tied up, but waning magic doesn't work so well on machines. Ari and I were more likely to cause an explosion than an ignition if we tried to pilot one of the big boats so we "liberated" a small unnamed dinghy and reluctantly climbed aboard. I sat down on the small wooden bench and sliced my palm with a knife I found in a box under the seat. I chanted the name "Alacrity" as I made a fist and shook a couple drops of my blood on the floor. Ari gave me a grim look and pushed off. I raked my bleeding hand through the Lethe as he rowed us out into the river, giving Estes a further offering for haste and speed.

I cannot imagine how long our journey would have taken had I not made these small offerings. As it was, the crossing was miserable. Ari wouldn't let me take a turn at rowing, arguing that even in his exhausted state he could row farther and faster than I could. My helplessness made me want to slash every part of my body and bleed out until my blood reached the mouth of the sea. But that type of sacrifice wouldn't be appreciated by an upstanding demon like Estes, and besides, little help I'd be to Night and Peter if I arrived dead on the north bank.

Sometime in the early morning, hours before sunrise, we reached the other side. By that point every muscle in Ari's body was shaking. I had to help him out of the boat. We found a public harmonic near the entrance to the docks and called Bryony. She agreed to meet us at the tomb. We had to walk a few blocks to find a cabriolet. Considering the time, I supposed it was Luck's hand that we found one at all. We scrambled into the backseat and my instinct was to scoop Ari up and put him on my lap. But that was laughable. His body was huge compared to mine. My heart ached though, thinking of him going into battle against a demon in his current exhausted state. I wanted to tell him to stay behind, but I knew what he would say. So I pressed myself against him and hoped Bryony was right behind us.

The cab dumped us in Sheol. The driver was pretty pissed about being stood up on the payment until I bared my demon mark and hissed at him to send me a bill. He took off, tires screeching. At that point, I was so worried about Night and Peter, I didn't even care. Ari looked expectantly at me and I blazed a blackened path through the woods that legions could have followed.

I retraced with Ari the steps Peter and I had taken. We crossed the same moonlit field, stopping to rest at the same place Peter and I had rested just before entering the forest. Unbidden, the memory of Peter's kiss came to mind. So desperately did I wish for him and Night to be okay that I probably would have kissed him again, right then and there, even in front of Ari, if I could have. Instead I turned into the forest, indiscriminately killing low brush, grass, and saplings alike. I picked up a dead tree limb and torched its end. My fire lit our way.

As before, we walked for what felt like hours, though it likely could not have been more than one. I knew when we got close because I could feel it, the nasty malignancy of the place that seemed to seep out of the ground. Just as we stepped into the clearing, our torches went out. Ari frowned at his and tried to relight it. I remembered how many times I'd tried to start a fire the night Peter and I had come.

"Don't bother," I said. "Nothing burns here."

Ari stared at me and said nothing. But the look on his face was enough to frighten me. Because he suddenly looked unsure of himself. He glanced around, taking in the broken rows of headstones, the decaying vegetation, and the ramshackle, collapsed grave keepers' house at the edge of the clearing.

"Noon, something's wrong."

"I know," I said, turning toward the house. But Ari grabbed my arm.

"*Nothing burns here?* Does our magic even work here?"

"I don't know," I said, staring into his eyes. Thankfully, his uncertainty melted into a mask of something I'd never seen. As I looked at him, I felt like I was looking in a mirror. *Battle rage,* I thought. *That's what I'm seeing; that's what I'm feeling.*

Fear and ferocity coursed through my veins in equal parts. "If our magic doesn't work here, neither does hers," I said, reaching for a sharp stick.

As we approached the house, I grew uneasy. I was well aware of the toxic effect of my surroundings. But this other thing I sensed was some niggling detail in my own subconscious. I ignored the feeling though. I didn't want any distractions. I concentrated on opening my signature as wide as possible so I could sense any demons who might be hiding. Ari's signature bumped up against mine, boiling hot, like the burning oil medieval Hyrkes had poured down on their enemies.

We reached the house and Ari went in first.

The dark was the first thing I noticed. Last time, strikes of lightning had periodically lit up the interior of the house, guiding my way. This time, it was pitch-black and eerily, intensely, silent. The rickety door slammed behind me and I jumped, bumping into Ari's back. I fumbled in my jacket pocket and pulled out a good old-fashioned electric hand torch. I switched it on and a white circular glow splashed across the floor sending hundreds of little black bugs skittering toward the walls.

The cold, wet, poisoned feel of the place was just as pronounced as before. We crept along the hallway and I fought the urge to cling to Ari's shirt. Entering this place purged my battle rage the way influenza flushed the intestines. My middle felt hollow and my limbs shook.

When we stepped into the back room where the tomb was, I heard breathing, but there was no accompanying demon signature, so I knew we'd found Night and Peter. I waved the torch frantically, splashing light across the piles of books, bells, carvings, and cradles that were still scattered throughout the room. In the corner, opposite the coffin lid, I saw them.

Peter was bound and gagged but otherwise looked fine. It was relatively easy to subdue one Angel if you caught him by surprise. Night, on the other hand, looked like he'd been tortured. His shirt was gone. Deep welts, oozing gashes, and purpling bruises covered every inch of his chest. His face looked like a gargoyle's with fat lips, swollen eyes, and puffy, bloated cheeks. I gave a muffled sob and ran to him, kneeling on the floor in front of him.

"Night," I cried, my voice breaking.

He didn't respond. I pressed my fingers against his neck and let my torch crash to the floor. Instantly, the light went out. I felt a weak pulse beneath my fingers and shook him, none too gently now that I knew he was alive. If we could get him out and into the woods, Bryony could heal him.

I heard Ari pick up my fallen light. He shook it as Peter screamed something incomprehensible beneath his gag. My stomach dropped as I felt a familiar signature. Hot pinpricks of pain needled my skin and a hornetlike buzz sounded in my ears. Cold sweat pooled at the base of my spine and, so great was the signature's psychological effect on me, I swiped at my ear, suddenly scared of what might be swarming in the darkness.

No. It couldn't be, I thought.

I heard Ari smack the torch against his palm. It relit and I turned my head. Sure enough, Nergal stood in the doorway. *His standing there made no sense,* I thought, *unless he was the demon responsible for abducting Night and Peter.*

I reached over and ripped the gag out of Peter's mouth. Immediately, he started casting a spell but Nergal struck him with an electric bolt of magic before he could complete it. Peter fell to the floor, smoking and stiff.

"Peter!" I shrieked, dropping to the floor. Beneath me, Peter lay still, his eyes open and unblinking, his fists curled like crow's feet, his lips frozen in the snarl of his half-cast spell.

Behind me, I felt a discharge of electric power from Ari and Nergal that was unlike anything I'd ever experienced. If this is what it felt like when two waning magic users fought without using fire, I couldn't imagine what Armageddon must have been like. No wonder Heaven had fallen.

I shielded Peter's body with my own, wondering if that would even help. Night was now too far away for me to reach. Light flashed irregularly as the fallen electric torch was kicked and spun, stopped and kicked again. Nergal's hands locked around Ari's neck and squeezed. Ari instinctively tried to defend himself with fire, which didn't work. Nergal threw another bolt of electricity at Ari, barely missing him. Ari tried to blast back but his earlier exhaustion slowed his reflexes. The two struggled, magically and physically, straining, sweating, joints popping, signatures grinding, until Nergal finally cracked his forehead against Ari's face. I heard a wet, pulpy, crunching sound. Blood flowed from Ari's nose and my vision swam.

Ari was seconds from passing out.

I grabbed the sharp stick I'd picked up from the ground outside. Blood pounding in my ears, I leapt onto Nergal's back and plunged the stick into his neck. He howled and threw me off. I crashed into the coffin lid and its enormous weight fell on me. I felt a popping sound in my arm and, suddenly, my elbow felt as if someone had shot an arrow through the joint.

I shrieked, but somehow kept my wits enough to remember not to throw fire. Instead, learning from Nergal, I blasted the coffin lid with an electric bolt. I expected it to go flying, so great was the blast I'd sent toward it, but it barely moved. The weight continued to press down on my chest. I panted. Nergal pulled the now grisly red and wet stick from his neck and turned toward Ari, who swayed on his feet. I howled beneath the coffin lid, twisting my body, thrashing my legs, desperately trying to get free. Tears coursed down my cheeks. The frustration and pain were driving me mad.

Nergal advanced on Ari and I pleaded to Luck, thinking that I'd do anything, *anything*, if he would help us. I was *this close* to praying to the Savior too, so great was my fear and desperation, when another demon crawled out of the open mouth of the tomb.

My mouth went dry. I stopped struggling and all thoughts fled.

It was Lamia and she was covered in blood, not the fresh, red blood that covered us, but rather the putrid, decaying blood of things that had already died. The smell of it, and the feel of her, was so awful, my stomach seized. I ground my teeth and somehow managed to wrench my legs free from the coffin lid.

Oh, great Luck below, she was the reason for this place's poisoned feel.

"You live here," I said, shaky with comprehension. I struggled to my feet and leaned against the wall. Nergal and Ari broke off and circled each other like two bulls, or two demons, ready to lock horns again.

"This is your home," I said to Nergal. "*This* is the spot of land you couldn't burn."

Until now, I realized, I'd been viewing everything through a pair of unfocused binoculars. I'd had two fields of vision, two areas of focus: my demon client and his aging, insane wife; and the demon who'd been attacking and abducting Mederies. The two views suddenly snapped together forming one singular, frightening perspective—they were one and the same.

There was no Vigilia, I thought breathlessly. Or rather, there had been at one time, but she was just as gone as the *Demon Register* had said she was. Who knew where she was? Dead? Off with her demon lover, Christos? It didn't matter. Because I suddenly knew which demon was responsible for the Mederi attacks: Lamia. The demon who'd been coughing up corn dolls on Bryde's Day. The demon who'd said the one thing, *the only thing*, she wanted was a child.

Nergal saw that I'd figured it out and he smiled at me, but just like a demon, his expression looked both sinister and sad at once. Like that optical illusion of the young maiden . . . or her old Mederi midwife.

"You said you walked for miles," I said, my voice almost dreamlike. My thoughts floated like unanchored buoys on a sea of disbelief, recollection, and awe. "You said that hours after sunset you finally found the spot of land that refused your touch—your fire. You saw a woman there, a beautiful woman." *Drawing water from a well,* I thought. *But it hadn't been a well. It had been the tomb.*

I turned to Lamia. It was almost impossible to believe she'd once been beautiful. In her hand, she clutched a ragged corn doll. The doll's dress was made of green wool scraps. It had real hair, hair that was a coppery gold color, and real blood smeared all over it. I swallowed. Had Laurel Scoria had red hair? *If not Laurel, then Amaryllis Apatite,* I thought. I clenched my fists, feeling absolute impotence.

Why hadn't I seen it? The corn dolls were mere effigies of Lamia's true offerings.

"I told Nergal not to contact the school clinic," Lamia said, stroking the doll's hair, "but he wouldn't listen." Her stroking became more manic and she raised the doll to her face and bared her pointed teeth at it. "I told him *you* couldn't help," she said, addressing the doll though, not me. "How could you?" She shook the doll viciously, causing its head to bobble up and down and scattering dried bits of blood everywhere.

"You're infested with death magic," she shrieked. "Same

as me." And then she began crooning and stroking the doll again, patting its head and smoothing its hair.

I bit my knuckles to keep from screaming.

How long had Lamia been Luck's grave keeper? Since the beginning? Since the Apocalypse? Or had she been spawned in his tomb in the centuries since? When had she made her first offerings to him? What were they? A silver bell? A lock of hair? What had she asked for in return? Beauty? Youth? When had simple offerings turned to live sacrifices?

When had she lost her mind?

I always thought I saw Luck's presence in every part of Halja life, except here. Nothing about this place felt right; from the moment I had stepped foot here, everything had felt wrong. It seemed that so much old magic had seeped into the ground; new magic couldn't even work anymore. This land seemed stuck in an unnatural eternal loop, like my mother's evergreens. But how could I find the cure when I didn't know the cause? Was it Lamia? Had a murderess come here to feed off of, and sustain, the remaining malignancy of war? Or was it the battleground itself? Had a young, devoted grave keeper been driven mad by the poisoned ground she was forced to guard? Was Lamia as much a victim of this place as everyone else who had died here?

I barked out a short laugh, on the edge of hysteria. We'd never know. None of these questions would ever be answered. I must have been mad myself to ever have thought I'd help clients like this by studying law books or legal precedents.

Despite all the unanswered questions though, I knew there was only one option, killing her. I didn't want to do it, but I didn't want to be a coward about it either. But as I prepared to send her a lethal blast, I made the mistake of looking at her. Lamia crooned to her corn doll as if it was a child and I chickened out. In that instant, I felt only pity. Lamia looked up at me and must have guessed what I'd intended. She was stark raving mad but her survival instincts were still intact.

I stalled when I should have thrown strong. If I hadn't

hesitated, Lamia wouldn't have had time to defend herself and she would be dead. Instead, I was the one who was going to die.

Seeing your own death approach is an interesting experience. Though I'd spent a considerable portion of my life shunning my true nature, I'd always assumed mine would be fiery. There was a sense of poetic justice about it: live by the flame; die by the flame. So it was surprising to see Lamia throw a spray of frost in my direction. But those little frozen magic crystals were the breath of death. I knew it as sure as I knew Lucifer's Morning Star would be the last star in the sky snuffed out by dawn.

Ari must have known it too because he threw himself in my direction. In the next instant, several things happened at once. Peter shook loose of the effects of Nergal's attack. His voice cracked but was capable enough. I felt the weight of a quickly cast protective spell fall over me like full plate armor. A second later, Ari's body crashed into mine. He landed on top of me, knocking the breath out of my lungs. For a moment I could do no more than stare numbly at the ceiling. When conscious thought returned, however, my immediate reaction was one of horrifying, utter, gut-wrenching denial. I refused to believe what had just happened. I wouldn't accept it. I couldn't.

There was just no way I could watch Ari die. But Luck didn't care. The frost settling over Ari had an immediate effect. The tiny grains of magic burned through his clothes, and from the look on his face, his skin as well. He grimaced as if he'd been doused with lye. His breath became hollow and raspy. He started bleeding from his nose and mouth. He grunted in pain as he shifted off of me and tried to turn away.

"No!" I cried, grabbing him and turning him onto his back. I ran my hand across his chest, as if I could somehow put him back together. *No not Ari please not Ari please not Ari anyone but him please Luck no not him no no—No!*

From the corner, I heard Peter cast a spell. I felt Lamia and Nergal's signatures dim. It would have been blessed relief if Ari weren't dying before my eyes. I looked up. The two demons appeared frozen, but otherwise fine. Lamia gazed adoringly down at her corn doll infant, her face suffused with joy. Nergal had been caught mid-shift, horns and claws barely breaching the surface of his skin. *The stasis spell,* I thought. Jonathan Aster's ancient spell would buy us time, but how long?

"Peter," I said, my voice roughened from crying, "help me lift him." I couldn't carry Ari by myself. And we had to get Night out too. "How much time do we have?"

"Probably just enough to get them out. If one of them could be healed enough to walk."

I made some wretched sound and lowered my forehead to Ari's, letting the tears flow. Then I raised my head. "Run outside," I said frantically. "There's a Mederi, Bryony. She was supposed to meet us here. Find her."

But Peter just stood there.

"Go!" I screamed, rounding on him, snarling in my anguish. He left.

Ari looked up at me, tears of blood weeping from his eyes. His gaze started to turn glassy. "Noon," he choked, "get out of here."

"No." I didn't want him to know how scared I was, but he must have felt it in my signature. "We're going to heal you."

He shook his head. "Take Night and go." He arched his back in pain. Stuff coming out of my nose dripped onto his shirt. I swiped at it with the back of my hand, fighting more tears.

"I'm not going to leave you."

"You shouldn't make promises lightly," Ari said, trying to laugh. It came out as a bloody half cough.

"I don't care," I said, grabbing his hand. "I won't leave you. I love you." I heard Peter return and looked up. He stared down at us, a peculiar expression on his face.

"Your Mederi wasn't out there," he said. "But I know how we can heal him."

Mederi magic was the only thing I knew that could heal

after a demon attack, but Peter had been pulling rabbits out of hats all semester so maybe he had another idea. "If you have a spell that can help him, what are you waiting for?"

Peter knelt down next to us. I should have known from the look on his face that his solution wouldn't be a cheap magic trick. The cost would be dear.

"I can't save him," Peter said, "but you can." Beneath me, Ari was fading in and out of consciousness. I couldn't tell how aware he was of what was going on around him, but after Peter's words he began convulsing, violently shaking his head from side to side.

"Shh," I said, laying my hand against his cheek. "Stop."

Around me, I felt Lamia and Nergal's signature heating up. It wouldn't be long before the stasis spell wore off. I knew what would happen then, but I no longer cared. I didn't want to live in a world without Ari. Suddenly, Joy's words came back to me. *There are worse fates than dying for someone you love.* Indeed. But maybe Luck didn't hate me that much after all. Maybe he'd spare me that fate and Ari and I would both perish in the next few moments. I became calm then, accepting, almost welcoming the inevitable. Until I heard Peter's next words. "I finished translating the Reversal Spell, Noon. I can cast it. Right now. *You* can heal Ari."

It was so simple. It was what I'd been waiting for my whole life. I paused for only a moment. Ari had made me realize that waning magic could be used as a force for good. Maegesters had a place and a purpose in Halja's life. Their role, in fact, was far greater than a Mederi's. Maegesters kept Halja from returning to the days of war. Far from being destructive, the greatest Maegesters sought to prevent mass destruction by maintaining peace and keeping order. But I paused for only a moment, because none of that mattered. I would have given anything to save Ari.

"No," Ari said. I had to strain to hear him. "It's too dangerous. Not worth it . . ." He panted furiously. "No idea . . . what might happen."

Peter scoffed. "Do you want to live?"

"Noon," Ari said, completely ignoring Peter. "Please don't. Please. Get out . . . now. Go. Promise me . . ."

"No," I said, my voice soft but firm. Ari's movements slowed and then stopped altogether. I could sense only the barest trickle of his signature now.

"There's just one thing," Peter said. I resisted the impulse to slap him and yell, *Now!*

"Promise that you'll leave Ari. Promise that you'll give me a chance."

I looked up at Peter, fighting to keep my magic in check. It was amazing how quickly your feelings for someone could change. But I wasn't the only one who'd changed. The Peter I'd known would never have forced me to make such a promise. The Peter I'd known had taken over a decade to work up the courage to kiss me. He would never have had the nerve to threaten me. I didn't want to give Peter a chance. I hated him suddenly for even asking me to. But when I'd said I'd do anything to save Ari, I'd meant it.

"Fine," I said, my voice cracking. "Do it. Cast the Reversal Spell and I'll walk out of here with you."

"Kiss me," Peter said, "to seal your promise."

I swallowed, my body suddenly hot and cold. At one time I'd been confused about whether I'd wanted this. No longer. Every part of me revolted. But I leaned over Ari's body and pressed my lips firmly to Peter's, wondering when exactly he'd become such a stranger. I felt Peter shiver as our lips touched and I broke off the kiss, refusing to look at him.

Peter wasted no time after that. He started casting the Reversal Spell just as the stasis spell was wearing off. Nergal twitched and Lamia's gaze shifted in our direction. I hoped I would instinctively know how to heal once Peter completed casting the Reversal Spell. If I could heal Ari enough, he and Peter could keep Lamia and Nergal at bay while I healed Night. Maybe, just maybe, we'd all make it out of here alive.

I laid my hands on Ari's chest, waiting for the spell to take effect. I felt the ancient magic stir. It was the most powerful spell I'd ever felt. The air vibrated with its presence; it seemed an entity in and of itself. After thousands of years of silence, it seemed to wake up and fly around the room, as if it were searching for something. *Me,* I thought. *I'm over here.* But it settled instead on the unlikeliest of people—Nergal. And instead of a healer, it turned him into a howling infant.

For a few seconds, I thought my eyes and ears were deceiving me. As if the whole thing was a demon illusion, or Luck's cruel joke. I shook my head, staring down at the wriggling infant on the floor. It was a little demon child, complete with horns and claws.

Lamia broke free from the final remains of the stasis spell, but instead of blasting us with further death magic, she stood transfixed, staring at the crying child. Peter let out a sound of disgust, momentarily shifting her attention to us. Lamia narrowed her eyes, preparing to throw something horrid, but I blasted first. I poured all of the anger and impotence I felt at this macabre, twisted, bizarre situation into that one blast. It was the most powerfully controlled blast I'd ever thrown. But nothing happened. Instinctively, I'd thrown fire, which had no effect here.

Lamia threw a spray of poison at us then, but her heart wasn't in it, and I easily shielded it with my magic. Ari's signature dimmed and I started sobbing uncontrollably. *Why had Luck forsaken me?* Lamia scooped up the infant Nergal and slipped into the mouth of the tomb. I tried to feel something positive, something life affirming, so that I would be able to control the power that was gathering within me. But it was impossible to feel hope or joy when Ari was dying before my eyes. So instead, I allowed every negative emotion I'd ever felt this past semester—pain, horror, hatred, fear, fury, grief, guilt, even recklessness—to gather within me and I melded them all into a great big ball of pure waning magic, undiluted by fire or electricity or any destructive force other than my sheer will. I poured *darkness* into that ball and I threw it toward the tomb, not caring if it was more than I had to give. Not caring now if I lived or died.

The world went black.

Chapter 26

ॐ

A few weeks later, I received news that I'd passed all of my classes, even Manipulation. Rochester and Seknecus decided (perhaps with some input from my father, whom I'd glimpsed once during finals hurrying toward their offices) that, although I hadn't completed my assignment, I'd demonstrated enough resilience in the field to overcome my former lack of experience. In fact, after the "altercation" at the tomb (the faculty's provocatively understated term for what had happened) I was ranked *Primoris*. I could have cared less.

When the semester ended, I returned to Etincelle and spent three whole days staring out of my bedroom window at my mother's blackened garden. It seemed as good a place as any for mourning. On the fourth day, I shoved my gilded mirror out the window. I watched as it fell, flipping end over end, until it finally crashed to the ground, splintering wood and shattering glass everywhere. The explosive sound of it was as gratifying as was the fact that the damage was irreparable. You didn't need magic to destroy, I smirked, thinking of my mother's gasoline can. A thousand jagged pieces of glass

winked up at me, their silvery edges glinting in the afternoon
sun. Aurelia came in then and put her arm around me. She
stared down at the wreckage looking almost as pleased as I
did. For once, I didn't flinch from her touch.

"I'm sorry," she said. "For everything."

"I know," I said, leaning my head on her shoulder.

My father showed up a few days later. As usual, there
was no "Hello" or "How have you been?" I forgave that
this time, however, because such inanities would have been
entirely inappropriate. Still, there were no words of sympathy
regarding Ari's injuries, which wounded me deeply, no congratulations on landing the *Primoris* position, which I would
have shunned anyway, and no mention of my smashed mirror, which still lay in pieces out in my mother's garden. She
seemed as content to leave it there as I did. Unlike before,
however, my father and I did talk shop for a few moments. He
asked what I would have done if my last dark, emotion-laden,
überpowerful, yet completely reckless and out-of-control
magic blast had not sealed Nergal forever (or at least for a
very long time) within the confines of Lucifer's Tomb. I ran
through a few arguments I might have made on his behalf
before the Council. Karanos appeared unimpressed with
these, but when I explained some of the things I'd wanted to
do to Nergal if he'd have continued to threaten me, my father
had smiled.

"Perhaps you are your mother's daughter after all," he'd
said, his expression as enigmatic as that legendary pre-
Apocalyptic sphinx. He then mentioned that I'd be assigned
a new client next semester, one that would provide some interesting new challenges.

The next week, mourning turned to healing. My best
friend was gone, but my boyfriend was alive and well. Bryony had arrived later that night and had nearly needed a
Mederi herself after she'd healed Ari, Night, and me from
our various injuries. Night had elected to finish recovering
with the Demeter Tribe. Linnaea had come to collect him

herself, fussing over him as if she were Androcles taming another lion. After what had happened at the tomb, I'd told Peter I never wanted to speak to him again. He told me I'd change my mind once he found the real Reversal Spell. True to my word though, I turned my back on him.

Curiosity had me making a few discreet inquiries, however, and I found out that, instead of the Reversal Spell, Peter had accidentally cast the Spell of Second Chances, a spell nearly as old, powerful, and illustrious as the Reversal Spell, and one which was giving Peter a lot of press over at the Joshua School. Apparently the Spell of Second Chances worked like medieval medicine. It bestowed its benefits on only the most sick. But the cure was often worse than the disease.

Lamia had been kidnapping Mederies, erroneously thinking that if they were tortured enough they might be able to create the impossible. Her madness had also given her a cold efficiency. Once they were dead, she'd used pieces of their hair and clothing to make her revolting corn dolls, which she ingested in the hopes that they could somehow make her barren womb fertile.

Nergal was worse though. He couldn't use madness as an excuse. He was perfectly sane when he'd first filed for the divorce he'd so desperately sought. He'd been motivated by all the things I'd accused him of. He'd fallen out of love with Lamia because she was ugly, old, and insane, but he'd also had a deeper, more pressing, motive—avoiding his own death. I'd nearly forgotten that demon lovers who married were bound by magic. They lived—*and died*—together, unless both agreed to end the marriage. Once Lamia's madness escalated to the point where she started killing Mederies, Nergal knew she'd eventually be killed for her sins. He hadn't wanted to die with her. Well, he hadn't. Instead, he'd gotten a life sentence in the bowels of Lucifer's Tomb. And Lamia had her longed for child.

I shuddered. *Be careful what you wish for.*

For my part I was done wishing for anything other than what I had. My childhood dream no longer appealed; my childhood friend was no longer a friend. Dropping the gilded mirror from my bedroom window had been cathartic, but I knew there was one more thing I had to do.

Early one summer morning, Ari and I took a cab to Sheol. Ari was still using a cane to walk so I wanted to allow sufficient time for what I had in mind. I tipped the cabdriver extra and he grinned at me, promising to come get us the next morning. I shouldered the immense backpack I'd brought, which held all our supplies. On the way over, Ari had argued nonstop about who was going to carry it. I finally got him to shut up by telling him that if he didn't, I'd re-schedule our excursion for a time when Fitz or Mercator could make it because I sure as hell wasn't going to let him carry it. He'd sulked for a mile or so but let it drop.

Once Ari had recovered enough to talk about what had happened, his whole take on it had been uncharacteristically naive and sweetly romantic. Perhaps that's what a brush with death did to a person. He'd stated, on multiple occasions, that the whole situation could have been avoided had Nergal simply been a better husband. While I felt this sweeping summary was entirely too idealistic, and managed to gloss over a few hard to hear truths, it did endear him to me even further.

When we got to the woods, I saw that our blackened path was still there. Grass had crept back over its outer edges and a few green stalks had shot up the middle. Still, the last thing I yearned for was the presence of an Angel to cast a spell of protection over these new growths. The forest as a whole would survive our presence and I'd had enough of spells. Besides, if what I had in mind worked, this path would become worn with the trampling of ordinary Hyrke feet before long.

We took our time. I made sure we stopped to rest often, including the spot just before the forest's edge where Peter had first kissed me. I kissed Ari long and hard there. I think he knew the trip was about excising demons—all kinds. His return kiss was ardent and enthusiastic.

Late in the afternoon, we reached the clearing. I paused before stepping onto the battlefield. It looked different during the day. The jagged headstones were still there. And the surrounding vegetation still appeared blighted. The house was, impossibly, still standing. But the light from the sinking sun coated everything with the warm glow of hope.

We spent the last daylight hours collecting all the deadwood. We piled it in a big heap at the front door of the house. Then I opened up my pack and pulled out the rest of our supplies: a large blanket, two huge covered mugs of ale, a couple slices of Innkeeper's Pie, and a box of matches. The days of staring at my mother's garden had given me the idea.

My plan was simple: purge this land with fire and bring it back to life, by committing the simple joyous acts of living on it. We would eat; we would drink; and we would be merry. I grinned to myself. I was particularly looking forward to that last part.

"Fire it up, Onyx," Ari called from the blanket. I struck the first match, nervously swallowing. What if it didn't work? But I had to believe.

I threw the match. *Lucem in tenebras ferimus.*
Into the darkness, we bring light.

From the "dark, rich, and sexy"*
Guardian Series from

MELJEAN BROOK

DEMON BLOOD

In an effort to save his people, the vampire Deacon
betrayed the demon-fighting Guardians. Now he lives
only for revenge. But Rosalia is in love with him and
willing to fight by his side—even if she has to stand
against her fellow Guardians to save him.

New York Times bestselling author Gena Showalter

penguin.com